PRIEST-KINGS
OF GOR

John Norman

BALLANTINE BOOKS • NEW YORK

SBN 345-24783-3-150

First U.S. Printing: December, 1968
Ninth U.S. Printing: October, 1975

First Canadian Printing: January, 1973

Printed in the United States of America

Cover Painting: Robert Foster

BALLANTINE BOOKS, INC.
201 East 50th Street, New York, N.Y. 10022.

CONTENTS

1
The Fair of En'Kara

I, Tarl Cabot, formerly of Earth, am one who is known to the Priest-Kings of Gor.

It came about late in the month of En'Kara in the year 10,117 from the founding of the City of Ar that I came to the Hall of Priest-Kings in the Sardar Mountains on the planet Gor, our Counter-Earth.

I had arrived four days before on tarnback at the black palisade that encircles the dreaded Sardar, those dark mountains, crowned with ice, consecrated to the Priest-Kings, forbidden to men, to mortals, to all creatures of flesh and blood.

The tarn, my gigantic, hawklike mount, had been unsaddled and freed, for it could not accompany me into the Sardar. Once it had tried to carry me over the palisade into the mountains, but never again would I have essayed that flight. It had been caught in the shield of the Priest-Kings, invisible, not to be evaded, undoubtedly a field of some sort, which had so acted on the bird, perhaps affecting the mechanism of the inner ear, that the creature had become incapable of controlling itself and had fallen disoriented and confused to the earth below. None of the animals of Gor, as far as I knew, could enter the Sardar. Only men could enter, and they did not return.

I regretted freeing the tarn, for it was a fine bird, powerful, intelligent, fierce, courageous, loyal. And, strangely, I think it cared for me. At least I cared for it. And only with harsh words could I drive it away, and when it disappeared in the distance, puzzled, perhaps hurt, I wept.

It was not far to the fair of En'Kara, one of the four great fairs held in the shadow of the Sardar during the Gorean year, and I soon walked slowly down the long central avenue between the tents, the booths and stalls, the pavilions and stockades of the fair, toward the high, brassbound timber gate, formed of black logs, beyond which lies the Sardar itself, the sanctuary of this world's gods, known to the men below the mountains, the mortals, only as Priest-Kings.

I would stop briefly at the fair, for I must purchase food for the journey into the Sardar and I must entrust a leatherbound package to some member of the Caste of Scribes, a package which contained an account of what had occurred at the City of Tharna in the past months, a short history of events which I thought should be recorded.*

----

* This is undoubtedly the manuscript which was subsequently published under the title *Outlaw of Gor*. One gathers from Cabot's remarks above that he was, at the time of writing, not aware of the fate of the manuscript. The title *Outlaw of Gor*, incidentally, is mine, not Cabot's. This is also the case, perhaps it should be mentioned, with the first book, *Tarnsman of Gor*, and the present book, *Priest-Kings of Gor*. For some reason Cabot never entitles his manuscripts. Perhaps he thinks of them not so much as books as personal records or histories, written perhaps as much for himself as for others. An account, incidentally, of how I came into possession of the ms. *Outlaw of Gor* precedes that book, which, like the others, I have had the privilege of editing. Suffice it here to say that the current manuscript, like the others, was tendered to me by my friend, and now my lawyer, young Harrison Smith of the city. Smith has had the pleasure of knowing Cabot personally, having originally met him several years ago in New England and having been able to renew the acquaintance briefly in New York City something over a year ago. Indeed, our first account of the Counter-Earth, *Tarnsman of Gor*, was entrusted to Smith personally by Cabot, who shortly thereafter disappeared. This manuscript, the third, was received, according to Smith, under substantially the same unusual conditions as the second, conditions which he kindly delineated in a preface contributed to

I wished that I had had longer to visit the fair for on another occasion at another time I should have sought eagerly to examine its wares, drink at its taverns, talk with its merchants and attend its contests, for these fairs are free ground for the many competitive, hostile Gorean cities, and provide almost the sole opportunity for the citizens of various cities to meet peaceably with one another.

It is little wonder then that the cities of Gor support and welcome the fairs. Sometimes they provide a common ground on which territorial and commercial disputes may be amicably resolved without loss of honor, plenipotentiaries of warring cities having apparently met by accident among the silken pavilions.

Further, members of castes such as the Physicians and Builders use the fairs for the dissemination of information and techniques among Caste Brothers, as is prescribed in their codes in spite of the fact that their respective cities may be hostile. And as might be expected members of the Caste of Scribes gather here to enter into dispute and examine and trade manuscripts.

My small friend, Torm of Ko-ro-ba, of the Caste of Scribes, had been to the fairs four times in his life. He informed me that in this time he had refuted seven hundred and eight scribes from fifty-seven cities, but I will not vouch for the accuracy of the report, as I sometimes suspect that Torm, like most members of his caste, and mine, tends to be a bit too sanguine in recounting his numerous victories. Moreover I have never been too clear as to the grounds on which the disputes of scribes are to be adjudicated, and it is

---

that volume. In all this I regret only that I have never had the pleasure of meeting Cabot personally. There is a real Cabot of course. I know that he exists, or existed. In so far as I have been able I have checked into these matters with great care. There was indeed a Tarl Cabot, answering the description of these accounts, who was raised in Bristol, and who attended Oxford and taught in the small New England college referred to in the first book, and who subsequently rented an apartment in midtown Manhattan at dates congruent with the accounts in the first and second books. In short, what can be confirmed, I have confirmed. Beyond this of course we have only the accounts of Cabot himself, brought to my attention by Smith, which we may or may not accept.—J. N.

not too infrequently that both disputants leave the field each fully convinced that he has had the best of the contest. In differences among members of my own caste, that of the Warriors, it is easier to tell who has carried the day, for the defeated one often lies wounded or slain at the victor's feet. In the contests of scribes, on the other hand, the blood that is spilled is invisible and the valiant foemen retire in good order, reviling their enemies and recouping their forces for the next day's campaign. I do not hold this against the contests of scribes; rather I commend it to the members of my own caste.

I missed Torm and wondered if I would ever see him again, bounding about excoriating the authors of dusty scrolls, knocking the inkwell from his desk with an imperial sweep of his blue robe, leaping on the table in birdlike fury denouncing one scribe or another for independently rediscovering an idea that had already appeared in a century-old manuscript known to Torm of course but not to the luckless scribe in question, rubbing his nose in his robe, shivering, leaping down to thrust his feet against the everpresent, overloaded charcoal brazier that invariably burned under his table, amid the litter of his scraps and parchments, regardless of whatever the outside temperature might be.

I supposed Torm might be anywhere, for those of Ko-ro-ba had been scattered by the Priest-Kings. I would not search the fair for him, nor if he were here would I make my presence known, for by the will of Priest-Kings no two men of Ko-ro-ba might stand together, and I had no wish to jeopardize the little scribe. Gor would be the poorer were it not for his furious eccentricities; the Counter-Earth would simply not be the same without belligerent, exasperated little Torm. I smiled to myself. If I should meet him I knew he would thrust himself upon me and insist on being taken into the Sardar, though he would know it would mean his death, and I would have to bundle him in his blue robes, hurl him into a rain barrel and make my escape. Perhaps it would be safer to drop him into a well. Torm had stumbled into more than one well in his life and no one who knew him would think it strange to find him sputtering about at the bottom of one.

The fairs incidentally are governed by Merchant Law and supported by booth rents and taxes levied on the items exchanged. The commercial facilities of these fairs, from money changing to general banking, are the finest I know of on Gor, save those in Ar's Street of Coins, and letters of credit are accepted and loans negotiated, though often at usurious rates, with what seems reckless indifference. Yet perhaps this is not so puzzling, for the Gorean cities will, within their own walls, enforce the Merchant Law when pertinent, even against their own citizens. If they did not, of course, the fairs would be closed to the citizens of that city.

The contests I mentioned which take place at the fairs are, as would be expected, peaceable, or I should say, at least do not involve contests of arms. Indeed it is considered a crime against the Priest-Kings to bloody one's weapons at the fairs. The Priest-Kings, I might note, seem to be more tolerant of bloodshed in other localities.

Contests of arms, fought to the death, whereas they may not take place at the fairs are not unknown on Gor, and are popular in some cities. Contests of this sort, most often involving criminals and impoverished soldiers of fortune, offer prizes of amnesty or gold and are customarily sponsored by rich men to win the approval of the populace of their cities. Sometimes these men are merchants who wish thereby to secure goodwill for their products; sometimes they are practitioners of the law, who hope to sway the votes of jury men; sometimes they are Ubars or High Initiates who find it in their interests to keep the crowds amused. Such contests, in which life is lost, used to be popular at Ar, for example, being sponsored in that city by the Caste of Initiates, who regard themselves as being intermediaries between Priest-Kings and men, though I suspect that, at least on the whole, they know as little about the Priest-Kings as do other men. These contests, it might be mentioned, were banned in Ar when Kazrak of Port Kar became administrator of that city. It was not an action which was popular with the powerful Caste of Initiates.

The contests at the fairs, however, I am pleased to say, offer nothing more dangerous than wrestling, with no holds to the death permitted. Most of the contests involve such

things as racing, feats of strength, and skill with bow and
spear. Other contests of interest pit choruses and poets and
players of various cities against one another in the several
theaters of the fair. I had a friend once, Andreas of the
desert city of Tor, of the Caste of Poets, who had once sung
at the fair and won a cap filled with gold. And perhaps it is
hardly necessary to add that the streets of the fair abound
with jugglers, puppeteers, musicians and acrobats who, far
from the theaters, compete in their ancient fashions for the
copper tarn disks of the broiling, turbulent crowds.

Many are the objects for sale at the fair. I passed among
wines and textiles and raw wool, silks, and brocades, copper-
ware and glazed pottery, carpets and tapestries, lumber, furs,
hides, salt, arms and arrows, saddles and harness, rings and
bracelets and necklaces, belts and sandals, lamps and oils,
medicines and meats and grains, animals such as the fierce
tarns, Gor's winged mounts, and tharlarions, her domesticated lizards, and long chains of miserable slaves, both male
and female.

Although no one may be enslaved at the fair, slaves may
be bought and sold within its precincts, and slavers do a
thriving business, exceeded perhaps only by that of Ar's
Street of Brands. The reason for this is not simply that here
is a fine market for such wares, since men from various cities
pass freely to and fro at the fair, but that each Gorean,
whether male or female, is expected to see the Sardar Mountains, in honor of the Priest-Kings, at least once in his life,
prior to his twenty-fifth year. Accordingly the pirates and
outlaws who beset the trade routes to ambush and attack the
caravans on the way to the fair, if successful, often have
more than inanimate metals and cloths to reward their
vicious labors.

This pilgrimage to the Sardar, enjoined by the Priest-Kings
according to the Caste of Initiates, undoubtedly plays its role
in the distribution of beauty among the hostile cities of Gor.
Whereas the males who accompany a caravan are often
killed in its defense or driven off, this fate, fortunate or not,
is seldom that of the caravan's women. It will be their sad lot
to be stripped and fitted with the collars and chains of slave
girls and forced to follow the wagons on foot to the fair, or

if the caravan's tharlarions have been killed or driven off, they will carry its goods on their backs. Thus one practical effect of the edict of the Priest-Kings is that each Gorean girl must, at least once in her life, leave her walls and take the very serious risk of becoming a slave girl, perhaps the prize of a pirate or outlaw.

The expeditions sent out from the cities are of course extremely well guarded, but pirates and outlaws too can band together in large numbers and sometimes, even more dangerously, one city's warriors, in force, will prey upon another city's caravans. This, incidentally, is one of the more frequent causes of war among these cities. The fact that warriors of one city sometimes wear the insignia of cities hostile to their own when they make these attacks further compounds the suspicions and internecine strife which afflicts the Gorean cities.

This chain of reflections was occasioned in my mind by sight of some men of Port Kar, a savage, coastal city on the Tamber Gulf, who were displaying a sullen chain of twenty freshly branded girls, many of them beautiful. They were from the island city of Cos and had undoubtedly been captured at sea, their vessel burned and sunk. Their considerable charms were fully revealed to the eye of appraising buyers who passed down the line. The girls were chained throat to throat, their wrists locked behind the small of their backs with slave bracelets, and they knelt in the customary position of Pleasure Slaves. When a possible buyer would stop in front of one, one of the bearded scoundrels from Port Kar would poke her with a slave whip and she would lift her head and numbly repeat the ritual phrase of the inspected slave girl, Buy Me, Master. They had thought to come to the Sardar as free women, discharging their obligation to the Priest-Kings. They would leave as slave girls. I turned away.

My business was with the Priest-Kings of Gor.

Indeed, I had come to the Sardar to encounter the fabled Priest-Kings, whose incomparable power so inextricably influences the destinies of the cities and men of the Counter-Earth.

It is said that the Priest-Kings know whatever transpires on their world and that the mere lifting of their hand can summon all the powers of the universe. I myself had seen the power of Priest-Kings and knew that such beings existed.. I myself had traveled in a ship of the Priest-Kings which had twice carried me to this world; I had seen their power so subtly exercised as to alter the movements of a compass needle, so grossly demonstrated as to destroy a city, leaving behind not even the stones of what had once been a dwelling place of men.

It is said that neither the physical intricacies of the cosmos nor the emotions of human beings are beyond the scope of their power, that the feelings of men and the motions of atoms and stars are as one to them, that they can control the very forces of gravity and invisibly sway the hearts of human beings, but of this latter claim I wonder, for once on a road to Ko-ro-ba, my city, I met one who had been a messenger of Priest-Kings, one who had been capable of disobeying them, one from the shards of whose burnt and blasted skull I had removed a handful of golden wire.

He had been destroyed by Priest-Kings as casually as one might jerk loose the thong of a sandal. He had disobeyed and he had been destroyed, immediately and with grotesque dispatch, but the important thing was, I told myself, that he had disobeyed, that he could disobey, that he had been able to disobey and choose the ignominious death he knew must follow. He had won his freedom though it had, as the Goreans say, led him to the Cities of Dust, where, I think, not even Priest-Kings care to follow. He had, as a man, lifted his fist against the might of Priest-Kings and so he had died, defiantly, though horribly, with great nobility.

I am of the Caste of Warriors, and it is in our codes that the only death fit for a man is that in battle, but I can no longer believe that this is true, for the man I met once on the road to Ko-ro-ba died well, and taught me that all wisdom and truth does not lie in my own codes.

My business with the Priest-Kings is simple, as are most matters of honor and blood. For some reason unbeknown to me they have destroyed my city, Ko-ro-ba, and scattered its peoples. I have been unable to learn the fate of my father, my friends, my warrior companions, and my beloved Talena, she who was the daughter of Marlenus, who had once been

Ubar of Ar—my sweet, fierce, wild, gentle, savage, beautiful love, she who is my Free Companion, my Talena, forever the Ubara of my heart, she who burns forever in the sweet, lonely darkness of my dreams. Yes, I have business with the Priest-Kings of Gor.

2
In the Sardar

I LOOKED DOWN THE LONG, broad avenue to the huge timber gate at its end, and beyond the gate to the black crags of the inhospitable Sardar Range.

It took not much time to purchase a small bundle of supplies to take into the Sardar, nor was it difficult to find a scribe to whom I might entrust the history of the events at Tharna. I did not ask his name nor he mine. I knew his caste, and he knew mine, and it was enough. He could not read the manuscript as it was written in English, a language as foreign to him as Gorean would be to most of you, but yet he would treasure the manuscript and guard it as though it were a most precious possession, for he was a scribe and it is the way of scribes to love the written word and keep it from harm, and if he could not read the manuscript, what did it matter—perhaps someone could someday, and then the words which had kept their secret for so long would at last enkindle the mystery of communication and what had been written would be heard and understood.

At last I stood before the towering gate of black logs, bound with its wide bands of brass. The fair lay behind me and the Sardar before. My garments and my shield bore no insignia, for my city had been destroyed. I wore my helmet. None would know who entered the Sardar.

At the gate I was met by one of the Caste of Initiates, a dour, thin-lipped, drawn man with deep sunken eyes, clad in the pure white robes of his caste.

"Do you wish to speak to Priest-Kings?" he asked.

"Yes," I said.

"Do you know what you do?" he asked.

"Yes," I said.

The Initiate and I gazed evenly at one another, and then he stepped aside, as he must have done many times. I would not be the first, of course, to enter the Sardar. Many men and sometimes women had entered these mountains but it is not known what they found. Sometimes these individuals are young idealists, rebels and champions of lost causes, who wish to protest to Priest-Kings; sometimes they are individuals who are old or diseased and are tired of life and wish to die; sometimes they are piteous or cunning or frightened wretches who think to find the secret of immortality in those barren crags; and sometimes they are outlaws fleeing from Gor's harsh justice, hoping to find at least brief sanctuary in the cruel, mysterious domain of Priest-Kings, a country into which they may be assured no mortal magistrate or vengeful band of human warriors will penetrate. I supposed the Initiate might account me one of the latter, for my habiliments bore no insignia.

He turned away from me and went to a small pedestal at one side. On the pedestal there was a silver bowl, filled with water, a vial of oil and a towel. He dipped his fingers in the bowl, poured a bit of oil on his hands, dipped his fingers again and then wiped his hands dry.

On each side of the huge gate there stood a great windlass and chain, and to each windlass a gang of blinded slaves was manacled.

The Initiate folded the towel carefully and replaced it on the pedestal.

"Let the gate be opened," he said.

The slaves obediently pressed their weight against the timber spokes of the two windlasses and they creaked and the chains tightened. Their naked feet slipped in the dirt and they pressed ever more tightly against the heavy, obdurate bars. Now their bodies humped with pain, clenching themselves against the spokes. Their blind eyes were fixed on nothing. The blood vessels in their necks and legs and arms began to distend until I feared they might burst open through the tortured flesh; the agonized muscles of their straining knotted bodies, like swollen leather, seemed to fill with pain as if pain were a fluid; their flesh seemed to fuse with the wood of the bars; the backs of their garments discolored with a scarlet sweat. Men had broken their own bones on the timber spokes of the Sardar windlasses.

At last there was a great creak and the vast portal parted a hand's breadth and then the width of a shoulder and the width of a man's body.

"It is enough," I said.

I entered immediately.

As I entered I heard the mournful tolling of the huge, hollow metal bar which stands some way from the gate. I had heard the tolling before, and knew that it signified that yet another mortal had entered the Sardar. It was a depressing sound, and not made less so by my realization that in this case it was I who had entered the mountains. As I listened it occurred to me that the purpose of the bar might not be simply to inform the men of the fair that the Sardar had been entered but to inform the Priest-Kings as well.

I looked behind myself in time to see the great gate close. It shut without a sound.

The journey to the Hall of Priest-Kings was not as difficult as I had anticipated. At places there were well-worn paths, at others even stairs had been cut in the sides of mountains, stairs worn smooth in the millenia by the passage of countless feet.

Here and there bones littered the path, human bones. Whether these were the remains of men who had starved or frozen in the barren Sardar, or had been destroyed by Priest-Kings, I did not know. Upon occasion some message would be found scratched in the cliffs along the path. Some of these were obscene, cursing the Priest-Kings; others were paeans in their praise; some were cheerful, if in a rather pessimistic way. One I remember was: "Eat, drink and be happy. The rest is nothing." Others were rather simple, and sometimes sad, such as "No food," I'm cold," "I'm afraid." One such read, "The mountains are empty. Rena I love you." I wondered who had written it, and when. The inscription was worn. It had been scratched out in the old Gorean script. It had weathered for perhaps better than a thousand years. But I knew that the mountains were not empty, for I had evidence of Priest-Kings. I continued my journey.

I encountered no animals, nor any growing thing, nothing

save the endless black rocks, the black cliffs, and the path cut before me in the dark stone. Gradually the air grew more chill and wisps of snow blew about me; frost began to appear on the steps and I trudged past crevices filled with ice, deposits which had perhaps lain as they were without melting for hundreds of years. I wrapped my cloak more firmly about myself and using my spear as a staff I forced my way upward.

Some four days into the mountains I heard for the first time in my journey the sound of a thing other than the wind, the sighing of snow and the groaning of ice; it was the sound of a living thing; the sound of a mountain larl.

The larl is a predator, clawed and fanged, quite large, often standing seven feet at the shoulder. I think it would be fair to say that it is substantially feline; at any rate its grace and sinuous power remind me of the smaller but similarly fearsome jungle cats of my old world.

The resemblance is, I suppose, due to the mechanics of convergent evolution, both animals having been shaped by the exigencies of the chase, the stealth of the approach and the sudden charge, and by the requirement of the swift and devastating kill. If there is an optimum configuration for a land predator, I suppose on my old world the palm must go to the Bengal tiger; but on Gor the prize belongs indisputably to the mountain larl; and I cannot but believe that the structural similarities between the two animals, though of different worlds, are more than a matter of accident.

The larl's head is broad, sometimes more than two feet across, and shaped roughly like a triangle, giving its skull something of the cast of a viper's save that of course it is furred and the pupils of the eyes like the cat's and unlike the viper's, can range from knifelike slits in the broad daylight to dark, inquisitive moons in the night.

The pelt of the larl is normally a tawny red or a sable black. The black larl, which is predominantly nocturnal, is maned, both male and female. The red larl, which hunts whenever hungry, regardless of the hour, and is the more common variety, possesses no mane. Females of both varieties tend generally to be slightly smaller than the males, but are quite as aggressive and sometimes even more dangerous, particularly in the late fall and winter of the year when they are likely to be hunting for their cubs. I had once killed a male red larl in the Voltai Range within pasangs of the city of Ar.

Now hearing the growl of such a beast I threw back my cloak, lifted my shield and held my spear ready. I was puzzled that I might encounter a larl in the Sardar. How could it have entered the mountains? Perhaps it was native. But on what could it live among these barren crags? For I had seen nothing on which it might prey, unless one might count the men who had entered the mountains, but their bones, scattered, white and frozen, were unsplintered and unfurrowed; they showed no evidence of having suffered the molestation of a larl's gnawing jaws. I then understood that the larl I had heard must be a larl of Priest-Kings, for no animal and no man enters or exists in the Sardar without the consent of Priest-Kings and if it was fed it must be at the hand of Priest-Kings or their servants.

In spite of my hatred of Priest-Kings I could not help but admire them. None of the men below the mountains, the mortals, had ever succeeded in taming a larl. Even larl cubs when found and raised by men would, on reaching their majority, on some night, in a sudden burst of atavistic fury slay their masters and under the three hurtling moons of Gor lope from the dwellings of men, driven by what instincts I know not, to seek the mountains where they were born. A case is known of a larl who traveled more than twenty-five hundred pasangs to seek a certain shallow crevice in the Voltai in which he had been whelped. He was slain at its mouth. Hunters had followed him. One among them, an old man who had originally been one of the party that had captured the animal, identified the place.

I advanced, my spear ready for its cast, my shield ready to be thrown over my body to protect it from the death throes of the thrashing beast should the cast be successful. My life was in my own hands and I was content that this should be so. I would have it no other way.

I smiled to myself. I was First Spear, for there were no others.

In the Voltai Range bands of hunters, usually from Ar,

stalk the larl with the mighty Gorean spear. Normally they do this in single file and he who leads the file is called First Spear, for his will be the first spear cast. As soon as he casts his weapon he throws himself to the ground and covers his body with his shield, as does each man successively behind him. This allows each man to have a clean cast at the beast and provides some protection once the spear is thrown.

The most significant reason, however, becomes clear when the rôle of the last man on the file, who is spoken of as Last Spear, is understood. Once Last Spear casts his weapon he may not throw himself to the ground. If he should, and any of his comrades survive, they will slay him. But this seldom occurs for the Gorean hunters fear cowardice more than the claws and fangs of larls. Last Spear must remain standing, and if the beast still lives, receive its charge with only his drawn sword. He does not hurl himself to the ground in order that he will remain conspicuously in the larl's field of vision and thus be the object of its wounded, maddened onslaught. It is thus that, should the spears miss their mark, he sacrifices his life for his companions who will, while the larl attacks him, make good their escape. This may seem cruel but in the long run it tends to be conservative of human life; it is better, as the Goreans say, for one man to die than many.

First Spear is normally the best of the spearmen because if the larl is not slain or seriously wounded with the first strike, the lives of all, and not simply that of Last Spear, stand in considerable jeopardy. Paradoxically perhaps, Last Spear is normally the weakest of the spearmen, the least skilled. Whether this is because Gorean hunting tradition favors the weak, protecting him with the stronger spears, or tradition scorns the weak, regarding him as the most expendable member of the party, I do not know. The origin of this hunting practice is lost in antiquity, being as old perhaps as men and weapons and larls.

I once asked a Gorean hunter whom I met in Ar why the larl was hunted at all. I have never forgotten his reply. "Because it is beautiful," he said, "and dangerous, and because we are Goreans."

I had not yet seen the beast whose growl I had heard. The path on which I trod turned a few yards ahead. It was about

a yard wide and hugged the side of a cliff, and to my left
there was a sheer precipice. The drop to its base must have
been at least a full pasang. I remembered that the boulders
below were huge but from my present height they looked like
grains of black sand. I wished the cliff were on my left rather
than my right in order to have a freer cast of my spear.

The path was steep but its ascent, here and there, was
lightened by high steps. I have never cared to have an enemy
above me, nor did I now, but I told myself that my spear
might more easily find a vulnerable spot if the larl leapt
downwards toward me than if I were above and had only the
base of its neck as my best target. From above I would try to
sever the vertebrae. The larl's skull is an even more difficult
cast, for its head is almost continually in motion. Moreover,
it possesses an unobtrusive bony ridge which runs from its
four nasal slits to the beginning of the backbone. This ridge
can be penetrated by the spear but anything less than a
perfect cast will result in the weapon's being deflected
through the cheek of the animal, inflicting a cruel but unimportant wound. On the other hand if I were under the larl I
would have a brief but clean strike at the great, pounding,
eight-valved heart that lies in the center of its breast.

My heart sank for I heard another growl, that of a second
beast.

I had but one spear.

I might kill one larl, but then I should almost certainly die
under the jaws of its mate.

For some reason I did not fear death but felt only anger
that these beasts might prevent me from keeping my rendez-
vous with the Priest-Kings of Gor.

I wondered how many men might have turned back at this
point, and I remembered the innumerable white, frozen
bones on the cliffs below. It occurred to me that I might
retreat, and return when the beasts had gone. It seemed
possible they might not yet have discovered me. I smiled as I
thought of the foolishness of this, for these beasts before me
must be the larls of Priest-Kings, guardians of the stronghold
of Gor's gods.

I loosened my sword in its sheath and continued upwards.

At last I came to the bend in the path and braced myself

for the sudden bolt about that corner in which I must cry aloud to startle them and in the same instant cast my spear at the nearest larl and set upon the other with my drawn sword.

I hesitated for a moment and then the fierce war cry of Ko-ro-ba burst from my lips in the clear, chill air of the Sardar and I threw myself into the open, my spear arm back, my shield high.

3
Parp

THERE WAS A SUDDEN STARTLED rattle of chains and I saw two huge, white larls frozen in the momentary paralysis of registering my presence, and then with but an instant's fleeting passage both beasts turned upon me and hurled themselves enraged to the lengths of their chains.

My spear had not left my hand.

Both animals were jerked up short as mighty chains, fastened to steel and bejeweled collars, terminated their vicious charge. One was thrown on its back, so violent was its rush, and the other stood wildly for a moment towering over me like a rearing giant stallion, its huge claws slashing the air, fighting the collar that held it from me.

Then at the length of their chains they crouched, snarling, regarding me balefully, occasionally lashing out with a clawed paw as if to sweep me into range of their fearsome jaws.

I was struck with wonder, though I was careful to keep beyond the range of their chains, for I had never seen white larls before.

They were gigantic beasts, superb specimens, perhaps eight feet at the shoulder.

Their upper canine fangs, like daggers mounted in their jaws, must have been at least a foot in length and extended well below their jaws in the manner of ancient saber-toothed tigers. The four nostril slits of each animal were flared and their great chests lifted and fell with the intensity of their excitement. Their tails, long and tufted at the end, lashed back and forth.

The larger of them unaccountably seemed to lose interest in me. He rose to his feet and sniffed the air, turning his side to me, and seemed ready to abandon any intentions of doing me harm. Only an instant later did I understand what was happening for suddenly turning he threw himself on his side and his head facing in the other direction hurled his hind legs at me. I lifted the shield for to my horror in reversing his position on the chain he had suddenly added some twenty feet to the fearful perimeter of the space alotted to him by that hated impediment. Two great clawed paws smote my shield and hurled me twenty feet against the cliff. I rolled and scrambled back further for the stroke of the larl had dashed me into the radius of its mate. My cloak and garments were torn from my back by the stroke of the second larl's claws.

I struggled to my feet.

"Well done," I said to the larl.

I had barely escaped with my life.

Now the two beasts were filled with a rage which dwarfed their previous fury, for they sensed that I would not again approach closely enough to permit them a repetition of their primitive stratagem. I admired the larls, for they seemed to me intelligent beasts. Yes, I said to myself, it was well done.

I examined my shield and saw ten wide furrows torn across its brassbound hide surface. My back felt wet with the blood from the second larl's claws. It should have felt warm, but it felt cold. I knew it was freezing on my back. There was no choice now but to go on, somehow, if I could. Without the small homely necessities of a needle and thread I should probably freeze. There was no wood in the Sardar with which to build a fire.

Yes, I repeated grimly to myself, glaring at the larls, though smiling, it was well done, too well done.

Then I heard the movement of chains and I saw that the two chains which fastened the larls were not hooked to rings in the stone but vanished within circular apertures. Now the chains were being slowly drawn in, much to the obvious frustration of the beasts.

The place in which I found myself was considerably wider than the path on which I had trod, for the path had given suddenly onto a fairly large circular area in which I had found the chained larls. One side of this area was formed by the sheer cliff which had been on my right and now curved about making a sort of cup of stone; the other side, on my left, lay partly open to the frightful drop below, but was partly enclosed by another cliff, the side of a second mountain, which impinged on the one I had been climbing. The circular apertures into which the larls' chains were being drawn were located in these two cliffs. As the chains were drawn back, the protesting larls were dragged to different sides. Thus a passage of sorts was cleared between them, but the passage led only, as far as I could see, to a blank wall of stone. Yet I supposed this seemingly impervious wall must house the portal of the Hall of Priest-Kings.

As the beasts had felt the tug of the chains they had slunk snarling back against the cliffs, and now they crouched down, their chains little more than massive leashes. I thought the snowy whiteness of their pelts was beautiful. Throaty growls menaced me, and an occasional paw, the claws extended, was lifted, but the beasts made no effort now to pull against the grim, jewel-set collars which bound them.

I had not long to wait for only a few moments later, perhaps no more than ten Gorean Ihn, a section of stone rolled silently back and upward revealing a rock passage beyond of perhaps some eight feet square.

I hesitated, for how did I know but that the chains of the larls might be loosed once I was between them. How did I know what might lie before me in that dark, quiet passage? As I hesitated that moment, I became aware of a motion inside the passage, which gradually became a white-clad rather short, rotund figure.

To my amazement a man stepped from the passage, blinking against the sun. He was clad in a white robe, somewhat resembling those of the Initiates. He wore sandals. His cheeks were red and his head bald. He had long whiskery sideburns which flared merrily from his muffinlike face. Small bright eyes twinkled under heavy white eyebrows. Most was I surprised to find him holding a tiny, round pipe from which curled a bright wisp of smoke. Tobacco is unknown on Gor, though there are certain habits or vices to take its place, in particular the stimulation afforded by chewing on the leaves of the Kanda plant, the roots of which, oddly enough, when ground and dried, constitute an extremely deadly poison.

I carefully regarded the small, rotund gentleman who stood framed so incongruously in the massive stone portal. I found it impossible to believe that he could be dangerous, that he could in any way be associated with the dreaded Priest-Kings of Gor. He was simply too cheerful, too open and ingenuous, too frank, and only too obviously pleased to see and welcome me. It was impossible not to be drawn to him; I found that I liked him, though I had just met him; and that I wanted him to like me, and that I felt he did, and that this pleased me.

If I had seen this man in my own world, this small, rotund, merry gentleman with his florid coloring and cheerful manner I would have thought him necessarily English, and of a sort one seldom encounters nowadays. If one had encountered him in the Eighteenth Century one might take him for a jolly, snuff-sniffing, roisterous country squire, knowing himself the salt of the earth, not above twitting the parson nor pinching the serving girls; in the Nineteenth Century he would have owned an old book shop and worked at a high desk, quite outdated, kept his money in a sock, distributed it indiscriminately to all who asked him for it, and publicly read Chaucer and Darwin to scandalize lady customers and the local clergy; in my own time such a man could only be a college professor, for there are few other refuges save wealth left in my world for men such as he; one could imagine him ensconced in a university chair, perhaps affluent enough for gout, reposing in his tenure, puffing on his pipe, a connoisseur of ales and castles, a gusty aficionado of bawdy Elizabethan drinking songs, which he would feel it his duty to bequeath, piously, as a portion of their rich literary heritage, to generations of recent, proper graduates of Eton and Harrow. The small eyes regarded me, twinkling.

With a start I noted that the pupils of his eyes were red.

When I started a momentary flicker of annoyance crossed his feaures, but in an instant he was again his chuckling, affable, bubbling self.

"Come, come," he said. "Come along, Cabot. We have been waiting for you."

He knew my name.

Who was waiting?

But of course he would know my name, and those who would be waiting would be the Priest-Kings of Gor.

I forgot about his eyes, for it did not seem important at the time, for some reason. I suppose that I thought that I had been mistaken. I had not been. He had now stepped back into the shadows of the passage.

"You are coming, aren't you?" he asked.

"Yes," I said.

"My name is Parp," he said, standing back in the passage. He puffed once on his pipe. "Parp," he repeated, puffing once again.

He had not extended his hand.

I looked at him without speaking.

It seemed a strange name for a Priest-King. I do not know what I expected. He seemed to sense my puzzlement.

"Yes," said the man, "Parp." He shrugged. "It's not much of a name for a Priest-King, but then I'm not much of a Priest-King." He chuckled.

"Are you a Priest-King?" I asked.

Again the momentary flicker of annoyance crossed his features. "Of course," he said.

It seemed that my heart stopped beating.

At that moment one of the larls gave a sudden roar. I shivered, but to my surprise the man who called himself Parp clutched his pipe in a white hand and seemed to give a start of terror. In a moment he was quite recovered. I found it strange that a Priest-King should fear a larl.

Without waiting to see if I would follow him he turned suddenly and went back down the passage.

I gathered my weapons and followed him. Only the rumbling growl of the now sullen mountain larls as I passed between them convinced me that I could not be dreaming, that I had come at last to the Hall of Priest-Kings.

4
The Hall of Priest-Kings

As I FOLLOWED THE MAN who called himself Parp down the
stone passage the portal behind me closed. I remember one
last glimpse of the Sardar Range, the path I had climbed, the
cold, blue sky and two snowy larls, one chained on either side
of the entrance.

My host did not speak but led the way with a merry stride,
an almost constant curl of smoke from his little round pipe
encircling his bald pate and muttonchop whiskers and drifting
back down the passage.

The passage was lit with energy bulbs, of the sort which I
had encountered in the tunnel of Marlenus which led beneath
the walls of Ar. There was nothing in the lighting of the
passage, or its construction, to suggest that the Priest-Kings'
Caste of Builders, if they had one, was any more advanced
than that of the men below the mountains. Too, the passage
was devoid of ornament, lacking the mosaics and tapestries
with which the beauty-loving Goreans below the mountains
are wont to glorify the places of their own habitation. The
Priest-Kings, as far as I could tell, had no art. Perhaps they
would regard it as a useless excrescence detracting from the
more sober values of life, such as, I supposed, study, medita-
tion and the manipulation of the lives of men.

I noted that the passage which I trod was well worn. It
had been polished by the sandals of countless men and
women who had walked before where I now walked, perhaps
thousands of years ago, perhaps yesterday, perhaps this
morning.

Then we came to a large hall. It was plain, but in its sheer
size it possessed a severe, lofty grandeur.

At the entrance to this room, or chamber, I stopped,
overcome with a certain sense of awe.

I found myself on the brink of entering what appeared to
be a great and perfect dome, having a diameter I am sure of
at least a thousand yards. I was pleased to see that its top
was a sparkling curvature of some transparent substance,

perhaps a special glass or plastic, for no glass or plastic with which I was familiar would be likely to withstand the stresses generated by such a structure. Beyond the dome I could see the welcome blue sky.

"Come, come, Cabot," remonstrated Parp.

I followed him.

In this great dome there was nothing save that at its very center there was a high dais and on this dais there was a large throne carved from a single block of stone.

It seemed to take us a long time to reach the dais. Our footsteps echoed hollowly across the great stone floor. At last we arrived.

"Wait here," said Parp, who pointed to an area outside a tiled ring which surrounded the dais.

I did not stand precisely where he asked but several feet away, but I did remain outside the tiled ring.

Parp puffed his way up the nine steps of the dais and climbed onto the stone throne. He was a strange contrast to the severe regality of the majestic seat on which he perched. His sandaled feet did not reach to the floor, and he made a slight grimace as he settled himself on the throne.

"Frankly," said Parp, "I think we make a mistake in sacrificing certain creature comforts in the Sardar." He tried to find some position that would satisfy him. "For example, a cushion would not be out of place on such a throne, do you think, Cabot?"

"On such a throne it would be out of place," I said.

"Ah yes," sighed Parp, "I suppose so."

Then, smartly, Parp cracked his pipe a few times against the side of the throne, scattering ashes and unsmoked tobacco about on the floor of the dais.

I regarded him without moving.

Then he began to fumble with the wallet which was slung from his belt, and removed a plastic envelope. I watched him closely, following every move. A frown crossed my face as I saw him take a pinch of tobacco from the bag and refill his pipe. Then he fumbled about a bit more and emerged with a narrow cylindrical, silverish object. For an instant it seemed to point at me.

I lifted my shield.

"Please, Cabot!" said Parp, with something of impatience, and used the silverish object to light his pipe.

I felt foolish.

Parp began to puff away contentedly on a new supply of tobacco. He had to turn slightly on the throne to look at me, as I had not chosen to stand directly where he had suggested.

"I do wish you would be more cooperative," he said.

Tapping the floor with the butt of my spear, I finally stood where he had directed.

Parp chuckled and puffed away.

I did not speak and he smoked one pipe. Then he cleaned it as before, knocking it against the side of the throne, and refilled it. He lit it again with the small, silverish object, and leaned back against the throne. He gazed up at the dome, so high above, and watched the smoke curl slowly upward.

"Did you have a good trip to the Sardar?" asked Parp.

"Where is my father?" I asked. "What of the city of Ko-ro-ba?" My voice choked. "What of the girl Talena, who was my Free Companion?"

"I hope you had a good trip," said Parp.

Then I began to feel rage creeping like hot, red vines through my blood.

Parp did not seem concerned.

"Not everyone has a good trip," said Parp.

My hand clenched on the spear.

I began to feel all the hatred of all the years that I had nursed against the Priest-Kings now uncontrollably, slowly, violently growing in my body, wild, fierce, those foliating scarlet vines of my fury that now seemed to encircle me, to enfold me, to engulf me, swelling, steaming, now writhing aflame about my body and before my eyes in the turbulent, burned air that separated me from the creature Parp and I cried, "Tell me what I want to know!"

"The primary difficulty besetting the traveler in the Sardar," continued Parp, "is probably the general harshness of the environment—for example, the inclemencies of the weather, particularly in the winter."

I lifted the spear and my eyes which must have been terrible in the apertures of my helmet were fixed on the heart of the man who sat upon the throne.

"Tell me!" I cried.

"The larls also," Parp went on, "are a not unformidable obstacle."

I cried with rage and strode forward to loose my spear but I wept and retained the weapon. I could not do murder.

Parp puffed away, smiling. "That was wise of you," he said.

I looked at him sullenly, my rage abated. I felt helpless.

"You could not have injured me, you know," said Parp.

I looked at him with wonder.

"No," he said. "Go ahead, if you wish, cast your spear."

I took the weapon and tossed it toward the foot of the dais. There was a sudden splintering burst of heat and I fell back, staggering. I shook my head to drive out the scarlet stars that seemed to race before my eyes.

At the foot of the dais there was a bit of soot and some droplets of melted bronze.

"You see," said Parp, "it would not have reached me."

I now understood the purpose of the tiled circle which surrounded the throne.

I removed my helmet and threw my shield to the floor.

"I am your prisoner," I said.

"Nonsense," said Parp, "you are my guest."

"I shall keep my sword," I said. "If you want it, you must take it from me."

Parp laughed merrily, his small round frame shaking on the heavy throne. "I assure you," he said, "I have no use for it." He looked at me, chuckling. "Nor have you," he added.

"Where are the others?" I asked.

"What others?" asked he.

"The other Priest-Kings," I said.

"I am afraid," said Parp, "that I am the Priest-Kings. All of them."

"But you said before 'We are waiting,' " I protested.

"Did I?" asked Parp.

"Yes," I said.

"Then it was merely a manner of speaking."

"I see," I said.

Parp seemed troubled. He seemed distracted.

He glanced up at the dome. It was getting late. He seemed

a bit nervous. His hands fumbled more with the pipe; a bit of tobacco spilled.

"Will you speak to me of my father, of my city, and of my love?" I asked.

"Perhaps," said Parp, "but now you are undoubtedly tired from your journey."

It was true that I was tired, and hungry.

"No," I said, "I would speak now."

For some reason Parp now seemed visibly uneasy. The sky above the dome was now gray and darkening. The Gorean night above, often black and beautiful with stars, now seemed to be approaching with swift stealth.

In the far distance, perhaps from some passage leading away from the Hall of Priest-Kings, I heard the roar of a larl.

Parp seemed to shiver on the throne.

"Is a Priest-King frightened of a larl?" I asked.

Parp chuckled, but not quite so merrily as usual. I could not understand his perturbation. "Do not be afraid," he said, "they are well secured."

"I am not afraid," I said, looking at him evenly.

"Myself," he said, "I'm forced to admit I've never quite gotten used to that awful racket they make."

"You are a Priest-King," I said, "why do you not simply lift your hand and destroy it?"

"Of what use is a dead larl?" asked Parp.

I did not reply.

I wondered why I had been allowed to reach the Sardar, to find the Hall of Priest-Kings, to stand before this throne.

Suddenly there was the sound of a distant, reverberating gong, a dull but penetrating sound which carried from somewhere even into the Hall of Priest-Kings.

Abruptly Parp stood up, his face white. "This interview," he said, "is at an end." He glanced about himself with ill-concealed terror.

"But what of me," I asked. "your prisoner?"

"My guest," insisted Parp irritably, nearly dropping his pipe. He pounded it once sharply against the throne and thrust it into the wallet he wore at his side.

"Your guest?" I asked.

"Yes," snapped Parp, darting his eyes from right to left, "—at least until it is time for you to be destroyed."

I stood without speaking.

"Yes," he repeated, looking down at me, "until it is time for you to be destroyed."

Then it seemed in the impending darkness in the Hall of Priest-Kings as he looked down on me that the pupils of his eyes for an instant glowed briefly, fiercely, like two tiny fiery disks of molten copper. I knew then that I had not been mistaken before. His eyes were unlike mine, or those of a human being. I knew then that Parp, whatever he might be, was not a man.

Then again came the sound of that great unseen gong, that distant sound, dull, penetrating, reverberating even in the vastness of the great hall in which we stood.

With a cry of terror Parp cast one last wild glance about the Hall of Priest-Kings and stumbled behind the great throne.

"Wait!" I cried.

But he had gone.

Wary of the tiled circle I traced its perimeter until I stood behind the throne. There was no sign of Parp. I walked the full ambit of the circle until I stood once more before the throne. I picked up my helmet and tossed it toward the dais. it clattered noisily against the first step. I followed it across the tiled circle which seemed harmless now that Parp had left.

Once more the distant and unseen gong rang out, and once more the Hall of Priest-Kings seemed filled with its ominous vibrations. It was the third stroke. I wondered why Parp had seemed to fear the coming of night, the sound of the gong.

I examined the throne and found no trace of a door behind it, but I knew that one must exist. Parp was, I was sure, though I had not touched him, as palpable as you or I. He could not simply have vanished.

It was now night outside.

Through the dome I could see the three moons of Gor and the bright stars above them.

They were very beautiful.

Then seized by an impulse I sat myself down on the great

throne in the Hall of Priest-Kings, drew my sword and placed it across my knees.

I recalled Parp's words, 'until it is time for you to be destroyed'.

For some reason I laughed and my laugh was the laugh of a warrior of Gor, full and mighty, unafraid, and it roared in the dark and lonely Hall of Priest-Kings.

5
Vika

I AWAKENED TO THE SOOTHING touch of a small sponge that bathed my forehead.

I grasped the hand that held the sponge and found that I held a girl's wrist.

"Who are you?" I asked.

I lay on my back on a large stone platform, some twelve feet square. Beneath me, twisted and tangled, lay heavy sleeping pelts, thick robes of fur, numerous sheets of scarlet silk. A cushion or two of yellow silk lay randomly on the platform.

The room in which I lay was large, perhaps forty feet square, and the sleeping platform lay at one end of the room but not touching the wall. The walls were of plain dark stone with energy bulbs fixed in them; the furnishings seemed to consist mostly of two or three large chests against one wall. There were no windows. The entire aspect was one of severity. There was no door on the room but there was a great portal, perhaps twelve feet wide and eighteen feet high. I could see a large passageway beyond.

"Please," said the girl.

I released her wrist.

She was comely to look on. Her hair was very light, the color of summer straw; it was straight and bound simply behind the back of her neck with a small fillet of white wool. Her eyes were blue, and sullen. Her full, red lips, which could have torn the heart of a man, seemed to pout; they were sensuous, unobtrusively rebellious, perhaps subtly contemptuous.

She knelt beside the platform.

Beside her, on the floor, rested a laver of polished bronze, filled with water, a towel and a straight-bladed Gorean shaving knife.

I rubbed my chin.

She had shaved me as I slept.

I shivered, thinking of the blade and my throat. "Your touch is light," I said.

She bowed her head.

She wore a long, simple sleeveless white robe, which fell gracefully about her in dignified classic folds. About her throat she had gracefully wrapped a scarf of white silk.

"I am Vika," she responded, "your slave."

I sat upright, cross-legged in the Gorean fashion, on the stone platform. I shook my head to clear it of sleep.

The girl rose and carried the bronze laver to a drain in one corner of the room and emptied it.

She walked well.

She then moved her hand past a glass disk in the wall and water emerged from a concealed aperture and curved into the shallow bowl. She rinsed the bowl and refilled it, and then took another towel of soft linen from a carved chest against the wall. She then again approached the stone platform and knelt before me, lifting the bowl. I took it and first drank from it and then set it on the stone platform before me, and washed. I wiped my face with the towel. She then gathered up the shaving knife, the towels I had used, and the bowl and went again to one side of the room.

She was very graceful, very lovely.

She rinsed the bowl again and set it against the wall to drain dry. She then rinsed and dried the shaving knife and put it in one of the chests. Then with a motion of her hand, which did not touch the wall, she opened a small, circular panel into which she dropped the two towels which I had used. When they had disappeared the circular panel closed.

She then returned into the vicinity of the stone platform, and knelt again before me, though some feet away.

We studied one another.

Neither spoke.

Her back was very straight and, kneeling, she rested back

on her heels. In her eyes there seemed to burn an irritable fury of helpless rage. I smiled at her, but she did not smile back but looked away, angrily.

When she looked again my eyes fixed on hers and we looked into one another's eyes for a long time until her lip trembled and her eyes fell before mine.

When she raised her head again I curtly gestured her nearer.

A look of angry defiance flashed in her eyes, but she rose to her feet and slowly approached me, and knelt beside the stone platform. I, still remaining cross-legged on the platform, reached forward and took her head in my hands, drawing it to mine. She knelt now but no longer on her heels and her face was brought forward and lifted to mine. The sensuous lips parted slightly and I became acutely conscious of her breathing, which seemed to deepen and quicken. I removed my hands from her head but she left it where I had placed it. I slowly unwrapped the white, silken scarf from her throat.

Her eyes seemed to cloud with angry tears.

As I had expected about her white throat there was fastened, graceful and gleaming, the slender, close-fitting collar of a Gorean slave girl.

It was a collar like most others, of steel, secured with a small, heavy lock which closed behind the girl's neck.

"You see," said the girl, "I did not lie to you."

"Your demeanor," I said, "does not suggest that of a slave girl."

She rose to her feet and backed away, her hands at the shoulders of her robe. "Nonetheless," she said, "I am a slave girl." She turned away. "Do you wish to see my brand?" she asked, contemptuously.

"No," I said.

So she was a slave girl.

But on her collar there was not written the name of her owner and his city, as I would have expected. Instead I had read there only the Gorean numeral which would correspond to '708'.

"You may do with me what you please," said the girl,

turning to face me. "As long as you are in this room I belong to you."

"I don't understand," I said.

"I am a Chamber Slave," she said.

"I don't understand," I said.

"It means," she said, irritably, "that I am confined to this room, and that I am the slave of whoever enters the room."

"But surely you can leave," I protested.

I gestured to the massive portal which, empty of a door or gate, led only too clearly into the corridor beyond.

"No," she said bitterly, "I cannot leave."

I arose and walked through the portal and found myself in a long stone passageway beyond it which stretched as far as I could see in either direction. It was lit with energy bulbs. In this passageway, placed regularly but staggered from one another, about fifty yards apart, were numerous portals like the one I had just passed through. From within any given room, one could not look into any other. None of these portals were hung with doors or gates, nor as far as I could see had they ever been hinged.

Standing in the passageway outside the room I extended my hand to the girl. "Come," I said, "there is no danger."

She ran to the far wall and crouched against it. "No," she cried.

I laughed and leaped into the room.

She crawled and stumbled away, for some reason terrified, until she found herself in the stone corner of the chamber.

She shrieked and clawed at the stone.

I gathered her in my arms and she fought like a she-larl, screaming. I wanted to convince her that there was no danger, that her fears were groundless. Her fingernails clawed across my face.

I was angered and I swept her from her feet so that she was helpless in my arms.

I began to carry her toward the portal.

"Please," she whispered, her voice hoarse with terror. "Please, Master, no, no, Master!"

She sounded so piteous that I abandoned my plan and released her, though I was irritated by her fear.

She collapsed at my feet, shaking and whimpering, and put her head to my knee.

"Please, no, Master," she begged.

"Very well," I said.

"Look!" she said, pointing to the great threshold.

I looked but I saw nothing other than the stone sides of the portal and on each side three rounded red domes, of perhaps four inches width apiece.

"They are harmless," I said, for I had passed them with safety. To demonstrate this I again left the chamber.

Outside the chamber, carved over the portal, I saw something I had not noted before. In Gorean notation, the numeral '708' was carved above the door. I now understood the meaning of the numeral on the girl's collar. I re-entered the chamber. "You see," I said, "they are harmless."

"For you," she said, "not for me."

"Why not?" I asked.

She turned away.

"Tell me," I said.

She shook her head.

"Tell me," I repeated, more sternly.

She looked at me. "Am I commanded?" she asked.

I did not wish to command her. "No," I said.

"Then," said she, "I shall not tell you."

"Very well," I said, "then you are commanded."

She looked at me through her tears and fear, with sudden defiance.

"Speak, Slave," I said.

She bit her lip with anger.

"Obey," I said.

"Perhaps," she said.

Angrily I strode to her and seized her by the arms. She looked up into my eyes and shivered. She saw that she must speak. She lowered her head in submission. "I obey," she said. "—Master."

I released her.

Again she turned away, going to the far wall.

"Long ago," she said, "when I first came to the Sardar and found the Hall of Priest-Kings, I was a young and foolish girl. I thought that the Priest-Kings possessed great wealth and that I, with my beauty—" she turned and looked at me and threw back her head— "for I am beautiful, am I not?"

I looked at her. And though her face was stained with the tears of her recent terror and her hair and robes were disarranged, she was beautiful, perhaps the more so because of her distress, which had at least shattered the icy aloofness with which she had originally regarded me. I knew that she now feared me, but for what reason I was uncertain. It had something to do with the door, with her fear that I might force her from the room.

"Yes," I said to her, "you are beautiful."

She laughed bitterly.

"Yes," she continued, "I, armed with my beauty, would come to the Sardar and wrest the riches and power of the Priest-Kings from them, for men had always sought to serve me, to give me what I wanted, and were the Priest-Kings not men?"

People had strange reasons for entering the Sardar, but the reason of the girl who called herself Vika seemed to me one of the most incredible. It was a plot which could have occurred only to a wild, spoiled, ambitious, arrogant girl, and perhaps as she had said, to one who was also young and foolish.

"I would be the Ubara of all Gor," she laughed, "with Priest-Kings at my beck and call, at my command all their riches and their untold powers!"

I said nothing.

"But when I came to the Sardar—" She shuddered. Her lips moved, but she seemed unable to speak.

I went to her and placed my arms about her shoulders, and she did not resist.

"There," she said, pointing to the small rounded domes set in the sides of the portal.

"I don't understand," I said.

She moved from my arms and approached the portal. When she was within perhaps a yard of the exit the small red domes began to glow.

"Here in the Sardar," she said, turning to face me, trembling, "they took me into the tunnels and locked over my head a hideous metal globe with lights and wires and when

they freed me they showed me a metal plate and told me
that the patterns of my brain, of my oldest and most primitive memories, were recorded on that plate . . ."

I listened intently, knowing that the girl could, even if of
High Caste, understand little of what had happened to her.
Those of the High Castes of Gor are permitted by the
Priest-Kings only the Second Knowledge, and those of the
lower castes are permitted only the more rudimentary First
Knowledge. I had speculated that there would be a Third
Knowledge, that reserved for Priest-Kings, and the girl's
account seemed to justify this conjecture. I myself would not
understand the intricate processes involved in the machine of
which she spoke but the purpose of the machine and the
theoretical principles that facilitated its purpose were reason-
ably clear. The machine she spoke of would be a brain-
scanner of some sort which would record three-dimensionally
the microstates of her brain, in particular those of the deeper, less alterable layers. If well done, the resulting plate
would be more individual than her fingerprints; it would be
as unique and personal as her own history; indeed, in a sense,
it would be a physical model of that same history, an isomor-
phic analog of her past as she had experienced it.

"That plate," she said, "is kept in the tunnels of the
Priest-Kings, but these—" and she shivered and indicated the
rounded domes, which were undoubtedly sensors of some
type, "are its eyes."

"There is a connection of some sort, though perhaps only a
beam of some type, between the plate and these cells," I
said, going to them and examining them.

"You speak strangely," she said.

"What would happen if you were to pass between them?" I
asked.

"They showed me," she said, her eyes filled with horror,
"by sending a girl between them who had not done her duty
as they thought she should."

Suddenly I started. "They?" I asked.

"The Priest-Kings," she replied simply.

"But there is only one Priest-King," I said, "who calls
himself Parp."

She smiled but did not respond to me. She shook her head sadly. "Ah, yes, Parp," she said.

I supposed at another time there might have been more Priest-Kings. Perhaps Parp was the last of the Priest-Kings? Surely it seemed likely that such massive structures as the Hall of Priest-Kings must have been the product of more than one being.

"What happened to the girl?" I asked.

Vika flinched. "It was like knives and fire," she said.

I now understood why she so feared to leave the room.

"Have you tried shielding yourself?" I asked, looking at the bronze laver which was drying against the wall.

"Yes," she said, "but the eye knows." She smiled ruefully. "It can see through metal."

I looked puzzled.

She went to the side of the room and picked up the bronze laver. Holding it before her as though to shield her face she approached the portal. Once more the rounded domes began to glow.

"You see," she said, "it knows. It can see through metal."

"I see," I said.

I silently congratulated the Priest-Kings on the efficacy of their devices. Apparently the rays which must emanate from the sensors, rays not within that portion of the spectrum visible to the human eye, must possess the power to penetrate at least common molecular structures, something like an X ray pierces flesh.

Vika glared at me sullenly. "I have been a prisoner in this room for nine years," she said.

"I am sorry," I said.

"I came to the Sardar," she laughed, "to conquer the Priest-Kings and rob them of their riches and power!"

She ran to the far wall, suddenly breaking into tears. Facing it she pounded on it weeping.

She spun to face me.

"And instead," she cried. "I have only these walls of stone and the steel collar of a slave girl!"

She helplessly, enraged, tried to tear the slender, graceful, obdurate band from her white throat. Her fingers tore at it in frenzy, in fury, and she wept with frustration, and at last she desisted. Of course she still wore the badge of her servitude. The steel of a Gorean slave collar is not made to be removed at a girl's pleasure.

She was quiet now.

She looked at me, curiously. "At one time," she said, "men sought to please me but now it is I who must please them."

I said nothing.

Her eyes regarded me, rather boldly I thought, as though inviting me to exercise my authority over her, to address to her any command I might see fit, a command which she of course would have no choice but to obey.

There was a long silence I did not feel I should break. Vika's life, in its way, had been hard, and I wished her no harm.

Her lips curled slightly in scorn.

I was well aware of the taunt of her flesh, the obvious challenge of her eyes and carriage.

She seemed to say to me, you cannot master me.

I wondered how many men had failed.

With a shrug she went to the side of the sleeping platform and picked up the white, silken scarf I had removed from her throat. She wrapped it again about her throat, concealing the collar.

"Do not wear the scarf," I said gently.

Her eyes sparkled with anger.

"You wish to see the collar," she hissed.

"You may wear the scarf if you wish," I said.

Her eyes clouded with bewilderment.

"But I do not think you should," I said.

"Why?" she asked.

"Because I think that you are more beautiful without it," I said, "but more importantly to hide a collar is not to remove it."

Rebellious fire flared in her eyes, and then she smiled. "No," she said, "I suppose not." She turned away bitterly. "When I am alone," she said, "I pretend that I am free, that I am a great lady, the Ubara of a great city, even of Ar—but when a man enters my chamber, then again I am only a slave." She slowly pulled the scarf from her throat and dropped it to the floor, and turned to face me. She lifted her head arrogantly and I saw that the collar was very beautiful on her throat.

"With me," I said gently, "you are free."

She looked at me scornfully. "There have been a hundred men in this chamber before you," she said, "and they have taught me—and taught me well—that I wear a collar."

"Nonetheless," I said, "with me you are free."

"And there will be a hundred after you," she said.

I supposed she spoke the truth. I smiled. "In the meantime," I said, "I grant you freedom."

She laughed. "To hide a collar," she said, in a mocking tone, "is not to remove it."

I laughed. She had had the best of the exchange. "Very well," I conceded, "you are a slave girl."

When I said this, though I spoke in jest, she stiffened as though I might have lashed her mouth with the back of my hand.

Her old insolence had returned. "Then use me," she said bitterly. "Teach me the meaning of the collar."

I marveled. Vika, in spite of her nine years of captivity, her confinement in this chamber, was still a headstrong, spoiled, arrogant girl, and one fully aware of her yet unconquered flesh, and the sinuous power which her beauty might exercise over men, its capacity to torture them and drive them wild, to bend them in the search for its smallest favors compliantly to her will. There stood before me insolently the beautiful, predatory girl who had come so long ago to the Sardar to exploit Priest-Kings.

"Later," I said.

She choked with fury.

I bore her no ill will but I found her as irritating as she was beautiful. I could understand that she, a proud, intelligent girl, could not but resent the indignities of her position, being forced to serve with the full offices of the slave girl whomsoever the Priest-Kings might see fit to send to her chamber, but yet I found in these grievances, great though they might be, no excuse for the deep hostility towards myself which seemed to suffuse her graceful being. After all, I, too, was a prisoner of Priest-Kings and I had not chosen to come to her chamber.

"How did I come to this chamber?" I asked.

"They brought you," she said.

"Priest-Kings?" I asked.

"Yes," she said.

"Parp?" I asked.

For answer she only laughed.

"How long did I sleep?" I asked.

"Long," she said.

"How long?" I asked.

"Fifteen Ahn," she said.

I whistled to myself. The Gorean day is divided into twenty Ahn. I had nearly slept around the clock.

"Well, Vika," I said, "I think I am now ready to make use of you."

"Very well, Master," said the girl, and the expression by which she had addressed me seemed dipped in irony. Her hand loosened the clasp by which her garment was secured over her left shoulder.

"Can you cook?" I asked.

She looked at me. "Yes," she snapped. She fumbled irritably with the clasp of her robe, but her fingers were clumsy with rage. She was unable to fasten the clasp.

I fastened it for her.

She looked up at me, her eyes blazing. "I will prepare food," she said.

"Be quick, Slave Girl," I said.

Her shoulders shook with rage.

"I see," I said, "that I must teach you the meaning of your collar." I took a step toward her and she turned stumbling with a cry and ran to the corner of the room.

My laugh was loud.

Almost instantly, reddening, Vika regained her composure and straightened herself, tossing her head and brushing back a melody of blond hair which had fallen across her forehead. The wool fillet she had worn to bind her hair had loosened. She fixed on me a look of the most lofty disdain and, standing against the wall, lifting her arms behind the back of her neck, she prepared to replace the fillet.

"No," I said.

I had decided I liked her better with her hair loose.

Deliberately, testing me, she continued to tie the fillet.

My eyes met hers.

Angrily she pulled the fillet from her hair and threw it to the floor, and turned away to busy herself with the preparation of my meal.

Her hair was very beautiful.

6
When Priest-Kings Walk

VIKA COULD COOK WELL AND I enjoyed the meal she prepared.

Stores of food were kept in concealed cabinets at one side of the room, which were opened in the same fashion as the other apertures I had observed earlier.

At my command Vika demonstrated for me the manner of opening and closing the storage and disposal areas in her unusual kitchen.

The temperature of the water which sprang from the wall tap, I learned, was regulated by the direction in which the shadow of a hand fell across a light-sensitive cell above the tap; the amount of water was correlated with the speed with which the hand passed before the sensor. I was interested to note that one received cold water by a shadow passing from right to left and hot water by a shadow passing from left to right. This reminded me of faucets on Earth, in which the hot water tap is on the left and the cold on the right. Undoubtedly there is a common reason underlying these similar arrangements on Gor and Earth. More cold water is used than hot, and most individuals using the water are right-handed.

The food which Vika withdrew from the storage apertures was not refrigerated but was protected by something resembling a foil of blue plastic. It was fresh and appetizing.

First she boiled and simmered a kettle of Sullage, a common Gorean soup consisting of three standard ingredients and, as it is said, whatever else may be found, saving only the rocks of the field. The principal ingredients of Sullage are the golden Sul, the starchy, golden-brown vine-borne fruit of the golden-leaved Sul plant; the curled, red, ovate leaves of the

Tur-Pah, a tree parasite, cultivated in host orchards of Tur trees; and the salty, blue secondary roots of the Kes Shrub, a small, deeply rooted plant which grows best in sandy soil.

The meat was a steak, cut from the loin of a bosk, a huge, shaggy, long-horned, ill-tempered bovine which shambles in large, slow-moving herds across the prairies of Gor. Vika seared this meat, as thick as the forearm of a warrior, on a small iron grill over a kindling of charcoal cylinders, so that the thin margin of the outside was black, crisp and flaky and sealed within by the touch of the fire was the blood-rich flesh, hot and fat with juice.

Beyond the Sullage and the bosk steak there was the inevitable flat, rounded loaf of the yellow Sa-Tarna bread. The meal was completed by a handful of grapes and a draught of water from the wall tap. The grapes were purple and, I suppose, Ta grapes from the lower vineyards of the terraced island of Cos some four hundred pasangs from Port Kar. I had tasted some only once before, having been introduced to them at a feast given in my honor by Lara, who was Tatrix of the city of Tharna. If they were indeed Ta grapes I supposed they must have come by galley from Cos to Port Kar, and from Port Kar to the Fair of En'Kar'a. Port Kar and Cos are hereditary enemies, but such traditions would not be likely to preclude some profitable smuggling. But perhaps they were not Ta grapes for Cos was far distant, and even if carried by tarns, the grapes would probably not seem so fresh. I dismissed the matter from my mind. I wondered why there was only water to drink, and none of the fermented beverages of Gor, such as Paga, Ka-la-na wine or Kal-da. I was sure that if these were available Vika would have set them before me.

I looked at her.

She had not prepared herself a portion but, after I had been served, had knelt silently to one side, back on her heels in the position of a Tower Slave, a slave to whom largely domestic duties would be allotted in the Gorean apartment cylinders.

On Gor, incidentally, chairs have special significance, and do not often occur in private dwellings. They tend to be reserved for significant personages, such as administrators and judges. Moreover, although you may find this hard to understand, they are not thought to be comfortable. Indeed, when I had returned to Earth from my first trip to Gor I had found that one of the minor inconveniences of my return was reaccustoming myself to the simple business of sitting on chairs. I felt, for some months, rather awkward, rather unsteady perched on a little wooden platform supported by four narrow sticks. Perhaps if you can imagine yourself suddenly being forced to sit on rather high end tables you can sense the feeling.

The Gorean male, at ease, usually sits cross-legged and the female kneels, resting back on her heels. The position of the Tower Slave, in which Vika knelt, differs from that of a free woman only in the position of the wrists which are held before her and, when not occupied, crossed as though for binding. A free woman's wrists are never so placed. The Older Tarl, who had been my mentor in arms years ago in Ko-ro-ba, had once told me the story of a free woman, desperately in love with a warrior, who, in the presence of her family was entertaining him, and whose wrists, unconsciously, had assumed the position of a slave. It was only with difficulty that she had been restrained from hurling herself in mortification from one of the high bridges. The Older Tarl had guffawed in recounting this anecdote and was scarcely less pleased by its sequel. It seems she thereafter, because of her embarrassment, would never see the warrior and he, at last, impatient and desiring her, carried her off as a slave girl, and returned to the city months later with her as his Free Companion. At the time that I had been in Ko-ro-ba the couple had still been living in the city. I wondered what had become of them.

The position of the Pleasure Slave, incidentally, differs from the position of both the free woman and the Tower Slave. The hands of a Pleasure Slave normally rest on her thighs but, in some cities, for example, Thentis, I believe, they are crossed behind her. More significantly, for the free woman's hands may also rest on her thighs, there is a difference in the placement of the knees. In all these kneeling positions, incidentally, even that of the Pleasure Slave, the Gorean woman carries herself well; her back is straight and her chin is high. She tends to be vital and beautiful to look upon.

"Why is there nothing but water to drink?" I asked Vika.

She shrugged. "I suppose," she said, "because the Chamber Slave is alone much of the time."

I looked at her, not fully understanding.

She gazed at me frankly. "It would be too easy then," she said.

I felt like a fool. Of course the Chamber Slaves would not be permitted the escape of intoxication, for if they were so allowed to lighten their bondage undoubtedly, in time, their beauty, their utility to the Priest-Kings would be diminished; they would become unreliable, lost in dreams and wines.

"I see," I said.

"Only twice a year is the food brought," she said.

"And it is brought by Priest-Kings?" I asked.

"I suppose," she said.

"But you do not know?"

"No," said she. "I awaken on some morning and there is food."

"I suppose Parp brings it," I said.

She looked at me, with a trace of amusement.

"Parp the Priest-King," I said.

"Did he tell you that?" she asked.

"Yes," I said.

"I see," she said.

The girl was apparently unwilling to speak more of this matter, and so I did not press her.

I had almost finished the meal. "You have done well," I congratulated her. "The meal is excellent."

"Please," she said, "I am hungry."

I looked at her dumbfounded. She had not prepared herself a portion and so I had assumed that she had eaten, or was not hungry, or would prepare her own meal later.

"Make yourself something," I said.

"I cannot," she said simply. "I can eat only what you give me."

I cursed myself for a fool.

Had I now become so much the Gorean warrior that I could disregard the feelings of a fellow creature, in particular those of a girl, who must be protected and cared for? Could it be that I had, as the Codes of my Caste recommended, not even considered her, but merely regarded her as a rightless animal, no more than a subject beast, an abject instrument to my interests and pleasures, a slave?

"I am sorry," I said.

"Was it not your intention to discipline me?" she asked.

"No," I said.

"Then my master is a fool," she said, reaching for the meat that I had left on my plate.

I caught her wrist.

"It is now my intention to discipline you," I said.

Her eyes briefly clouded with tears. "Very well," she said, withdrawing her hand.

Vika would go hungry that night.

Although it was late, according to the chamber chronometer, fixed in the lid of one of the chests, I prepared to leave the room. Unfortunately there was no natural light in the room and so one could not judge the time by the sun or the stars and moons of Gor. I missed them. Since I had awakened, the energy bulbs had continued to burn at a constant and undiminished rate.

I had washed as well as I could squatting in the stream of water which emerged from the wall.

In one of the chests against the wall I had found, among the garments of various other castes, a warrior's tunic. I donned this, as my own had been torn by the larl's claws.

Vika had unrolled a straw mat which she placed on the floor at the foot of the great stone couch in the chamber. On this, wrapped in a light blanket, her chin on her knees, she sat watching me.

A heavy slave ring was set in the bottom of the couch to which I might have, had I pleased, chained her.

I buckled on my sword.

"You are not going to leave the chamber, are you?" asked Vika, the first words she had said to me since the meal.

"Yes," I said.

"But you may not," she said.

"Why?" I asked, alert.

"It is forbidden," she said.

"I see," I said.

I started for the door.

"When the Priest-Kings wish you, they will come for you," she said. "Until then you must wait."

"I do not care to wait," I said.

"But you must," she insisted, standing.

I went to her and placed my hands on her shoulders. "Do not fear the Priest-Kings so," I said.

She saw that my resolve was not altered.

"If you go," she said, "return at least before the second gong."

"Why?" I asked.

"For yourself," she said, looking down.

"I am not afraid," I said.

"Then for me," she said, not raising her eyes.

"But why?" I asked.

She seemed confused. "I am afraid to be alone," she said.

"But you have been alone many nights," I pointed out.

She looked up at me and I could not read the expression in her troubled eyes. "One does not cease to be afraid," she said.

"I must go," I said.

Suddenly in the distance I heard the rumble of the gong which I had heard before in the Hall of Priest-Kings.

Vika smiled up at me. "You see," she said in relief, "it is too late. Now you must remain."

"Why?" I asked.

She looked away, avoiding my eyes. "Because the energy bulbs will soon be dimmed," she said, "and it will be the hours allotted for sleep."

She seemed unwilling to speak further.

"Why must I remain?" I asked.

I held her shoulders more firmly and shook her to force her to speak. "Why?" I insisted.

Fear crept into her eyes.

"Why?" I demanded.

Then came the second rumbling stroke of the distant gong, and Vika seemed to tremble in my arms.

Her eyes were wide with fear.

I shook her again, savagely. "Why?" I cried.

She could hardly speak. Her voice was scarcely a whisper. "Because after the gong—" she said.

"Yes?" I demanded.

"—they walk," she said.

"Who!" I demanded.

"The Priest-Kings!" she cried and turned from me.

"I am not afraid of Parp," I said.

She turned and looked at me. "He is not a Priest-King," she said quietly.

And then came the third and final stroke of that distant gong and at the same instant the energy bulbs in the room dimmed and I understood that now somewhere in the long corridors of that vast edifice there walked the Priest-Kings of Gor.

7
I Hunt for Priest-Kings

IN SPITE OF VIKA'S PROTESTS it was with a light heart that I strode into the passageway beyond her chamber. I would seek the Priest-Kings of Gor.

She followed me almost to the portal, and I can remember how the sensors set in that great threshold in the dimmed light of the energy bulbs began to glow and pulse as she neared them.

I could see her white garment and sense the pale beauty of her skin as she stood back from the portal in the semidarkened chamber.

"Please do not go," she called to me.

"I must," I said.

"Come back," she cried.

I did not answer her but began to prowl down the hallway.

"I'm afraid," I heard her call.

I assumed she would be safe, as she had been on countless nights and so I went on.

I thought I heard her weep, and supposed that she did so for herself, because she was frightened.

I continued down the passageway.

My business was not to console her, not to tell her not to

be afraid, not to give her the comfort of another human presence. My business was with the dread denizens of these dim passageways which had so inspired her terror; my business was not that of the comforter or friend, but that of the warrior.

As I went down the passageway I looked into the various chambers, identical with my own, which lined it. Each, like mine, lacked a gate or door, and had for its entrance only that massive portal, perhaps some twelve feet wide and eighteen feet high. I would not have enjoyed sleeping in such a room, for there was no way to protect oneself from the hall, and of course eventually one would need sleep.

Almost all of the chambers I passed, and I passed many, seemed to be empty.

Two, however, housed Chamber Slaves, girls like Vika, clad and collared identically. I supposed the only difference in the attire of the three girls would have been the numerals engraved on their collars. Vika of course had worn a scarf and these girls did not, but now Vika no longer wore her scarf; now her collar, steel and gleaming, locked, encircling her fair throat, was as evident and beautiful as theirs, proclaiming her to the eyes of all, like them, only a slave girl.

The first girl was a short, sturdy wench with thick ankles and wide, exciting shoulders, probably of peasant stock. Her hair had been braided and looped over her right shoulder; it was hard in the light to determine its color. She had risen from her mat at the foot of the couch unbelievingly, blinking and rubbing her heavy-lidded, ovoid eyes. As far as I could tell she was alone in the chamber. When she approached the portal its sensors began to glow and pulse as had Vika's.

"Who are you?" asked the girl, her accent suggesting the Sa-Tarna fields above Ar and toward the Tamber Gulf.

"Have you seen Priest-Kings?" I asked.

"Not this night," she said.

"I am Cabot of Ko-ro-ba," I said and went on.

The second girl was tall, fragile and willowy, with slender ankles and large, hurt eyes; she had dark, curling hair that fell about her shoulders and stood out against the white of her garment; she may have been of High Caste; without speaking to her it would be hard to tell; even then it might be difficult to be sure, for the accents of some of the higher artisan castes approximate pure High Caste Gorean; she stood with her back against the far wall, the palms of her hands against it, her eyes fastened on me, frightened, scarcely breathing. As far as I could tell she too was alone.

"Have you seen Priest-Kings?" I asked.

She shook her head vigorously, No.

Still wondering if she were of High Caste, and smiling to myself, I continued down the passageway.

Both of the girls had in their way been beautiful but I found Vika superior to both.

My Chamber Slave's accent had been pure High Caste Gorean though I could not place the city. Probably her caste had been that of the Builders or Physicians, for had her people been Scribes I would have expected a greater subtlety of inflections, the use of less common grammatical cases; and had her people been of the Warriors I would have expected a blunter speech, rather belligerently simple, expressed in great reliance on the indicative mood and, habitually, a rather arrogant refusal to venture beyond the most straightforward of sentence structures. On the other hand these generalizations are imperfect, for Gorean speech is no less complex than that of any of the great natural language communities of the Earth nor are its speakers any the less diverse. It is, incidentally, a beautiful language; it can be as subtle as Greek; as direct as Latin; as expressive as Russian; as rich as English; as forceful as German. To the Goreans it is always, simply, The Language, as though there were no others, and those who do not speak it are regarded immediately as barbarians. This sweet, fierce, liquid speech is the common bond that tends to hold together the Gorean world. It is the common property of the Administrator of Ar, a herdsman beside the Vosk, a peasant from Tor, a scribe from Thentis, a metalworker from Tharna, a physician from Cos, a pirate from Port Kar, a warrior from Ko-ro-ba.

I found it difficult to remove from my mind the image of the two Chamber Slaves, and that of Vika, perhaps because the plight of these girls touched my heart, perhaps because each, though differently, was beautiful. I found myself congratulating myself that I had been taken to the chamber of

Vika, for I had thought her the most beautiful. Then I wondered if my having been brought to her chamber, and not to that of one of the others had been simply my good fortune. It occurred to me that Vika, in some ways, resembled Lara, who was Tatrix of Tharna, for whom I had cared. She was shorter than Lara and more fully bodied but they would have been considered of the same general physical type. Vika's eyes were a sullen, smoldering, taunting blue; the blue of Lara's eyes had been brighter, as clear and, when not impassioned, as soft as the summer sky over Ko-ro-ba; when impassioned they had burned as fiercely, as beautifully, as helplessly as the walls of a raped city. Lara's lips had been rich and fine, sensitive and curious, tender, eager, hungry; the lips of Vika were maddening; I recalled those lips, full and red, pouting, defiant, scornful, scarlet with a slave girl's challenge to my blood; I wondered if Vika might be a bred slave, a Passion Slave, one of those girls bred for beauty and passion over generations by the zealous owners of the great Slave Houses of Ar, for lips such as Vika's were a feature often bred into Passion Slaves; they were lips formed for the kiss of a master.

And as I pondered these things I sensed that it had not been accident that I had been carried to Vika's chamber but that this had been part of a plan by the Priest-Kings. I had sensed that Vika had defeated and broken many men, and I sensed that the Priest-Kings might be curious to see how I might fare with her. I wondered if Vika herself had been instructed by Priest-Kings to subdue me. I gathered that she had not. It was not the way of Priest-Kings. Vika would be all unconscious of their machinations; she would simply be herself, which is what the Priest-Kings would desire. She would simply be Vika, insolent, aloof, contemptuous, provocative, untamed though collared, determined to be the master though she were the slave. I wondered how many men had fallen at her feet, how many men she had forced to sleep at the foot of the great stone couch, in the shadow of the slave ring, while she herself reclined on the pelts and silks of the master.

After some hours I found myself again in the Hall of

Priest-Kings. I was gladdened to see once more the moons and stars of Gor hurtling in the sky above the dome.

My footsteps rang hollowly on the stones of the floor. The great chamber reposed in vastness and stillness. The empty throne loomed silent and awesome.

"I am here!" I cried. "I am Tarl Cabot. I am a warrior of Ko-ro-ba and I issue the challenge of a warrior to the Priest-Kings of Gor! Let us do battle! Let us make war!"

My voice echoed for a long time in the vast chamber, but I received no response to my challenge.

I called out again and again there was no response.

I decided to return to Vika's chamber.

On another night I might explore further, for there were other passageways, other portals visible from where I stood. It might take days to pursue them all.

I set out on my way back to Vika's chamber.

I had walked perhaps an Ahn and was deep inside one of the long, dimly lit passageways which led in the direction of her chamber when I seemed somehow to sense a presence behind me.

I spun quickly about drawing my sword in the same motion.

The corridor behind me was empty.

I slammed the blade back in the sheath and continued on.

I had not walked far when I again became uneasy. This time I did not turn, but walked slowly ahead, listening behind me with every fiber I could bend to the effort. When I came to a bend in the passageway I rounded it, and then pressed myself against the wall and waited.

Slowly, very slowly, I drew the sword, taking care that it made no sound as it left its sheath.

I waited but nothing occurred.

I have the patience of a warrior and I waited for a long time. When men stalk one another with weapons it is well to have patience, great patience.

It of course occurred to me a hundred times that I was foolish for actually I was conscious of having heard nothing. Yet my awareness or sense that something followed me in the corridor might well have been occasioned by some tiny sound which my conscious mind had not even registered, but yet which had impinged on my senses, leaving as its only conscious trace a vague wind of suspicion. At last I decided to force the game. My decision was motivated in part by the fact that the hall allowed few concealments for ambush and I would presumably see my pursuer almost as soon as he saw me. If he were not carrying a missile weapon it would make little difference. And if he had been carrying such a weapon why had he not slain me before? I smiled grimly. If it were a matter of waiting I acknowledged that the Priest-King, if such it were, who followed me had had the best of things. For all I knew a Priest-King could wait like a stone or tree, nerveless until necessary. I had waited perhaps better than an Ahn and I was covered with sweat. My muscles ached for motion. It occurred to me that whatever followed might have heard the cessation of my footsteps. That it knew that I was waiting. How acute would be the senses of Priest-Kings? Perhaps they would be relatively feeble, having grown accustomed to reliance on instrumentation; perhaps they would be other than the senses of men, sharper if only from a differing genetic heritage, capable of discriminating and interpreting sensory cues that would not even be available to the primitive five senses of men. Never before had I been so aware of the thin margin of reality admitted into the human nervous system, little more than a razor's width of apprehension given the multiple, and complex physical processes which formed our environment. The safest thing for me would be to continue on as I had been doing, a pattern of action which would give me the benefit of the shield formed by the turn in the passage. But I had no wish to continue on. I tensed myself for the leap and cry that would fling me into the open, the sudden interruption in the stillness of the passageway that might be sufficient to impair the steadiness of a spear arm, the calm setting of a crossbow's iron quarrel on its guide.

And so I uttered the war cry of Ko-ro-ba and leaped, sword ready, to face what might follow me.

A howl of bitter rage escaped my lips as I saw that the passageway was empty.

Maddened beyond understanding I began to race down the passageway, retracing my steps to confront what might be in the passage. I had run for perhaps a half pasang when I stopped, panting and furious with myself.

"Come out!" I cried. "Come out!"

The stillness of the passageway taunted me.

I remembered Vika's words, When the Priest-Kings wish you, they will come for you.

Angrily I stood alone in the passageway in the dimmed light of its energy bulbs, my unused sword grasped futilely in my hand.

Then I sensed something.

My nostrils flared slightly and then as carefully as one might examine an object by eye I smelled the air of the passageway.

I had never much relied on this sense.

Surely I had enjoyed the scent of flowers and women, of hot, fresh bread, roasted meat, Paga and wines, harness leather, the oil with which I protected the blade of my sword from rust, of green fields and storm winds, but seldom had I considered the sense of smell in the way one would consider that of vision or touch, and yet it too had its often neglected store of information ready for the man who was ready to make use of it.

And so I smelled the passageway and to my nostrils, vague but undeniable, there came an odor that I had never before encountered. It was, as far as I could tell at that time, a simple odor, though later I would learn that it was the complex product of odors yet more simple than itself. I find it impossible to describe this odor, much as one might find it difficult to describe the taste of a citrus fruit to one who had never tasted it or anything much akin to it. It was however slightly acrid, irritating to my nostrils. It reminded me vaguely of the odor of an expended cartridge.

Although there was nothing now with me in the passage it had left its trace.

I knew now that I had not been alone.

I had caught the scent of a Priest-King.

I resheathed my sword and returned to Vika's chamber. I hummed a warrior's tune, for somehow I was happy.

8
Vika Leaves the Chamber

"WAKE UP, WENCH!" I CRIED, striding into Vika's chamber, clapping my hands sharply twice.

The startled girl cried out and leaped to her feet. She had been lying on the straw mat at the foot of the stone couch. So suddenly had she arisen that she had struck her knee against the couch and this had not much pleased her. I had meant to scare her half to death and I was pleased to see that I had.

She looked at me angrily. "I was not asleep," she said.

I strode to her and held her head in my hands, looking at her eyes. She had spoken the truth.

"You see!" she said.

I laughed.

She lowered her head, and then looked up shyly. "I am happy," she said, "that you have returned."

I looked at her and sensed that she was.

"I suppose," I said, "that in my absence you have been in the pantry."

"No," she said, "I have not," adding as an acrimonious afterthought, "—Master."

I had offended her pride.

"Vika," I said, "I think it is time that some changes were made around here."

"Nothing ever changes here," she said.

I looked around the room. The sensors in the room interested me. I examined them again. I was elated. Then, methodically, I began to search the room. Although the sensors and the mode of their application were fiendish and beyond my immediate competence to fully understand, they suggested nothing ultimately mysterious, nothing which might not eventually be explained. There was nothing about them to encourage me to believe that the Priest-Kings, or King as it might be, were ultimately unfathomable or incomprehensible beings.

Moreover in the corridor beyond I had sensed the traces,

tangible traces, of a Priest-King. I laughed. Yes, I had smelled a Priest-King, or its effects. The thought amused me.

More fully than ever before I then understood how much the forces of superstition have depressed and injured men. No wonder the Priest-Kings hid behind their palisade in the Sardar and let the myths of the Initiates build a wall of human terror about them, no wonder they let their nature and ends be secret, no wonder they took such pains to conceal and obscure their plans and purposes, their devices, their instrumentation, their limitations! I laughed aloud.

Vika watched me, puzzled, surely convinced that I must have lost my mind.

I cracked my fist into my open palm. "Where is it?" I cried.

"What?" whispered Vika.

"The Priest-Kings see and the Priest-Kings hear!" I cried. "But how?"

"By their power," said Vika, moving back to the wall.

I had examined the entire room as well as I could. It might be possible, of course, to use some type of penetrating beam which if subtly enough adjusted might permit the reception of signals through walls and then relay these to a distant screen, but I doubted that such a device, though perhaps within the capacities of the Priest-Kings, would be used in the relatively trivial domestic surveillance of these chambers.

Then my eye saw, directly in the center of the ceiling, another energy bulb, like those in the walls, only the bulb was not lit. That was a mistake on the Priest-Kings' part. But of course the device could be in any of the bulbs. Perhaps one of the almost inexhaustible energy bulbs, which can burn for years, had as a simple matter of fact at last burned out.

I leaped to the center of the stone platform. I cried to the girl, "Bring me the laver."

She was convinced I was mad.

"Quickly!" I shouted, and she fairly leapt to fetch the bronze bowl.

I seized the bowl from her hand and hurled it underhanded up against the bulb which, though it had apparently burned out, shattered with a great flash and hiss of smoke and

sparks. Vika screamed and crouched behind the stone platform. Down from the cavity where the energy bulb had been
there hung, blasted and smoking, a tangle of wires, a rup-
tured metal diaphragm and a conical receptacle which might
once have held a lens.

"Come here," I said to Vika, but the poor girl cringed
beside the platform. Impatient, I seized her by the arm and
yanked her to the platform and held her there in my arms.
"Look up!" I said. But she kept her face resolutely down. I
thrust my fist in her hair and she cried out and looked up.
"See!" I cried.

"What is it?" she whimpered.

"It was an eye," I said.

"An eye?" she whimpered.

"Yes," I said, "something like the 'eye' in the door." I
wanted her to understand.

"Whose eye?" she asked.

"The eye of Priest-Kings," I laughed. "But it is now shut."

Vika trembled against me and in my joy with my fist still
in her hair I bent my face to hers and kissed her full on those
magnificent lips and she cried out helpless in my arms and
wept but did not resist.

It was the first kiss I had taken from the lips of my slave
girl, and it had been a kiss of mad joy, one that astonished
her, that she could not understand.

I leaped from the couch and went to the portal.

She remained standing on the stone platform, bewildered,
her fingers at her lips.

Her eyes regarded me strangely.

"Vika," I cried, "would you like to leave this room?"

"Of course," she said. Her voice trembled.

"Very well," I said, "you shall do so."

She shrank back.

I laughed and went to the portal. Once again I examined
the six red, domed sensors, three on a side, which were fixed
there. It would be, in a way, a shame to destroy them, for
they were rather beautiful.

I drew my sword.

"Stop!" cried Vika, in terror.

She leaped from the stone couch and ran to me, seizing my

sword arm but with my left hand I flung her back and she fell stumbling back against the side of the stone couch.

"Don't!" she cried, kneeling there, her hands outstretched.

Six times the hilt of my sword struck against the sensors and six times there was a hissing pop like the explosion of hot glass and a bright shower of scarlet sparks. The sensors had been shattered, their lenses broken and the wired apertures behind them a tangle of black, fused wire.

I resheathed my sword and wiped my face with the back of my forearm. I could taste a little blood and knew that some of the fragments from the sensors had cut my face.

Vika knelt beside the couch numbly.

I smiled at her. "You may now leave the room," I said, "should you wish to do so."

Slowly she rose to her feet. Her eyes looked to the portal and its shattered sensors. Then she looked at me, something of wonder and fear in her eyes.

She shook herself.

"My master is hurt," she said.

"I am Tarl Cabot of Ko-ro-ba," I said to her, telling her my name and city for the first time.

"My city is Treve," she said, for the first time telling me the name of her city.

I smiled as I watched her go to fetch a towel from one of the chests against the wall.

So Vika was from Treve.

That explained much.

Treve was a warlike city somewhere in the trackless magnificence of the Voltai Range. I had never been there but I knew her reputation. Her warriors were said to be fierce and brave, her women proud and beautiful. Her tarnsmen were ranked with those of Thentis, famed for its tarn flocks, and Ko-ro-ba, even great Ar itself.

Vika returned with the towel and began dabbing at my face.

It was seldom a girl from Treve ascended the auction block. I supposed Vika would have been costly had I purchased her in Ar or Ko-ro-ba. Even when not beautiful, because of their rarity, they are prized by collectors.

Treve was alleged to lie above Ar, some seven hundred

pasangs distant, and toward the Sardar. I had never seen the city located on a map but I had seen the territory she claimed so marked. The precise location of Treve was not known to me and was perhaps known to few save its citizens. Trade routes did not lead to the city and those who entered its territory did not often return.

There was said to be no access to Treve save on tarnback and this would suggest that it must be as much a mountain stronghold as a city.

She was said to have no agriculture, and this may be true. Each year in the fall legions of tarnsmen from Treve were said to emerge from the Voltai like locusts and fall on the fields of one city or another, different cities in different years, harvesting what they needed and burning the rest in order that a long, retaliatory winter campaign could not be launched against them. A century ago the tarnsmen of Treve had even managed to stand off the tarnsmen of Ar in a fierce battle fought in the stormy sky over the crags of the Voltai. I had heard poets sing of it. Since that time her depredations had gone unchecked, although perhaps it should be added that never again did the men of Treve despoil the fields of Ar.

"Does it hurt?" asked Vika.

"No," I said.

"Of course it hurts," she sniffed.

I wondered if many of Treve's women were as beautiful as Vika. If they were it was surprising that tarnsmen from all the cities of Gor would not have descended on the place, as the saying goes, to try chain luck.

"Are all the women of Treve as beautiful as you?" I asked.

"Of course not," she said irritably.

"Are you the most beautiful?" I asked.

"I don't know," she said simply, and then she smiled and added, "perhaps . . ."

With a graceful movement she rose and went back again to the chests against the wall. She returned with a small tube of ointment.

"They are deeper than I thought," she said.

With the tip of her finger she began to work the ointment into the cuts. It burned quite a bit.

"Does it hurt?" she asked.

"No," I said.

She laughed, and it pleased me to hear her laugh.

"I hope you know what you are doing," I said.

"My father," she said, "was of the Caste of Physicians."

So I thought to myself, I had placed her accent rather well, either Builders or Physicians, and had I thought careful-ly enough about it, I might have recognized her accent as being a bit too refined for the Builders. I chuckled to myself. In effect, I had probably merely scored a lucky hit.

"I didn't know they had physicians in Treve," I said.

"We have all the High Castes in Treve," she said, angrily.

The only two cities, other than Ar, which I knew that Treve did not periodically attack were mountainous Thentis, famed for its tarn flocks, and Ko-ro-ba, my own city.

If the issue was grain, of course, there would be little point in going to Thentis, for she imports her own, but her primary wealth, her tarn flocks, is not negligible, and she also possesses silver, though her mines are not as rich as those of Tharna. Perhaps Treve has never attacked Thentis because she, too, is a mountain city, lying in the Mountains of Thentis, or more likely because the men of Treve respect her tarnsmen almost as much as they do their own.

The cessation of attacks on Ko-ro-ba began during the time my father, Matthew Cabot, was Ubar of that city.

He organized a system of far-flung beacons, set in fortified towers, which would give the alarm when unwelcome forces entered the territory of Ko-ro-ba. At the sight of raiders one tower would set its beacon aflame, glittering by night, or dampen it with green branches by day to produce a white smoke, and this signal would be relayed from tower to tower. Thus when the tarnsmen of Treve came to the grain fields of Ko-ro-ba, which lie for the most part some pasangs from the city, toward the Vosk and Tamber Gulf, they would find her tarnsmen arrayed against them. Having come for grain and not war, the men of Treve would then turn back, and seek out the fields of a less well-defended city.

There was also a system of signals whereby the towers could communicate with one another and the city. Thus if one tower failed to report when expected the alarm bars of

Ko-ro-ba would soon ring and her tarnsmen would saddle and be aflight.

Cities, of course, would pursue the raiders from Treve, and carry the pursuit vigorously as far as the foothills of the Voltai, but there they would surrender the chase, turning back, not caring to risk their tarnsmen in the rugged, formidable territory of their rival, whose legendary ferocity among her own crags once gave pause long ago even to the mighty forces of Ar.

Treve's other needs seemed to be satisfied much in the same way as her agricultural ones, for her raiders were known from the borders of the Fair of En'Kara, in the very shadow of the Sardar, to the delta of the Vosk and the islands beyond, such as Tyros and Cos. The results of these raids might be returned to Treve or sold, perhaps even at the Fair of En'Kara, or another of the four great Sardar Fairs, or if not, they could always be disposed of easily without question in distant, crowded, malignant Port Kar.

"How do the people of Treve live?" I asked Vika.

"We raise the verr," she said.

I smiled.

The verr was a mountain goat indigenous to the Voltai. It was a wild, agile, ill-tempered beast, long-haired and spiral-horned. Among the Voltai crags it would be worth one's life to come within twenty yards of one.

"Then you are a simple, domestic folk," I said.

"Yes," said Vika.

"Mountain herdsmen," I said.

"Yes," said Vika.

And then we laughed together, neither of us able to restrain ourselves.

Yes, I knew the reputation of Treve. It was a city rich in plunder, probably as lofty, inaccessible and impregnable as a tarn's nest. Indeed, Treve was known as the Tarn of the Voltai. It was an arrogant, never-conquered citadel, a stronghold of men whose way of life was banditry, whose women lived on the spoils of a hundred cities.

And it was the city from which Vika had come.

I believed it.

But yet tonight she had been gentle, and I had been kind to her.

Tonight we had been friends.

She went to the chest against the wall, to replace the tube of ointment.

"The ointment will soon be absorbed," she said. "In a few minutes there will be no trace of it, nor of the cuts."

I whistled.

"The physicians of Treve," I said, "have marvelous medicines."

"It is an ointment of Priest-Kings," she said.

I was pleased to hear this, for it suggested vulnerability. "Then the Priest-Kings can be injured?" I asked.

"Their slaves can," said Vika.

"I see," I said.

"Let us not speak of Priest-Kings," said the girl.

I looked at her, standing across the room, lovely, facing me in the dim light.

"Vika," I asked, "was your father truly of the Caste of Physicians?"

"Yes," she said, "why do you ask?"

"It does not matter," I said.

"But why?" she insisted.

"Because," I said, "I thought you might have been a bred Pleasure Slave."

It was a foolish thing to say, and I regretted it immediately. She stiffened. "You flatter me," she said, and turned away. I had hurt her.

I made a move to approach her but without turning, she said, "Please do not touch me."

And then she seemed to straighten and turned to face me, once again the old and scornful Vika, challenging, hostile. "But of course you may touch me," she said, "for you are my master."

"Forgive me," I said.

She laughed bitterly, scornfully.

It was truly a woman of Treve who stood before me now.

I saw her as I had never seen her before.

Vika was a bandit princess, accustomed to be clad in silk and jewels from a thousand looted caravans, to sleep on the richest furs and sup on the most delicate viands, all purloined from galleys, beached and burnt, from the ravished storerooms of outlying, smoking cylinders, from the tables and treasure chests of homes whose men were slain, whose daughters wore the chains of slave girls, only now she herself, Vika, this bandit princess, proud Vika, a woman of lofty, opulent Treve, had fallen spoils herself in the harsh games of Gor, and felt on her own throat the same encircling band of steel with which the men of her city had so often graced the throats of their fair, weeping captives.

Vika was now property.

My property.

Her eyes regarded me with fury.

Insolently she approached me, slowly, gracefully, as silken in her menace as the she-larl, and then to my astonishment when she stood before me, she knelt, her hands on her thighs, her knees in the position of the Pleasure Slave, and dropped her head in scornful submission.

She raised her head and her taunting blue eyes regarded me boldly. "Here, Master," she said, "is your Pleasure Slave."

"Rise," I said.

She rose gracefully and put her arms about my neck and moved her lips close to mine. "You kissed me before," she said. "Now I shall kiss you."

I looked into those blue eyes and they looked into mine, and I wondered how many men had been burned, and had died, in that smoldering, sullen fire.

Those magnificent lips brushed mine.

"Here," she said softly, imperiously, "is the kiss of your Pleasure Slave."

I disengaged her arms from my neck.

She looked at me in bewilderment.

I walked from the room into the dimly lit hall. In the passageway, I extended my hand to her, that she might come and take it.

"Do I not please you?" she asked.

"Vika," I said, "come here and take the hand of a fool."

When she saw what I intended she shook her head slowly, numbly. "No," she said. "I cannot leave the chamber."

"Please," I said.

She shook with fear.

"Come," I said, "take my hand."

Slowly, trembling, moving as though in a dream, the girl approached the portal, and this time the sensors could not glow.

She looked at me.

"Please," I said.

She looked again at the sensors, which stared out of the wall like black, gutted metal eyes. They were burned and still, shattered, and even the wall in their vicinity showed the seared, scarlet stain of their abrupt termination.

"They can hurt you no longer," I said.

Vika took another step and then it seemed her legs would fail her and she might swoon. She put out her hand to me. Her eyes were wide with fear.

"The women of Treve," I said, "are brave, as well as beautiful and proud."

She stepped through the portal and fell fainting in my arms.

I lifted her and carried her to the stone couch.

I regarded the ruined sensors in the portal and the wreckage of the surveillance device which had been concealed in the energy bulb.

Perhaps now I would not have so long to wait for the Priest-Kings of Gor.

Vika had said that when they wished me, they would come for me.

I chuckled.

Perhaps now they would be encouraged to hasten their appointment.

I gently placed Vika on the great stone couch.

9
The Priest-King

I WOULD ALLOW VIKA TO share the great stone couch, its sleeping pelts, and silken sheets.

This was unusual, however, for normally the Gorean slave girl sleeps at the foot of her master's couch, often on a straw mat with only a thin, cottonlike blanket, woven from the soft fibers of the Rep Plant, to protect her from the cold.

If she has not pleased her master of late, she may be, of course, as a disciplinary measure, simply chained nude to the slave ring in the bottom of the couch, sans both blanket and mat. The stones of the floor are hard and the Gorean nights are cold and it is a rare girl who, when unchained in the morning, does not seek more dutifully to serve her master.

This harsh treatment, incidentally, when she is thought to deserve it, may even be inflicted on a Free Companion, in spite of the fact that she is free and usually much loved. According to the Gorean way of looking at things a taste of the slave ring is thought to be occasionally beneficial to all women, even the exalted Free Companions.

Thus when she has been irritable or otherwise troublesome even a Free Companion may find herself at the foot of the couch looking forward to a pleasant night on the stones, stripped, with neither mat nor blanket, chained to a slave ring precisely as though she were a lowly slave girl.

It is the Gorean way of reminding her, should she need to be reminded, that she, too, is a woman, and thus to be dominated, to be subject to men. Should she be tempted to forget this basic fact of Gorean life the slave ring set in the bottom of each Gorean couch is there to refresh her memory. Gor is a man's world.

And yet on this world I have seen great numbers of women who were both beautiful and splendid.

The Gorean woman, for reasons that are not altogether clear to me, considering the culture, rejoices in being a woman. She is often an exciting, magnificent, glorious creature, outspoken, talkative, vital, active, spirited. On the whole

I find her more joyful than many of her earth-inhabiting sisters who, theoretically at least, enjoy a more lofty status, although it is surely true that on my old world I have met several women with something of the Gorean zest for acknowledging the radiant truth of their sex, the gifts of joy, grace and beauty, tenderness, and fathoms of love that we poor men, I suspect, may sometimes and tragically fail to understand, to comprehend.

Yet with all due respect and regard for the most astounding and marvelous sex, I suspect that, perhaps partly because of my Gorean training, it is true that a touch of the slave ring is occasionally beneficial.

Of custom, a slave girl may not even ascend the couch to serve her master's pleasure. The point of this restriction, I suppose, is to draw a clearer distinction between her status and that of a Free Companion. At any rate the dignities of the couch are, by custom, reserved for the Free Companion.

When a master wishes to make use of a slave girl he tells her to light the lamp of love which she obediently does, placing it in the window of his chamber that they may not be disturbed. Then with his own hand he throws upon the stone floor of his chamber luxurious love furs, perhaps from the larl itself, and commands her to them.

I had placed Vika gently on the great stone couch.

I kissed her gently on the forehead.

Her eyes opened.

"Did I leave the chamber?" she asked.

"Yes," I said.

She regarded me for a long time. "How can I conquer you?" she asked. "I love you, Tarl Cabot."

"You are only grateful," I said.

"No," she said, "I love you."

"You must not," I said.

"I do," she said.

I wondered how I should speak to her, for I must disabuse her of the illusion that there could be love between us. In the house of Priest-Kings there could be no love, nor could she know her own mind in these matters, and there was always Talena, whose image would never be eradicated from my heart.

"But you are a woman of Treve," I said, smiling.

"You thought I was a Passion Slave," she chided.

I shrugged.

She looked away from me, toward the wall. "You were right in a way, Tarl Cabot."

"How is that?" I asked.

She looked at me directly. "My mother," she said bitterly, "—was a Passion Slave—bred in the pens of Ar."

"She must have been very beautiful," I said.

Vika looked at me strangely. "Yes," she said, "I suppose she was."

"Do you not remember her?" I asked.

"No," she said, "for she died when I was very young."

"I'm sorry," I said.

"It doesn't matter," said Vika, "for she was only an animal bred in the pens of Ar."

"Do you despise her so?" I asked.

"She was a bred slave," said Vika.

I said nothing.

"But my father," said Vika, "whose slave she was, and who was of the Caste of Physicians of Treve, loved her very much and asked her to be his Free Companion." Vika laughed softly. "For three years she refused him," she said.

"Why?" I asked.

"Because she loved him," said Vika, "and did not wish him to take for his Free Companion only a lowly Passion Slave."

"She was a very deep and noble woman," I said.

Vika made a gesture of disgust. "She was a fool," she said. "How often would a bred slave have a chance of freedom?"

"Seldom indeed," I admitted.

"But in the end," said Vika, "fearing he would slay himself she consented to become his Free Companion." Vika regarded me closely. Her eyes met mine very directly. "I was born free," she said. "You must understand that. I am not a bred slave."

"I understand," I said. "Perhaps," I suggested, "your mother was not only beautiful, but proud and brave and fine."

"How could that be?" laughed Vika scornfully. "I have told you she was only a bred slave, an animal from the pens of Ar."

"But you never knew her," I said.

"I know what she was," said Vika.

"What of your father?" I asked.

"In a way," she said, "he is dead too."

"What do you mean, in a way?" I asked.

"Nothing," she said.

I looked about the room, at the chests against the wall dim in the reduced light of the energy bulbs, at the walls, at the shattered device in the ceiling, at the broken sensors, at the great, empty portal that led into the passageway beyond.

"He must have loved you very much, after your mother died," I said.

"Yes," said Vika, "I suppose so—but he was a fool."

"Why do you say that?" I asked.

"He followed me into the Sardar, to try and save me," she said.

"He must have been a very brave man," I said.

She rolled away from me and stared at the wall. After a time she spoke, her words cruel with contempt.

"He was a pompous little fool," she said, "and afraid even of the cry of a larl."

She sniffed.

Suddenly she rolled back to face me. "How," she asked, "could my mother have loved him? He was only a fat, pompous little fool."

"Perhaps he was kind to her," I suggested, "—when others were not."

"Why would anyone be kind to a Passion Slave?" asked Vika.

I shrugged.

"For the Passion Slave," she said, "it is the belled ankle, perfume, the whip and the furs of love."

"Perhaps he was kind to her," I suggested again, "—when others were not."

"I don't understand," said Vika.

"Perhaps," I said, "he cared for her and spoke to her and was gentle—and loved her."

"Perhaps," said Vika. "But would that be enough?"

"Perhaps," I said.

"I wonder," said Vika. "I have often wondered about that."

"What became of him," I asked, "when he entered the Sardar?"

Vika would not speak.

"Do you know?" I asked.

"Yes," she said.

"Then what?" I asked.

She shook her head bitterly. "Do not ask me," she said.

I would not press her further on the matter.

"How is it," I asked, "that he allowed you to come to the Sardar?"

"He did not," said Vika. "He tried to prevent me but I sought out the Initiates of Treve, proposing myself as an offering to the Priest-Kings. I did not, of course, tell them my true reason for desiring to come to the Sardar." She paused. "I wonder if they knew," she mused.

"It is not improbable," I said.

"My father would not hear of it, of course," she said. She laughed. "He locked me in my chambers, but the High Initiate of the City came with warriors and they broke into our compartments and beat my father until he could not move and I went gladly with them." She laughed again. "Oh how pleased I was when they beat him and he cried out," she said, "for I hated him—so much I hated him—for he was not a true man and even though of the Caste of Physicians could not stand pain. He could not even bear to hear the cry of a larl."

I knew that Gorean caste lines, though largely following birth, were not inflexible, and that a man who did not care for his caste might be allowed to change caste, if approved by the High Council of his city, an approval usually contingent on his qualifications for the work of another caste and the willingness of the members of the new caste to accept him as a Caste Brother.

"Perhaps," I suggested, "it was because he could not stand pain that he remained a member of the Caste of Physicians."

"Perhaps," said Vika. "He always wanted to stop suffering, even that of an animal or slave."

I smiled.

"You see," she said, "he was weak."

"I see," I said.

Vika lay back on the silks and furs. "You are the first of the men in this chamber," she said, "who have spoken to me of these things."

I did not reply.

"I love you, Tarl Cabot," she said.

"I think not," I said gently.

"I do!" she insisted.

"Someday," I said, "you will love—but I do not think it will be a warrior of Ko-ro-ba."

"Do you think I cannot love?" she challenged.

"I think someday you will love," I said, "and I think you will love greatly."

"Can you love?" she challenged.

"I don't know," I said. I smiled. "Once—long ago—I thought I loved."

"Who was she?" asked Vika, not too pleasantly.

"A slender, dark-haired girl," I said, "whose name was Talena."

"Was she beautiful?" asked Vika.

"Yes," I said.

"As beautiful as I?" asked Vika.

"You are both very beautiful," I said.

"Was she a slave?" asked Vika.

"No," I said, "—she was the daughter of a Ubar."

Rage transfigured Vika's features and she leaped from the couch and strode to the side of the room, her fingers angrily inside her collar, as though they might pull it from her throat. "I see!" she said. "And I—Vika—am only a slave girl!"

"Do not be angry," I said.

"Where is she?" demanded Vika.

"I don't know," I admitted.

"How long has it been since you have seen her?" demanded Vika.

"It has been more than seven years," I said.

Vika laughed cruelly. "Then," she gloated, "she is in the Cities of Dust."

"Perhaps," I admitted.

"I—Vika—" she said, "am here."

"I know," I said.

I turned away.

I heard her voice over my shoulder. "I will make you forget her," she said.

Her voice had borne the cruel, icy, confident, passionate menace of a woman from Treve, accustomed to have what she wanted, who would not be denied.

I turned to face Vika once more, and I no longer saw the girl to whom I had been speaking but a woman of High Caste, from the bandit kingdom of Treve, insolent and imperious, though collared.

Casually Vika reached to the clasp on the left shoulder of her garment and loosened it, and the garment fell to her ankles.

She was branded.

"You thought I was a Passion Slave," she said.

I regarded the woman who stood before me, the sullen eyes, the pouting lips, the collar, the brand.

"Am I not beautiful enough," she asked, "to be the daughter of a Ubar?"

"Yes," I said, "you are that beautiful."

She looked at me mockingly. "Do you know what a Passion Slave is?" she asked.

"Yes," I said.

"It is a female of the human kind," she said, "but bred like a beast for its beauty and its passion."

"I know," I said.

"It is an animal," she said, "bred for the pleasure of men, bred for the pleasure of a master."

I said nothing.

"In my veins," she said, "flows the blood of such an animal. In my veins flows the blood of a Passion Slave." She laughed. "And you, Tarl Cabot," she said, "are its master. You, Tarl Cabot, are my master."

"No," I said.

Amused, tauntingly, she approached me. "I will serve you as a Passion Slave," she said.

"No," I said.

"Yes," she said, "for you I will be an obedient Passion Slave." She lifted her lips to mine.

My hands on her arms held her from me.

"Taste me," she said.

"No," I said.

She laughed. "You cannot reject me," she said.

"Why not?" I asked.

"I shall not allow you to do so," she said. "You see, Tarl Cabot, I have decided that you shall be my slave."

I thrust her from me.

"Very well," she cried, her eyes flashing. "Very well, Cabot," she said, "then I shall conquer you!"

And she seized my head in her hands and pressed her lips to mine.

In that moment I sensed once more that slightly acrid scent which I had experienced in the corridors beyond the chamber, and I pressed my mouth hard into Vika's until her lips were cut by my teeth and I had pressed her back until only my arm kept her from falling to the stones of the floor, and I heard her cry of surprise and pain, and then I hurled her angrily from me to the straw slave mat which lay at the foot of the stone couch.

Now it seemed to me that I understood but they had come too soon! She had not had a chance to do her work. It might go hard with her but I was not concerned.

Still I did not turn to that giant portal.

The scent was now strong.

Vika crouched terrified on the slave mat at the foot of the couch, in the very shadow of the slave ring.

"What is the matter?" she asked. "What is wrong?"

"So you were to conquer me for them, were you?" I demanded.

"I don't understand," she stammered.

"You are a poor tool for Priest-Kings," I said.

"No," she said, "no!"

"How many men have you conquered for Priest-Kings?" I asked. I seized her by the hair and twisted her head to face me. "How many?" I cried.

"Please!" she wept.

I found myself tempted to break her head against the foot

of the stone couch, for she was worthless, treacherous, seductive, cruel, vicious, worthy only of the collar, irons and the whip!

She shook her head numbly as though denying charges I had not voiced.

"You don't understand," she said. "I love you!"

With loathing I cast her from me.

Yet still did I not turn to face that portal.

Vika lay at my feet, a streak of blood at the corner of those lips that bore still the marks of my fierce kiss. She looked up at me, tears welling in her eyes.

"Please," she said.

The scent was strong. I knew that it was near. How was it that the girl was not aware of it? How was it that she did not know? Was it not part of her plan?

"Please," she said, looking up at me, lifting her hand to me. Her face was tear-stained; her voice a broken sob. "I love you," she said.

"Silence, Slave Girl," I said.

She lowered her head to the stones and wept.

I knew now that it was here.

The scent was now overpowering, unmistakable.

I watched Vika and suddenly she seemed too to know and her head lifted and her eyes widened with horror and she crept to her knees, her hands before her face as though to shield herself and she shuddered and suddenly uttered a wild, long, terrible scream of abject fear.

I drew my sword and turned.

It stood framed in the doorway.

In its way it was very beautiful, golden and tall, looming over me, framed in that massive portal. It was not more than a yard wide but its head nearly touched the top of the portal and so I would judge that, standing as it did, it must have been nearly eighteen feet high.

It had six legs and a great head like a globe of gold with eyes like vast luminous disks. Its two forelegs, poised and alert, were lifted delicately in front of its body. Its jaws opened and closed once. They moved laterally.

From its head there extended two fragile, jointed appendages, long and covered with short quivering strands of golden hair. These two appendages, like eyes, swept the room once and then seemed to focus on me.

They curved toward me like delicate golden pincers and each of the countless golden strands on those appendages straightened and pointed toward me like a quivering golden needle.

I could not conjecture the nature of the creature's experience but I knew that I stood within the center of its sensory field.

About its neck there hung a small circular device, a translator of some sort, similar to but more compact than those I had hitherto seen.

I sensed a new set of odors, secreted by what stood before me.

Almost simultaneously a mechanically reproduced voice began to emanate from the translator.

It spoke in Gorean.

I knew what it would say.

"Lo Sardar," it said. "I am a Priest-King."

"I am Tarl Cabot of Ko-ro-ba," I said.

A moment after I spoke I sensed another set of odors, which emanated perhaps from the device which hung about the neck of what stood before me.

The two sensory appendages of the creature seemed to register this information.

A new scent came to my nostrils.

"Follow me," said the mechanically reproduced voice, and the creature turned from the portal.

I went to the portal.

It was stalking in long, delicate steps down the passageway.

I looked once more at Vika, who lifted her hand to me. "Don't go." she said.

I turned scornfully from her and followed the creature.

Behind me I heard her weep.

Let her weep, I said to myself, for she has failed her masters the Priest-Kings, and undoubtedly her punishment will not be light.

Had I the time, had I not more urgent business, I might have punished her myself, teaching her without mercy what could be the meaning of her collar, using her as objectively and ruthlessly as she deserved, brutally administering the discipline of a Gorean master to a treacherous slave girl.

We would see then who would conquer.

I shook these thoughts from my head and continued down the passageway.

I must forget the treacherous, vicious wench. There were more important matters to attend to. The slave girl was nothing.

I hated Vika.

I followed a Priest-King.

10
Misk the Priest-King

THE PRIEST-KINGS HAVE LITTLE or no scent of their own which is detectable by the human nostrils, though one gathers there is a nest odor by which they may identify one another, and that the variations in this nest odor permit identifications of individuals.

What in the passageways I had taken to be the scent of Priest-Kings had actually been the residue of odor-signals which Priest-Kings, like certain social insects of our world, use in communicating with one another.

The slightly acrid odor I had noticed tends to be a common property of all such signals, much as there is a common property to the sound of a human voice, whether it be that of an Englishman, a Bushman, a Chinese or a Gorean, which sets it apart from, say, the growling of animals, the hiss of snakes, the cry of birds.

The Priest-Kings have eyes, which are compound and many-faceted, but they do not much rely on these organs. They are, for them, something like our ears and nose, used as secondary sensors to be relied upon when the most pertinent information in the environment is not relayed by vision, or, in the case of the Priest-Kings, by scent. Accordingly the two golden-haired, jointed appendages protruding from their globelike heads, above the rounded, disklike eyes, are their primary sensory organs. I gather that these appendages are

sensitive not only to odors but, due to a modification of some
of the golden hairs, may also transform sound vibrations into
something meaningful in their experience. Thus, if one
wishes, one may speak of them not only as smelling but
hearing through these appendages. Apparently hearing is not
of great importance, however, to them, considering the small
number of hairs modified for this purpose. Oddly enough few
of the Priest-Kings whom I questioned on this matter seemed
to draw the distinction clearly between hearing and smelling.
I find this incredible, but I have no reason to believe they
deceived me. They recognize that we have different sensory
arrangements than they and I suspect that they are as unclear
as to the nature of our experience as we are of theirs. In
fact, though I speak of hearing and smelling, I am not sure
that these expressions are altogether meaningful when applied
to Priest-Kings. I speak of them smelling and hearing
through the sensory appendages, but what the quality of their
experience may be I am uncertain. For example, does a
Priest-King have the same qualitative experience that I do
when we are confronted by the same scent? I am inclined to
doubt it, for their music, which consists of rhapsodies of
odors produced by instruments constructed for this purpose,
and often played by Priest-Kings, some of whom I am told
are far more skillful than others, is intolerable to my ear, or
I should say, nose.

Communication by odor-signals can in certain circumstances be extremely efficient, though it can be disadvanta-
geous in others. For example, an odor can carry, to the sensory
appendages of a Priest-King, much farther than can the
shout or cry of a man to another man. Moreover, if not too
much time is allowed to elapse, a Priest-King may leave a
message in his chamber or in a corridor for another Priest-
King, and the other may arrive later and interpret it. A
disadvantage of this mode of communication, of course, is
that the message may be understood by strangers or others
for whom it is not intended. One must be careful of what one
says in the tunnels of Priest-Kings for one's words may linger
after one, until they sufficiently dissipate to be little more than
a meaningless blur of scent.

For longer periods of time there are various devices for

recording a message, without relying on complex mechanical devices. The simplest and one of the most fascinating is a chemically treated rope of clothlike material which the Priest-King, beginning at an end bearing a certain scent, saturates with the odors of his message. This coiled message-rope then retains the odors indefinitely and when another Priest-King wishes to read the message he unrolls it slowly scanning it serially with the jointed sensory appendages.

I am told that the phonemes of the language of Priest-Kings or, better, what in their language would correspond to phonemes in ours, since their "phonemes" have to do with scent and not sound, number seventy-three. Their number is, of course, potentially infinite, as would be the number of possible phonemes in English, but just as we take a subset of sounds to be English sounds and form our utterances from them, so they take a subset of odors as similarly basic to their speech. The number of English phonemes, incidentally, is in the neighborhood of fifty.

The morphemes of the language of Priest-Kings, those smallest intelligible information bits, in particular roots and affixes, are, of course, like the morphemes of English, extremely numerous. The normal morpheme, in their language as in ours, consists of a sequence of phonemes. For example, in English 'bit' is one morpheme but three phonemes, as will appear clear if given some reflection. Similarly in the language of the Priest-Kings, the seveny-three "phonemes" or basic scents are used to form the meaning units of the language, and a single morpheme of Priest-Kings may consist of a complex set of odors.

I do not know whether there are more morphemes in the language of the Priest-Kings or in English, but both are apparently rich languages, and, of course, the strict morpheme count is not necessarily a reliable index to the complexity of the lexicon, because of combinations of morphemes to form new words. German, for example, tends to rely somewhat more on morpheme combination than does English or French. I was told, incidentally, that the language of the Priest-Kings does possess more morphemes than English but I do not know if the report is truthful or not, for Priest-Kings tend to be somewhat touchy on the matter of any comparisons, particularly those to their disadvantage or putative disadvantage, with organisms of what they regard as the lower orders. On the other hand it may well be the case that, as a matter of fact, the morpheme set of the language of Priest-Kings is indeed larger than that of English. I simply do not know. The translator tapes, incidentally, are approximately the same size, but this is no help, since the tapes represent pairings of approximate equivalents, and there are several English morphemes not translatable into the language of Priest-Kings, and, as I learned, morphemes in their language for which no English equivalents exist. One English expression for which no natural "word" in their language exists is, oddly enough, 'friendship', and certain of its cognates. There is an expression in their language which translates into English as 'Nest Trust', however, and seems to play something of the same role in their thinking. The notion of friendship, it seems to me, has to do with a reliance and affection between two or more individuals; the notion of Nest Trust, as nearly as I can understand it, is more of a communal notion, a sense of relying on the practices and traditions of an institution, accepting them and living in terms of them.

I followed the Priest-King for a long time through the passages.

For all its size it moved with a delicate, predatory grace. It was perhaps very light for its bulk, or very strong, perhaps both. It moved with a certain deliberate, stalking movement; its tread was regal and yet it seemed almost dainty, almost fastidious; it was almost as if the creature did not care to soil itself by contact with the floor of the passage.

It walked on four extremely long, slender, four-jointed stalks that were its supporting legs, and carried its far more muscular, four-jointed grasping legs, or appendages, extremely high, almost level with its jaw, and in front of its body. Each of these grasping appendages terminated in four much smaller, delicate hooklike prehensile appendages, the tips of which normally touched one another. I would learn later that in the ball at the end of its forelegs from which the smaller prehensile appendages extended, there was a curved, bladed, hornlike structure that could spring forward; this happens spontaneously when the leg's tip is inverted, a motion which at once exposes the hornlike blade and withdraws the four prehensile appendages into the protected area beneath it.

The Priest-King halted before what appeared to be a blind wall.

He lifted one foreleg high over his head and touched something high in the wall which I could not see.

A panel slid back and the Priest-King stepped into what seemed to be a closed room.

I followed him, and the panel closed.

The floor seemed to drop beneath me and my hand grasped my sword.

The Priest-King looked down at me and the antennae quivered as though in curiosity.

I resheathed my sword.

I was in an elevator.

After perhaps four or five minutes the elevator stopped and the Priest-King and I emerged.

The Priest-King rested back on the two posterior supporting appendages and with a small cleaning hook behind the third joint of one of his forelegs began to comb his antennae.

"These are the tunnels of the Priest-Kings," it said.

I looked about me and found myself on a high, railed platform, overlooking a vast circular artificial canyon, lined with bridges and terraces, In the depths of this canyon and on the terraces that mounted its sides were innumerable structures, largely geometrical solids—cones, cylinders, lofty cubes, domes, spheres and such—of various sizes, colors and illuminations, many of which were windowed and possessed of numerous floors, some of which even towered to the level of the platform where I stood, some of which soared even higher into the lofty reaches of the vast dome that arched over the canyon like a stone sky.

I stood on the platform, my hands clenched on the railing, staggered by what I saw.

The light of energy bulbs set in the walls and in the dome like stars shed a brilliant light on the entire canyon.

"This," said the Priest-King, still grooming the golden hairs of his antennae, "is the vestibule of our dominion."

From my position on the platform I could see numerous

tunnels at many levels leading out of the canyon, perhaps to other such monstrous cavities, filled with more structures.

I wondered what would be the function of the structures, probably barracks, factories, storehouses.

"Notice the energy bulbs," said the Priest-King. "They are for the benefit of certain species such as yourself. Priest-Kings do not need them."

"Then there are creatures other than Priest-Kings who live here," I said.

"Of course," it replied.

At that moment to my horror a large, perhaps eight feet long and a yard high, multilegged, segmented arthropod scuttled near, its eyes weaving on stalks.

"It's harmless," said the Priest-King.

The arthropod stopped and the eyes leaned toward us and then its pincers clicked twice.

I reached for my sword.

Without turning it scuttled backwards away, its body plates rustling like plastic armor.

"See what you have done," said the Priest-King. "You have frightened it."

My hand left the sword hilt and I wiped the sweat from my palm on my tunic.

"They are timid creatures," said the Priest-King, "and I am afraid they have never been able to accustom themselves to the sight of your kind."

The Priest-King's antennae shuddered a bit as they regarded me.

"Your kind is terribly ugly," it said.

I laughed, not so much because I supposed what it said was absurd, but because I supposed that, from the viewpoint of a Priest-King, what it said might well be true.

"It is interesting," said the Priest-King. "What you have just said does not translate."

"It was a laugh," I said.

"What is a laugh?" asked the Priest-King.

"It is something men sometimes do when they are amused," I said.

The creature seemed puzzled.

I wondered to myself. Perhaps men did not much laugh in

the tunnels of the Priest-Kings and it was not accustomed to this human practice. Or perhaps a Priest-King simply could not understand the notion of amusement, it being perhaps genetically removed from his comprehension. Yet I said to myself the Priest-Kings are intelligent and I found it difficult to believe there could exist an intelligent race without humor.

"I think I understand," said the Priest-King. "It is like shaking and curling your antennae?"

"Perhaps," I said, now more puzzled than the Priest-King.

"How stupid I am," said the Priest-King.

And then to my amazement the creature, resting back on its posterior appendages, began to shake, beginning at its abdomen and continuing upward through its trunk to its thorax and head and at last its antennae began to tremble and, curling, they wrapped about one another.

Then the Priest-King ceased to rock and its antennae uncurled, almost reluctantly I thought, and it once again rested quietly back on its posterior appendages and regarded me.

Once again it addressed itself to the patient, meticulous combing of its antennae hairs.

Somehow I imagined it was thinking.

Suddenly it stopped grooming its antennae and the antennae looked down at me.

"Thank you," it said, "for not attacking me in the elevator."

I was dumbfounded.

"You're welcome." I said.

"I did not think the anesthesia would be necessary," it said.

"It would have been foolish to attack you," I said.

"Irrational, yes," agreed the Priest-King, "but the lower orders are often irrational.

"Now," it said, "I may still look forward someday to the Pleasures of the Golden Beetle."

I said nothing.

"Sarm thought the anesthesia would be necessary," it said.

"Is Sarm a Priest-King?" I asked.

"Yes," it said.

"Then a Priest-King may be mistaken," I said. This seemed

to me significant, far more significant than the mere fact that a Priest-King might not understand a human laugh.

"Of course," said the creature.

"Could I have slain you?" I asked.

"Possibly," said the creature.

I looked over the rail at the marvelous complexity which confronted me.

"But it would not have mattered," said the Priest-King.

"No?" I asked.

"No," it said. "Only the Nest matters."

My eyes still did not leave the dominion which lay below me. Its diameter might have been ten pasangs in width.

"This is the Nest?" I asked.

"It is the beginning of the Nest," said the Priest-King.

"What is your name?" I asked.

"Misk," it said.

11
Sarm the Priest-King

I TURNED FROM THE RAILING to observe the great ramp which for pasangs in a great spiral approached the platform on which I stood.

Another Priest-King, mounted on a low, oval disk which seemed to slide up the ramp, was approaching.

The new Priest-King looked a great deal like Misk, save that he was larger. I wondered if men of my species would have difficulty telling Priest-Kings apart. I would later learn to do so easily but at first I was often confused. The Priest-Kings themselves distinguish one another by scent but I, of course, would do so by eye.

The oval disk glided to within some forty feet of us, and the golden creature which had ridden it stepped delicately to the ramp.

It approached me, its antennae scrutinizing me carefully. Then it backed away perhaps some twenty feet.

It seemed to me much like Misk except in size.

Like Misk it wore no clothing and carried no weapons, and

its only accouterment was a translator which dangled from its neck.

I would learn later that in scent it wore its rank, caste and station as clearly on its body as an officer in one of the armies of Earth might wear his distinguishing braid and metal bars.

"Why has it not been anesthetized?" asked the new creature, training its antennae on Misk.

"I did not think it would be necessary," said Misk.

"It was my recommendation that it be anesthetized," said the newcomer.

"I know," said Misk.

"This will be recorded," said the newcomer.

Misk seemed to shrug. His head turned, his laterally opening jaws opened and closed slowly, his shoulders rustled and the two antennae twitched once as though in irritation, and then idly they began to examine the roof of the dome.

"The Nest was not jeopardized," came from Misk's translator.

The newcomer's antennae were now trembling, perhaps with anger.

It turned a knob on its own translator and in a moment the air was filled with the sharp odors of what I take might have been a reprimand. I heard nothing for the creature had snapped off his translator.

When Misk replied he too turned off his translator.

I observed their antennae and the general posturing and carriage of their long, graceful bodies.

They stalked about one another and some of their motions were almost whiplike. Upon occasion, undoubtedly as a sign of irritation, the tips of the forelegs were inverted, and I caught my first glimpse of the bladed, hornlike structures therein concealed.

I would learn to interpret the emotions and states of Priest-Kings by such signs. Many of these signs would be far less obvious than the ones now displayed in the throes of anger. Impatience, for example, is often indicated by a tremor in the tactile hair on the supporting appendages, as though the creature could not wait to be off; a wandering of attention can be shown by the unconscious movement of the cleaning hooks from behind the third joints of the forelegs, suggesting perhaps the creature is thinking of grooming, an occupation in which Priest-Kings, to my mind, spend an inordinate amount of time; I might note, however, in deference to them, that they consider humans a particularly unclean animal and in the tunnels normally confine them for sanitary purposes to carefully restricted areas; the subtlety of these signs might well be illuminated if the indications for a wandering of attention, mentioned above, are contrasted with the superficially similar signs which give evidence that a Priest-King is well or favorably disposed toward another Priest-King, or other creature of any type. In this case there is again the unconscious movement of the cleaning hooks but there is in addition an incipient, but restrained, extension of the forelegs in the direction of the object toward which the Priest-King is well disposed; this suggests to me that the Priest-King is willing to put its cleaning hooks at the disposal of the other, that he is willing to groom it. This may become more comprehensible when it is mentioned that Priest-Kings, with their cleaning hooks, their jaws and their tongues, often groom one another as well as themselves. Hunger, incidentally, is indicated by an acidic exudate which forms at the edges of the jaws giving them a certain moist appearance; thirst, interestingly enough, is indicated by a certain stiffness in the appendages, evident in their movements, and by a certain brownish tarnish that seems to infect the gold of the thorax and abdomen. The most sensitive indicators of mood and attention, of course, as you would probably gather, are the motions and tensility of the antennae.

The translator, incidentally, supposing it to be turned on, would provide only the translation of what was said, and the words, unless the volume control was manipulated during the message, would always occur at the same sound level. An analogue to listening to a translator would be to imagine words as pictures which, in the same type face and size, flash serially on a screen. There would be no clue in the individual pictures, *per se,* of the rhythm of the language or the mood of the speaker. The translator can tell you that the speaker is angry but it cannot show you that he is angry.

After a minute or two the Priest-Kings stopped circling

one another and turned to face me. As one creature, they turned on their translators.

"You are Tarl Cabot of the City of Ko-ro-ba," said the larger.

"Yes," I said.

"I am Sarm," it said, "beloved of the Mother and First Born."

"Are you the leader of the Priest-Kings?" I asked.

"Yes," said Sarm.

"No," said Misk.

Sarm's antennae darted in Misk's direction.

"Greatest in the Nest is the Mother." said Misk.

Sarm's antennae relaxed. "True," said Sarm.

"I have much to speak of with Priest-Kings," I said. "If the one whom you call the Mother is chief among you, I wish to see her."

Sarm rested back on his posterior appendages. His antennae touched one another in a slightly curling movement. "None may see the Mother save her caste attendants and the High Priest-Kings," said Sarm, "the First, Second, Third, Fourth and Fifth Born."

"Except on the three great holidays," said Misk.

Sarm's antennae twitched angrily.

"What are the three great holidays?" I asked.

"The Nest Feast Cycle," said Misk, "Tola, Tolam and Tolama."

"What are these feasts?" I asked.

"They are the Anniversary of the Nuptial Flight," said Misk, "the Feast of the Deposition of the First Egg and the Celebration of the Hatching of the First Egg."

"Are these holidays near?" I asked.

"Yes," said Misk.

"But," said Sarm, "even on such feasts none of the lower orders may view the Mother—only Priest-Kings."

"True," said Misk.

Anger suffused my countenance. Sarm seemed not to notice this change but Misk's antennae perked up immediately. Perhaps it had had experience with human anger.

"Do not think badly of us, Tarl Cabot," said Misk, "for on the holidays those of the lower orders who labor for us—be it even in the pastures or fungus trays—are given surcease from their labors."

"The Priest-Kings are generous," I said.

"Do the men below the mountains do as much for their animals?" asked Misk.

"No," I said. "But men are not animals."

"Are men Priest-Kings?" asked Sarm.

"No," I said.

"Then they are animals," said Sarm.

I drew my sword and faced Sarm. The motion was extremely rapid and must have startled him.

At any rate Sarm leaped backward on his jointed, stalklike legs with almost incredible speed.

He now stood almost forty feet from me.

"If I cannot speak to the one you call the Mother," I said, "perhaps I can speak to you."

I took a step toward Sarm.

Sarm pranced angrily backward, his antennae twitching with agitation.

We faced one another.

I noticed the tips of his forelegs were inverted, unsheathing the two curved, hornlike blades which reposed there.

We watched one another carefully.

From behind me I heard the mechanical voice of Misk's translator: "But she is the Mother," it said, "and we of the Nest are all her children."

I smiled.

Sarm saw that I did not intend to advance further and his agitation decreased, although his general attitude of awareness was not relaxed.

It was at this time that I first saw how Priest-Kings breathed, probably because Sarm's respiratory movements were now more pronounced than they had been hitherto. Muscular contractions in the abdomen take place with the result that air is sucked into the system through four small holes on each side of the abdomen, the same holes serving also as exhalation vents. Usually the breathing cycle, unless one is quite close and listens carefully, cannot be heard, but in the present case I could hear quite clearly from a distance of several feet the quick intake of air through the eight tiny, tubular mouths in Sarm's abdomen, and its almost immediate expellation through the same apertures.

Now the muscular contractions in Sarm's abdomen became almost unnoticeable and I could no longer hear the evidence of his respiratory cycle. The tips of his forelegs were no longer inverted, with the result that the bladed structures had disappeared and the small, four-jointed, hooklike prehensile appendages were again fully visible. Their tips delicately touched one another. Sarm's antennae were calm.

He regarded me.

He did not move.

I would never find myself fully able to adjust to the incredible stillness with which a Priest-King can stand.

He reminded me vaguely of the blade of a golden knife.

Suddenly Sarm's antennae pointed at Misk. "You should have anesthetized it," he said.

"Perhaps," said Misk.

For some reason this hurt me. I felt that I had betrayed Misk's trust in me, that I had behaved as a not fully rational creature, that I had behaved as Sarm had expected me to.

"I'm sorry," I said to Sarm, resheathing my sword.

"You see," said Misk.

"It's dangerous," said Sarm.

I laughed.

"What is that?" asked Sarm, lifting his antennae.

"It is shaking and curling his antennae," said Misk.

On the receipt of this information Sarm did not shake nor did his antennae curl; rather the bladelike structures snapped out and back, and his antennae twitched in irritation. I gathered one did not shake and curl one's antennae at Priest-Kings.

"Mount the disk, Tarl Cabot of Ko-ro-ba," said Misk, gesturing with his foreleg to the flat oval disk which had brought Sarm to our level.

I hesitated.

"He is afraid," said Sarm.

"He has much to fear," said Misk.

"I am not afraid," I said.

"Then mount the disk," said Misk.

I did so, and the two Priest-Kings stepped delicately onto

the disk to join me, in such a way that one stood on each side and slightly behind me. Scarcely had they placed their weight on the disk when it began to smoothly and silently accelerate down the long ramp which led toward the bottom of the canyon.

The disk moved with great swiftness and it was with some difficulty that I managed to stand on my feet, leaning into the blast of air which rushed past me. To my annoyance both of the Priest-Kings seemed immobile, leaning alertly forward into the wind, their forelegs lifted high, their antennae lying flat, streaming backwards.

12
Two Muls

ON A MARBLE CIRCLE OF some half pasang in width, in the bottom of that vast, brilliantly lit, many-colored artificial canyon the oval disk diminished its speed and drew to a stop.

I found myself in some sort of plaza, surrounded by the fantastic architecture of the Nest of Priest-Kings. The plaza was crowded, not only with Priest-Kings but even more with various creatures of other forms and natures. Among them I saw men and women, barefoot with shaven heads, clad in short purple tunics that reflected the various lights of the plaza as though they might have been formed of some reflective plastic.

I stepped aside as a flat, sluglike creature, clinging with several legs to a small transportation disk, swept by.

"We must hurry," said Sarm.

"I see human beings here," I said to Misk. "Are they slaves?"

"Yes," said Misk.

"They wear no collars," I pointed out.

"It is not necessary to mark a distinction between slave and free within the Nest," said Misk, "for in the Nest all humans are slaves."

"Why are they shaven and clad as they are?" I asked.

"It is more sanitary," said Misk.

"Let us leave the plaza," said Sarm.

I would learn later that his agitation was principally due to his fear of contracting filth in this public place. Humans walked here.

"Why do the slaves wear purple?" I asked Misk. "That is the color of the robes of a Ubar."

"Because it is a great honor to be the slave of Priest-Kings," said Misk.

"Is it your intention," I asked, "that I should be so shaved and clad?"

My hand was on my sword hilt.

"Perhaps not," said Sarm. "It may be that you are to be destroyed immediately. I must check the scent-tapes."

"He is not to be destroyed immediately," said Misk, "nor is he to be shaved and clad as a slave."

"Why not?" asked Sarm.

"It is the wish of the Mother," said Misk.

"What has she to do with it?" asked Sarm.

"Much," said Misk.

Sarm seemed puzzled. He stopped. His antennae twitched nervously. "Was he brought to the tunnels for some purpose?"

"I came of my own accord," I avowed.

"Don't be foolish," said Misk to me.

"For what purpose was he brought to the tunnels?" asked Sarm.

"The purpose is known to the Mother," said Misk.

"I am the First Born," said Sarm.

"She is the Mother," said Misk.

"Very well," said Sarm, and turned away. I sensed he was not much pleased.

At that moment a human girl walked near and wide-eyed circled us, looking at me. Although her head was shaved she was pretty and the brief plastic sheath she wore did not conceal her charms.

A shudder of repulsion seemed to course through Sarm.

"Hurry," he said, and we followed him as he scurried from the plaza.

"Your sword," said Misk, extending one foreleg down to me.

"Never," I said, backing away.

"Please," said Misk.

For some reason I unbuckled the sword belt and reluctant-ly handed the weapon to Misk.

Sarm, who stood in the long room on an oval dais, seemed satisfied with this transaction. He turned to the walls behind him which were covered with thousands of tiny illuminated knobs. He pulled certain of these out from the wall and they seemed to be attached to slender cords which he passed between his antennae. He spent perhaps an Ahn in this activity and then, exasperated, turned to face me.

I had been pacing back and forth in the long room, nervous without the feel of the sword steel at my thigh.

Misk during all this time had not moved but had remained standing in that incredible fixity perhaps unique to Priest-Kings.

"The scent-tapes are silent," said Sarm.

"Of course," said Misk.

"What is to be the disposition of this creature?" asked Sarm.

"For the time," said Misk, "it is the wish of the Mother that it be permitted to live as a Matok."

"What is that?" I asked.

"You speak much for one of the lower orders," said Sarm.

"What is a Matok?" I asked.

"A creature that is in the Nest but is not of the Nest," said Misk.

"Like the arthropod?" I asked.

"Precisely," said Misk.

"If I had my wish," said Sarm, "he would be sent to the vivarium or the dissection chambers."

"But that is not the wish of the Mother," said Misk.

"I see," said Sarm.

"Thus," said Misk, "it is not the wish of the Nest."

"Of course," said Sarm, "for the wish of the Mother is the wish of the Nest."

"The Mother is the Nest and the Nest is the Mother," said Misk.

"Yes," said Sarm, and the two Priest-Kings approached one another, bowed and gently locked their antennae.

When they disengaged themselves, Sarm turned to face me. "Nonetheless," he said, "I shall speak to the Mother about this matter."

"Of course," said Misk.

"I should have been consulted," said Sarm, "for I am First Born."

"Perhaps," said Misk.

Sarm looked down at me. I think he had not forgiven me the start I had given him on the platform high above the canyon, near the elevator.

"It is dangerous," he said. "It should be destroyed."

"Perhaps," said Misk.

"And it curled its antennae at me," said Sarm.

Misk was silent.

"Yes," said Sarm. "It should be destroyed."

Sarm then turned from me and with his left, forward supporting appendage depressed a recessed button in the dais on which he stood.

Hardly had his delicate foot touched the button than a panel slid aside and two handsome men, of the most symmetrical form and features with shaven heads and clad in the purple, plastic tunics of slaves, entered the room and prostrated themselves before the dais.

At a signal from Sarm they leaped to their feet and stood alertly beside the dais, their feet spread, their heads high, their arms folded.

"Behold these two," said Sarm.

Neither of the two men who had entered the room had seemed to notice me.

I now approached them.

"I am Tarl Cabot of Ko-ro-ba," I said to them, extending my hand.

If they saw my hand they made no effort to accept it.

I assumed they must be identical twins. They had wide, fine heads, strong, broad bodies, and a carriage that suggested calmness and strength.

Both were a bit shorter than I but were somewhat more squarely built.

"You may speak," said Sarm.

"I am Mul-Al-Ka," said one, "honored slave of the glorious Priest-Kings."

"I am Mul-Ba-Ta," said the other, "honored slave of the glorious Priest-Kings."

"In the Nest," said Misk, "the expression 'Mul' is used to designate a human slave."

I nodded. The rest of it I did not need to be told. The expressions 'Al-Ka' and 'Ba-Ta' are the first two letters of the Gorean alphabet. In effect these men had no names, but were simply known as Slave A and Slave B.

I turned to Sarm.

"I assume," I said, "you have more than twenty-eight human slaves." There were twenty-eight characters in the Gorean alphabet. I had intended my remark to be rather vicious but Sarm took no offense.

"Others are numbered," he said. "When one dies or is destroyed, his number is assigned to another."

"Some of the low numbers," volunteered Misk, "have been assigned as many as a thousand times."

"Why do these slaves not have numbers?" I asked.

"They are special," said Misk.

I regarded them closely. They seemed splendid specimens of mankind. Perhaps Misk had meant merely that they were unusually excellent representatives of the human type.

"Can you guess," asked Sarm, "which one has been synthesized?"

I must have given quite a start.

Sarm's antennae giggled.

"Yes," said Sarm, "one was synthesized, beginning with the synthesis of the protein molecules, and was formed molecule by molecule. It is an artificially constructed human being. It is not of much scientific interest but it has considerable curiosity value. It was built over a period of two centuries by Kusk, the Priest-King, as a way of escaping in his leisure hours from the burdens of his serious biological investigations."

I shuddered.

"What of the other?" I asked.

"It too," said Sarm, "is not without interest and is also

bestowed upon us by the avocational whims of Kusk, one of the greatest of our Nest."

"Is the other also synthesized?" I asked.

"No," said Sarm, "it is the product of genetic manipulation, artificial control and alteration of the hereditary coils in gametes."

I was sweating.

"Not the least interesting aspect of this matter," said Sarm, "is the match."

To be sure I could not tell the two men, if they were men, apart.

"That is the evidence of real skill," said Sarm.

"Kusk," said Misk, "is one of the greatest of the Nest."

"Which of these slaves," I asked, "is the one who was synthesized?"

"Can't you tell?" asked Sarm.

"No," I said.

Sarm's antennae shivered and wrapped themselves about one another. He was shaking with the signs I knew now to be associated with amusement.

"I will not tell you," he said.

"It is growing late," said Misk, "and the Matok, if he is to remain in the Nest, must be processed."

"Yes," said Sarm, but he seemed in no hurry to conclude his gloating. He pointed one long, jointed foreleg at the Muls. "Gaze upon them with awe, Matok," said he, "for they are the product of Priest-Kings and the most perfect specimens of your race ever to exist."

I wondered about what Misk meant by 'processing' but Sarm's words irritated me, as did the two grave, handsome fellows who had so spontaneously groveled before his dais. "How is that?" I asked.

"Is it not obvious?" asked Sarm.

"No," I said.

"They are symmetrically formed," said Sarm. "Moreover they are intelligent, strong and in good health." Sarm seemed to wait for my reply but there was none. "And," said Sarm, "they live on fungus and water, and wash themselves twelve times a day."

I laughed. "By the Priest-Kings!" I roared, the rather

blasphemous Gorean oath slipping out, somehow incongruously considering my present location and predicament. Neither Priest-King however seemed in the least disturbed by
this oath which might have brought tears to the eyes of a
member of the Caste of Initiates.

"Why do you curl your antennae?" asked Sarm.

"You call these perfect human beings?" I asked, waving
my arms toward the two slaves.

"Of course," said Sarm.

"Of course," said Misk.

"Perfect slaves!" I said.

"The most perfect human being is of course the most
perfect slave," said Sarm.

"The most perfect human being," I said, "is free."

A look of puzzlement seemed to appear in the eyes of the
two slaves.

"They have no wish to be free," said Misk. He then
addressed the slaves. "What is your greatest joy, Muls?" he
asked.

"To be the slaves of Priest-Kings," they said.

"You see?" asked Misk.

"Yes," I said. "I see now that they are not men."

Sarm's antennae twitched angrily.

"Why do you not," I challenged, "have your Kusk, or
whoever he is, synthesize a Priest-King?"

Sarm seemed to shiver with rage. The bladed hornlike
projections snapped into view on his forelegs.

Misk had not moved. "It would be immoral," he said.

Sarm turned to Misk. "Would the Mother object if the
Matok's arms and legs were broken?"

"Yes," said Misk.

"Would the Mother object if its organs were damaged?"
asked Sarm.

"Undoubtedly," said Misk.

"But surely," said Sarm, "it can be punished."

"Yes," said Misk, "undoubtedly it will have to be disciplined sometime."

"Very well," said Sarm and directed his antennae at the
two shaven-headed, plastic-clad slaves. "Punish the Matok,"
said Sarm, "but do not break its bones nor injure its organs."

No sooner had these words been emitted from Sarm's translator than the two slaves leaped toward me to seize me.

In the same instant I leaped toward them, taking them by surprise and compounding the momentum of my blow. I thrust one aside with my left arm and crushed my fist into the face of the second. His head snapped to the side and his knees buckled. He crumpled to the floor. Before the other could regain his balance, I had leaped to him and seized him in my hands and lifted him high over my head and hurled him on his back to the stone flooring of the long chamber. Had it been combat to the death in that brief instant I would have finished him leaping over him and gouging my heels into his stomach rupturing the diaphragm. But I had no wish to kill him, nor a matter of fact to injure him severely. He managed to roll over on his stomach. I could have snapped his neck then with my heel. The thought occurred to me that these slaves had not been well trained to administer discipline. They seemed to know almost nothing. Now the man was on his knees, gasping, supporting himself on the palm of his right hand. If he was right-handed, that seemed foolish. Also he made no effort to cover his throat.

I looked up at Sarm and Misk, who, observing, stood in that slightly inclined, infuriatingly still posture.

"Do not injure them further," said Misk.

"I will not," I said.

"Perhaps the Matok is right," said Misk to Sarm. "Perhaps they are not perfect human beings."

"Perhaps," admitted Sarm.

Now the slave who was conscious lifted his hand piteously to the Priest-Kings. His eyes were filled with tears.

"Please," he begged, "let us go to the dissection chambers."

I was dumbfounded.

Now the other had regained consciousness and, on his knees, joined his fellow. "Please," he cried, "let us go to the dissection chambers."

My astonishment could not be concealed.

"They feel they have failed the Priest-Kings and wish to die," said Misk.

Sarm regarded the two slaves. "I am kind," he said, "and it

is near the Feast of Tola." He lifted his foreleg with a gentle, permissive gesture, almost a benediction. "You may go to the dissection chambers."

To my amazement, gratitude transfigured the features of the two slaves and, helping one another, they prepared to leave the room.

"Stop!" I cried.

The two slaves stopped and looked at me.

My eyes were fixed however on Sarm and Misk. "You can't send them to their deaths," I said.

Sarm seemed puzzled.

Misk's antennae shrugged.

Frantically I groped about for a plausible objection. "Kusk would surely be displeased if his creatures were to be destroyed," I said. I hoped it would do.

Sarm and Misk touched antennae.

"The Matok is right," said Misk.

"True," said Sarm.

I breathed a sigh of relief.

Sarm then turned to the two slaves. "You may not go to the dissection chambers," he said.

Once more the two slaves, this time apparently without emotion, folded their arms and stood, legs apart, beside the dais. Nothing might have happened in the last few moments save that one was breathing heavily and the other's face was splattered with his own blood.

Neither of them showed any gratitude at being reprieved nor did either evince any resentment at my having interfered with their executions.

I was, as you might suppose, puzzled. The responses and behavior of the two slaves seemed to be incomprehensible.

"You must understand, Tarl Cabot of Ko-ro-ba," said Misk, apparently sensing my puzzlement, "that it is the greatest joy of Muls to love and serve Priest-Kings. If it is the wish of a Priest-King that they die they do so with great joy; if it is the wish of a Priest-King that they live, they are similarly delighted."

I noted that neither of the two slaves looked particularly delighted.

"You see," continued Misk, "these Muls have been formed to love and serve Priest-Kings."

"They have been made that way," I said.

"Precisely," said Misk.

"And yet you say they are human," I said.

"Of course," said Sarm.

And then to my surprise one of the slaves, though which one I could not have told, looked at me and spoke. "We are human," it said very simply.

I approached him and held out my hand. "I hope I did not hurt you," I said.

It took my hand and awkwardly held it, not knowing how to shake hands apparently.

"I too am human," said the other, looking at me rather directly.

He held his hand out with the back of his hand up. I took the hand and turned it and shook it.

"I have feelings," said the first man.

"I, too, have feelings," said the second man.

"We all do," I said.

"Of course," said the first man, "for we are human."

I looked at them very carefully. "Which of you," I asked, "has been synthesized?"

"We do not know," said the first man.

"No," said the second man. "We have never been told."

The two Priest-Kings had watched this small concourse with some interest, but now the voice of Sarm's translator was heard: "It is growing late," it said, "let the Matok be processed."

"Follow me," said the first man and turned, and I followed him, leaving the room, the second man falling into stride beside me.

13
The Slime Worm

I FOLLOWED MUL-AL-KA AND MUL-BA-TA through several rooms and down a long corridor.

"This is the Hall of Processing," said one of them.

We passed several high steel portals in the hallway and on each of these, about twenty feet high, at the antennae level of a Priest-King, were certain dots, which I was later to learn were scent-dots.

If the scent-dots were themselves not scented one might be tempted to think of them as graphemes in the language of the Priest-Kings, but since they themselves are scented they are best construed as analogous to uttered phonemes or phoneme combinations, direct expressions of the oral sylla-bary of the Priest-Kings.

When surrounded by scent-dots one might suppose the Priest-King to be subjected to a cacophony of stimulation, much as we might be if environed by dozens of blaring radios and television sets, but this is apparently not the case; the better analogy would seem to be our experience of walking down a quiet city street surrounded by printed signs which we might notice but to which we do not pay much attention.

In our sense there is no distinction between a spoken and written language for the Priest-Kings, though there is an analogous distinction between linguistic patterns that are ac-tually sensed and those which are potentially to be sensed, an example of the latter being the scents of a yet uncoiled scent-tape.

"You will not much care for the processing," said one of my guides.

"But it will be good for you," said the other.

"Why must I be processed?" I asked.

"To protect the Nest from contamination," said the first.

Scents, of course, will fade in time, but the specially prepared synthetic products of the Priest-Kings can last for thousands of years and, in the long run, will surely outlast the fading print of human books, the disintegrating celluloid of our films, perhaps even the carved, weathering stones so imperishably attesting the incomparable glories of our nu-merous kings, conquerors and potentates.

Scent-dots, incidentally, are arranged in rows constituting a geometrical square, and are read beginning with the top row from left to right, then right to left, and then left to right and so on again.

Gorean, I might note, is somewhat similar, and though I

speak Gorean fluently, I find it very difficult to write, largely because of the even-numbered lines which, from my point of view, must be written backwards. Torm, my friend of the Caste of Scribes, never forgave me this and to this day, if he lives, he undoubtedly considers me partly illiterate. As he said, I would never make a Scribe. "It is simple," he said. "You just write it forward but in the other direction."

The syllabary of Priest-Kings, not to be confused with their set of seventy-three "phonemes," consists of what seems to me to be a somewhat unwieldy four hundred and eleven characters, each of which stands of course for a phoneme or phoneme combination, normally a combination. Certain juxtapositions of these phonemes and phoneme combinations, naturally, form words. I would have supposed a simpler syllabary, or even an experimentation with a nonscented perhaps alphabetic graphic script, would have been desirable linguistic ventures for the Priest-Kings, but as far as I know they were never made.

With respect to the rather complex syllabary, I originally supposed that it had never been simplified because the Priest-King, with his intelligence, would absorb the four hundred and eleven characters of his syllabary more rapidly than would a human child his alphabet of less than thirty letters, and thus that the difference to him between more than four hundred signs and less than thirty would be negligible.

As far as it goes this was not bad guesswork on my part, but deeper reasons underlay the matter. First, I did not know then how Priest-Kings learned. They do not learn as we do. Second, they tend in many matters to have a penchant for complexity, regarding it as more elegant than simplicity. One practical result of this seems to be that they have never been tempted to oversimplify physical reality, biological processes or the operations of a functioning mind. It would never occur to them that nature is ultimately simple, and if they found it so they would be rather disappointed. They view nature as a set of interrelated continua rather than as a visually oriented organism is tempted to do, as a network of discrete objects which must be somehow, mysteriously, related to one another. Their basic mathematics, incidentally, begins with ordinal and not cardinal numbers, and the mathematics of cardinal numbers is regarded as a limiting case imposed on more intuitively acceptable ordinalities. Most significantly however I suspect that the syllabary of Priest-Kings remains complex, and that experiments with unscented graphemes were never conducted, because, except for lexical additions, they wish to keep their language much as it was in the ancient past. The Priest-King, for all his intelligence, tends to be fond of established patterns, at least in basic cultural matters such as Nest mores and language, subscribing to them however not because of genetic necessity but rather a certain undoubtedly genetically based preference for that which is comfortable and familiar. The Priest-King, somewhat like men, can change its ways but seldom cares to do so.

And yet there is probably more to these matters than the above considerations would suggest.

I once asked Misk why the syllabary of Priest-Kings was not simplified, and he responded, "If this were done we would have to give up certain signs, and we could not bear to do so, for they are all very beautiful."

Beneath the scent-dots on each high portal which Mul-Al-Ka and Mul-Ba-Ta and I passed there was, perhaps for the benefit of humans or others, a stylized outline picture of a form of creature.

On none of the doors that we had passed thus far was the stylized outline picture of a human.

Down the hall running towards us, not frantically but rather deliberately, at a steady pace, came a young human female, of perhaps eighteen years of age, with shaved head and clad in the brief plastic tunic of a Mul.

"Do not obstruct her," said one of my guides.

I stepped aside.

Scarcely noticing us and clutching two scent-tapes in her hands the girl passed.

She had brown eyes and, I thought, in spite of her shaved head, was attractive.

Neither of my companions showed, or seemed to show, the least interest in her.

For some reason this annoyed me.

I watched her continue on down the passageway, listened to the slap of her bare feet on the floor.

"Who is she?" I asked.

"A Mul," said one of the slaves.

"Of course she is a Mul," I said.

"Then why did you ask?" he asked.

I found myself nastily hoping that he was the one who had been synthesized.

"She is a Messenger," said the other, "who carries scent-tapes between portals in the Hall of Processing."

"Oh," said the first slave. "He is interested in things like that."

"He is new in the tunnels," said the second slave.

I was curious. I looked directly at the first slave. "She had good legs, didn't she?" I said.

He seemed puzzled. "Yes," he said, "very strong."

"She was attractive," I said to the second.

"Attractive?" he asked.

"Yes," I said.

"Yes," he said, "she is healthy."

"Perhaps she is someone's mate?" I asked.

"No," said the first slave.

"How do you know?" I asked.

"She is not in the breeding cases," said the man.

Somehow these laconic responses and the unquestioning acceptance of the apparent barbarities of the rule of Priest-Kings infuriated me.

"I wonder how she would feel in one's arms," I said.

The two men looked at me and at one another.

"One must not wonder about that," said one.

"Why not?" I asked.

"It is forbidden," said the other.

"But surely," I said, "you must have wondered about that?"

One of the men smiled at me. "Yes," he said, "I have sometimes wondered about that."

"So have I," said the other.

Then all three of us turned to watch the girl, who was now no more than a bluish speck under the energy bulbs far down the hall.

"Why is she running?" I asked.

"The journeys between portals are timed," said the first slave, "and if she dallies she will be given a record-scar."

"Yes," said the other, "five record-scars and she will be destroyed."

"A record-scar," I said, "is some sort of mark on your records?"

"Yes," said the first slave, "it is entered on your scent-tape and also, in odor, inscribed on your tunic."

"The tunic," said the other, "is inscribed with much information, and it is by means of the tunic that Priest-Kings can recognize us."

"Yes," said the first slave, "otherwise I am afraid we would appear much alike to them."

I stored this information away, hoping that someday it might prove useful.

"Well," I said, still looking down the hall, "I would have supposed that the mighty Priest-Kings could have devised a quicker way of transporting scent-tapes."

"Of course," said the first slave, "but there is no better way, for Muls are extremely inexpensive and are easily replaced."

"Speed in such matters," said one, "is of little interest to Priest-Kings."

"Yes," said the other, "they are very patient."

"Why have they not given her a transportation device?" I asked.

"She is only a Mul," said the first slave.

All three of us stared down the hall after the girl, but she had now disappeared in the distance.

"But she is a healthy Mul," said one.

"Yes," said the other, "and she has strong legs."

I laughed and clapped both of the slaves on the shoulders, and the three of us, arm in arm, walked down the hall.

We had not walked far when we passed a long, wormlike animal, eyeless, with a small red mouth, that inched its way along the corridor, hugging the angle between the wall and floor.

Neither of my two guides paid the animal any attention.

Indeed, even I myself, after my experience of the arthropod on the platform and the flat, sluglike beast on its transportation disk in the plaza, was growing accustomed to finding strange creatures in the Nest of the Priest-Kings.

"What is it?" I asked.

"A Matok," said one of the slaves.

"Yes," said the other, "it is in the Nest but not of the Nest."

"But I thought I was a Matok," I said.

"You are," said one of the slaves.

We continued on.

"What do you call it?" I asked.

"Oh," said one of the slaves. "It is a Slime Worm."

"What does it do?" I asked.

"Long ago it functioned in the Nest," said one of the slaves, "as a sewerage device, but it has not served that function in many thousands of years."

"But yet it remains in the Nest."

"Of course," said one of the slaves, "the Priest-Kings are tolerant."

"Yes," said the other, "and they are fond of it, and are themselves creatures of great reverence for tradition."

"The Slime Worm has earned its place in the Nest," said the other.

"How does it live?" I asked.

"It scavenges on the kills of the Golden Beetle," said the first slave.

"What does the Golden Beetle kill?" I asked.

"Priest-Kings," said the second slave.

I would surely have pressed forward this inquiry but at that very moment we arrived at a tall steel portal in the hallway.

Looking up I saw beneath the square of scent-dots fixed high on the steel door the stylized outline picture of what was unmistakably a human being.

"This is the place," said one of my companions. "It is here that you will be processed."

"We will wait for you," said the other.

14
The Secret Chamber of Misk

THE ARMS OF THE METAL device seized me and I found myself held helplessly by the arms suspended some feet above the floor.

Behind me the panel had slid shut.

The room was rather large, bleak and coated with plastic. It seemed to be bare except that at one end there were several metal disks in the wall and, high in the wall, there was a transparent shield. Viewing me antiseptically through this shield was the face of a Priest-King.

"May you bathe in the dung of Slime Worms," I called to him cheerfully. I hoped he had a translator.

Two circular metal plates in the wall beneath the shield had slid upward and suddenly long metal arms had telescoped outwards and reached for me.

For an instant I had considered scrambling out of their reach but then I had sensed that there would be no escape in the smooth, closed, carefully prepared room in which I found myself.

The metal arms had locked on me and lifted me from the floor.

The Priest-King behind the shield did not seem to notice my remark. I supposed he did not have a translator.

As I dangled there to my irritation further devices manipulated by the Priest-King emerged from the wall and extended towards me.

One of these with maddening delicacy snipped the clothing from my body, even cutting the thongs of my sandals. Another deftly forced a large, ugly pellet down my throat.

Considering the size of a Priest-King and the comparatively small scale of these operations I gathered that the reduction gearing on the mechanical appendages must be considerable. Moreover the accuracy with which the operations were performed suggested a magnification of some sort. I would learn later that practically the entire wall which faced me was such a device, being in effect a very large scent-reinforcer. But at the time I was in no mood to admire the engineering talents of my captors.

"May your antennae be soaked in grease!" I called to my tormentor.

His antennae stiffened and then curled a bit at the tips.

I was pleased. Apparently he did have a translator.

I was considering my next insult when the two arms which held me swung me over a metal cage with a double floor, the higher consisting of narrow bars set in a wide mesh and the lower consisting simply of a white plastic tray.

The metal appendages which held me suddenly sprang open and I was dropped into the cage.

I sprang to my feet but the top of the cage had clicked shut.

I wanted to try the bars but already I felt sick and I sank to the bottom of the cage.

I was no longer interested in insulting Priest-Kings.

I remember looking up and seeing its antennae curling.

It took only two or three minutes for the pellet to do its work and it is not with pleasure that I recall those minutes.

Finally the plastic tray neatly slid out from beneath the cage and swiftly disappeared through a low, wide panel in the left wall.

I gratefully noted its departure.

Then the entire cage, on a track of some sort, began to move through an opening which appeared in the right wall.

In the following journey the cage was successively submerged in various solutions of various temperatures and densities, some of which, perhaps because I was still ill, I found exceedingly noxious.

Had I been less ill I would undoubtedly have been more offended.

At last after I, sputtering and choking, had been duly cleansed and rinsed several times, and then it seemed several times again, the cage began to move slowly, mercifully, between vents from which blasts of hot air issued, and, eventually, it passed slowly between an assortment of humming projection points for wide-beam rays, some of which were visible to my eye, being yellow, red and a refulgent green.

I would later learn that these rays, which passed through my body as easily and harmlessly as sunlight through glass, were indexed to the metabolic physiology of various organisms which can infect Priest-Kings. I would also learn that the last known free instance of such an organism had occurred more than four thousand years before. In the next few weeks in the Nest I would occasionally come upon diseased Muls. The organisms which afflict them are apparently harmless to Priest-Kings and thus allowed to survive. Indeed, they are regarded as Matoks, in the Nest, but not of the Nest, and are thus to be tolerated with equanimity.

I was still quite ill when, clad in a red plastic tunic, I rejoined the two slaves in the hall outside the door.

"You look much better," said one of them.

"They left the threadlike growths on your head," said the other.

"Hair," I said, leaning against the portal.

"Strange," said one of the slaves. "The only fibrous body growths permitted Muls are the lashes of the eyes."

This, I supposed, would have to do with protecting the eyes from particles. Idly, not feeling well, I wondered if there were any particles.

"But he is a Matok," said one.

"That is true," said the other.

I was glad that the tunic I wore was not of the Ubar's purple which would proclaim me a slave of Priest-Kings.

"Perhaps if you are very zealous," said one, "you can become a Mul."

"Yes," said the other, "then you would be not only in the Nest but of the Nest."

I did not respond.

"That is best," said one.

"Yes," said the other.

I leaned back against the portal of the Hall of Processing, my eyes closed, and took several slow, deep breaths.

"You have been assigned quarters," said one of the two slaves, "a case in the chamber of Misk."

I opened my eyes.

"We will take you there," said the other.

I looked at them blankly. "A case?" I asked.

"He is not well," said one of the slaves.

"It is quite comfortable," said the other, "with fungus and water."

I closed my eyes again and shook my head. I could feel them gently take my arms and I accompanied them slowly down the hall.

"You will feel much better," said one of them, "when you have had a bit of fungus."

"Yes," said the other.

It is not hard to get used to Mul-Fungus, for it has almost no taste, being an extremely bland, pale, whitish, fibrous vegetablelike matter. I know of no one who is moved much in one direction or the other by its taste. Even the Muls, many of whom have been bred in the Nest, do not particularly like it, nor despise it. It is eaten with much the same lack of attention that we normally breathe air.

Muls feed four times a day. In the first meal, Mul-Fungus is ground and mixed with water, forming a porridge of sorts; for the second meal it is chopped into rough two-inch cubes; for the third meal it is minced with Mul-Pellets and served as a sort of cold hash; the Mul-Pellets are undoubtedly some type of dietary supplement; at the final meal Mul-Fungus is pressed into a large, flat cake and sprinkled with a few grains of salt.

Misk told me, and I believe him, that Muls had occasionally slain one another for a handful of salt.

The Mul-Fungus, as far as I can tell, is not much different from the fungus, raised under ideal conditions from specially selected spores, which graces the feed troughs of the Priest-Kings themselves, a tiny sample of which was once given me by Misk. It was perhaps a bit less coarse than Mul-Fungus. Misk was much annoyed that I could not detect the difference. I was much annoyed when I found out later that the major difference between high-quality fungus and the lower-grade Mul-Fungus was simply the smell. I was in the Nest, incidentally, for more than five weeks before I could even vaguely detect the odor difference which seemed so significant to Misk. And then it did not strike me as being better or worse than that of the low-grade Mul-Fungus.

The longer I stayed in the Nest the more acute became my sense of smell, and it was an embarrassing revelation to me to discover how unaware I had been of these varied, rich sensory cues so abundantly available in my environment. I was given a translator by Misk and I would utter Gorean expressions into it and then wait for the translation into the language of the Priest-Kings, and in this way, after a time, I became capable of recognizing numerous meaningful odors. The first odor I came to recognize was Misk's name, and it was delightful to then discover, as I became more practiced and sensitive, that the odor was the same as his own.

One of the things I did was run the translator over the red plastic tunic I had been issued and listen to the information which had been recorded on it. There was not much save my name and city, that I was a Matok under the supervision of Misk, that I had no record-scars and that I might be dangerous.

I smiled at the latter caution.

I did not even have a sword, and I was sure that, in any battle with Priest-Kings, I would constitute but a moment's work for their fierce mandibles and the bladed, hornlike projections on their forelegs.

The case which I was to occupy in Misk's chamber was not as bad as I had anticipated.

Indeed, it seemed to me far more luxurious than the appointments in Misk's own chamber, which seemed utterly bare except for the feed trough and numerous compartments, dials, switches and plugs mounted in one wall. The Priest-Kings eat and sleep standing and never lie down, except perhaps it be to die.

The bareness of Misk's chamber was, however, as it turned out, only an apparent bareness to a visually oriented organism such as myself. Actually the walls, ceiling and floor were covered with what, to a Priest-King, were excruciatingly beautiful scent-patterns. Indeed, Misk informed me that the patterns in his chamber had been laid down by some of the greatest artists in the Nest.

My case was a transparent plastic cube of perhaps eight feet square, with ventilation holes and a sliding plastic door.

There was no lock on the door and thus I could come and go as I pleased.

Inside the cube there were canisters of Mul-Fungus, a bowl, a ladle, a wooden-bladed Fungus-Knife; a wooden-headed Fungus-Mallet; a convenient tube of Mul-Pellets, which discharged its contents one at a time following my depressing a lever in the bottom of the tube; and a large, inverted jar of water, by means of which an attached, somewhat shallow, watering pan was kept filled.

In one corner of the case there was a large, circular padding a few inches deep of soft, rough-cut, reddish moss which was not uncomfortable and was changed daily.

Adjoining the cube, reached from the cube by sliding plastic panels, were a lavatory facility and a washing-booth.

The washing-booth was remarkably like the showers with which we are familiar except that one may not regulate the flow of fluid. One turns on the fluid by stepping into the booth and its amount and temperature are controlled automatically. I had naturally supposed the fluid to be simply water which it closely resembled in appearance, and once had tried to fill my bowl for the morning meal there, rather than ladling the water out of the water pan. Choking, my mouth burning, I spat it out in the booth.

"It is fortunate," said Misk, "that you did not swallow it for the washing fluid contains a cleansing additive that is highly toxic to human physiology."

Misk and I got on rather well together after a few small initial frictions, particularly having to do with the salt ration and the number of times a day the washing-booth was to be used. If I had been a Mul I would have received a record-scar for each day on which I had not washed completely twelve times. Washing-booths, incidentally, are found in all Mul-cases and often, for convenience, along the tunnels and in public places, such as plazas, shaving-parlors, pellet-dispensaries, and fungus commissaries. Since I was a Matok I insisted that I should be exempted from the Duty of the Twelve Joys, as it is known. In the beginning I held out for one shower a day as quite sufficient but poor Misk seemed so upset that I agreed to up my proposal to two. He would still hear nothing of this and seemed firm that I should not fall below ten. At last, feeling that I perhaps owed something to Misk's acceptance of me in his chamber, I suggested a compromise at five, and, for an extra salt packet, six on alternate days. At last Misk threw in two extra salt packets a day and I agreed to six washings. He himself, of course, did not use a washing-booth but groomed and cleaned himself in the age-old fashions of Priest-Kings, with his cleaning hooks and mouth. Occasionally after we got to know one another better, he would even allow me to groom him, and the first time he allowed me, with the small grooming fork used by favored Muls, to comb his antennae I knew that he trusted me, and liked me, though for what reason I could not tell.

I myself grew rather fond of Misk.

"Did you know," said Misk once to me, "that humans are among the most intelligent of the lower orders?"

"I'm glad to hear it," I said.

Misk was quiet and his antennae quivered nostalgically.

"I once had a pet Mul," he said.

I looked at my case.

"No," said Misk, "when a pet Mul dies the case is always destroyed, lest there be contamination."

"What happened to him?" I asked.

"It was a small female," said Misk. "It was slain by Sarm."

I felt a tension in the foreleg of Misk which I was grooming as though it were involuntarily preparing to invert, bringing out the bladelike projection.

"Why?" I asked.

Misk said nothing for a long time, and then he dejectedly lowered his head, delicately extending his antennae to me for grooming. After I had combed them for a bit, I sensed he was ready to speak.

"It was my fault," said Misk. "She wanted to let the threadlike growths on her head emerge, for she was not bred in the Nest." Misk's voice came from the translator as consecutively and mechanically as ever, but his whole body trembled. I removed the grooming fork from his antennae in order that the sensory hairs not be injured. "I was indulgent," said Misk, straightening up so that his long body now loomed over me, inclined forward slightly from the vertical in the characteristic stance of Priest-Kings. "So that it was actually I who killed her."

"I think not," I said. "You tried to be kind."

"And it occurred on the day on which she saved my life," said Misk.

"Tell me about it," I said.

"I was on an errand for Sarm," said Misk, "which took me to unfrequented tunnels and for company I took the girl with me. We came upon a Golden Beetle though none had ever been seen in that place and I wanted to go to the Beetle and I put down my head and approached it but the girl seized my antennae and dragged me away, thus saving my life."

Misk lowered his head again and extended his antennae for grooming.

"The pain was excruciating," said Misk, "and I could not but follow her in spite of the fact that I wanted to go to the Golden Beetle. In an Ahn of course I no longer wanted to go to the Beetle and I knew then she had saved my life. It was the same day that Sarm ordered her given five record-scars for the growths on her head and had her destroyed."

"Is it always five record-scars for such an offense?" I asked.

"No," said Misk. "I do not know why Sarm acted as he did."

"It seems to me," I said, "that you should not blame yourself for the girl's death, but Sarm."

"No," said Misk. "I was too indulgent."

"Is it not possible," I asked, "that Sarm wished you to die by the Golden Beetle?"

"Of course," said Misk. "It was undoubtedly his intention."

I puzzled to myself why Sarm might want Misk to be killed. Undoubtedly there was some type of rivalry or political division between them. To my human mind, used to the cruelties with which selfish men can implement their schemes, I saw nothing incomprehensible in the fact that Sarm would have attempted to engineer Misk's death. I would learn later however that this simple fact was indeed almost incomprehensible to Priest-Kings, and that Misk, though he readily accepted it as a fact in his mind, could not bring himself, so to speak, in the furthest reaches of his heart to acknowledge it as true, for were not both he and Sarm of the Nest, and would not such an action be a violation of Nest Trust?

"Sarm is the First Born," said Misk, "whereas I am the Fifth Born. The first five born of the Mother are the High Council of the Nest. The Second, Third and Fourth Born, in the long ages, have, one by one, succumbed to the Pleasures of the Golden Beetle. Only Sarm and I are left of the Five."

"Then," I suggested, "he wants you to die so that he will be the only remaining member of the Council and thus have absolute power."

"The Mother is greater than he," said Misk.

"Still," I suggested, "his power would be considerably augmented."

Misk looked at me and his antennae had a certain lack of resilience and the golden hairs had seemed to lose some of their sheen.

"You are sad," I said.

Misk bent down until his long body was horizontal and then inclined downward yet more towards me. He laid his antennae gently on my shoulders, almost as though a man might have put his hands on them.

"You must not understand these things," said Misk, "in terms of what you know of men. It is different."

"It seems no different to me," I said.

"These things," said Misk, "are deeper and greater than you know, than you can now understand."

"They seem simple enough to me," I remarked.

"No," said Misk. "You do not understand." Misk's antennae pressed a bit on my shoulders. "But you will understand," he said.

The Priest-King then straightened and stalked to my case. With his two forelegs he gently lifted it and moved it aside. The ease with which he did this astonished me for I am sure its weight must have been several hundred pounds. Beneath the case I saw a flat stone with a recessed ring. Misk bent down and lifted this ring.

"I dug this chamber myself," he said, "and day by day over the lifetimes of many Muls I took a bit of rock dust away and scattered it here and there unobserved in the tunnels."

I looked down into the cavern which was now revealed.

"I requisitioned as little as possible, you see," said Misk. "Even the portal must be moved by mechanical force."

He then went to a compartment in the wall and withdrew a slender black rod. He broke the end of the rod off and it began to burn with a bluish flame.

"This is a Mul-Torch," said Misk, "used by the Muls who raise fungus in darkened chambers. You will need it to see."

I knew that the Priest-King had no need of the torch.

"Please," said Misk, gesturing toward the opening.

15
In the Secret Chamber

HOLDING THE SLENDER MUL-TORCH over my head I peered into the cavern now revealed in the floor of Misk's chamber. From a ring on the underside of the floor, the ceiling of the chamber, there dangled a knotted rope.

There seemed to be very little heat from the bluish flame of the Mul-Torch but, considering the size of the flame, a surprising amount of light.

"The workers of the Fungus-Trays," said Misk, "break off both ends of the torch and climb about on the trays with the torch in their teeth."

I had no mind to do this, but I did grasp the torch in my teeth with one end lit and, hand over hand, lower myself down the knotted rope.

One side of my face began to sweat. I closed my right eye.

A circle of eerie, blue, descending light flickered on the walls of the passage down which I lowered myself. The walls a few feet below the level of Misk's compartment became damp. The temperature fell several degrees. I could see the discolorations of slime molds, probably white, but seeming blue in the light, on the walls. I sensed a film of moisture forming on the plastic of my tunic. Here and there a trickle of water traced its dark pattern downward to the floor where it crept along the wall and, continuing its journey, disappeared into one crevice or another.

When I arrived at the bottom of the rope, some forty feet below, I held the torch over my head and found myself in a bare, simple chamber.

Looking up I saw Misk, disdaining the rope, bend himself backwards through the aperture in the ceiling and, step by dainty step, walk across the ceiling upside down and then back himself nimbly down the side of the wall.

In a moment he stood beside me.

"You must never speak of what I am going to show you," said Misk.

I said nothing.

Misk hesitated.

"Let there be Nest Trust between us," I said.

"But you are not of the Nest," said Misk.

"Nonetheless," I said, "let there be Nest Trust between us."

"Very well," said Misk, and he bent forward, extending his antennae towards me.

I wondered for a moment what was to be done but then it seemed I sensed what he wanted. I thrust the torch I carried into a crevice in the wall and, standing before Misk, I raised my arms over my head, extending them towards him.

With extreme gentleness, almost tenderness, the Priest-King touched the palms of my hands with his antennae.

"Let there be Nest Trust between us," he said.

"Yes," I said, "let there be Nest Trust between us."

It was the nearest I could come to locking antennae.

Briskly Misk straightened up.

"Somewhere here," he said, "but unscented and toward the floor, where a Priest-King would not be likely to find it, is a small knob which will look much like a pebble. Find this knob and twist it."

It was but a moment's work to locate the knob of which he spoke though I gathered from what he said that it might have been well concealed from the typical sensory awareness of a Priest-King.

I turned the knob and a portion of the wall swung back.

"Enter," said Misk, and I did so.

Scarcely were we inside when Misk touched a button I could not see several feet over my head and the door swung smoothly closed.

The only light in the chamber was from my bluish torch.

I gazed about myself with wonder.

The room was apparently large, for portions of it were lost in the shadows from the torch. What I could see suggested paneling and instrumentation, banks of scent-needles and gauges, numerous tiered decks of wiring and copper plating. There were on one side of the room, racks of scent-tapes, some of which were spinning slowly, unwinding their tapes through slowly rotating translucent, glowing spheres. These spheres in turn were connected by slender, woven cables of wire to a large, heavy boxlike assembly, made of steel and rather squarish, which was set on wheels. In the front of this assembly, one by one, thin metal disks would snap into place, a light would flash as some energy transaction occurred, and then the disk would snap aside, immediately to be replaced by another. Eight wires led from this box into the body of a Priest-King which lay on its back, inert, in the center of the room on a moss-softened stone table.

I held the torch high and looked at the Priest-King, who was rather small for a Priest-King, being only about twelve feet long.

What most astonished me was that he had wings, long, slender, beautiful, golden, translucent wings, folded against his back.

He was not strapped down.

He seemed to be completely unconscious.

I bent my ears to the air tubes in his abdomen and I could hear the slight whispers of respiration.

"I had to design this equipment myself," said Misk, "and for that reason it is inexcusably primitive, but there was no possibility to apply for standard instrumentation in this case."

I didn't understand.

"No," said Misk, "and observe I had to make my own mnemonic disks, devising a transducer to read the scent-tapes, which fortunately are easily available, and record their signals on blank receptor-plating, from there to be transformed into impulses for generating and regulating the appropriate neural alignments."

"I don't understand," I said.

"Of course," said Misk, "for you are a human."

I looked at the long, golden wings of the creature. "Is it a mutation?" I asked.

"Of course not," said Misk.

"Then what is it?" I asked.

"A male," said Misk. He paused for a long time and the antennae regarded the inert figure on the stone table. "It is the first male born in the Nest in eight thousand years."

"Aren't you a male?" I asked.

"No," said Misk, "nor are the others."

"Then you are female," I said.

"No," said Misk, "in the Nest only the Mother is female."

"But surely," I said, "there must be other females."

"Occasionally," said Misk, "an egg occurred which was female but these were ordered destroyed by Sarm. I myself know of no female egg in the Nest, and I know of only one which has occurred in the last six thousand years."

"How long," I asked, "does a Priest-King live?"

"Long ago," said Misk, "Priest-Kings discovered the secrets of cell replacement without pattern deterioration, and accordingly, unless we meet with injury or accident, we will live until we are found by the Golden Beetle."

"How old are you?" I asked.

"I myself was hatched," said Misk, "before we brought our world into your solar system." He looked down at me. "That was more than two million years ago," he said.

"Then," I said, "the Nest will never die."

"It is dying now," said Misk. "One by one we succumb to the Pleasures of the Golden Beetle. We grow old and there is little left for us. At one time we were rich and filled with life and in that time our great patterns were formed and in another time our arts flourished and then for a very long time our only passion was scientific curiosity, but now even that lessens, even that lessens."

"Why do you not slay the Golden Beetles?" I asked.

"It would be wrong," said Misk.

"But they kill you," I said.

"It is well for us to die," said Misk, "for otherwise the Nest would be eternal and the Nest must not be eternal for how could we love it if it were so?"

I could not follow all of what Misk was saying, and I found it hard to take my eyes from the inert figure of the young male Priest-King which lay on the stone table.

"There must be a new Nest," said Misk. "And there must be a new Mother, and there must be the new First Born. I myself am willing to die but the race of Priest-Kings must not die."

"Would Sarm have this male killed if he knew he were here?" I asked.

"Yes," said Misk.

"Why?" I asked.

"He does not wish to pass," said Misk simply.

I puzzled on the machine in the room, the wiring that seemed to feed into the young Priest-King's body at eight points. "What are you doing to him?" I asked.

"I am teaching him," said Misk.

"I don't understand," I said.

"What you know—even a creature such as yourself—" said Misk, "depends on the charges and microstates of your neural tissue, and, customarily, you obtain these charges and microstates in the process of registering and assimilating sensory stimuli from your environment, as for example when you directly experience something, or perhaps as when you are given information by others or you peruse a scent-tape. This device you see then is merely a contrivance for producing these charges and microstates without the necessity for the time-consuming external stimulation."

My torch lifted, I regarded with awe the inert body of the young Priest-King on the stone table.

I watched the tiny flashes of light, the rapid, efficient placement of the disks and their almost immediate withdrawal.

The instrumentation and the paneling of the room seemed to loom about me.

I considered the impulses that must be transmitted by those eight wires into the body of the creature that lay before us.

"Then you are literally altering its brain," I whispered.

"He is a Priest-King," said Misk, "and has eight brains, modifications of the ganglionic net, whereas a creature such as yourself, limited by vertebrae, is likely to develop only one brain."

"It is very strange to me," I said.

"Of course," said Misk, "for the lower orders instruct their young differently, accomplishing only an infinitesimal fraction of this in a lifetime of study."

"Who decides what he learns?" I asked.

"Customarily," said Misk, "the mnemonic plates are standardized by the Keepers of the Tradition, chief of whom is Sarm." Misk straightened and his antennae curled a bit. "As you might suppose I could not obtain a set of standardized plates and so I have inscribed my own, using my own judgment."

"I don't like the idea of altering its brain," I said.

"Brains," said Misk.

"I don't like it," I said.

"Do not be foolish," said Misk. His antennae curled. "All creatures who instruct their young alter their brains. How else could learning take place? This device is merely a comparatively considerate, swift and efficient means to an end that is universally regarded as desirable by rational creatures."

"I am uneasy," I said.

"I see," said Misk, "you fear he is becoming a kind of machine."

"Yes," I said.

"You must remember," said Misk, "that he is a Priest-King and thus a rational creature and that we could not turn him into a machine without neutralizing certain critical and perceptive areas, without which he would no longer be a Priest-King."

"But he would be a self-governing machine," I said.

"We are all such machines," said Misk, "with fewer or a greater number of random elements." His antennae touched me. "We do what we must," he said, "and the ultimate control is never in the mnemonic disk."

"I do not know if these things are true," I said.

"Nor do I," said Misk. "It is a difficult and obscure matter."

"And what do you do in the meantime?" I asked.

"Once," said Misk, "we rejoiced and lived, but now though we remain young in body we are old in mind, and one wonders more often, from time to time, on the Pleasures of the Golden Beetle."

"Do Priest-Kings believe in a life after death?" I asked.

"Of course," said Misk, "for after one dies the Nest continues."

"No," I said, "I mean individual life."

"Consciousness," said Misk, "seems to be a function of the ganglionic net."

"I see," I said. "And yet you say you are willing to, as you said, pass."

"Of course," said Misk. "I have lived. Now there must be others."

I looked again at the young Priest-King lying on the stone table.

"Will he remember learning these things?" I asked.

"No," said Misk, "for his external sensors are now being bypassed, but he will understand that he has learned things in this fashion for a mnemonic disk has been inscribed to that effect."

"What is he being taught?" I asked.

"Basic information, as you might expect, pertains to language, mathematics, and the sciences, but he is also being taught the history and literature of Priest-Kings, Nest mores, social customs; mechanical, agricultural, and husbanding procedures, and other types of information."

"But will he continue to learn later?"

"Of course," said Misk, "but he will build on a rather complete knowledge of what his ancestors have learned in the past. No time is wasted in consciously absorbing old information, and one's time is thus released for the discovery of new information. When new information is discovered it is also included on mnemonic disks."

"But what if the mnemonic disks contain some false information?" I asked.

"Undoubtedly they do," said Misk, "but the disks are continually in the process of revision and are kept as current as possible."

16
The Plot of Misk

I TOOK MY EYES FROM THE young Priest-King and looked up at Misk. I could see the disklike eyes in that golden head above me and see the flicker of the blue torch on their myriad surfaces.

"I must tell you, Misk," I said slowly, "that I came to the Sardar to slay Priest-Kings, to take vengeance for the destruction of my city and its people."

I thought it only fair to let Misk know that I was no ally of his, that he should learn of my hatred for Priest-Kings and my determination to punish them, to the extent that it lay within my abilities, for the evil which they had done.

"No," said Misk. "You have come to the Sardar to save the race of Priest-Kings."

I looked at him dumbfounded.

"It is for that purpose that you were brought here," said Misk.

"I came of my own free will!" I cried. "Because my city was destroyed!"

"That is why your city was destroyed," said Misk, "that you would come to the Sardar."

I turned away. Tears burned in my eyes and my body trembled. I turned in rage on the tall, gentle creature who stood, unmoving, behind that strange table and that still form of the young Priest-King.

"If I had my sword," I said, pointing to the young Priest-King, "I would kill it!"

"No, you would not," said Misk, "and that is why you and not another were chosen to come to the Sardar."

I rushed to the figure on the table, the torch held as though to strike it.

But I could not.

"You will not hurt it because it is innocent," said Misk. "I know that."

"How can you know that?"

"Because you are of the Cabots and we know them. For more than four hundred years we have known them, and since your birth we have watched you."

"You killed my father!" I cried.

"No," said Misk, "he is alive and so are others of your city, but they are scattered to the ends of Gor."

"And Talena?"

"As far as I know she is still alive," said Misk, "but we cannot scan for her, or for others of Ko-ro-ba, without raising the suspicion that we are solicitous for you—or are bargaining with you."

"Why not simply bring me here?" I challenged. "Why destroy a city?"

"To conceal our motivation from Sarm," said Misk.

"I don't understand," I said.

"Occasionally on Gor we destroy a city, selecting it by means of a random selection device. This teaches the lower orders the might of Priest-Kings and encourages them to keep our laws."

"But what if the city has done no wrong?" I asked.

"So much the better," said Misk, "for the Men below the Mountains are then confused and fear us even more—but the members of the Caste of Initiates, we have found, will produce an explanation of why the city was destroyed. They invent one and if it seems plausible they soon believe it. For example, we allowed them to suppose that it was through some fault of yours—disrespect for Priest-Kings as I recall—that your city was destroyed."

"Why when first I came to Gor, more than seven years ago, did you not do this?" I asked.

"It was necessary to test you."

"And the seige of Ar," I asked, "and the Empire of Marlenus?"

"They provided a suitable test," said Misk. "From Sarm's point of view of course your utilization there was simply to curtail the spread of the Empire of Ar, for we prefer humans to dwell in isolated communities. It is better for observing their variations, from the scientific point of view, and it is safer for us if they remain disunited, for being rational they might develop a science, and being subrational it might be dangerous for us and for themselves if they did so."

"That is the reason then for your limitations of their weaponry and technology?"

"Of course," said Misk, "but we have allowed them to develop in many areas—in medicine, for example, where something approximating the Stabilization Serums has been independently developed."

"What is that?" I asked.

"You have surely not failed to notice," said Misk, "that though you came to the Counter-Earth more than seven years ago you have undergone no significant physical alteration in that time."

"I have noticed," I said, "and I wondered on this."

"Of course," said Misk, "their serums are not as effective as ours and sometimes do not function, and sometimes the effect wears off after only a few hundred years."

"This was kind of you," I said.

"Perhaps," said Misk. "There is dispute on the matter." He peered intently down at me. "On the whole," he said, "we Priest-Kings do not interfere in the affairs of men. We leave them free to love and slay one another, which seems to be what they most enjoy doing."

"But the Voyages of Acquisition?" I said.

"We keep in touch with the earth," said Misk, "for it might, in time, become a threat to us and then we would have to limit it, or destroy it or leave the solar system."

"Which will you do?" I asked.

"None, I suspect," said Misk. "According to our calculations, which may of course be mistaken, life as you know it on the earth will destroy itself within the next thousand years."

I shook my head sadly.

"As I said," went on Misk, "man is subrational. Consider what would happen if we allowed him free technological development on our world."

I nodded. I could see that from the Priest-Kings' point of view it would be more dangerous than handing out automatic weapons to chimpanzees and gorillas. Man had not proved himself worthy of a superior technology to the Priest-Kings. I mused that man had not proved himself worthy of such a technology even to himself.

"Indeed," said Misk, "it was partly because of this tendency that we brought man to the Counter-Earth, for he is an interesting species and it would be sad to us if he disappeared from the universe."

"I suppose we are to be grateful," I said.

"No," said Misk, "we have similarly brought various species to the Counter-Earth, from other locations."

"I have seen few of these 'other species'," I said.

Misk shrugged his antennae.

"I do remember," I said, "a Spider in the Swamp Forests of Ar."

"The Spider People are a gentle race," said Misk, "except the female at the time of mating."

"His name was Nar," I said, "and he would rather have died than injure a rational creature."

"The Spider People are soft," said Misk. "They are not Priest-Kings."

"I see," I said.

"The Voyages of Acquisition," said Misk, "take place normally when we need fresh material from Earth, for our purposes."

"I was the object of one such voyage," I said.

"Obviously," said Misk.

"It is said below the mountains that Priest-Kings know all that occurs on Gor."

"Nonsense," said Misk. "But perhaps I shall show you the Scanning Room someday. We have four hundred Priest-Kings who operate the scanners, and we are accordingly well informed. For example, if there is a violation of our weapons laws we usually, sooner or later, discover it and after determining the coordinates put into effect the Flame Death Mechanism."

I had once seen a man die the Flame Death, the High Initiate of Ar, on the roof of Ar's Cylinder of Justice. I shivered involuntarily.

"Yes," I said simply, "sometime I would like to see the Scanning Room."

"But much of our knowledge comes from our implants," said Misk. "We implant humans with a control web and transmitting device. The lenses of their eyes are altered in such a way that what they see is registered by means of transducers on scent-screens in the scanning room. We can also speak and act by means of them, when the control web is activated in the Sardar."

"The eyes look different?" I asked.

"Sometimes not," said Misk, "sometimes yes."

"Was the creature Parp so implanted?" I asked, remembering his eyes.

"Yes," said Misk, "as was the man from Ar whom you met on the road long ago near Ko-ro-ba."

"But he threw off the control web," I said, "and spoke as he wished."

"Perhaps the webbing was faulty," said Misk.

"But if it was not?" I asked.

"Then he was most remarkable," said Misk. "Most remarkable."

"You spoke of knowing the Cabots for four hundred years," I said.

"Yes," said Misk, "and your father, who is a brave and noble man, has served us upon occasion, though he dealt only, unknowingly, with Implanted Ones. He first came to Gor more than six hundred years ago."

"Impossible!" I cried.

"Not with the stabilization serums," remarked Misk.

I was shaken by this information. I was sweating. The torch seemed to tremble in my hand.

"I have been working against Sarm and the others for millenia," said Misk, "and at last—more than three hundred years ago—I managed to obtain the egg from which this male emerged." Misk looked down at the young Priest-King on the stone table. "I then, by means of an Implanted Agent, unconscious of the message being read through him, instructed your father to write the letter which you found in the mountains on your native world."

My head was spinning.

"But I was not even born then!" I exclaimed.

"Your father was instructed to call you Tarl, and lest he might speak to you of the Counter-Earth or attempt to dissuade you from our purpose, he was returned to Gor before you were of an age to understand."

"I thought he deserted my mother," I said.

"She knew," said Misk, "for though she was a woman of Earth she had been to Gor."

"Never did she speak to me of these things," I said.

"Matthew Cabot on Gor," said Misk, "was a hostage for her silence."

"My mother," I said, "died when I was very young . . ."

"Yes," said Misk, "because of a petty bacillus in your contaminated atmosphere, a victim to the inadequacies of your infantile bacteriology."

I was silent. My eyes smarted, I suppose from some heat or fume of the Mul-Torch.

"It was difficult to foresee," said Misk. "I am truly sorry."

"Yes," I said. I shook my head and wiped my eyes. I still held the memory of the lonely, beautiful woman whom I had known so briefly in my childhood, who in those short years had so loved me. Inwardly I cursed the Mul-Torch that had brought tears to the eyes of a Warrior of Ko-ro-ba.

"Why did she not remain on Gor?" I asked.

"It frightened her," said Misk, "and your father asked that she be allowed to return to Earth, for loving her he wished her to be happy and also perhaps he wanted you to know something of his old world."

"But I found the letter in the mountains, where I had made camp by accident," I said.

"When it was clear where you would camp the letter was placed there," said Misk.

"Then it did not lie there for more than three hundred years?"

"Of course not," said Misk, "the risk of discovery would have been too great."

"The letter itself was destroyed, and nearly took me with it," I said.

"You were warned to discard the letter," said Misk. "It

was saturated with Flame Lock, and its combustion index was set for twenty Ehn following opening."

"When I opened the letter it was like switching on a bomb," I said.

"You were warned to discard the letter," said Misk.

"And the compass needle?" I asked, remembering its erratic behavior which had so unnerved me.

"It is a simple matter," said Misk, "to disrupt a magnetic field."

"But I returned to the same place I had fled from," I said.

"The frightened human, when fleeing and disoriented, tends to circle," said Misk. "But it would not have mattered. I could have picked you up had you not returned. I think that you may have sensed there was no escape and thus, perhaps as an act of pride, returned to the scene of the letter."

"I was simply frightened," I said.

"No one is ever simply frightened," said Misk.

"When I entered the ship I fell unconscious," I said.

"You were anesthetized," said Misk.

"Was the ship operated from the Sardar?" I asked.

"It could have been," said Misk, "but I could not risk that."

"Then it was manned," I said.

"Yes," said Misk.

I looked at him.

"Yes," said Misk. "It was I who manned it." He looked down at me. "Now it is late, past the sleeping time. You are tired."

I shook my head. "There is little," I said, "which was left to chance."

"Chance does not exist," said Misk, "ignorance exists."

"You cannot know that," I said.

"No," said Misk, "I cannot know it." The tips of Misk's antennae gently dipped towards me. "You must rest now," he said.

"No," I said. "Was the fact that I was placed in the chamber of the girl Vika of Treve considered?"

"Sarm suspects," said Misk, "and it was he who arranged your quarters, in order that you might succumb to her charms, that she might enthrall you, that she might bend you helplessly, pliantly to her will and whim as she had a hundred men before you, turning them—brave, proud warriors all—into the slaves of a slave, into the slaves of a mere girl, herself only a slave."

"Can this be true?" I asked.

"A hundred men," said Misk, "allowed themselves to be chained to the foot of her couch where she would upon occasion, that they might not die, cast them scraps of food as though they might have been pet sleen."

My old hatred of Vika now began once again to enfuse my blood, and my hands ached to grip her and shake her until her bones might break and then throw her to my feet.

"What became of them?" I asked.

"They were used as Muls," said Misk.

My fists clenched.

"I am glad that such a creature," said Misk, "is not of my species."

"I am sorry," I said, "that she is of mine."

"When you broke the surveillance device in the chamber," said Misk, "I felt I had to act quickly."

I laughed. "Then," I said, "you actually thought you were saving me?"

"I did," said Misk.

"I wonder," I said.

"At any rate," said Misk, "it was not a risk we cared to take."

"You speak of 'we'?"

"Yes," said Misk.

"And who is the other?" I asked.

"The greatest in the Nest," said Misk.

"The Mother?"

"Of course."

Misk touched me lightly on the shoulder with his antennae. "Come now," he said. "Let us return to the chamber above."

"Why," I asked, "was I returned to Earth after the siege of Ar?"

"To fill you with hatred for Priest-Kings," said Misk. "Thus you would be more willing to come to the Sardar to find us."

"But why seven years?" I asked. They had been long, cruel, lonely years.

"We were waiting," said Misk.

"But for what?" I demanded.

"For there to be a female egg," said Misk.

"Is there now such an egg?"

"Yes," said Misk, "but I do not know where it is."

"Then who knows?" I asked.

"The Mother," said Misk.

"But what have I to do with all this?" I demanded.

"You are not of the Nest," said Misk, "and thus you can do what is necessary."

"What is necessary?" I asked.

"Sarm must die," said Misk.

"I have no wish to kill Sarm," I said.

"Very well," said Misk.

I puzzled on the many things which Misk had told me, and then I looked up at him, lifting my torch that I might better see that great head with its rich, disklike, luminous eyes.

"Why is this one egg so important?" I asked. "You have the stabilization serums. Surely there will be many eggs, and others will be female."

"It is the last egg," said Misk.

"Why is that?" I demanded.

"The Mother was hatched and flew her Nuptial Flight long before the discovery of the stabilization serums," said Misk. "We have managed to retard her aging considerably but eon by eon it has been apparent that our efforts have been less and less successful, and now there are no more eggs."

"I don't understand," I said.

"The Mother is dying," said Misk.

I was silent and Misk did not speak and the only noise in that paneled metallic laboratory that was the cradle of a Priest-King was the soft crackle of the blue torch I held.

"Yes," said Misk, "it is the end of the Nest."

I shook my head. "This is no business of mine," I said.

"That is true," said Misk.

We faced one another. "Well," I said, "are you not going to threaten me?"

"No," said Misk.

"Are you not going to hunt down my father or my Free Companion and kill them if I do not serve you?"

"No," said Misk. "No."

"Why not?" I demanded. "Are you not a Priest-King?"

"Because I am a Priest-King," said Misk.

I was thunderstruck.

"All Priest-Kings are not as Sarm," said Misk. He looked down at me. "Come," he said, "it is late and you will be tired. Let us retire to the chamber above."

Misk left the room and I, bearing the torch, followed him.

17
The Scanning Room

THOUGH THE MOSS IN THE case was soft I had great difficulty in falling asleep that night, for I could not rid my mind of the turbulence which had been occasioned in it by the disclosures of Misk, the Priest-King. I could not forget the winged figure on the stone table. I could not forget the plot of Misk, the threat which loomed over the Nest of the Priest-Kings. In fevered sleep it seemed I saw Sarm's great head with its powerful, laterally moving jaws hovering over me, that I heard the cry of larls and saw the burning pupils of Parp's eyes and his reaching toward me with instruments and a golden net, and I found myself chained to the foot of Vika's couch and heard her laugh and I cried aloud and shouted and sat up on the moss startled.

"You are awake," said a voice on a translator.

I rubbed my eyes and stood up, and through the transparent plastic of the case I saw a Priest-King. I slid the door open and stepped into the room.

"Greetings, Noble Sarm," I said.

"Greetings, Matok," said Sarm.

"Where is Misk?" I asked.

"He has duties elsewhere," said Sarm.

"What are you doing here?" I asked.

"It is near the Feast of Tola," said Sarm, "and it is a time of pleasure and hospitality in the Nest of Priest-Kings, a time in which Priest-Kings are well disposed to all living things, whatever be their order."

"I am pleased to hear this," I said. "What are the duties of Misk which keep him from his chamber?"

"In honor of the Feast of Tola," said Sarm, "he is now pleased to retain Gur."

"I don't understand," I said.

Sarm looked about himself. "It is a beautiful compartment which Misk has here," he said, examining the visually bare walls with his antennae, admiring the scent-patterns which had been placed on them.

"What do you want?" I asked.

"I want to be your friend," said Sarm.

I made no move but I was startled to hear the Gorean expression for 'friend' emanate from Sarm's translator. I knew there was no expression in the language of the Priest-Kings which was a satisfactory equivalent for the expression. I had tried to find it on the translator and lexical tapes which Misk had placed at my disposal. Literally what hearing the expression from Sarm meant was that he had had the item specially entered into his translator tapes and correlated with a random odor, much as if we had decided to invent a name to stand for some novel relation or object. I wondered if Sarm had much idea of the meaning of the expression 'friend' or if it were merely used because he calculated that it would produce a favorable impression on me. He might have asked Mul Translator Engineers for such an expression and an explanation of it, and I supposed they might have given him the expression 'friend' and explained it for him, more or less adequately, in terms of the normal consequences of the relation designated, such things as tending to be well disposed toward one, tending to want to do well by one, and so on. The occurrence of the expression on Sarm's translator tape, simple as it was, indicated that he had gone to a good deal of trouble, and that the matter, for some reason, was rather important to him. I did not, however, betray my surprise and acted as though I did not know that the expression was a new addition to the Gorcan lexicon on his tapes.

"I am honored," I said simply.

Sarm looked at the case. "You were of the Caste of

Warriors," he said. "Perhaps you would like to be given a female Mul?"

"No," I said.

"You may have more than one if you wish," said Sarm.

"Sarm is generous," I said, "but I decline his kind offer."

"Perhaps you would like a supply of scarce metals and stones?"

"No," I said.

"Perhaps you would like to be the Mul-supervisor of a warehouse or fungus farm?"

"No," I said.

"What would you like?" asked Sarm.

"My freedom," I said, "the restoration of the City of Ko-ro-ba, the safety of its people—to see my father again, my friends, my Free Companion."

"Perhaps these things can be arranged," said Sarm.

"What must I do?" I asked.

"Tell me why you have been brought to the Nest," said Sarm, and suddenly his antennae snapped downward towards me like whips, and now rigid, they seemed to be trained on me, as though they might be weapons.

"I have no idea," I said.

The antennae quivered briefly in anger and the bladelike structures at the tips of Sarm's forelegs snapped out and back, but then the antennae relaxed and once again the four hooklike grasping appendages at the termination of each foreleg lightly, almost meditatively, touched one another. "I see," came from Sarm's translator.

"Would you care for a bit of fungus?" I asked.

"Misk has had time to speak to you," said Sarm. "What did he say?"

"There is Nest Trust between us," I said.

"Nest Trust with a human?" asked Sarm.

"Yes," I said.

"An interesting concept," said Sarm.

"You will excuse me if I wash?" I asked.

"Of course," said Sarm, "please do."

I stayed a long time in the washing-booth and when I came out and donned my plastic tunic it took quite some time to make the Mul-Fungus Porridge of just the consistency at which I preferred it, and then, since I had finally managed to make it the way in which it was least unpalatable, I took some time to, as one might say, almost enjoy it.

If these tactics were calculated to have some effect on Sarm I think they most miserably failed of that effect, for during the entire time I took, which was considerable, he stood motionless in the room, save for an occasional movement of his antennae, frozen in that maddening, immobile but alert posture of Priest-Kings.

At last I emerged from the case.

"I want to be your friend," said Sarm.

I was silent.

"Perhaps you would like to see the Nest?" asked Sarm.

"Yes," I said, "I would enjoy that."

"Good," said Sarm.

I did not ask to see the Mother, for I knew that was forbidden to those of the human kind, but I found Sarm a most attentive and gracious guide, quick to answer my questions and suggest places of interest. Part of the time we rode on a transportation disk, and he showed me how to operate it. The disk flows on a tread of volatile gas and is itself lightened by its construction from a partially gravitationally resistant metal, of which I shall speak later. Its speed is controlled by the placement of the feet along double accelerator strips which lie flush with the surface of the disk; its direction is controlled by the rider who bends and turns his body, thereby transmitting force to the lightly riding disk, the principles involved being no more unusual than those employed in such homely devices as roller skates or the now vanishing skate boards once popular with Earth children. One stops the disk by stepping off the accelerator strips, which brings the disk to a smooth halt depending on the area available for braking. There is a cell in the forward portion of the disk which casts an invisible beam ahead and if the area for stopping is small, the stop is accordingly more abrupt. This cell, however, does not function if the accelerator strips are depressed. I would have thought that some type of cells for avoiding collisions when the accelerator strips are depressed might have been useful or that a bumper of gas, or a field of some sort, might have been practical improvements but Sarm felt that such refinements would be excessive. "No one is ever injured by a transportation disk," he told me, "except an occasional Mul."

At my request Sarm took me to the Scanning Room, whence the surface of Gor is kept under selective surveillance by the Priest-Kings.

Patterns of small ships, not satellites, invisible from the ground and remotely controlled, carry the lenses and receptors which beam information to the Sardar. I suggested to Sarm that satellites would be less expensive to maintain in flight but he denied this. I would not have made this suggestion at a later time but then I did not understand the Priest-Kings' utilization of gravity.

"The reason for observation within the atmosphere," said Sarm, "is that it is simpler to get more definition in the signal because of greater proximity to its source. To get comparable definition in an extra-atmospheric surveillance device would require more refined equipment."

The receptors on the surveillance craft were equipped to handle patterns of light, sound and scent, which, selectively collected and reconcentrated, were beamed to the Sardar for processing and analysis. Reconstituted in large observation cubes these patterns might then be monitored by Priest-Kings. Provisions were available also, as you might suppose, for taping the transmissions of the surveillance craft.

"We use random scanning patterns," said Sarm, "for we find in the long run, over centuries, they are more effective than following fixed scanning schedules. Of course, if we know that something of interest or importance to us is occurring we lock onto its coordinates and follow its developments."

"Did you make a tape," I asked, "of the destruction of the City of Ko-ro-ba?"

"No," said Sarm, "it was not of sufficient interest or importance to us."

My fists clenched, and I noted that Sarm's antennae curled slightly.

"I once saw a man die the Flame Death," I said. "Is that mechanism also in this room?"

"Yes," said Sarm, indicating with one foreleg a quiet-looking metal cabinet to one side possessing several dials and knobs. "The projection points for the Flame Death are located in the surveillance craft," said Sarm, "but the coordinates are fixed and the firing signal is relayed from this room. The system is synchronized, of course, with the scanning apparatus and may be activated from any of the control panels at the observation cubes."

"Of course," I said.

I looked about the room. It was an exceedingly long chamber and built on four levels, almost like steps. Along each of these levels, spaced a few feet from one another, were the observation cubes, which resembled cubes of transparent glass, and were approximately sixteen feet square. I was told by Sarm that there were four hundred such cubes in the room, and monitoring each, I could see a Priest-King, tall, alert, unmoving. I walked along one of the levels, gazing into the cubes. Most of them were simply filled with the passing scenery of Gor; once I saw a city, but what city it was I could not tell.

"This might interest you," said Sarm, indicating one of the observation cubes.

I regarded the cube.

The angle from which the lens was functioning was unlike that of most of the other cubes. The lens was apparently parallel to rather than above the scene.

It was merely a scene of a road, bordered by some trees, which seemed to slowly approach the lens and then pass behind it.

"You are seeing through the eyes of an Implanted One," said Sarm.

I gasped.

Sarm's antennae curled. "Yes," he said, "the pupils of his eyes have been replaced with lenses and a control net and transmitting device have been fused with his brain tissue. He himself is now unconscious for the control net is activated. Later we will allow him to rest, and he will see and hear and think again for himself."

The thought of Parp crossed my mind.

Once again I looked into the observation cube.

I wondered of the man through whose eyes I was now seeing, who he was, what he had been, that unknown Implanted
One who now walked some lonely road somewhere on Gor, a
device of Priest-Kings.

"Surely," I said bitterly, "with all the knowledge and power of Priest-Kings you could build something mechanical, a
robot, which might resemble a man and do this work for
you."

"Of course," said Sarm, "but such an instrument, if it were
to be a genuinely satisfactory substitute for an Implanted
One, would have to be extremely complex—consider provisions for the self-repair of damaged tissue alone—and thus,
in the end, would itself have to approximate a humanoid
organism. Accordingly with humans themselves so plentiful
the construction of such a device would be nothing but an
irrational misuse of our resources."

Once again I looked into the observation cube, and wondered about that unknown man, or what had been a man,
through whose eyes I now looked. I, in the very Nest of
Priest-Kings, was more free than he who walked the stones
of some road in the bright sun, somewhere beyond the
palisade, far from the mountains of Priest-Kings yet still in
the shadow of the Sardar.

"Can he disobey you?" I asked.

"Sometimes there is a struggle to resist the net or regain
consciousness," said Sarm.

"Could a man so resist you that he could throw off the
power of the net?"

"I doubt it," said Sarm, "unless the net were faulty."

"If it could be done," I said, "what would you do?"

"It is a simple matter," said Sarm, "to overload the net's
power capacity."

"You would kill the man?"

"It is only a human," said Sarm.

"Is this what was done once on the road to Ko-ro-ba, to a
man from Ar, who spoke to me in the name of Priest-
Kings?"

"Of course," said Sarm.

"His net was faulty?" I asked.

"I suppose so," said Sarm.

"You are a murderer," I said.

"No," said Sarm, "I am a Priest-King."

Sarm and I passed further on down one of the long levels, looking into one or another of the observation cubes.

Suddenly one of the cubes we passed locked onto a given scene and no more did the scenery move past me as though in a three-dimensional screen. Rather the magnification was suddenly increased and the air became suddenly filled with more intense odors.

On a green field somewhere, I had no idea where, a man in the garments of the Caste of Builders, emerged from what was apparently an underground cave. He looked furtively about himself as though he feared he might be observed. Then, satisfied that he was alone, he returned to the cave and emerged once more carrying what resembled a hollow pipe. From a hole in the top of this pipe there protruded what resembled the wick of a lamp.

The man from the Caste of Builders then sat cross-legged on the ground and took from the pouch slung at his waist a tiny, cylindrical Gorean fire-maker, a small silverish tube commonly used for igniting cooking fires. He unscrewed the cap and I could see the tip of the implement, as it was exposed to the air, begin to glow a fiery red. He touched the fire-maker to the wicklike projection in the hollow tube and, screwing the fire-maker shut, replaced it in his pouch. The wick burned slowly downward toward the hole in the pipe. When it was almost there the man stood up and holding the pipe in both hands trained it at a nearby rock. There was a sudden flash of fire and a crack of sound from the hollow tube as some projectile hurtled through it and shattered against the rock. The face of the rock was blackened and some stone had been chipped from its surface. The quarrel of a crossbow would have done more damage.

"Forbidden weapon," said Sarm.

The Priest-King monitoring the observation cube touched a knob on his control panel.

"Stop!" I cried.

Before my horrified eyes in the observation cube the man

seemed suddenly to vaporize in a sudden blasting flash of blue fire. The man had disappeared. Another brief incandescent flash destroyed the primitive tube he had carried. Then once again, aside from the blackened grass and stone, the scene was peaceful. A small, curious bird darted to the top of the stone, and then hopped from it to the blackened grass to hunt for grubs.

"You killed that man," I said.

"He may have been carrying on forbidden experiments for years," said Sarm. "We were fortunate to catch him. Sometimes we must wait until others are using the device for purposes of war and then destroy many men. It is better this way, more economical of material."

"But you killed him," I said.

"Of course," said Sarm, "he broke the law of Priest-Kings."

"What right have you to make the law for him?" I asked.

"The right of a higher-order organism to control a lower-order organism," said Sarm. "The same right you have to slaughter the bosk and the tabuk, to feed on the flesh of the tarsk."

"But those are not rational animals," I said.

"They are sentient," said Sarm.

"We kill them swiftly," I said.

Sarm's antennae curled. "And so too do we Priest-Kings commonly kill swiftly and yet you complain of our doing so."

"We need food," I said.

"You could eat fungus and other vegetables," said Sarm.

I was silent.

"The truth is," said Sarm, "that the human is a dangerous and predatory species."

"But those animals," I said, "are not rational."

"Is that so important?" asked Sarm.

"I don't know," I said. "What if I claimed it was?"

"Then I should reply," said Sarm, "that nothing below a Priest-King is truly rational." He looked down at me. "Remember that as you are to the bosk and the sleen so are we to you." He paused. "But I see that you are distressed by the Scanning Room. You must remember it was at your own request that I brought you here. I did not wish you to be unhappy. Do not think badly of Priest-Kings. I wish you to be my friend."

18
I Speak with Sarm

IN THE NEXT DAYS, WHEN I could escape from the attentions of Sarm, on occasions when he was undoubtedly drawn elsewhere by his numerous duties and responsibilities, I searched the Nest by myself, on a transportation disk furnished by Sarm, looking for Misk, but I found no trace of him. I knew only that he had been, as Sarm had put it, pleased to retain Gur.

No one to whom I spoke, principally Muls, would explain the meaning of this to me. I gathered that the Muls to whom I spoke, who seemed well enough disposed towards me, simply did not know what was meant, in spite of the fact that several of them had been bred in the Nest, in the breeding cases located in certain special vivaria set aside for the purpose. I even approached Priest-Kings on this subject and they, since I was a Matok and not a Mul, gave me of their attention, but politely refused to furnish me with the information I sought. "It has to do with the Feast of Tola," they said, "and is not the concern of humans."

Sometimes on these excursions Mul-Al-Ka and Mul-Ba-Ta would accompany me. On the first time they accompanied me I obtained a marking stick, used by Mul clerks in various commissaries and warehouses, and inscribed their appropriate letters on the left shoulders of their plastic tunics. Now I could tell them apart. The visual mark was plain to human eyes but it would not be likely to be noticed by Priest-Kings, any more than a small, insignificant sound is likely to be noticed by a human who is not listening for it and is attending to other things.

One afternoon, as I judged by the feeding times, for the energy bulbs always keep the Nest of Priest-Kings at a constant level of illumination, Mul-Al-Ka and Mul-Ba-Ta and

I were swiftly passing through one tunnel on my transportation disk.

"It is pleasant to ride thusly, Cabot," said Mul-Al-Ka.

"Yes, it is pleasant," agreed Mul-Ba-Ta.

"You speak much alike," I said.

"We are much alike," pointed out Mul-Al-Ka.

"Are you the Muls of the biologist Kusk?" I asked.

"No," said Mul-Al-Ka, "we were given by Kusk to Sarm as a gift."

I stiffened on the transportation disk and it nearly ran into the wall of the tunnel.

A startled Mul had leaped back against the wall. Looking back I could see him shaking his fist and shouting with rage. I smiled. I gathered he had not been bred in the Nest.

"Then," I said to the Muls who rode with me, "you are spying on me for Sarm."

"Yes," said Mul-Al-Ka.

"It is our duty," said Mul-Ba-Ta.

"But," said Mul-Al-Ka, "should you wish to do something which Sarm will not know of, simply let us know and we will avert our eyes."

"Yes," said Mul-Ba-Ta, "or stop the disk and we will get off and wait for you. You can pick us up on your way back."

"That sounds fair enough," I said.

"Good," said Mul-Al-Ka.

"Is it human to be fair?" asked Mul-Ba-Ta.

"Sometimes," I said.

"Good," said Mul-Al-Ka.

"Yes," said Mul-Ba-Ta, "we wish to be human."

"Perhaps you will teach us someday how to be human?" asked Mul-Al-Ka.

The transportation disk sped on and none of us spoke for some time.

"I am not sure I know how myself," I said.

"It must be very hard," said Mul-Al-Ka.

"Yes," I said, "it is very hard."

"Must a Priest-King learn to be a Priest-King?" asked Mul-Ba-Ta.

"Yes," I said.

"That must be even more difficult," said Mul-Al-Ka.

"Probably," I said, "I don't know."

I swung the transportation disk in a graceful arc to one side of the tunnel to avoid running into a crablike organism covered with overlapping plating and then swung the disk back in another sweeping arc to avoid slicing into a stalking Priest-King who lifted his antennae quizzically as we shot past.

"The one who was not a Priest-King," quickly said Mul-Al-Ka, "was a Matok and is called a Toos and lives on discarded fungus spores."

"We know you are interested in things like that," said Mul-Ba-Ta.

"Yes, I am," I said. "Thank you."

"You are welcome," said Mul-Al-Ka.

"Yes," said Mul-Ba-Ta.

For a while we rode on in silence.

"But you will teach us about being human, will you not?" asked Mul-Al-Ka.

"I do not know a great deal about it," I said.

"But more than we, surely," said Mul-Ba-Ta.

I shrugged.

The disk flowed on down the tunnel.

I was wondering if a certain maneuver was possible.

"Watch this!" I said, and turning my body I swung the transportation disk in a sudden, abrupt complete circle and continued on in the same direction we had been traveling.

All of us nearly lost our footing.

"Marvelous," cried Mul-Al-Ka.

"You are very skilled," said Mul-Ba-Ta.

"I have never seen even a Priest-King do that," said Mul-Al-Ka with something of awe in his voice.

I had been wondering if such a turn was possible with a transportation disk and I was rather pleased with myself that I had accomplished it. The fact that I had nearly thrown myself and my two passengers off the disk at high speed onto the flooring of the tunnel did not occur to me at the time.

"Would you like to try guiding the transportation disk?" I asked.

"Yes!" said Mul-Al-Ka.

"Yes," said Mul-Ba-Ta, "we would like that very much!"

"But first," asked Mul-Al-Ka, "will you not show us how to be human?"

"Why, how foolish you are!" scolded Mul-Ba-Ta. "He is already showing us."

"I don't understand," said Mul-Al-Ka.

"Then you are probably not the one who was synthesized," said Mul-Ba-Ta.

"Perhaps not," said Mul-Al-Ka, "but I still do not understand."

"Do you think," said Mul-Ba-Ta loftily, "that a Priest-King would have done so foolish a thing with a transportation disk?"

"No," said Mul-Al-Ka, his face beaming.

"You see," said Mul-Ba-Ta. "He is teaching us to be human."

I reddened.

"Teach us more about these things," said Mul-Al-Ka.

"I told you," I said, "I don't know much about it."

"If you should learn, inform us," said Mul-Al-Ka.

"Yes, do," said Mul-Ba-Ta.

"Very well," I said.

"That is fair enough," said Mul-Al-Ka.

"Yes," said Mul-Ba-Ta.

"In the meantime," said Mul-Al-Ka, gazing with unconcealed fascination at the accelerator strips in the transportation disk, "let us concentrate on the matter of the transportation disk."

"Yes," said Mul-Ba-Ta, "that will be quite enough for us for now—Tarl Cabot."

I did not object to the time I spent with Sarm, however, for he taught me far more of the Nest in a much shorter time than would have otherwise been possible. With him at my side I had access to many areas which would otherwise have been closed to a human.

One of the latter was the power source of the Priest-Kings, the great plant wherein the basic energy is generated for their many works and machines.

"Sometimes this is spoken of as the Home Stone of all Gor," said Sarm, as we walked the long, winding, iron spiral that clung to the side of a vast, transparent blue dome. Within that dome, burning and glowing, emitting a bluish, combustive refulgence, was a huge, crystalline reticulated hemisphere.

"The analogy, of course," said Sarm, "is incorrect for there is no Home Stone as such in the Nest of Priest-Kings, the Home Stone being a barbarous artifact generally common to the cities and homes of Gorean humans."

I was somewhat annoyed to find the Home Stones, taken so seriously in the cities of Gor that a man might be slain if he did not rise when speaking of the Home Stone of his city, so airily dismissed by the lofty Sarm.

"You find it hard to understand the love of a man for his Home Stone," I said.

"A cultural oddity," said Sarm, "which I understand perfectly but find slightly preposterous."

"You have nothing like the Home Stone in the Nest?" I asked.

"Of course not," said Sarm. I noticed an involuntary, almost spasmlike twitch of the tips of the forelegs, but the bladed projections did not emerge.

"There is of course the Mother," I said innocently.

Sarm stopped on the narrow iron railing circling the huge, glassy blue dome and straightened himself and turned to face me. With one brush of a foreleg he might have sent me hurtling to my death some hundreds of feet below. Briefly the antennae flattened themselves on his head and the bladelike projections snapped into view, and then the antennae raised and the bladelike projections disappeared.

"That is very different," said Sarm.

"Yes, it is different," I said.

Sarm regarded me for a moment and then turned and continued to lead the way.

At last we had reached the very apex of the great blue dome and I could see the glowing, bluish, refulgent, reticulated hemisphere far below me.

Surrounding the bluish dome, in a greater concentric dome of stone I saw walkway upon walkway of paneling and instrumentation. Here and there Priest-Kings moved lightly about, occasionally noting the movements of scent-needles, sometimes delicately adjusting a dial with the nimble, hook-like appendages at the tips of their forelegs.

I supposed the dome to be a reactor of some sort.

I looked down through the dome beneath us. "So this is the source of the Priest-Kings' power," I said.

"No," said Sarm.

I looked up at him.

He moved his forelegs in a strange parallel pattern, touching himself with each leg at three places on the thorax and one behind the eyes. "Here," he said, "is the true source of our power."

I then realized that he had touched himself at the points of entry taken by the wires which had been infixed in the young Priest-King's body on the stone table in the secret compartment below Misk's chamber. Sarm had pointed to his eight brains.

"Yes," I said, "you are right."

Sarm regarded me. "You know then of the modifications of the ganglionic net?"

"Yes," I said, "Misk told me."

"It is well," said Sarm. "I want you to learn of Priest-Kings."

"In the past days," I said, "you have taught me much, and I am grateful."

Sarm, standing on that high platform with me, over the bluish dome, over the refulgent power source so far below, lifted his antennae and turned, sweeping them over this vast, intricate, beautiful, formidable domain.

"Yet," said Sarm, "there are those who would destroy all this."

I wondered if hurling my weight against Sarm I might have tumbled him from that platform to his death far below.

"I know why you were brought to the Nest," said Sarm.

"Then you know more than I do," I said.

"You were brought here to kill me," said Sarm, looking down.

I started.

"There are those," he said, "who do not love the Nest, who would wish to see it pass."

I said nothing.

"The Nest is eternal," said Sarm. "It cannot die. I will not let it die."

"I don't understand," I said.

"You understand, Tarl Cabot," said Sarm. "Do not lie to me."

He turned to me and the antennae lowered themselves toward me, the slender, golden hairs on the antennae slightly oscillating. "You would not wish to see this beauty and this power pass from our common world, would you?" asked Sarm.

I looked about myself at the incredible complex which lay below me. "I don't know," I said. "I suppose if I were a Priest-King I would not wish to see it pass."

"Precisely," said Sarm, "and yet there is one among us— himself incredibly enough a Priest-King—who could betray his own kind, who would be willing to see this glory vanish."

"Do you know his name?" I asked.

"Of course," said Sarm. "We—both of us—know his name. It is Misk."

"I know nothing of these matters," I said.

"I see," said Sarm. He paused. "Misk believes that he brought you to the Nest for his own purposes, and I have allowed him to suppose so. I allowed him also to suppose that I suspected—but not that I knew—of his plot, for I had you placed in the chamber of Vika of Treve, and it was there he proved his guilt beyond doubt by rushing to protect you."

"And had he not entered the room?" I asked.

"The girl Vika of Treve has never failed me," said Sarm.

My fists clenched on the railing and bitterness choked in my throat, and the old hatred I had felt for the girl of Treve lit once again its dark fires in my breast.

"What good would I be to you chained to her slave ring?" I asked.

"After a time, perhaps a year," said Sarm, "when you were ready, I would free you on the condition that you would do my bidding."

"And what would that be?" I asked.

"Slay Misk," said Sarm.

"Why do you not slay him yourself?" I asked.

"That would be murder," said Sarm. "He for all his guilt and treason is yet a Priest-King."

"There is Nest Trust between myself and Misk," I said.

"There can be no Nest Trust between a Priest-King and a human," said Sarm.

"I see," I said. I looked up at Sarm. "And supposing I had agreed to do your bidding, what would have been my reward for all this?"

"Vika of Treve," said Sarm. "I would have placed her at your feet naked and in slave chains."

"Not so pleasant for Vika of Treve," I said.

"She is only a female Mul," said Sarm.

I thought of Vika and of the hatred I bore her.

"Do you still wish me to slay Misk?" I asked.

"Yes," said Sarm. "It was for that purpose I brought you to the Nest."

"Then give me my sword," I said, "and take me to him."

"Good," said Sarm, and we began to trace our way downward around that vast bluish globe that sheltered the power source of Priest-Kings.

19
Die, Tarl Cabot

NOW ONCE AGAIN I WOULD have my sword in my hands and at last I would be able to find Misk, for whose safety I feared.

Beyond this I had no definite plan.

Sarm did not act as quickly as I had anticipated and, from the room of the power source had simply returned me to Misk's compartment, where my case was kept.

I spent an uneasy night on the moss.

Why had we not gotten on directly with the business at hand?

In the morning, after the hour of the first feeding, Sarm entered Misk's compartment, where I was waiting for him. To my surprise his head was crowned with an aromatic wreath of green leaves, the first thing green I had seen in the Nest, and about his neck there hung, besides the invariable translator, a necklace, perhaps of accouterments, perhaps of pure ornaments, small pieces of metal, some shallow and rounded like tiny scoops, others rounded and pointed, others slender and bladed. His entire person I also noted was annointed with unusual and penetrating scents.

"It is the Feast of Tola—the Feast of the Nuptial Flight," said Sarm. "It is fitting that your work should be done today."

I regarded him.

"Are you ready?" he asked.

"Yes," I said.

"Good," said Sarm, and went to one of the high cabinets in Misk's chamber and touching a button in a certain sequence of long and short presses opened it. Sarm was apparently familiar with Misk's compartment. I wondered if the compartments of all Priest-Kings were so similar, or if he had investigated it at various times in the past. I wondered if he knew about the chamber which lay beneath my case. From the high cabinet Sarm withdrew my sword belt, my scabbard, and the short, sharp blade of Gorean steel which I had earlier yielded at the request of Misk.

The weapon felt good again in my hand.

I calculated the distance between myself and Sarm and wondered if I could reach him and kill him before he could bring his jaws into play, or those formidable blades on his forelegs. Where would one strike a Priest-King?

To my surprise Sarm then jerked at the door of the compartment from which he had withdrawn my sword. He bent it outward and downward and then, with one of the pieces of metal hanging from the necklace at his throat he scraped at the front edge of the door and bent it a bit outward; following this he attacked the interior edge of the cabinet similarly.

"What are you doing?" I asked.

"I am making sure," said Sarm, "that no one will lock your sword up again in this compartment." He added, as an afterthought, "I am your friend."

"I am indeed fortunate to have such a friend," I said. It was obvious that the compartment was being fixed in such a way as to suggest that it had been broken open.

"Why," I asked, "are you adorned as you are today?"

"It is the Feast of Tola," said Sarm, "the Feast of the Nuptial Flight."

"Where did you get green leaves?" I asked.

"We grow them in special chambers under lamps," said Sarm. "They are worn on Tola by all Priest-Kings in memory of the Nuptial Flight, for the Nuptial Flight takes place above the ground in the sun and there on the surface there are many things which are green."

"I see," I said.

Sarm's foreleg touched the metals dangling from his necklace. "These, too," he said, "have their significance."

"They are an ornament," I suggested, "in honor of the Feast of Tola."

"More than that," said Sarm, "look at them closely."

I approached Sarm and regarded the pieces of metal. Some of them reminded me of shallow scoops, others of awls, others of knives.

"They are tools," I said.

"Long ago," said Sarm, "in Nests long before this one, in times of which you cannot conceive, it was by means of these small things that my people began the journey that led in time to Priest-Kings."

"But what of the modifications of the ganglionic net?" I asked.

"These things," said Sarm, "may even be older than the modifications of the net. It is possible that had it not been for them and the changes they wrought in an ancient form of life there might have been no such modifications, for such modifications might then have been of little practical utility and thus, if they had occurred, might not have been perpetuated."

"Then it might seem," I proposed, somewhat maliciously, "that from one point of view, contrary to your suggestion of yesterday, that these tiny pieces of metal—and not the modifications of the ganglionic net—are the true and ultimate source of the Priest-Kings' power."

Sarm's antennae twitched irritably.

"We had to pick them up and use them, and later make them," said Sarm.

"But they may have come before the modifications of the net, you said," I reminded him.

"The matter is obscure," said Sarm.

"Yes, I suppose so," I said.

Sarm's bladelike projections snapped into view and disappeared again.

"Very well," said Sarm, "the true source of the Priest-Kings' power lies in the microparticles of the universe."

"Very well," I agreed.

I was pleased to note that it was only with genuine effort that Sarm managed to control himself. His entire body seemed to tremble with rage. He pressed the tips of his forelegs forcibly together to prevent the spontaneous triggering of the bladed projections.

"By the way," I asked, "how does one kill a Priest-King?" As I asked this I found myself unconsciously measuring my distance from Sarm.

Sarm relaxed.

"It will not be easy with your tiny weapon," he said, "but Misk will be unable to resist you and so you may take as much time as you wish."

"You mean I could simply butcher him?"

"Strike at the brain-nodes in the thorax and head," said Sarm. "It will probably not take more than half a hundred strokes to cut through."

My heart fell.

For all practical purposes it now seemed that Priest-Kings would be invulnerable to my blade, though I supposed I might have injured them severely if I sliced at the sensory hairs on the legs, at the trunk joining thorax and abdomen, at the eyes and antennae if I could reach them.

Then it occurred to me that there must be some vital center not mentioned by Sarm, probably a crucial organ or organs for pumping the body fluids of the Priest-Kings, most simply something corresponding to the heart. But of course he would not tell me of this, nor of its location. Rather than reveal this information he would undoubtedly prefer that I hack away at doomed Misk as though he were a block of insensate fungus. Not only would I not do this because of my affection for Misk but even if I intended to kill him I surely would not have done so in this manner, for it is not the way a trained warrior kills. I would expect to find the heart, or its correspondent organ or organs, in the thorax, but then I would have supposed that the respiratory cavities were also in the thorax and I knew that they were actually in the abdomen. I wished I had had time to investigate certain of Misk's scent-charts, but even if I had had the time, I might not have found helpful charts and, anyway, my translator scanning them could read only labels. It would be simpler, when I approached Misk with my sword in hand, to see if he would volunteer the information. For some reason I smiled as I considered this.

"Will you accompany me," I asked, "to the slaying of Misk?"

"No," said Sarm, "for it is Tola and I must give Gur to the Mother."

"What does that mean?" I asked.

"It is not a matter of concern for humans," said Sarm.

"Very well," I said.

"Outside," said Sarm, "you will find a transportation disk and the two Muls, Mul-Al-Ka and Mul-Ba-Ta. They will take you to Misk and later will direct you as to the disposal of the body."

"I can depend on them?" I asked.

"Of course," said Sarm. "They are loyal to me."

"And the girl?" I asked.

"Vika of Treve?"

"Of course."

Sarm's antennae curled. "Mul-Al-Ka and Mul-Ba-Ta will tell you where to find her."

"Is it necessary for them to accompany me?" I asked.

"Yes," said Sarm, "to ensure that you do your work well."

"But it will be too many who will know of the thing," I suggested.

"No," said Sarm, "for I have instructed them to report to the dissection chambers following the completion of your work."

I said nothing for a moment, but simply looked at the Priest-King who loomed above me.

"Kusk," said Sarm, anticipating me, "may be displeased for

a time, but it cannot be helped, and he may always produce others if he pleases."

"I see," I said.

"Besides," said Sarm, "he gave them to me and I may do with them as I please."

"I understand," I said.

"Do not worry about Kusk," said Sarm.

"Very well," I said, "I shall try not to worry about Kusk."

Sarm pranced backwards on those long, delicate, jointed legs, clearing the passage to the door. He lifted his long, bladelike body almost to the vertical.

"I wish you good fortune in this venture," he said. "In the accomplishing of this matter you do a great service to the Nest and to Priest-Kings, and thereby will you gain great glory for yourself and a life of honor and riches, the first of which will be the slave girl Vika of Treve."

"Sarm is most generous," I said.

"Sarm is your friend," came from the Priest-King's translator.

As I turned to leave the chamber I noted that the grasping appendages on Sarm's right foreleg turned off his translator.

He then raised the limb in what appeared to be a magnanimous, benevolent salute, a wishing of me well in my venture.

I lifted my right arm somewhat ironically to return the gesture.

To my nostrils, now alert to the signals of Priest-Kings and trained by my practice with the translator Misk had allowed me to use, there came a single brief odor, the components of which I had little difficulty in discriminating. It was a very simple message and was of course not carried by Sarm's translator. It was: "Die, Tarl Cabot."

I smiled to myself and left the chamber.

20
Collar 708

OUTSIDE I ENCOUNTERED MUL-AL-KA AND Mul-Ba-Ta.

Although they stood on a transportation disk and this would customarily have been enough to delight both of them, today, and for good reason as I recognized, neither of them looked particularly pleased.

"We are instructed," said Mul-Al-Ka, "to take you to the Priest-King Misk, whom you are to slay."

"We are further instructed," said Mul-Ba-Ta, "to help you dispose of the body in a place of which we have been informed."

"We are also instructed," said Mul-Al-Ka, "to express our encouragement for you in this fearsome undertaking and to remind you of the honors and riches that await you upon its successful termination."

"Not the least of which, we are requested to point out," said Mul-Ba-Ta, "is the enjoyment of the female Mul Vika of Treve."

I smiled and boarded the transportation disk.

Mul-Al-Ka and Mul-Ba-Ta took up positions in front of me, but standing with their backs to me. It would have been easy to fling both of them from the disk. Mul-Al-Ka stepped on the accelerator strips and guided the disk from the vicinity of Misk's portal and out into the broad, smooth thoroughfare of the tunnel. The disk flowed silently down the tunnel on its wide gaseous tread. The air of the tunnel moved against us and the portals we passed slid behind in a soft blur.

"It seems to me," I said, "you have well discharged your instructions." I clapped them on the shoulders. "Now tell me what you really wish."

"I wish that we could, Tarl Cabot," said Mul-Al-Ka.

"But undoubtedly it would be improper," said Mul-Ba-Ta.

"Oh," I said.

We rode on for a while more.

"You will note," said Mul-Al-Ka, "that we are standing in such a way that you might, without our being able to stop you, hurl us both from the transportation disk."

"Yes," I said, "I noted that."

"Increase the speed of the transportation disk," said Mul-Ba-Ta, "in order that his action may be the more effective."

"I don't wish to throw you from the disk," I said.

"Oh," said Mul-Al-Ka.

"It seemed a good idea to us," said Mul-Ba-Ta.

"Perhaps," I said, "but why should you wish to be thrown from the disk?"

Mul-Ba-Ta looked at me. "Well, Tarl Cabot," he said, "that way you would have some time to run and hide. You would be found, of course, but you might survive for a while longer."

"But I am supposed to have honors and riches," I reminded them.

Neither of the Muls spoke further but they seemed plunged into a sadness that I found in its way touching, but yet I could scarcely refrain from smiling for they looked so precisely similar.

"Look, Tarl Cabot," said Mul-Al-Ka suddenly, "we want to show you something."

"Yes," said Mul-Ba-Ta.

Mul-Al-Ka swung the transportation disk suddenly down a side tunnel and, accelerating fiercely, flowed like sound down the tunnel for several portals and then stepped off the accelerator strips and, as the disk slowed and stopped, brought it neatly to rest at a tall steel portal. I admired his skill. He was really rather good with the disk. I would have liked to have raced him.

"What is it you wish to show me?" I asked.

Mul-Al-Ka and Mul-Ba-Ta said nothing but stepped from the transportation disk and, pressing the portal switch, opened the steel portal. I followed them inside.

"We have been instructed not to speak to you," said Mul-Al-Ka.

"Were you instructed to bring me here?" I asked.

"No," said Mul-Ba-Ta.

"Then why have you brought me here?"

"It seemed good for us to do so," said Mul-Al-Ka.

"Yes," said Mul-Ba-Ta. "This has to do with honors and riches and Priest-Kings."

The room in which we found ourselves was substantially empty, and not too much different in size and shape from the room in which my processing had been initiated. There was, however, no observation screen and no wall disks.

The only object in the room other than ourselves was a

heavy, globelike contrivance, high over our heads, attached to a set of jointed extensions fastened in the ceiling of the chamber. In the floor side of the globelike contrivance there was an adjustable opening which was now of a diameter of perhaps six inches. Numerous wires extended from the globe along the metal extensions and into a panel in the ceiling. Also, the globe itself bristled with various devices, nodes, switches, coils, disks, lights.

Vaguely I sensed that I had heard of this thing somewhere before.

In another chamber I heard a girl cry out.

My hand went to my sword.

"No," said Mul-Al-Ka, placing his hand on my wrist.

Now I knew the purpose of the device in the room—why it was there and what it did—but why had Mul-Al-Ka and Mul-Ba-Ta brought me here?

A panel to the side slid open and two plastic-clad Muls entered. Leaning forward they were pushing a large, flat circular disk. The disk floated on a thin gas cushion. They placed the disk directly under the globelike object in the ceiling. On the disk there was mounted a narrow, closed cylinder of transparent plastic. It was approximately eighteen inches in diameter and apparently constructed so that it might be opened along its vertical axis, although it was now securely locked. In the cylinder, save for her head which was held in place by a circular opening in the top of the cylinder, was a girl, clad in the traditional robes of concealment, even to the veil, whose gloved hands pressed helplessly against the interior of the cylinder.

Her terrified eyes fell on Mul-Al-Ka, Mul-Ba-Ta and myself. "Save me!" she cried.

Mul-Al-Ka's hand touched my wrist. I did not draw my sword.

"Greetings, Honored Muls," said one of the two attendants.

"Greetings," said Mul-Al-Ka.

"Who is the other?" asked one of the attendants.

"Tarl Cabot of the City of Ko-ro-ba," said Mul-Ba-Ta.

"I have never heard of it," said the other attendant.

"It is on the surface," said Mul-Al-Ka.

"Ah well," said the attendant, "I was bred in the Nest."

"He is our friend," said Mul-Ba-Ta.

"Friendship between Muls is forbidden," said the first attendant.

"We know," said Mul-Al-Ka, "but we are going to the dissection chambers anyway."

"I am sorry to hear that," said the other attendant.

"Yes," said Mul-Al-Ka, "we were sorry to hear it too."

I gazed at my companions with amazement.

"On the other hand," said Mul-Ba-Ta, "it is the wish of a Priest-King and thus we also rejoice."

"Of course," said the first attendant.

"What was your crime?" asked the second attendant.

"We do not know," said Mul-Al-Ka.

"That is always annoying," said the first attendant.

"Yes," agreed Mul-Ba-Ta, "but not important."

"True," agreed the first attendant.

The attendants now busied themselves with their work. One of them climbed onto the disk beside the plastic cylinder. The other went to a panel at the side of the room and by pushing certain buttons and turning a dial, began to lower the globe object down toward the girl's head.

I pitied her as she turned her head up and saw the large object, with an electronic hum, descend slowly towards her. She gave a long, frantic, terrified, wild scream and squirmed about in the cylinder, her small gloved fists striking futilely at the strong, curved plastic walls that confined her.

The attendant who stood on the disk then, to her horror, pushed back the hood of her garment and the ornate, beautiful veils that masked her features, face-stripping her as casually as one might remove a scarf. She trembled in the cylinder, pressing her small hands against it, and wept. I noted that her hair was brown and fine, her eyes dark and longly lashed. Her mouth was lovely, her throat white and beautiful. Her final scream was muffled as the attendant adjusted the heavy globe over her head and locked it in place. His companion then snapped a switch at the wall panel and the globe seemed to come alive, humming and clicking, coils suddenly glowing and tiny signal lights flashing on and off.

I wondered if the girl knew that a plate of her brain traces was being prepared, which would be correlated with the sensors guarding the quarters of a Chamber Slave.

While the globe did its work, and held the girl's head in place, the attendant at the cylinder unlocked the five latches which held it shut and swung it open. Swiftly and efficiently he placed her wrists in retaining devices mounted in the cylinder and, with a small, curved knife, removed her clothing, which he cast aside. Bending to a panel in the disk he took out three objects: the long, classic, white garment of a Chamber Slave, which was contained in a wrapper of blue plastic; a slave collar; and an object of which I did not immediately grasp the import, a small, flat boxlike object which bore the upraised figure that, in cursive Gorean script, is the first letter in the expression for 'slave girl'.

On the latter object he pressed a switch and almost immediately, before I became aware of it, the upraised portion turned white with heat.

I lunged forward but Mul-Al-Ka and Mul-Ba-Ta, sensing my intention, seized my arms and before I could shake them off I heard, muffled but agonized from within that terrible metal globe, the cry of a branded slave girl.

I felt helpless.

It was too late.

"Is your companion well?" asked the attendant at the wall.

"Yes," said Mul-Al-Ka, "he is quite well, thank you."

"If he is not well," said the attendant on the disk, "he should report to the infirmary for destruction."

"He is quite well," said Mul-Ba-Ta.

"Why did he say 'destruction'?" I asked Mul-Al-Ka.

"Infected Muls are disposed of," said Mul-Al-Ka. "It is better for the Nest."

The attendant on the disk had now broken open the blue plastic wrapper that held, fresh and folded, the garment of a Chamber Slave. This, with its clasp on the left shoulder, he fastened on the girl. He then sprung her wrists free of the retaining devices and reclosed the plastic cylinder, locking her inside once again. She was now contained precisely as she had been originally save that she had exchanged the thick, multitudinous, ornate Robes of Concealment, the proud, cumbersome insignia of the free woman of Gor, for the simple garment of a Chamber Slave and a burning wound on her left thigh.

The globelike object which had been fastened over her head now stopped humming and flashing, and the attendant on the disk opened it, releasing the girl's head. He shoved the globe up and a foot or so to the side and then with a quick movement reclosed it in such a way that once again its floorside aperture described an opening of approximately six inches in diameter. The attendant at the wall panel then pressed a button and the entire apparatus raised on its extension arms to the ceiling.

As well as she could, sobbing and trembling, the girl looked downward through the transparent top of the plastic cylinder and regarded herself. She now saw herself in a strange garment. She touched her left hand to her thigh and cried out in pain.

She shook her head, her eyes bursting with tears. "You don't understand," she whimpered, "I am an offering to the Priest-Kings from the Initiates of Ar."

The attendant on the disk then bent down and picked up the slender, graceful metal collar.

These collars are normally measured individually to the girl as is most slave steel. The collar is regarded not simply as a designation of slavery and a means for identifying the girl's owner and his city but as an ornament as well. Accordingly the Gorean master is often extremely concerned that the fit of the graceful band will be neither too tight nor too loose. The collar is normally worn snugly, indeed so much so that if the snap of a slave leash is used the girl will normally suffer some discomfort.

The girl continued to shake her head. "No," she said, "no, you do not understand." She tried to twist away as the attendant's hands lifted the collar towards her. "But I came to the Sardar," she cried, "in order that I might never be a slave girl—never a slave girl!"

The collar made a small, heavy click as it closed about her throat.

"You are a slave girl," said the attendant.

She screamed.

"Take her away," said the attendant by the wall panel.

Obediently the attendant on the disk lightly jumped down and began to push the disk and its cylinder from the room.

As it passed from the chamber, followed by the attendant who had operated the wall panel, I could see the dazed, confused girl, sobbing and in pain, trying to reach the collar through the plastic of the cylinder's top. "No, no," she said, "you do not understand." She threw me one last look, not comprehending, hopeless, wild, reproachful.

My hand tightened on the hilt of my sword.

"There is nothing you can do," said Mul-Al-Ka.

I supposed that he might well be right. Should I kill the innocent attendants, merely Muls who were performing the tasks allotted to them by Priest-Kings? Would I then have to slay Mul-Al-Ka and Mul-Ba-Ta as well? And what would I do with the girl in the Nest of Priest-Kings? And what of Misk? Would I not then lose my opportunity, if any, of saving him?

I was angered toward Mul-Al-Ka and Mul-Ba-Ta.

"Why did you bring me here?" I demanded.

"Why," said Mul-Al-Ka, "did you not notice her collar?"

"It was a slave collar," I said.

"But the engraving was large and very plain," he said.

"Did you not read it?" asked Mul-Ba-Ta.

"No," I said irritably, "I did not."

"It was the numeral '708'," said Mul-Al-Ka.

I started and did not speak. 708 had been the number of Vika's collar. There was now a new slave for her chamber. What did this mean?

"That was the collar number of Vika of Treve," I said.

"Precisely," said Mul-Al-Ka, "she whom Sarm promised to you as part of the riches accruing from your part in his plan to slay Misk."

"The number, as you see," said Mul-Ba-Ta, "has been reassigned."

"What does that mean?" I asked.

"It means," said Mul-Al-Ka, "that Vika of Treve no longer exists."

I suddenly felt as though a hammer had struck me, for though I hated Vika of Treve I would not have wished her dead. Somehow, unaccountably in spite of my great hatred for her, I was shaking, sweating and trembling. "Perhaps she has been given a new collar?" I asked.

"No," said Mul-Al-Ka.

"Then she is dead?" I asked.

"As good as dead," said Mul-Ba-Ta.

"What do you mean!" I cried, seizing him by the shoulders and shaking him.

"He means," said Mul-Al-Ka, "that she has been sent to the tunnels of the Golden Beetle."

"But why?" I demanded.

"She was useless any longer as a servant to Priest-Kings," said Mul-Ba-Ta.

"But why!" I insisted.

"I think we have said enough," said Mul-Al-Ka.

"That is true," said Mul-Ba-Ta. "Perhaps we should not have spoken even this much to you, Tarl Cabot."

I placed my hands gently on the shoulders of the two Muls.

"Thank you, my friends," I said. "I understand what you have done here. You have proved to me that Sarm does not intend to keep his promises, that he will betray me."

"Remember," said Mul-Al-Ka, "we have not told you that."

"That is true," I said, "but you have showed me."

"We only promised Sarm," said Mul-Ba-Ta, "that we would not tell you."

I smiled at the two Muls, my friends.

"After I have finished with Misk are you then to kill me?" I asked.

"No," said Mul-Al-Ka, "we are simply to tell you that Vika of Treve awaits you in the tunnels of the Golden Beetle."

"That is the weak part of Sarm's plan," said Mul-Ba-Ta,

"for you would never go to the tunnels of the Golden Beetle to seek a female Mul."

"True," said Mul-Al-Ka, "it is the first mistake I have known Sarm to make."

"You will not go to the tunnels of the Golden Beetle," said Mul-Ba-Ta, "because it is death to do so."

"But I will go," I said.

The two Muls looked at one another sadly and shook their heads.

"Sarm is wiser than we," said Mul-Al-Ka.

Mul-Ba-Ta nodded his head. "See how he uses the instincts of humans against themselves," he said to his companion.

"A true Priest-King," said Mul-Al-Ka.

I smiled to myself for I thought how incredible that I should find myself naturally and without a second thought considering going to the rescue of the worthless, vicious wench, Vika of Treve.

And yet it was not a strange thing, particularly not on Gor, where bravery is highly esteemed and to save a female's life is in effect to win title to it, for it is the option of a Gorean male to enslave any woman whose life he has saved, a right which is seldom denied even by the citizens of the girl's city or her family. Indeed, there have been cases in which a girl's brothers have had her clad as a slave, bound in slave bracelets, and handed over to her rescuer, in order that the honor of the family and her city not be besmirched. There is, of course, a natural tendency in the rescued female to feel and demonstrate great gratitude to the man who has saved her life, and the Gorean custom is perhaps no more than an institutionalization of this customary response. There are cases where a free woman in the vicinity of a man she desired has deliberately placed herself in jeopardy. The man then, after having been forced to risk his life, is seldom in a mood to use the girl other than as his slave. I have wondered upon occasion about this practice so different on Gor than on Earth. On my old world when a woman is saved by a man she may, I understand, with propriety bestow upon him a grateful kiss and perhaps, if we may believe the tales in these matters, consider him more seriously because of his action as a possible, eventual companion in wedlock. One of these girls, if rescued on Gor, would probably be dumbfounded at what would happen to her. After her kiss of gratitude which might last a good deal longer than she had anticipated she would find herself forced to kneel and be collared and then, stripped, her wrists confined behind her back in slave bracelets, she would find herself led stumbling away on a slave leash from the field of her champion's valor. Yes, undoubtedly our Earth girls would find this most surprising. On the other hand the Gorean attitude is that she would be dead were it not for his brave action and thus it is his right, now that he has won her life, to make her live it for him precisely as he pleases, which is usually, it must unfortunately be noted, as his slave girl, for the privileges of a Free Companionship are never bestowed lightly. Also of course a Free Companionship might be refused, in all Gorean right, by the girl, and thus a warrior can hardly be blamed, after risking his life, for not wanting to risk losing the precious prize which he has just, at great peril to himself, succeeded in winning. The Gorean man, as a man, cheerfully and dutifully attends to the rescuing of his female in distress, but as a Gorean, as a true Gorean, he feels, perhaps justifiably and being somewhat less or more romantic than ourselves, that he should have something more for his pains than her kiss of gratitude and so, in typical Gorean fashion, puts his chain on the wench, claiming both her and her body as his payment.

"I thought you hated her," said Mul-Al-Ka.

"I do," I said.

"Is it human to act as you do?" inquired Mul-Ba-Ta.

"Yes," I said, "it is the part of a man to protect a female of the human kind, regardless of who she may be."

"Is it enough that she be merely a female of our kind?" asked Mul-Ba-Ta.

"Yes," I said.

"Even a female Mul?" asked Mul-Al-Ka.

"Yes," I said.

"Interesting," said Mul-Ba-Ta. "Then we should accompany you for we too wish to learn to be men."

"No," I said, "you should not accompany me."

"Ah," said Mul-Al-Ka bitterly, "you do not truly regard us yet as men."

"I do," I said. "You have proved that by informing me of Sarm's intentions."

"Then we may accompany you?" asked Mul-Ba-Ta.

"No," I said, "for I think you will be able to help me in other matters."

"That would be pleasant," said Mul-Al-Ka.

"But we will not have much time," said Mul-Ba-Ta.

"That is true," said Mul-Al-Ka, "for we must soon report to the dissection chambers."

The two Muls looked understandably dejected.

I thought about things for a moment or so and then I shrugged and fixed on them both a look of what I hoped would be a somewhat poignant disappointment.

"You may if you wish," I said, "but it is not really very human on your part."

"No?" asked Mul-Al-Ka, perking up.

"No?" asked Mul-Ba-Ta, showing sudden interest.

"No," I said, "definitely not."

"Are you sure?" inquired Mul-Al-Ka.

"Truly sure?" pressed Mul-Ba-Ta.

"I am positive," I said. "It is simply not human at all to just go off and report to the dissection chambers."

The two Muls looked at me for a long time, and at themselves, and at me again, and seemed to reach some sort of accord.

"Well then," said Mul-Al-Ka, "we shall not do so."

"No," said Mul-Ba-Ta rather firmly.

"Good," I said.

"What will you do now, Tarl Cabot?" asked Mul-Al-Ka.

"Take me to Misk," I said.

21
I Find Misk

I FOLLOWED MUL-AL-KA AND MUL-BA-TA into a damp, high, vaulted chamber, unlit by energy bulbs. The sides of the chamber were formed of some rough cementlike substance in which numerous rocks of various sizes and shapes inhered as in a conglomerate mass.

At the entrance to the chamber, from a rack, Mul-Al-Ka had taken a Mul-Torch and broken off its end. Holding this over his head he illuminated those portions of the chamber to which the light of the torch would reach.

"This must be a very old portion of the Nest," said Mul-Al-Ka.

"Where is Misk?" I asked.

"He is here somewhere," said Mul-Ba-Ta, "for so we were told by Sarm."

As far as I could tell the chamber seemed empty. In impatience I fingered the chain of the translator I had had the two Muls pick up on the way to Misk's prison. I was not sure that Misk would have been allowed to retain his translator and I wished to be able to communicate with him.

My eyes drifted upward and I froze for an instant and then, scarcely moving, touched Mul-Ba-Ta's arm.

"Up there," I whispered.

Mul-Al-Ka lifted the torch as high as he could.

Clinging to the ceiling of the chamber were numerous dark, distended shapes, apparently Priest-Kings but with abdomens swollen grotesquely. They did not move.

I turned on the translator. "Misk," I said into it. Almost instantly I recognized the familiar odor.

There was a rustling among the dark, distended shapes that clung to the ceiling.

No response came from my translator.

"He is not here," proposed Mul-Al-Ka.

"Probably not," said Mul-Ba-Ta, "for had he replied I think your translator would have picked up his response."

"Let us look elsewhere," said Mul-Al-Ka.

"Give me the torch," I said.

I took the torch and went around to the edges of the room. By the door I saw a series of short bars which emerged from the wall, which might be used as a ladder. Taking the torch in my teeth I prepared to climb the set of bars.

Suddenly I stopped, my hands on one of the bars.

"What is the matter?" asked Mul-Al-Ka.

"Listen," I said.

We listened carefully and in the distance it seemed we heard, incredibly enough, the mournful singing of human voices, as though of many men, and the sound was as we determined by listening for a minute or two gradually nearing.

"Perhaps they are coming here," said Mul-Al-Ka.

"We had better hide," said Mul-Ba-Ta.

I left the bars and led the two Muls to the far side of the room. There I directed them to take cover as well as they could behind some of the conglomerate material which had crumbled from the wall and lay at its base. Grinding out the Mul-torch on the stones I crouched down with them behind some of this debris and together we watched the door.

The singing grew louder.

It was a sad song, mournful and slow, almost a dirgelike chant.

The words were in archaic Gorean which I find very difficult to understand. On the surface it is spoken by none but members of the Caste of Initiates who use it primarily in their numerous and complex rituals. As nearly as I could make it out the song, though sad, was a paean of some sort to Priest-Kings, and mentioned the Feast of Tola and Gur. The refrain, almost constantly repeated, was something to the effect that We Have Come for Gur, On the Feast of Tola We Have Come for Gur, We Rejoice For on the Feast of Tola We Have Come for Gur.

Then, as we crouched in the darkness of the far side of the chamber, the doors opposite us swung open and we observed two long lines of strange men, marching abreast, each of whom carried a Mul-Torch in one hand and in the other by a handle what resembled a deflated wineskin of golden leather.

I heard Mul-Al-Ka draw in his breath quickly beside me.

"Look, Tarl Cabot," whispered Mul-Ba-Ta.

"Yes," I said, cautioning him to silence, "I see."

The men who came through the door in the long mournful procession may have been of the human kind or they may not have been. They were shaven and clad in plastic as are all Muls of the Nest, but their torsos seemed smaller and rounder than those of a human being and their legs and arms seemed extraordinarily long for their body size and the hands and feet seemed unusually wide. The feet had no toes but were rather disklike, fleshy cushions on which they padded silently along, and similarly on the palms of their wide hands there seemed to be a fleshy disk, which glistened in the blue light of the Mul-Torches. Most strange perhaps was the shape and width of the eyes, for they were very large, perhaps three inches in width, and were round and dark and shining, much like the eyes of a nocturnal animal.

I wondered at what manner of creatures they were.

As more of them filed abreast into the room the increased torchlight well illuminated the chamber and I quietly warned my companions to make no movement.

I could now see the Priest-Kings clearly where they clung upside down to the ceiling, their great swollen abdomens almost dwarfing their thoraxes and heads.

Then to my amazement, one by one, the strange creatures, disdaining the bars near the door began simply to pad up the almost vertical walls to the Priest-Kings and then, astonishingly, began to walk upside down on the ceiling. Where they stepped I could see a glistening disk of exudate which they had undoubtedly secreted from the fleshy pads which served them as feet. While the creatures remaining on the floor continued their mournful paean, their fellow creatures on the walls and ceiling, still carrying their torches, and scattering wild shadows of their own bodies and those of swollen Priest-Kings against the ceiling, began to fill their golden vessels from the mouths of the Priest-Kings. Many times was a golden vessel held for a Priest-King as it slowly yielded whatever had been stored in its abdomen to the Muls.

There seemed to be almost an indefinite number of the Muls and of clinging Priest-Kings there were perhaps a hundred. The strange procession to and fro up the walls and across the ceiling to Priest-Kings and back down to the floor, continued for more than an hour, during which time the Muls who stood below, some of them having returned with a full vessel, never ceased to chant their mournful paean.

The Muls made no use of the bars and from this I gathered that they might have been placed where they were in ancient times before there were such creatures to serve Priest-Kings.

I assumed that the exudate or whatever it might be that had been taken from the Priest-Kings was Gur, and that I now understood what it was to retain Gur.

Finally the last of the unusual Muls stood below on the stone flooring.

In all this time not one of them had so much as glanced in our direction, so single-minded were they in their work. When not actively engaged in gathering Gur their round dark eyes were lifted like dark curves to the Priest-Kings who clung to the ceiling far over their heads.

At last I saw one Priest-King move from the ceiling and climb backwards down the wall. His abdomen drained of Gur was now normal and he stalked regally to the door, moving on those light, feathery feet with the delicate steps of one of nature's masters. When there several Muls flanked him on either side, still singing, and holding their torches and carrying their vessels which now brimmed with a pale, milky substance, something like white, diluted honey. The Priest-King, escorted by Muls, then began to move slowly, step by majestic step, down the passage outside of the chamber. He was followed by another Priest-King, and then another, until all but one Priest-King had departed the chamber. In the light of the last torches which left the chamber I could see that there remained one Priest-King who, though emptied of Gur, still clung to the ceiling. A heavy chain, fastened to a ring in the ceiling, led to a thick metal band which was locked about his narrow trunk between the thorax and the abdomen.

It was Misk.

I broke off the other end of the Mul-Torch, igniting it, and walked to the center of the chamber.

I lifted it as far over my head as I could.

"Welcome, Tarl Cabot," came from my translator. "I am ready to die."

22
To the Tunnels of the Golden Beetle

I SLUNG THE TRANSLATOR ON its chain over my shoulder and went to the bars near the door. Putting the torch in my teeth, I began to climb the bars rapidly. One or two of them, rusted through, broke away in my hands, and I was nearly plunged to the rocky floor beneath. The bars were apparently very old and had never been kept in a state of repair or replaced when defective.

When I reached the ceiling I saw, to my relief, that further bars projected downwards from the ceiling and that the bottom of each was bent outwards in a flat, horizontal projection that would afford me a place to put my feet. Still holding the Mul-Torch in my teeth because I wanted both hands free I began to make my way toward Misk, hand and foot, across these metal extensions.

I could see the figures of Mul-Al-Ka and Mul-Ba-Ta beneath me, perhaps a hundred and fifty feet below.

Suddenly one of the extensions, the fourth I believe, slipped with a grating sound from the ceiling and I leaped wildly for the next bar, just managing to catch it in my fall. I heard the other bar drop with a great clang to the floor. For a moment I hung there sweating. My mouth seemed to be filled with carbon and I realized I must have almost bitten through the Mul-Torch.

Then the bar to which I clung moved an inch from the ceiling.

I moved a bit and it slipped another inch.

If I drew myself up on it I was afraid it would fall altogether.

I hung there and it slipped a bit more, perhaps the fraction of an inch.

I swung forward and back on the bar and felt it loosen almost entirely in the ceiling but on the next forward swing I released it and seized the next bar. I heard the bar I had just left slide out and fall like its predecessor to the stone floor below.

I looked down and saw Mul-Al-Ka and Mul-Ba-Ta standing below, looking up. Concern for me was written on their faces. The two fallen bars lay almost at their feet.

The bar to which I now clung seemed relatively stable and with relief I drew myself up onto it, and then stepped carefully to the next.

In a moment I stood by Misk's side.

I took the Mul-Torch out of my mouth and spit out some particles of carbon. I lifted the torch and looked at Misk.

He, hanging there upside down, reflected in the blue torchlight, regarded me calmly.

"Greetings, Tarl Cabot," said Misk.

"Greetings, Misk," I said.

"You were very noisy," said Misk.

"Yes," I said.

"Sarm should have had those bars checked," said Misk.

"I suppose so," I said.

"But it is difficult to think of everything," said Misk.

"Yes, it is," I agreed.

"Well," said Misk. "I think perhaps you should get busy and kill me now."

"I do not even know how to go about it," I said.

"Yes," said Misk, "it will be difficult, but with perseverance I think it may be accomplished."

"Is there some central organ that I might attack?" I queried. "A heart for example?"

"Nothing that will be of great use," said Misk. "In the lower abdomen there is a dorsal organ which serves to circulate the body fluids but since our tissues are, on the whole, directly bathed in body fluid, injuring it would not produce death for some time, at least not for a few Ehn.

"On the other hand," said Misk, "I suppose you have the time."

"Yes," I said.

"My own recommendation," said Misk, "would be the brain-nodes."

"Then there is no swift way to kill a Priest-King?" I asked.

"Not really with your weapon," said Misk. "You might however, after some time, sever the trunk or head."

"I had hoped," I said, "that there would be a quicker way to kill Priest-Kings."

"I am sorry," said Misk.

"I guess it can't be helped," I said.

"No," agreed Misk. And he added, "And under the circumstances I wish it could."

My eye fell on a metal device, a square rod with some tiny projections at one end. The device hung from a hook about a foot out of Misk's reach.

"What is that?" I asked.

"A key to my chain," said Misk.

"Good," I said and walked over a few bars to get the device, and returned to Misk's side. After a moment's difficulty I managed to insert the key into the lock on Misk's trunk band.

"Frankly," said Misk, "it would be my recommendation to slay me first and then unlock the band and dispose of my body, for otherwise I might be tempted to defend myself."

I turned the key in the lock, springing it open.

"But I have not come to kill you," I said.

"But did Sarm not send you?"

"Yes," I said.

"Then why do you not kill me?"

"I do not wish to do so," I said. "Besides, there is Nest Trust between us."

"That is true," agreed Misk and with his forelegs removed the metal band from his trunk and let it dangle from the chain. "On the other hand you will now be killed by Sarm."

"I think that would have happened anyway," I said.

Misk seemed to think a moment. "Yes," he said. "Undoubtedly." Then Misk looked down at Mul-Al-Ka and Mul-Ba-Ta. "Sarm will have to dispose of them also," he observed.

"He has ordered them to report to the dissection chambers," I said, adding, "but they have decided not to do so."

"Remarkable," said Misk.

"They are just being human," I said.

"I suppose it is their privilege," said Misk.

"Yes, I think so," I said.

Then, almost tenderly, Misk reached out with one foreleg and gathered me from the bar on which I stood. I found myself pressed up tightly against his thorax. "This will be a great deal safer," he said, and added, unnecessarily to my mind, "and probably a good deal less noisy." Then, clutching me securely, he scampered away across the ceiling and backed down the wall.

Misk, the Muls and I now stood on the stone floor of the chamber near the door.

I thrust the Mul-Torch which I still carried into a narrow iron receptacle, consisting mainly of two connected rings and a base plate, which was bolted to the wall. There were several of these, I noted, around the walls and they seemed obviously intended to hold Mul-torches or some similar illuminating device.

I turned to the Priest-King.

"You must hide yourself somewhere," I said.

"Yes," said Mul-Al-Ka, "find yourself some secret place and stay, and perhaps someday Sarm will succumb to the Pleasures of the Golden Beetle and you can emerge in safety."

"We will bring you food and water," volunteered Mul-Ba-Ta.

"That is very kind of you," responded Misk, peering down at us, "but it is of course impossible to do so."

The two Muls stood back aghast.

"Why?" I asked, bewildered.

Misk drew himself up to his proud, almost eighteen feet of height, save that he inclined slightly forward from the vertical, and fixed on us with his antennae what I had come to recognize in the last few weeks as a look of rather patient, gentle reproach.

"It is the Feast of Tola," he said.

"So?" I asked.

"Well," said Misk, "it being the Feast of Tola I must give Gur to the Mother."

"You will be discovered and slain," I said. "Sarm if he finds you are alive will simply bring about your destruction as soon as possible."

"Naturally," said Misk.

"Then you will hide?" I asked.

"Don't be foolish," said Misk, "it is the Feast of Tola and I must give Gur to the Mother."

I sensed there was no arguing with Misk, but his decision saddened me.

"I am sorry," I said.

"What was sad," said Misk, "was that I might not have been able to give Gur to the Mother, and that thought troubled me grievously for the days in which I retained Gur, but now thanks to you I will be able to give Gur to the Mother and I will stand forever in your debt until I am slain by Sarm or succumb to the Pleasures of the Golden Beetle."

He placed his antennae lightly on my shoulders and then lifted them and I held up my arms and he touched the palms of my hands with the tips of his antennae, and once again we had, in so far as we could, locked our antennae.

He extended his antennae toward the two Muls but they withdrew in shame. "No," said Mul-Al-Ka, "we are only Muls."

"Let there be Nest Trust between a Priest-King and two Muls," said Misk.

"There can be no Nest Trust between a Priest-King and Muls," said Mul-Ba-Ta.

"Then," said Misk, "between a Priest-King and two of the human kind."

Slowly, fearfully, Mul-Al-Ka and Mul-Ba-Ta lifted their hands and Misk touched them with his antennae.

"I will die for you," said Mul-Al-Ka.

"And I," said Mul-Ba-Ta.

"No," said Misk, "you must hide and try to live."

The Muls looked at me, stricken, and I nodded. "Yes," I said, "hide and teach others who are of the human kind."

"What will we teach them?" asked Mul-Al-Ka.

"To be human," I said.

"But what is it to be human," begged Mul-Ba-Ta, "for you have never told us."

"You must decide that for yourself," I said. "You must yourself decide what it is to be human."

"It is much the same thing with a Priest-King," said Misk.

"We will come with you, Tarl Cabot," said Mul-Al-Ka, "to fight the Golden Beetle."

"What is this?" asked Misk.

"The girl Vika of Treve lies in the tunnels of the Golden Beetle," I said. "I go to her succor."

"You will be too late," said Misk, "for the hatching time is at hand."

"What do you mean?" I asked.

"Are you going?" asked Misk.

"Yes," I said.

"Then," said he, "what I said will be evident."

We looked at one another.

"Do not go, Tarl Cabot," he said. "You will die."

"I must go," I said.

"I see," said Misk, "it is like giving Gur to the Mother."

"Perhaps," I said, "I don't know."

"We will go with you," said Mul-Al-Ka.

"No," I said, "you must go to the human kind."

"Even to those who carried Gur?" asked Mul-Ba-Ta, shivering at the thought of those small round bodies and the strange arms and legs, and eyes.

"They are mutations," said Misk, "bred long ago for service in the darkened tunnels, now preserved for ceremonial purposes and for the sake of tradition."

"Yes," I said to Mul-Ba-Ta, "even to those who carried Gur."

"I understand," said Mul-Ba-Ta, smiling.

"Everywhere in the Nest," I said, "you must go everywhere that there is something human to be found."

"Even in the Fungus Chambers and the Pastures?" asked Mul-Al-Ka.

"Yes," I said, "wherever there is something human—wherever it is to be found and however it is found."

"I understand," said Mul-Al-Ka.

"And I too," said Mul-Ba-Ta.

"Good," I said.

With a last handclasp the two men turned and ran toward the exit.

Misk and I stood alone.

"That will mean trouble," said Misk.

"Yes," I said, "I suppose it will."

"And you will be responsible," said Misk.

"In part," I said, "but mostly what it means will be decided by Priest-Kings and men."

I looked up at him.

"You are foolish," I said, "to go to the Mother."

"You are foolish," he said, "to go to the tunnels of the Golden Beetle."

I drew my sword, lifting it easily from the sheath. It cleared the leather as easily and swiftly as a larl might have bared its fangs. In the blue torchlight I examined the blade and the light coat of oil that protected it. I tried the balance, and dropped the steel back into its sheath. I was satisfied.

I liked the blade which seemed so simple and efficient compared to the manifold variations in sword steel that were possible. I supposed one of the reasons for the short blade was that it could clear the sheath a fraction of a second before a longer blade. Another advantage was that it could be moved with greater swiftness than a longer blade. The primary advantage I supposed was that it allowed the Gorean warrior to work close to his man. The brief reach of the blade tended to be more than compensated for by the rapidity with which it might be wielded and the ease with which it might work beneath the guard of a longer weapon. If the swordsman with a longer weapon could not finish the fight in the first thrust or two he was a dead man.

"Where are the tunnels of the Golden Beetle?" I asked.

"Inquire," said Misk. "They are well known to all within the Nest."

"Is it as difficult to slay a Golden Beetle as a Priest-King?" I asked.

"I do not know," said Misk. "We have never slain a Golden Beetle, nor have we studied them."

"Why not?" I asked.

"It is not done," said Misk. "And," he said, peering down at me, his luminous eyes intent, "it would be a great crime to kill one."

"I see," I said.

I turned to go but then turned once again to face the Priest-King. "Could you, Misk," I asked, "with those bladelike structures on your forelegs slay a Priest-King?"

Misk inverted his forelegs and examined the blades. "Yes," he said. "I could."

He seemed lost in thought.

"But it has not been done in more than a million years," he said.

I lifted my arm to Misk. "I wish you well," I said, using the traditional Gorean farewell.

Misk lifted one foreleg in salute, the bladelike projection disappearing. His antennae inclined toward me and the golden hairs with which the antennae glistened extended towards me as though to touch me. "And I, Tarl Cabot," he said, "wish you well."

And we turned, the Priest-King and I, and went our separate ways.

23
I Find Vika

I GATHERED THAT I HAD arrived too late to save Vika of Treve.

Deep in the unlit tunnels of the Golden Beetle, those unadorned, tortuous passages through the solid rock, I came upon her body.

I held the Mul-Torch over my head and beheld the foul cavern in which she lay on a bedding of soiled mosses and stems.

She wore only brief rags, the remains of her once long and beautiful garment, torn and stained by what must have been her terrified flight through these dark, rocky tunnels, running, stumbling, screaming, futilely trying to escape the pursuing jaws of the implacable Golden Beetle.

Her throat, I was pleased to see, no longer wore the collar of a slave.

I wondered if her collar had been the same as that placed on the girl I had seen. If the sizes had matched I supposed it would have been. The Priest-Kings often practice such small economies, jealously conserving the inanimate resources of the Nest.

I wondered if the removal of the collar meant that Vika had been freed before being closed within the tunnels of the Golden Beetle. I recalled vaguely that Misk had once said to me that in deference to the Golden Beetle it was given only free women.

The cavern in which she lay reeked of the spoor of the Golden Beetle, which I had not yet encountered. Its contrast with the fastidiously clean tunnels of the Nest of Priest-Kings made it seem all the more repulsive in its filth and litter.

In one corner there were scattered bones and among them the shards of a human skull. The bones had been split and the marrow sucked from them.

How long Vika had been dead I had no way of judging, though I cursed myself for it would not have appeared to be a matter of more than a few hours. Her body, though rigid in the appearance of recent death, did not have the coldness I would have expected. She was unmoving and her eyes seemed fixed on me with all the horror of the last moment in which the jaws of the Golden Beetle must have closed upon her. I wondered if in the darkness she would have been able to see what had attacked her. I found myself almost hoping that she had not, for it would have been more than enough to have heard it following in the tunnels. Yet I myself I knew would have preferred to see the assailant and so I found myself wishing that this brief, terrible privilege had been Vika of Treve's, for I remembered her as a woman of courage and pride.

Her skin seemed slightly dry but not desiccated.

Because of the lack of coldness in the body I listened for a long time for a heartbeat. Holding her wrist I felt for the slightest sign of a pulse. I could detect neither heartbeat nor pulse.

Though I had hated Vika of Treve I would not have

wanted this fate to be hers, nor could I believe that any man, even those whom she had injured, could have wished it to be so. As I looked upon her now I felt strangely sad, and there was nothing left in my bosom of the bitterness with which I had earlier regarded her. I saw her now as only a girl, surely too innocent for this, who had met the Golden Beetle and had in consequence died one of the most horrible of deaths. She was of the human kind and whatever might have been her faults, she could not have deserved this grotesque, macabre fate, the jaws and cavern of the Golden Beetle. And looking upon her I now realized too that somehow, not fully understanding, I had cared for her.

"I am sorry," I said, "I am sorry, Vika of Treve."

Strangely there did not seem to be severe wounds on her body.

I wondered if it were possible that she had died of fear.

There were no lacerations or bruises that might not have been caused by her flight through the tunnels. Her body and arms and legs, though cut and injured, were neither torn nor broken.

I found nothing that could have caused her death unless perhaps a small puncture on her left side, through which some poison might have been injected.

There were, however, though I could not conceive of how they could have killed her, five large round swellings on her body. These extended in a line along her left side, reaching from the interior of her left thigh to her waist to a few inches below her shoulder. These swellings, hard, round and smooth, seemed to lie just beneath the skin and to be roughly the size of one's fist. I supposed they might have been some unusual physiological reaction to the poison which I conjectured had been injected into her system through the small, livid puncture, also on her left side.

I wiped the back of my forearm across my eyes.

There was nothing I could do for her now, save perhaps hunt for the Golden Beetle.

I wondered if I could bury the body somewhere, but dismissed the thought in view of the stony passages I had just traversed. I might move it from the filth of the Golden Beetle's den but it, until the creature itself was slain, would

never be safe from its despoiling jaws. I turned my back on
Vika of Treve, and carrying the torch left the cavern. As I
did so I seemed almost to hear a silent, horrible, pleading
shriek but there was of course no sound. I returned and held
the torch and her body was the same as before, the eyes fixed
with the same expression of frozen horror, so I left the
chamber.

I continued to search the stony passages of the tunnels of
the Golden Beetle but I saw no sign of the creature.

I held my sword in my right hand and the Mul-Torch in
my left.

When I made a turn I would take the hilt of the sword, in
order to protect the blade, and scratch a small sign indicating
the direction from which I had come.

It was a long, eerie search, in the blue light of the Mul-
Torch, thrusting it into one crevice and another, trying one
passage and then the next.

As I wandered through these passages my sorrow for Vika
of Treve struggled with my hatred for the Golden Beetle
until I forced myself to clear my head of emotion and
concentrate on the task at hand.

But still, as the Mul-Torch burned lower and I yet
encountered no sign of the Golden Beetle, my thoughts
turned ever and again to the still form of Vika lying in the
cavern of the Golden Beetle.

It had been weeks since I had last seen her and I supposed
it would have been at least days since she had been closed in
the tunnels of the Golden Beetle. How was it that she had
been captured only so recently by the creature? And if it
were true that she had been captured only recently how
would she have managed to live in the caverns for those
days? Perhaps she might have found a sump of water but
what would there have been to eat, I wondered? Perhaps, I
told myself, she, like the Slime Worm, would have been
forced to scavenge on the previous kills of the Beetle but I
found this hard to believe, for the condition of her body did
not suggest an ugly, protracted, degrading battle with the
worms of starvation.

And how was it, I asked myself, that the Golden Beetle had

not already feasted on the delicate flesh of the proud beauty of Treve?

And I wondered on the five strange protuberances that nested so grotesquely in her lovely body.

And Misk had said to me he thought I would be too late for it was near hatching time.

A cry of horror from the bottom of my heart broke from my lips in that dark passage and I turned and raced madly back down the path I had come.

Time and time again I stumbled against outcroppings of rock and bruised my shoulders and thighs but never once did I diminish my speed in my headlong race back to the cavern of the Golden Beetle. I found I did not even have to stop and search for the small signs I had scratched in the walls of the passages to guide my way for as I ran it seemed I knew each bend and turn of that passageway as though it had suddenly leaped alive flaming in my memory.

I burst into the cavern of the Golden Beetle and held the torch high.

"Forgive me, Vika of Treve!" I cried. "Forgive me!"

I fell to my knees beside her and thrust the Mul-Torch into a space between two stones in the floor.

From her flesh at one point I could see the gleaming eyes of a small organism, golden and about the size of a child's turtle, scrambling, trying to pull itself from the leathery shell. With my sword I dug out the egg and crushed it and its occupant with the heel of my sandal on the stone floor.

Carefully, methodically, I removed a second egg. I held it to my ear. Inside it I could hear a persistent, ugly scratching, sense the movement of a tiny, energetic organism. I broke this egg too, stamping it with my heel, not stopping until what squirmed inside was dead.

The next three eggs I disposed of similarly.

I then took my sword and wiped the oil from one side of the blade and set the shining steel against the lips of the girl from Treve. When I removed it I cried out with pleasure for a bit of moisture had formed on the blade.

I gathered her in my arms and held her against me.

"My girl of Treve," I said. "You live."

24
The Golden Beetle

AT THAT INSTANT I HEARD a slight noise and looked up to see peering at me from the darkness of one of the tunnels leading from the cavern, two flaming, luminous eyes.

The Golden Beetle was not nearly as tall as a Priest-King, but it was probably considerably heavier. It was about the size of a rhinoceros and the first thing I noticed after the glowing eyes were two multiply hooked, tubular, hollow, pincerlike extensions that met at the tips perhaps a yard beyond its body. They seemed clearly some aberrant mutation of its jaws. Its antennae, unlike those of Priest-Kings, were very short. They curved and were tipped with a fluff of golden hair. Most strangely perhaps were several long, golden strands, almost a mane, which extended from the creature's head over its domed, golden back and fell almost to the floor behind it. The back itself seemed divided into two thick casings which might once, ages before, have been horny wings, but now the tissues had, at the points of touching together, fused in such a way as to form what was for all practical purposes a thick, immobile golden shell. The creature's head was even now withdrawn beneath the shell but its eyes were clearly visible and of course the extensions of its jaws.

I knew the thing before me could slay Priest-Kings.

Most I feared for the safety of Vika of Treve.

I stood before her body my sword drawn.

The creature seemed to be puzzled and made no move to attack. Undoubtedly in its long life it had never encountered anything like this in its tunnels. It backed up a bit and withdrew its head further beneath the shell of its fused, golden wings. It lifted its hooked, tubular jaws before its eyes as though to shield them from the light.

It occurred to me then that the light of the Mul-Torch burning in the invariably dark tunnels of its domain may have temporarily blinded or disoriented the creature. More likely the smell of the torch's oxidation products suddenly

permeating its delicate antennae would have been as caco-
phonous to it as some protracted, discordant bedlam of
noises might have been to us.

It seemed clear the creature did not yet understand what
had taken place within its cavern.

I seized the Mul-Torch from between the stones where I
had placed it and, with a great shout, thrust it towards the
creature's face.

I would have expected it to retreat with rapidity, but it
made no move whatsoever other than to lift its tubular,
pincerlike jaws to me.

It seemed to me most unnatural, as though the creature
might have been a living rock, or a blind, carnivorous growth.

One thing was clear. The creature did not fear me nor the
flame.

I withdrew a step and it, on its six short legs, moved
forward a step.

It seemed to me that it would be very difficult to injure the
Golden Beetle, particularly when its head was withdrawn
beneath the shell of its enclosing wings. This withdrawal on
its part, of course, would not in the least prevent it from
using its great jaws to attack, but it would, I supposed,
somewhat narrow the area of its sensory awareness. It would
most certainly limit its vision but I did not suppose that the
Golden Beetle, any more than a Priest-King, much depended
on this sense. Both would be quite at home, incomprehensibly
to a visually oriented organism, in utter darkness. On the
other hand I could hope that somehow the sensory field of
the antennae might be similarly, at least partially, restricted
by their withdrawal beneath the casing of the fused, horny
wings.

I slipped my sword into its sheath and knelt beside Vika's
body, not taking my eyes off the creature who stood about
four yards distant.

By feeling I closed the lids of her eyes in order that they
might no longer stare blindly out with that look of frozen
horror.

Her body was stiff yet from the venom which had induced
the paralysis, but now, perhaps because of the removal of the

five eggs, it seemed somewhat warmer and more yielding than before.

As I touched the girl the Beetle took another step forward. It began to hiss.

This noise unnerved me for a moment because I had been used to the uncanny silence of Priest-Kings.

Now the Beetle began to poke its head out from beneath the shelter of those domed, golden wings and its short antennae, tufted with golden fluff, thrust out and began to explore the chamber.

With my right hand I lifted Vika to my shoulder and stood up.

The hissing now became more intense.

Apparently the creature did not wish me to remove Vika from the cavern.

Walking backwards, Vika on my shoulder, the Mul-Torch in my hand, I slowly retreated from the cavern of the Golden Beetle.

When the creature, following me, crawled over the pile of soiled moss and stems on which Vika had lain, it stopped and began to poke about among the shattered remains of the eggs I had crushed.

I had no notion of the speed of the creature but at this point I turned and began to jog away down the passage, back toward the entrance to the tunnels of the Golden Beetle. I hoped, considering the size and shape and probable weight of the creature, and the comparative tininess of its legs, that it would not be able to move quickly, at least not for a sustained period.

About an Ehn after I had turned and begun to move away from the cavern, Vika on my shoulder, I heard from the cavern one of the strangest and most horrifying sounds I had ever heard in my life, a long, weird, frantic, enraged rush of sound, more than a rush of air, more than a wild hiss, almost a cry of pain, of comprehension and agony.

I stopped for a moment and listened.

Now, scrambling after me in the tunnel, I could hear the approach of the Golden Beetle.

I turned and jogged on.

After a few Ehn I stopped again and once more listened.

Apparently my conjecture as to the mobility of the Golden Beetle had been correct and the speed of its pursuit had quickly slackened. Yet I knew that somewhere back there it would still be coming, that it would not yield its vengeance and its prey so easily. It was still coming, somewhere back there in the darkness, slowly, patiently, implacably, like the coming of winter or the weathering of a stone.

I wondered at the nature of the Beetle's pursuit of his prey.

How horrible I thought it would be to be trapped in these tunnels, waiting for the Beetle, able to avoid it perhaps for hours, perhaps days, but not daring to sleep or to stop, not knowing if one were going down a blind passage, if the Beetle were suddenly to confront one at the next turn.

No, I supposed the Beetle did not need speed in its tunnels.

I set Vika down.

I leaned the Mul-Torch against the side of the passage.

And yet it seemed strange to me to think of the Beetle as pursuing its prey in these tunnels for hours, perhaps days. It seemed foolish, unlikely, a puzzle of nature. But I myself had seen its body and knew now that it was incapable of prolonged, rapid movement. How was it then, I asked myself, that such a slow, awkward, clumsy creature, no matter how formidable at close range, could capture and slay an organism as alert and swift as a Priest-King?

I moved Vika's limbs and rubbed her hands to see if I could restore her circulation to a more normal level.

Bending my ear to her heart I was pleased to detect its faint beat. Holding her wrist I sensed a tiny movement of blood in her veins.

There did not seem to be much air in the tunnels of the Golden Beetle.

I supposed they were not ventilated as well as the tunnels of the Priest-Kings. There was an odor in the tunnels of the Golden Beetle, perhaps of its spoor or various exudates. The odor seemed somewhat oppressive. I had not noticed it much before. Now I became aware of how long I had been in its tunnels, how long without food and how tired I was. Surely there would be time to sleep. The Beetle was far behind.

Surely there would be time, if not to sleep, to close my eyes for a moment.

I awoke with a start.

The odor was now insufferable and close.

The Mul-Torch was little more now than a glowing stub.

I saw the peering eyes.

The golden strands on its back were lifted and quivering, and it was from them that the odor came.

I cried out as I felt two long, hard, curved objects close on my body.

25
The Vivarium

MY HANDS SEIZED THE NARROW, hollow, pincerlike jaws of the Golden Beetle and tried to force them from my body, but those relentless, hollow, chitinous hooks closed ever more tightly. They had now entered my skin and to my horror I felt a pull against my tissues and knew that the creature was now sucking through those foul tubes, but I was a man, a mammal, and not a Priest-King, and my body fluids were locked within the circulatory system of another form of being, and I thrust against the vicious hooked tubes that were the jaws of the Golden Beetle, and they budged out an inch and the creature began to hiss and the pressure of the jaws became even more cruel, but I managed to thrust them out of my skin and inch by inch I separated them until I held them at last almost at my arms' length and then I thrust yet more, forcing them yet further apart, slowly, as implacably as the Beetle itself, and then at my arms' length with a sickening, snapping sound they broke from its face and fell to the stone floor of the passage.

The hissing stopped.

The Beetle wavered, its entire shell of golden, fused wings trembling, and it seemed as if those fused wings shook as though to separate and fly but they could not, and it pulled its head back under the shelter of the wings. It began to back away from me on its six short legs. I leaped forward and thrust my hand under the wing shell and seized the short, tufted antennae and with one hand on them twisting and the other beneath the shell I slowly managed, lifting and twisting, to force the struggling creature onto its back and when it lay on its back, rocking, its short legs writhing impotently, I drew my sword and plunged it a dozen times into its vulnerable, exposed belly, and at last the thing stopped squirming and lay still.

I shuddered.

The odor of the golden hairs still lingered in the passages and, fearing I might once again succumb to whatever drug they released into the air, I determined to make my departure.

The Mul-Torch began to sputter.

I did not wish to resheath my sword for it was coated with the body fluids of the Golden Beetle.

I wondered how many more such creatures might dwell in similar passages and caverns near the tunnels of the Priest-Kings.

The plastic tunic I wore did not provide an absorbent surface with which to clean the blade.

I thought for a moment I might clean it on the golden strands of the Beetle's strange mane but I discovered these were wet with foul, glutinous exudate, the source of that unpleasant, narcotic odor which still permeated the passage-way.

My eyes fell on Vika of Treve.

She had not yet made her contribution to the business of the day.

So I tore a handful of cloth from her garment and on this I wiped my hands and the blade.

I wondered how proud Vika would have responded to that.

I smiled to myself for I could always tell her, and truthfully, that having saved her life she was now mine by Gorean law, so brief had been her freedom, and that it was up to me to determine the extent and nature of her clothing, and indeed, whether or not she would be allowed clothing at all.

Well could I imagine her fury upon the receipt of this announcement, a fury not diminished in the least by the knowledge that the words I spoke were simply and prosaically true.

But now it was important to get her from the tunnels, to find her a place of refuge and safety where I hoped she might recover from the venom of the Golden Beetle.

I worried, for where could I find such a place?

By now it might be well known to Sarm that I had refused to slay Misk and the Nest would no longer be safe for me, or for anyone associated with me.

For whether I wished it or not my action had placed me in the party of Misk.

As I prepared to resheath the sword I heard a slight noise in the passage and, in the light of the dying Mul-Torch, without moving, I waited.

What approached was not another Golden Beetle, though I supposed there might have been several in those tunnels, but another inhabitant of those dismal passages, the whitish, long, slow, blind Slime Worm.

Its tiny mouth on the underside of its body touched the stone flooring here and there like the poking finger of a blind man and the long, whitish, rubbery body gathered itself and pushed forward and gathered itself and pushed forward again until it lay but a yard from my sandal, almost under the shell of the slain Beetle.

The Slime Worm lifted the forward portion of its long, tubular body and the tiny red mouth on its underside seemed to peer up at me.

"No," I said, "the Golden Beetle has not made a kill in this place."

The tiny red mouth seemed to continue to peer at me for perhaps a moment or two more and then it slowly turned away from me to the carcass of the Golden Beetle.

I shook myself and resheathed my sword.

I had been long enough in this place.

I lifted the girl Vika of Treve in my arms. I could feel the tremble of life in her body and the touch of her breath on my cheek made me happy.

The Mul-Torch suddenly sputtered out leaving us in darkness.

Gently I kissed her cheek.

I was happy. We were both alive.

I turned and with the girl in my arms began to trace my way slowly down the passage.

Behind me in the darkness I could hear the feeding of the Slime Worm.

Although it was slow work I had little difficulty in finding my way back to where I had entered the tunnels of the Golden Beetle.

When I had entered I had immediately marked my passage with small arrows scratched by the hilt of my sword at eye level on the left side of the passages. Now, by touch, I was able to retrace my journey. I had made the marks because, unlike others who had entered the tunnels, I fully intended to return.

When I came to the portal where I had entered I found it closed as I had known it would be and there was, as I knew, no handle or obvious device for opening the door on this side, for no one returned, supposedly, from the tunnels of the Golden Beetle. The portals were opened occasionally to allow the Beetle its run of the Nest but I had no idea when this might occur again.

Although the portal was thick I supposed that I might have been heard on the outside if I had pounded on it with the hilt of my sword.

On the other hand I had been informed, graciously, by the Muls who manned the portal that it might not be opened by them to release me once I had decided to enter. As they put it, they simply were not permitted to do so. It was the law of Priest-Kings. I was not certain whether, as a matter of fact, they would open the door or not, but I thought it best that both of them could honestly report that they had seen me enter the tunnels and had not seen me return.

It had been Sarm's intention apparently that I should enter the tunnels of the Golden Beetle and die there and so I thought it expedient to allow him to believe I had done so.

I knew the tunnels of the Golden Beetle, like those of the Nest itself, were ventilated and I hoped to be able to use one of the shafts to leave the tunnels undetected. If this were not possible I would explore the tunnels seeking some other exit, and if worse came to worst, I was sure that Vika and I, now that I knew the dangers and strengths and weaknesses of the Golden Beetle, might manage to survive indefinitely in the tunnels, however despicably, and escape eventually when the portal was opened to release yet another of the Priest-Kings' golden assassins.

In the vicinity of the portal itself I remembered, when I had had the Mul-Torch, seeing a ventilation shaft some twenty or thirty yards inside the passage and fixed in the ceiling of the passage some nine feet from the floor. A metal grille had been bolted over the shaft but it was fairly light and I did not expect much difficulty in wrenching it loose.

The problem would be Vika.

I could now feel a bit of fresh air and, in the darkness, Vika in my arms, I walked until I could feel it best, and it seemed to be blowing directly down upon me. I then set Vika to one side and prepared to leap up to seize the grille.

A shattering flash of energy seemed to explode in my face and burn through my body as my fingers touched the metal grille.

Shivering and numb and disoriented I crumpled to the floor beneath it.

In the flash of light I had seen the mesh clearly and the shaft beyond and the rings set in the shaft used by Muls who upon occasion clean the shafts and spray them with bactericides.

My limbs shaking, clouds of yellow and red fire moving in tangled afterimages across my field of vision in the darkness, I struggled to my feet.

I walked a bit up and down in the shaft rubbing my arms and shaking my head until I felt ready to try again.

This time, with luck, I could hook my fingers in the grille and hang on.

I leaped again and this time managed to fasten my fingers in the grille and cried out in pain turning my face away from the heat and fire that seemed to transform its surface erupting over my head with torturing, savage incandescence. Then I could no longer release the grille had I wanted to and I hung there agonized, a prisoner of the charges flashing through my body and the bolts wrenched loose from the ceiling, and I fell again to the floor, the grille clattering beside me, my fingers still hooked in its mesh.

I pulled my hands free and crawled in the darkness to one side of the passage and lay down against the wall. My body ached and trembled and I could not control the involuntary movements of its muscles. I shut my eyes but to no avail against the burning universes that seemed to float and explode before my eyes.

I do not know if I lost consciousness or not but I suppose I may have for the next thing I remember was that the pain had gone from my body and that I lay against the wall weak and sick. I crawled to my knees and threw up in the passage. I stood up then unsteadily and walked beneath the shaft and stood there with my head back drawing in the welcome fresh air that blew down towards me.

I shook myself and moved my limbs.

Then, gathering my strength, I leaped up and easily seized one of the rings inside the chamber shaft, held it for a moment and then released it and dropped back to the floor.

I went to Vika's side.

I could hear the clear beat of her heart, and the pulse was now strong. Perhaps the fresh air in the vicinity of the shaft was doing its part in reviving her.

I shook her. "Wake up," I said. "Wake up!" I shook her again, harder, but she could not regain consciousness. I carried her beneath the shaft and tried to hold her upright, but her legs crumpled.

Strangely I sensed that somehow within her she was vaguely conscious of what was occurring.

I lifted her to her feet again and slapped her face four times, savagely, sharply. "Wake up!" I cried, but though her head jerked from side to side and my hand felt afire she did not regain consciousness.

I kissed her and lowered her gently to the floor.

I had no wish to remain indefinitely in the passage, nor could I bring myself to abandon the girl.

There seemed to be but one thing to do.

I took off my sword belt and, rebuckling it, made a loop which I managed to hook over the closest ring in the shaft. I then removed the thongs from my sandals. With one thong I

tied them together about my neck. With the other thong I
bound Vika's wrists securely together before her body and
placed her arms about my neck and left shoulder. Thus
carrying her I climbed the sword belt and soon had attained
the first ring. Once in the shaft I rebuckled the belt about my
waist and, still carrying Vika as before, began to climb.

After perhaps two hundred feet of climbing the rings in
the shaft I was pleased to reach two branching shafts which
led horizontally from the vertical shaft which I had just
ascended.

I removed Vika's arms from my neck and shoulder and
carried her in my arms down the shaft which led, to the best
of my reckoning, in the general direction of the major
complexes of the Nest.

A slight moan escaped the girl and her lips moved.

She was regaining consciousness.

For perhaps an Ahn I carried her through the network of
ventilation shafts, sometimes walking on the level, sometimes
climbing. Occasionally we would pass an opening in the shaft
where, through a grille, I could see portions of the Nest. The
light entering at these openings was very welcome to me.

At last we came to an opening which gave onto something
of the sort for which I was looking, a rather small complex
of buildings, where I saw several Muls at work but no
Priest-Kings.

I also noted, against the far wall of the brilliantly lit area,
tiers and tiers of plastic cases, much like the one I had
occupied in Misk's compartment. Some of these cases were
occupied by Muls, male or female, sometimes both. Unlike
the case in Misk's compartment and others I had seen, these
were apparently locked.

Fungus, water and pellets, and whatever else was needed,
were apparently administered to the occupants of these cases
from the outside by the Muls who attended them.

I was reminded a bit of a zoo with its cages. Indeed, as I
spied through the grille I saw that not all of the cases were
occupied by humans but some by a variety of other organisms, some of the types with which I was familiar in the Nest
but others not, and some of the others were, as far as I could
tell, even mammals.

There was, I could see, a pair of sleen in one case, and two larls in another pair of cases, with a sliding partition between them. I saw one humanoid creature, small with a receding forehead and excessively hairy face and body, bounding about in one case, racing along and leaping with his feet against the wall and then with the momentum established dashing along the next wall of the case and then dropping to the floor to repeat again this peculiar circuit.

In a vast low case, on the floor of which apparently grew real grass, I saw a pair of shaggy, long-horned bosk grazing, and in the same case but in a different corner was a small herd, no more than five adult animals, a proud male and four does, of tabuk, the single-horned, golden Gorean antelope. When one of the does moved I saw that moving beside her with dainty steps were two young tabuk, the first I had ever seen, for the young of the tabuk seldom venture far from the shaded, leafy bowers of their birth in the tangled Ka-la-na thickets of Gor. Their single horns were little more than velvety stubs on their foreheads and I saw that their hide, unlike that of the adults, was a mottled yellow and brown. When one of the attendant Muls happened to pass near the case the two little tabuk immediately froze, becoming almost invisible, and the mother, her bright golden pelt gleaming, began to prance away from them, while the angry male lowered his head against the Mul and trotted in a threatening manner to the plastic barrier.

There were several other creatures in the cases but I am not sure of their classification. I could, however, recognize a row of brown varts, clinging upside down like large matted fists of teeth and fur and leather on the heavy, bare, scarred branch in their case. I saw bones, perhaps human bones, in the bottom of their case.

There was a huge, apparently flightless bird stalking about in another case. From its beak I judged it to be carnivorous.

In another case, somnolent and swollen, I saw a rare golden hith, a Gorean python whose body, even when unfed, it would be difficult for a full-grown man to encircle with his arms.

In none of the cases did I spy a tarn, one of the great, predatory saddle birds of Gor, perhaps because they do not thrive well in captivity. To live a tarn must fly, high, far and often. A Gorean saying has it that they are brothers of the wind, and how could one expect such a creature to survive confinement? Like its brother the wind when the tarn is not free it has no choice but to die.

As I gazed on this strange assemblage of creatures in the tiered cases it seemed clear to me that I must be gazing upon one of the vivaria of which I had heard Sarm speak.

Such a complex might ideally serve my purpose of the moment.

I heard a groan from Vika and I turned to face her.

She lay on her side against the wall of the shaft, some seven or eight feet back from the grille.

The light pouring through the grille formed a reticulated pattern of shadows on her body.

I stood to one side, back a bit from the grille so as not to be observed from the outside, and watched her.

Her wrists of course were still bound.

She was very beautiful and the brief rags that were all that remained of her once long and lovely garment left little of her beauty to conjecture.

She struggled to her hands and knees, her head hanging down, her hair falling over her head to the floor of the shaft. Slowly she lifted her head and shook it, a small beautiful movement that threw her hair back from her face. Her eyes fell on me and opened wide in disbelief. Her lips trembled but no word escaped them.

"Is it the custom of the proud women of Treve," I asked, "to appear so scantily clad before men?"

She looked down at the brief rags she wore, insufficient even for a slave girl, and at her bound wrists.

She looked up and her eyes were wide and her words were scarcely a whisper. "You brought me," she said, "from the tunnels of the Golden Beetle."

"Yes," I said.

Now that Vika was recovering I suddenly became aware of the difficulties that might ensue. The last time I had seen this woman conscious had been in the chamber where she had tried with the snares of her beauty to capture and conquer me for my archenemy, Sarm the Priest-King. I knew that she was faithless, vicious, treacherous and because of her glorious beauty a thousand times more dangerous than a foe armed only with the reed of a Gorean spear and the innocence of sword steel.

As she gazed upon me her eyes held a strange light which I did not understand.

Her lips trembled. "I am pleased to see you live," she whispered.

"And I," I said sternly, "am pleased to see that you live."

She smiled ruefully.

"You have risked a great deal," she said, "to thong the wrists of a girl."

She lifted her bound wrists.

"Your vengeance must be very precious to you," she said.

I said nothing.

"I see," she said, "that even though I was once a proud woman of the high city of Treve you have not honored me with binding fiber but have bound my limbs only with the thong of your sandal, as though I might be the lowest tavern slave in Ar—carried off on a wager, a whim or caprice."

"Are you, Vika of Treve," I asked, "higher than she of whom you speak, the lowest tavern slave in Ar?"

Her answer astounded me. She lowered her head. "No," she said, "I am not.

"Is it your intention to slay me?" she asked.

I laughed.

"I see," she said.

"I have saved your life," I said.

"I will be obedient," she said.

I extended my hands to her and her eyes met mine, blue and beautiful and calm, and she lifted her bound wrists and placed them in my hands and kneeling before me lowered her head between her arms and said softly, very clearly, "I the girl Vika of Treve submit myself—completely—to the man Tarl Cabot of Ko-ro-ba."

She looked up at me.

"Now, Tarl Cabot," she said, "I am your slave girl and I must do whatever you wish."

I smiled at her. If I had had a collar I would then have locked it on her beautiful throat.

"I have no collar," I said.

To my amazement her eyes as they looked up into mine were tender, moist, submissive, yielding. "Nonetheless, Tarl Cabot," she said, "I wear your collar."

"I do not understand," I said.

She dropped her head.

"Speak, Slave Girl," I said.

She had no choice but to obey.

The words were spoken very softly, very slowly, haltingly, painfully, and it must have cost the proud girl of Treve much to speak them. "I have dreamed," she said, "since first I met you, Tarl Cabot, of wearing—your collar and your chains. I have dreamed since first I met you of sleeping beneath the slave ring—chained at the foot of your couch."

It seemed to me incomprehensible what she had said.

"I do not understand," I said.

She shook her head sadly. "It means nothing," she said.

My hand fixed itself in her hair and gently turned her face up to mine.

"—Master?" she asked.

My stern gaze demanded an answer.

She smiled, my hand in her hair. Her eyes were moist. "It means only," she said, "that I am your slave girl—forever."

I released her head and she dropped it again.

To my surprise I saw her lips gently kiss the cruel leather thong which so tightly bound her wrists.

She looked up. "It means, Tarl Cabot," she said, her eyes wet with tears, "that I love you."

I untied her wrists and kissed her.

26
The Safekeeping of Vika of Treve

IT WAS HARD TO BELIEVE that the gentle, obedient girl who nestled in my arms, who had so leaped and sobbed with pleasure, was the proud Vika of Treve.

I still had not determined to my satisfaction that she might be fully trusted, much to her distress, and I would take no chances with her for I knew who she was, the bandit princess of the lofty plundering Treve of the Voltai Range. No, I would take no chances with this girl, whom I knew to be as treacherous and vicious as the nocturnal, sinuous, predatory sleen.

"Cabot," she begged, "what must I do that you will trust me?"

"I know you," I said.

"No, dear Cabot," she said, "you do not know me." She shook her head sadly.

I began to move the grille at one corner to allow us to drop to the floor beneath in the vivarium chamber. Fortunately this grille was not charged, and I had not supposed it would be.

"I love you," she said, touching my shoulder.

I pushed her back roughly.

It seemed to me I now understood her treacherous plan and something of the same bitterness with which I had earlier regarded this woman tended to fill my breast.

"But I do," she said.

I turned and regarded her coldly. "You play your role well," I said, "and nearly was I fooled, Vika of Treve."

"I don't understand," she stammered.

I was irritated. How convincing she had been in her role of the enamoured slave girl, hopelessly, desperately mine, undoubtedly waiting her chance to betray me.

"Be silent, Slave," I told her.

She blushed with shame and hung her head, her hands before her face, and sank to her knees weeping softly, her body shaken with sobs.

For a moment I almost yielded, but I steeled myself against her trickery and continued my work.

She would be treated with the coldness and harshness which she deserved as what she was, a beautiful and treacherous slave girl.

At last I moved the corner of the large grille sufficiently to allow me to slip through to the floor beneath and then Vika followed me and I helped her to the floor.

The grille snapped back into place.

I was rather pleased with the discovery of the network of ventilator shafts for it suggested to me almost a private and extensive highway to any place in the Nest I might wish to reach.

Vika was still crying a bit, but I took her hair and wiped her face and told her to stop her noise. She bit her lip and choked back a sob and stopped crying, though her eyes still brimmed with tears.

I regarded her garment which, however soiled and torn, was still recognizably that of a Chamber Slave.

It would never do. It would be a clue to her identity. It would surely provoke curiosity, perhaps suspicion.

My plan was a bold one.

I looked at Vika sternly. "You must do whatever I say," I said, "and quickly, and without question."

She hung her head. "I will be obedient," she said softly, "—Master."

"You will be a girl brought from the surface," I said, "for you are still unshaved, and you are to be delivered to the vivarium on the orders of Sarm, the Priest-King."

"I do not understand," she said.

"But you will obey," I said.

"Yes," she said.

"I will be your keeper," I said, "and I am bringing you as a new female Mul to the breeding cases."

"A Mul?" she asked. "Breeding cases?"

"Remove your clothing," I commanded, "and place your hands behind your back."

Vika looked at me with surprise.

"Quickly!" I said.

She did as I commanded and I thonged her wrists behind her back.

I then took the handful of rags she had worn and discarded them in a nearby waste container, a convenience with which the Nest was, to my mind, excessively provided.

In a few moments, putting on something of an air of authority, I presented Vika to the Chief Attendant of the Vivarium.

He looked at her unshaved head and long, beautiful hair with disgust. "How ugly she is," he said.

I gathered he had been bred in the Nest and therein had formed his concepts of female beauty.

Vika, I was pleased to note, was considerably shaken by his appraisal, and I supposed it was the first time a man had ever looked upon her with disfavor.

"Surely there is some mistake?" asked the Attendant.

"None," I said. "Here is a new female Mul from the surface. On the orders of Sarm shave her and clothe her suitably and place her in a breeding case, alone and locked. You will receive further orders later."

It was a most miserable and bewildered Vika of Treve whom I bundled into a small but comfortable plastic case on the fourth tier of the Vivarium. She wore the brief tunic of purple plastic allotted to female Muls in the nest and save for her eyelashes her hair had been completely removed.

She saw her reflection in the side of her plastic case and screamed, throwing her hands before her face.

Actually she was not unattractive and she had a well-shaped head.

It must have been a great shock for Vika to see herself as she now was.

She moaned and leaned against the side of the case, her eyes closed.

I took her briefly in my arms.

This seemed to surprise her.

She looked up at me. "What have you done to me?" she whispered.

I felt that I might tell her that what I had done was perhaps to save her life, at least for a time, but I did not say this to her. Rather I looked rather sternly down into her eyes and said simply, "What I wished."

"Of course," she said, looking away bitterly, "for I am only a slave girl."

But then she looked up at me and there was no bitterness in her eyes, no reproach, only a question. "But how can I please my Master," she asked, "—like this?"

"It pleases me," I said.

She stepped back. "Ah yes," she said, "I forgot—your vengeance." She looked at me. "Earlier," she said, "I thought—" but she did not finish her sentence and her eyes clouded briefly with tears. "My Master is clever," she said, straightening herself proudly. "He well knows how to punish a treacherous slave."

She turned away.

I heard her voice from over her shoulder and I could see her reflection in the side of the plastic case before which she stood. "Am I now to be abandoned?" she asked. "Or are you not yet done with me?"

I would have responded, in spite of my better judgment, to reassure her of my intentions to free her as soon as practicable, and to tell her that I believed her greatest chance of safety lay in the anonymity of a specimen in the Vivarium, but it would have been foolish to inform her, treacherous as she was, of my plans, and fortunately there was no opportunity to do so because the Chief Attendant at that moment approached the case and handed me a leather loop on which dangled the key to Vika's case.

"I will keep her well fed and watered," said the Attendant.

At these words Vika suddenly turned to face me, desperately, her back against the plastic side of the case, the palms of her hands against it.

"I beg of you, Cabot," she said, "please do not leave me here."

"It is here you will stay," I said.

In my hand she saw the key to her case.

She shook her head slowly, numbly. "No, Cabot," she said, "—please."

I had made my decision and I was now in no mood to debate the matter with the slave girl, so I did not respond.

"Cabot," she said, "—what if my request were on the lips of a woman of High Caste and of one of the high cities of all Gor—could you refuse it then?"

"I don't understand," I said.

She looked about herself at the plastic walls, and shivered. Her eyes met mine. I could see that not only did she not wish to stay in this place but that she was terrified to do so.

Suddenly she fell on her knees, her eyes filled with tears, and extended her hands to me. "Look, Warrior of Ko-ro-ba," she said, "a woman of High Caste of the lofty city of Treve kneels before you and begs of you that you will not leave her here."

"I see at my feet," I said, "only a slave girl." And I added, "And it is here that she will stay."

"No, no," said Vika.

Her eyes were fixed on the key that dangled from the leather loop in my hand.

"Please—" she said.

"I have made my decision," I said.

Vika fell to her hands and slumped to the floor moaning, unable to stand.

"She is actually quite beautiful," said the Attendant, appraisingly.

Vika looked up at him dully as though she could not comprehend what he had said.

"Yes," I said, "she is quite beautiful."

"It is amazing how proper clothing and a removal of the threadlike growths improve a female Mul," observed the Attendant.

"Yes," I agreed, "it is truly amazing."

Vika lowered her head to the floor again and moaned.

"Is there another key?" I asked the Attendant.

"No," he said.

"What if I should lose this?" I asked.

"The plastic of the case," said the Attendant, "is cage plastic and the lock is a cage lock, so it would be better not to lose it."

"But if I should?" I asked.

"In time I think we could cut through with heat torches," said the Attendant.

"I see," I said. "Has it ever been done?" I asked.

"Once," said the Attendant, "and it took several months but there is no danger because we feed and water them from the outside."

"Very well," I said.

"Besides," said the Attendant, "a key is never lost. Nothing in the Nest is ever lost." He laughed. "Not even a Mul."

I smiled, but rather grimly.

Entering the case I checked the containers of fungus.

Vika had now regained her feet and was wiping her eyes with her arm in one corner of the case.

"You can't leave me here, Cabot," she said, quite simply as though very sure of it.

"Why not?" I asked.

She looked at me. "For one thing," she said, "I belong to you."

"I think my property will be safe here," I said.

"You're joking," she said, sniffing.

She watched me lifting the lids of the fungus containers. The materials in the containers seemed fresh and of good sort.

"What is in the containers?" she asked.

"Fungus," I said.

"What for?" she asked.

"You eat it," I said.

"Never," she said. "I'll starve first."

"You will eat it," I said, "when you are hungry enough."

Vika looked at me with horror for a moment and then, to my astonishment, she laughed. She stood back against the rear of the case scarcely able to stand. "Oh Cabot," she cried with relief, reproachfully, "how frightened I was!" She stepped to my side and lifted her eyes to mine and gently placed her hand on my arm. "I understand now," she said, almost weeping with relief, "but you frightened me so."

"What do you mean?" I asked.

She laughed. "Fungus indeed!" she sniffed.

"It's not bad when you get used to it," I said, "but on the other hand it is not really particularly good either."

She shook her head. "Please, Cabot," she said, "your joke has gone far enough." She smiled. "Have pity," she said, "if not on Vika of Treve—on a poor girl who is only your slave."

"I'm not joking," I told her.

She did not believe me.

I checked the tube of Mul-Pellets and the inverted jar of water. "We do not have the luxuries in the Nest that you had in your chamber," I said, "but I think you will manage quite well."

"Cabot," she laughed, "please!"

I turned to the Attendant. "She is to have a double salt ration each evening," I told him.

"Very well," he said.

"You will explain to her the washings?" I asked.

"Of course," he said, "and the exercises."

"Exercises?" I asked.

"Of course," he said, "it is important to exercise in confinement."

"Of course," I admitted.

Vika came up behind me and placed her arms around me. She kissed me on the back of the neck. She laughed softly. "You have had your joke, Cabot," she said, "now let us leave this place for I do not like it."

There was no scarlet moss in the case but there was a straw mat on one side. It was better than the one she had had in her own chamber.

I looked about the case and it seemed that everything, considering the circumstances, was quite comfortable.

I stepped to the door and Vika, holding my arm, smiling and looking up into my eyes, accompanied me.

At the door I stopped and as she made as if to pass through the door my hand on her arm stopped her.

"No," I said, "you remain here."

"You are joking," she said.

"No," I said, "I am not."

"Yes you are!" she laughed, clinging ever more tightly to my arm.

"Release my arm," I said.

"You cannot seriously mean to leave me here," she said, shaking her head. "No," she said, "you can't—you simply can't leave me here, not Vika of Treve." She laughed and looked up at me. "I will simply not permit it," she said.

I looked at her.

The smile fled from her eyes and the laugh died in her lovely throat.

"You will not permit it?" I asked.

My voice was the voice of her Gorean master.

She removed her hand from my arm and stepped back, trembling, her eyes frightened. The color had drained from her face. "I did not think of what I was saying," she said.

Terrified, she, as the expression is, knelt to the whip, assuming the position of the slave girl who is to be punished, her wrists crossed beneath her as though bound and her head touching the floor, leaving the bow of her back exposed.

"I have no wish to punish you," I said.

Bewildered she lifted her head and there were tears in her eyes.

"Beat me if you wish," she begged, "but please—please—take me with you."

"I told you," I said, "my decision has been made."

"But you could change your decision, Master," she said, wheedling, "—for me."

"I do not," I said.

Vika struggled to restrain her tears. I wondered if this were perhaps the first time in her life in a matter of importance to her that she had not had her way with a man.

At a gesture from me she rose timidly to her feet. She wiped her eyes and looked at me. "May your girl ask a question, Master?" she asked.

"Yes," I said.

"Why must I stay here?" she asked.

"Because I do not trust you," I said simply.

She reacted as if struck and tears welled in her eyes. I could not understand why this assertion of mine should have troubled one of Vika's proud and treacherous nature but she seemed somehow more hurt than if I had administered to her when she had knelt the blows of a slave whip or the lashings of my sword belt.

I looked upon her.

She stood, very much alone, in the center of the smooth plastic case, numb, not moving. There were tears in her eyes.

I was forced to remind myself in no uncertain terms of the cleverness of this consummate actress, and how so many men had weakened to her insidious blandishments. Yet I knew that I would not weaken, though I was sorely tempted to believe that she might be trusted, that the feelings she expressed were truly those she felt.

"Is this," I asked, "how you chained men to your slave ring?"

"Oh Cabot," she moaned, "Cabot—"

Saying nothing further I stepped outside.

Vika shook her head slowly and numbly looked about

herself disbelievingly—at the mat, the jar of water, the canisters along the wall.

I reached up to slide the plastic door downward.

This gesture seemed to shake Vika and her entire frame suddenly trembled with all the panic of a beautiful, trapped animal.

"No!" she cried. "Please Master!"

She rushed across the case and into my arms. I held her for a moment and kissed her and her kiss met mine wet and warm, sweet and hot and salty with the tears that had coursed down her cheeks and then I threw her back and she stumbled across the case and fell to her knees against the wall on the opposite side. She turned to face me there, on her hands and knees. She shook her head in denial of what was happening and her eyes filled with tears. She lifted her hands to me. "No, Cabot," she said. "No!"

I slid the plastic door down and clicked it into place.

I turned the key in the lock and heard the firm, heavy snap of the mechanism.

Vika of Treve was my prisoner.

With a cry she leaped to her feet and threw herself against the door, her face suddenly wild with tears, and pounded on it madly with her small fists. "Master! Master!" she cried.

I slung the key on its leather loop around my neck.

"Good-bye, Vika of Treve," I said.

She stopped pounding on the plastic partition and stared out at me, her face stained with tears, her hands pressed against the plastic.

Then to my amazement she smiled and wiped back a tear, and shook her head as though to throw the hair from her eyes and smiled at the foolishness of the gesture.

She looked out at me.

"You are truly leaving," she said.

I could hear her voice through the vent holes in the plastic. It did not sound much different.

"Yes," I said.

"I knew before," she said, "that I was truly your slave but I did not know until now that you were truly my master." She looked up at me through the plastic, shaken. "It is a strange feeling," she said, "to know that someone—truly—is

your master, to know that not only has he the right to do
with you as he pleases but that he will, that your will is
nothing to him, that it is your will and not his that must
bend, that you are helpless and must—and will—do what he
says, that you must obey."

It made me a bit sad to hear Vika recount the woes of
female slavery.

Then to my astonishment she smiled up at me. "It is good
to belong to you, Tarl Cabot," she said. "I love belonging to
you."

"I don't understand," I said.

"I am a woman," she said, "and you are a man, and
stronger than I and I am yours and this you knew and now I
have learned it too."

I was puzzled.

Vika dropped her head. "Every woman in her heart," said
Vika, "wants to wear the chains of a man."

This seemed to me quite doubtful.

Vika looked up and smiled. "Of course," she said, "we
would like to choose the man."

This seemed to me only a bit less doubtful.

"I would choose you, Cabot," she said.

"Women wish to be free," I told her.

"Yes," she said, "we also wish to be free." She smiled. "In
every woman," she said, "there is something of the Free
Companion and something of the Slave Girl."

I wondered at the things she said to me for they seemed
strange, perhaps more so to my ears than they would have to
one bred and raised from infancy as a Gorean, one as much
accustomed to the submission of women as to the tides of the
gleaming Thassa or the phases of the three moons.

As the girl spoke and I tried to lightly dismiss her words I
wondered at the long processes of evolution that had nur-
tured over thousands of generations what had in time become
the human kind. I wondered of the struggles of my own
world as well as on Gor, struggles which over millenia had
shaped the blood and inmost being of my species, perhaps
conflicts over tunnels in cliffs to be fought with the savage
cave bear, long dangerous weeks spent hunting the same
game as the saber-toothed tiger, perhaps years spent protect-

ing one's mate and brood from the depredations of carnivores and the raids of one's fellow creatures.

As I thought of our primeval ancestor standing in the mouth of his cave one hand gripping a chipped stone and perhaps the other a torch, his mate behind him and his young hidden in the mosses at the back of the cave I wondered at the genetic gifts that would insure the survival of man in so hostile a world, and I wondered if among them would not be the strength and the aggressiveness and the swiftness of eye and hand and the courage of the male and on the part of the woman—what?

What would have been the genetic truths in her blood without which she and accordingly man himself might have been overlooked in the vicious war of a species to remain alive and hold its place on an unkind and savage planet?

It seemed possible to me that one trait of high survival value might be the desire on the part of the woman to belong—utterly—to a man.

It seemed clear that woman would, if the race were to survive, have to be sheltered and defended and fed—and forced to reproduce her kind.

If she were too independent she would die in such a world and if she did not mate her race would die.

That she might survive it seemed plausible that evolution would have favored not only the woman attractive to men but the one who had an unusual set of traits—among them perhaps the literally instinctual desire to be his, to belong to him, to seek him out for her mate and submit herself to him. Perhaps if she were thrown by her hair to the back of the cave and raped on furs in the light of the animal fire at its mouth this would have been to her little more than the proof of her mate's regard for her, the expected culmination of her innate desire to be dominated and his.

I smiled to myself as I thought of the small things on my old world that at such remoteness perhaps reenacted the ancient ceremony of the caves, the carrying of the bride over the threshhold, perhaps as a prisoner, the tiny wedding bands, perhaps a small reminder of the primitive thongs that bound the wrists of the first bride, or perhaps later of the golden manacles fastened on the wrists of the daughters of

kings, captive maidens led in triumph through cheering
streets to the bondage of slave girls.

Yes, I said to myself, the words Vika spoke were perhaps
not as strange as I had thought.

I looked at her gently. "I must go," I said.

"When first I saw you, Cabot," she said, "I knew you
owned me." She looked up at me. "I wanted to be free but I
knew that you owned me—though you had not touched me
nor kissed me—I knew that I was from that moment your
slave; your eyes told me that I was owned and my most
secret heart acknowledged it."

I turned to go.

"I love you, Tarl Cabot," she said suddenly, and then, as
though confused and perhaps a bit frightened, she suddenly
dropped her head humbly. "I mean—" she said, "I love
you—Master."

I smiled at Vika's very natural correction of her mode of
addressing me, for a slave girl is seldom permitted, at least
publicly, to address her master by his name, only his title.
The privilege of using his name, of having it on her lips, is,
according to the most approved custom, reserved for that of
a free woman, in particular a Free Companion. Gorean
thinking on this matter tends to be expressed by the saying
that a slave girl grows bold if her lips are allowed to touch
the name of her master. On the other hand, I, like many
Gorean masters, provided the girl was not testing or challenging me, and provided that free women, or others, were not
present whom I had no wish to offend or upset, preferred as
a matter of fact to have my own name on the girl's lips, for I
think, with acknowledged vanity, that there are few sounds as
pleasurable as the sound of one's own name on the lips of a
beautiful woman.

Vika's eyes were worried and her hands moved as though
she wanted to touch me through the plastic.

"May I ask," she queried, "where my master goes?"

I considered the matter and smiled at her.

"I go," I said, "to give Gur to the Mother."

"What does that mean?" she asked, wide-eyed.

"I don't know," I said, "but I intend to find out."

"Must you go?" she asked.

"Yes," I replied, "I have a friend who may be in danger."

"A slave girl is pleased," she said, "that such a man as you is her master."

I turned to go.

I heard her voice over my shoulder. "I wish you well, Master," she said.

I briefly turned to face her again and almost unconsciously I kissed the tips of my fingers and pressed them against the plastic. Vika kissed the plastic opposite where my fingers had touched.

She was a strange girl.

Had I not known how vicious and deceitful she was, how cruel and treacherous, I might have permitted myself a word of kindness to her. I regretted that I had touched the plastic for it seemed to express a concern for her which I had intended to mask.

Her performance had been superb, almost convincing. She had almost led me to believe she cared.

"Yes," I said, "Vika of Treve—Slave Girl—you play your part well."

"No," she said, "no—Master—I love you!"

Angered at how nearly I had been deceived I laughed at her.

Now undoubtedly realizing her game was known she covered her eyes with her hands and sank weeping to her knees behind the heavy transparent plastic partition.

I turned away, having more important things to attend to than the faithless wench from Treve.

"I will keep the female Mul well fed and watered," said the Attendant.

"If you wish," I said, and turned away.

27
In the Chamber of the Mother

It was still the Feast of Tola.

Though the time was now past the fourth feeding.

It was almost eight Gorean Ahn, or about ten Earth

hours, since I had separated from Misk and Mul-Al-Ka and
Mul-Ba-Ta early this morning.

The transportation disk which had originally taken me to
the chamber where I had found Misk I had taken to the
entrance to the tunnels of the Golden Beetle and I thought it
well that it should stay there, as if witnessing my entrance
and my supposed failure to return.

I was less pleased to have left the translator with the disk
but it seemed the better thing to do, for one would not have
taken a translator into the tunnels of the Golden Beetle and
if it were found missing from the disk it might occasion
speculation not that I had returned from the tunnels of the
Golden Beetle but more likely that I had only pretended to
enter. The word of the two Muls by the portal might or
might not carry weight with their Priest-King Masters.

I had not walked far from the Vivarium before I was able
to regather my general directions in the Nest and, as I
walked impatiently along, I spied a transportation disk
docked, so to speak, hovering on its cushion of gas, outside
one of the tall steel portals of the Hall of Commissaries. The
disk was of course, untended, for in the enclosed, regulated
life of the Nest theft, save for an occasional handful of salt,
was unknown.

Therefore I may have been setting something of a
precedent when I leaped on the transportation disk and
stepped to the accelerator strips.

I was soon gliding rapidly down the hall on my, let us say,
considering the significance and urgency of my mission, com-
mandeered vehicle.

I had gone not more than a pasang or so when I spun the
disk to a stop before another portal in the Hall of Commissaries. I entered the portal and in a few moments emerged
wearing the purple of a Mul. The clerk, at my request
writing the expense down to Sarm, informed me that I would
promptly have to have the new tunic imprinted with the
scent-patterns pertaining to my identity, record-scars, etc. I
assured him I would give the matter serious consideration
and departed, hearing him congratulate me on my good
fortune in having been permitted to become a Mul rather

than having to remain a lowly Matok. "You will now be of
the Nest as well as in it," he beamed.

Outside I thrust the red plastic garment I had worn into
the first disposal chute I found whence it would be whisked
away pneumatically to the distant incinerators that burned
somewhere below the Nest.

I then leaped again on the transportation disk and swept
away to Misk's compartment.

There I took a few minutes to replenish my energies from
the containers of Mul-Fungus and I took a long welcome
draught of water from the inverted jar in my case. As I ate
the fungus and sat in the case I considered my future course
of action. I must try to find Misk. Probably to die with him,
or to die in the attempt to avenge him.

My thoughts wandered to Vika in her own case, though
hers, unlike mine, was her prison. I fingered the key to her
case which hung on its leather loop about my throat. I found
myself hoping that she might not be too distressed by her
captivity, and then I scorned myself this weakness and insisted to myself that I welcomed the thought that whatever
miseries she endured would be richly deserved. I dropped the
metal key back inside my tunic. I considered the heavy,
transparent case on the fourth tier of the Vivarium. Yes, the
hours would be long and lonely for the caged, shorn Vika of
Treve.

I wondered what had become of Mul-Al-Ka and Mul-Ba-
Ta. They, like myself, having disobeyed Sarm, were now
outlaws in the Nest. I hoped they might be able to hide and
find or steal enough food to live. I did not give much for
their chances but even a piteous alternative to the dissection
chambers was welcome.

I wondered about the young male Priest-King in the
secret chamber below Misk's compartment. I supposed my
best way of serving Misk might be to abandon him to his
death and try to protect the young male, but these were
matters in which I had little interest. I did not know the
location of the female egg nor could I have tended it had I
known; and, further, that the race of Priest-Kings should
wither and die did not seem the proper business of a human,
particularly considering my hatred for them, and my rejec-

tion of their mode of regulating in so many important respects the lives of men in this world. Had they not destroyed my city? Had they not scattered its people? Had they not destroyed men by Flame Death and brought them, willing or no, to their own world on the Voyages of Acquisition? Had they not implanted their control nets in human beings and spun the hideous mutations of the Gur Carriers off the stock of which I was a specimen? Did they not regard us as a lower order of animal and one suitably placed at the disposal of their lofty excellence? And what of the Muls and the Chamber Slaves and all those of the human kind who were forced to serve them or die? No, I said to myself, it is good for my kind that Priest-Kings should die. But Misk was different, for he was my friend. There was Nest Trust between us and accordingly, as a warrior and a man, I stood ready to give my life for him.

I checked the sword in its sheath and left Misk's compartment, stepped to the transportation disk and swept silently, rapidly, down the tunnel in the direction in which I knew lay the Chamber of the Mother.

I had spent but a few Ehn on the disk before I came to the barricade of heavy steel bars which separated those portions of the Nest open to Muls from those which were prohibited to them.

There was a Priest-King on guard whose antennae waved quizzically about as I drew the disk to a stop not twelve feet from him. His head was garlanded by a wreath of green leaves as had been that of Sarm, and also, like Sarm, there was about his neck, as well as his translator, the ceremonial string of tiny metal tools.

It took a moment for me to understand the Priest-King's consternation.

The tunic I wore carried no scent-patterns and for a moment he had thought that the transportation disk I rode was actually without a driver.

I could see the lenses of the compound eyes almost flickering as it strained to see, much as we might have strained to hear some small sound.

His reactions were almost those that a human might have

had if he could hear something in the room with him but had not yet been able to see it.

At last his antennae fastened on me but I am sure the Priest-King was annoyed that he did not receive the strong signals he would have if I had been wearing my own scent-infixed tunic. Without the tunic I had worn I probably did not seem much different to him from any other male Mul he had encountered in the Nest. To another human, of course, my hair alone, which is a shaggy, bright red, would have been a clearly recognizable feature, but Priest-Kings, as I may have indicated, tend to have extremely casual visual discrimination and are, moreover, I would gather, color blind. The colors that are found in the Nest are always in the areas frequented by Muls. The only Priest-King in the Nest who could have recognized me immediately, and perhaps from a distance, was probably Misk, who knew me not as a Mul but a friend.

"You are undoubtedly the Noble Guard of the Chamber where I may have my tunic fixed with scent-marks," I called jovially.

The Priest-King seemed relieved to hear me speak.

"No," he said, "I guard the entrance to the tunnels of the Mother, and you may not enter."

Well, I said to myself, this is the right place.

"Where can I have my tunic marked?" I inquired.

"Return to whence you came and inquire," said the Priest-King.

"Thank you, Noble One!" I cried and turned the transportation disk almost as if it had a vertical central axis and sped off. I glanced over my shoulder and I could see the Priest-King still straining to sense me.

I quickly turned the disk down a side tunnel and began to hunt for a ventilator shaft.

In perhaps two or three Ehn I found one which appeared to be quite suitable. I drove the disk about a half pasang away and stopped it by an open portal within which I could see busy Muls stirring vats of bubbling plastic with huge wooden paddles.

I quickly retraced my steps to the ventilator shaft, pried open the bottom of the grille, squeezed inside and soon found

myself making my way rapidly through the ventilating system
in the direction of the Chamber of the Mother.

From time to time I would pass an opening in the shaft
and peer out. From one of these openings I could see that I
was already behind the steel barricade with its Priest-King
guard, who was standing as I would have expected, in that
almost vertical, slender, golden fixity that was so characteristic of his kind.

There was no sound to celebrate the Feast of Tola but I
had little difficulty in locating the scene of the celebration for
I soon encountered a shaft, one of those through which used
air is pumped out of the tunnels, which was rich in unusual
and penetrating scents, of a sort which my stay with Misk
had taught me were regarded by Priest-Kings as being of
great beauty.

I followed these scents and soon found myself peering into
an immense chamber. Its ceiling was only perhaps a hundred
feet high but its length and width were considerable and it
was filled with golden Priest-Kings, garlanded in green and
wearing about their necks that shining, jangling circle of tiny,
silverish tools.

There were perhaps a thousand Priest-Kings in the Nest,
and I supposed that this might be almost all the Priest-Kings
in the Nest, save perhaps those that might be essentially
placed at a few minimum posts, such as the guard at the
steel barricade and perhaps some in the Scanning Chamber
or, more likely, the Power Plant.

Much of the business of the Nest, of course, even relatively technical matters, was carried on by trained Muls.

The Priest-Kings stood motionless in great circling, tiered
rows which spread concentrically outward as though from a
stage in an ancient theater. To one side I could see four
Priest-Kings handling the knobs of a large scent-producer,
about the size of a steel room. There were perhaps hundreds
of knobs on each side and one Priest-King on each side with
great skill and apparent rhythm touched one knob after
another in intricate patterns.

I had little doubt but that these Priest-Kings were the most
highly regarded musicians of the Nest, that they should be
chosen to play together on the great Feast of Tola.

The antennae of the thousand Priest-Kings seemed almost motionless so intent were they on the beauties of the music.

Inching forward I saw, on the raised platform at this end of the room, the Mother.

For a moment I could not believe that it was real or alive.

It was undoubtedly of the Priest-King kind, and it now was unwinged, but the most incredible feature was the fantastic extent of the abdomen. Its head was little larger than that of an ordinary Priest-King, or its thorax, but its trunk was conjoined to an abdomen which if swollen with eggs might have been scarcely smaller than a city bus. But now this monstrous abdomen, depleted and wrinkled, no longer possessing whatever tensility it might once have had, lay collapsed behind the creature like a flattened sack of brownly tarnished golden ancient leather.

Even with the abdomen empty her legs could not support its weight and she lay on the dais with her jointed legs folded beside her.

Her coloring was not that of the normal Priest-King but darker, more brownish, and here and there black stains discolored her thorax and abdomen.

Her antennae seemed unalert and lacked resilience. They lay back over her head.

Her eyes seemed dull and brown.

I wondered if she were blind.

It was a most ancient creature on which I gazed, the Mother of the Nest.

It was hard to imagine her, uncounted generations ago, with wings of gold in the open air, in the blue sky of Gor, glistening and turning with her lover borne on the high, glorious, swift winds of this distant, savage world. How golden she would have been.

There was no male, no Father of the Nest, and I supposed the male had died, or had not lived long after her mating. I wondered if, among Priest-Kings, he would have helped her, or if there would have been others from the former Nest, or if she alone would have fallen to earth, to eat the wings that had borne her, and to burrow beneath the mountains to begin the lonely work of the Mother, the creation of the new Nest.

I wondered why there had not been more females.

If Sarm had killed them, how was it that the Mother had not learned of this and had him destroyed?

Or was it her wish that there should be no others?

But if so why was she, if it were true, in league with Misk to perpetuate the race of Priest-Kings?

I looked again through the grille on the shaft. It opened about thirty feet over the floor of the chamber and a bit to one side of the Platform of the Mother. I surmised there might be a similar shaft on the other side of her platform, knowing the symmetry that tends to mark the engineering aesthetics of Priest-Kings.

As the musicians continued to produce their rhapsodic, involute rhythms of aroma on the scent-producer, one Priest-King at a time, one after the other, would slowly stalk forward and approach the Platform of the Mother.

There, from a great golden bowl, about five feet deep and with a diameter of perhaps twenty feet, setting on a heavy tripod, he would take a bit of whitish liquid, undoubtedly Gur, in his mouth.

He took no more than a taste and the bowl, though the Feast of Tola was well advanced, was still almost brimming. He would then approach the Mother very slowly and lower his head to hers. With great gentleness he would then touch her head with his antennae. She would extend her head to him and then with a delicacy hard to imagine in so large a creature he would transfer a tiny drop of the precious fluid from his mouth to hers. He would then back away and return to his place where he would stand as immobile as before.

He had given Gur to the Mother.

I did not know at the time but Gur is a product originally secreted by large, gray, domesticated, hemispheric arthropods which are, in the morning, taken out to pasture where they feed on special Sim plants, extensive, rambling, tangled vine-like plants with huge, rolling leaves raised under square energy lamps fixed in the ceilings of the broad pasture chambers, and at night are returned to their stable cells where they are milked by Muls. The special Gur used on the Feast of Tola is, in the ancient fashion, kept for weeks in the social stomachs of specially chosen Priest-Kings to mellow and reach the exact flavor and consistency desired, which Priest-Kings are then spoken of as retaining Gur.

I watched as one Priest-King and then another approached the Mother and repeated the Gur Ceremony.

I was perhaps the first human who had ever beheld this ceremony.

Considering the number of Priest-Kings and the time it took for each to give Gur to the Mother, I conjectured that the ceremony must have begun hours ago. Indeed, it did not seem incredible to me at all that the giving of Gur might well last an entire day.

I was already familiar with the astounding patience of Priest-Kings and so I was not surprised at the almost total lack of movement in the lines of that golden pattern, formed of Priest-Kings, which radiated out from the Platform of the Mother. But I now understood as I observed the slight, almost enraptured tremor of their antennae responding to the scent-music of the musicians that this was not a simple demonstration of their patience but a time of exaltation for them, of gathering, of bringing the Nest together, of reminding them of their common, remote origins and their long, shared history, of reminding them of their very being and nature, of what they perhaps alone in all the universe were—Priest-Kings.

I looked at the golden rows of Priest-Kings, alert, immobile, their heads wreathed in green leaves, about their necks dangling the tiny, primitive, silverish tools telling of a distant, simpler time before the Scanning Chamber, the Power Plant and the Flame Death.

I could not to my emotional satisfaction conjecture the ancientness of this people on which I gazed, and I could but dimly understand their powers, what they might feel, what they might hope or dream, supposing that so old and wise a people were still akin to the simple dream, the vagrant, insuppressible perhaps, folly of hope.

The Nest, had said Sarm, is eternal.

But on the platform before which these golden creatures stood there lay the Mother, perhaps blind, almost insensate, the large, feeble thing they revered, weak, brownish, withered, the huge worn body at last wrinkled and empty.

You are dying, Priest-Kings, I said to myself.

I strained my eyes to see if I could pick out either Sarm or Misk in those golden rows.

I had watched for perhaps an hour and then it seemed that the ceremony might be over, for some minutes passed and no further Priest-King approached the Mother.

Then almost at the same time I saw Sarm and Misk together.

The rows of the Priest-Kings separated forming an aisle down the middle of the chamber and the Priest-Kings now stood facing this aisle, and down the aisle together came Sarm and Misk.

I gathered that perhaps this was the culmination of the Feast of Tola, the giving of Gur by the greatest of the Priest-Kings, the First Five Born, save that of that number there were only two left, the First Born and the Fifth, Sarm and Misk. As it turned out later I was correct in this surmise and the moment of the ceremony is known as the March of the First Five Born, in which these five march abreast to the Mother and give her Gur in inverse order of their priority.

Misk of course lacked the wreath of green leaves and the chain of tools about his neck.

If Sarm were disturbed at finding Misk, whom he thought to have had killed, at his side, he gave no sign to this effect.

Together, in silence to human ears but to the swelling intensities of scent-music, in stately, stalking procession the two Priest-Kings approached the Mother, and I saw Misk, first, dip his mouth to the great golden bowl on its tripod and then approach her.

As his antennae touched her head her antennae lifted and seemed to tremble and the ancient, brownish creature lifted her head and on her ready tongue from his own mouth Misk, her child, delicately and with supreme gentleness placed a glistening drop of Gur.

He backed away from her.

Now did Sarm, the First Born, approach the Mother and dip his jaws too to the golden bowl and stalk to the Mother and place his antennae gently on her head, and once again the old creature's antennae lifted but this time they seemed to retract.

Sarm placed his jaws to the mouth of the Mother but she did not lift her head to him.

She turned her face away.

The scent-music suddenly stopped and the Priest-Kings seemed to rustle as though an unseen wind had suddenly stirred the leaves of autumn and I heard even the surprised jangling of those tiny metal tools.

Well could I now read the signs of consternation in the rows of Priest-Kings, the startled antennae, the shifting of the supporting appendages, the sudden intense inclination of the head and body, the straining of the antennae toward the Platform of the Mother.

Once again Sarm thrust his jaws at the face of the Mother and once again she moved her head away from him.

She had refused to accept Gur.

Misk stood by, immobile.

Sarm pranced backwards from the Mother. He stood as though stunned. His antennae seemed to move almost randomly. His entire frame, that long, slender golden blade, seemed to shudder.

Trembling, with none of that delicate grace that so typically characterizes the movements of Priest-Kings, he once again tried to approach the Mother. His movements were awkward, uncertain, clumsy, halting.

This time even before he was near her she again turned aside that ancient, brownish, discolored head.

Once again Sarm retreated.

Now there was no movement among the rows of Priest-Kings and they stood in that uncanny frozen stance regarding Sarm.

Slowly Sarm turned toward Misk.

No longer was Sarm trembling or shaken but he had drawn his frame to its full and golden height.

Before the Platform of the Mother, facing Misk, rearing perhaps two feet over him, Sarm stood with what, even for a Priest-King, seemed a most terrible quietude.

For a long moment the antennae of the two Priest-Kings regarded one another and then Sarm's antennae flattened themselves over his head and so, too, did Misk's.

Almost at the same time the bladelike projections on their forelegs snapped into view.

Slowly the Priest-Kings began to circle one another in a ritual more ancient perhaps even than the Feast of Tola, a ritual perhaps older than even the days and objects celebrated by the string of metal tools that hung jangling about the neck of Sarm.

With a speed that I still find hard to comprehend Sarm rushed upon Misk and after a blurring moment I saw them on their posterior supporting appendages locked together rocking slowly back and forth, trying to bring those great golden, laterally chopping jaws into play.

I knew the unusual strength of Priest-Kings and I could well imagine the stresses and pressures that throbbed in the frames of those locked creatures as they rocked back and forth, to one side and another, each pressing and seeking for the advantage that would mean death to the other.

Sarm broke away and began to circle again, and Misk turned slowly, watching him, his antennae still flattened.

I could now hear the sucking in of air through the breathing tubes of both creatures.

Suddenly Sarm charged at Misk and slashed down at him with one of those bladelike projections on his forelegs and leaped away even before I saw the green-filled wound opening on the left side of one of those great, compound luminous disks on Misk's head.

Again Sarm charged and again I saw a long greenish-wet opening appear as if by magic on the side of Misk's huge golden head, and again Sarm, whose speed was almost unbelievable, leaped away before Misk could touch him and was again circling and watching.

Once more Sarm leaped to attack and this time a green-flowing wound sprang into view on the right side of Misk's thorax in the neighborhood of one of the brain-nodes.

I wondered how long it would take to kill a Priest-King.

Misk seemed stunned and slow, his head dropped and the antennae seemed to flutter, exposing themselves.

I noted that already the green exudate which flowed from Misk's wounds was turning into a green, frozen sludge on his body, stanching the flow from the wounds.

The thought crossed my mind that Misk, in spite of his apparently broken and helpless condition, had actually lost very little body fluid.

I told myself that perhaps the stroke in the vicinity of the brain-nodes had been his undoing.

Cautiously Sarm watched Misk's fluttering, piteous, exposed antennae.

Then slowly one of Misk's legs seemed to give way beneath him and he tilted crazily to one side.

In the frenzy of the battle I had apparently failed to note the injury to the leg.

Perhaps so too had Sarm.

I wondered if Sarm, considering Misk's desperate condition and plight, would offer quarter.

Once again Sarm leaped in, his bladed projection lifted to strike, but this time Misk suddenly straightened himself promptly on the leg which had seemed to fail him and whipped his antennae back behind his head an instant before the stroke of Sarm's blade and when Sarm struck he found his appendage gripped in the hooklike projections on the end of Misk's foreleg.

Sarm seemed to tremble and he struck with his other foreleg but this one too Misk seized with his other foreleg and once again they stood rocking on their posterior appendages for Misk, having learned their strengths in the first grappling, and lacking the swiftness of Sarm, had decided to close with his antagonist.

Their jaws locked together, the great heads twisting.

Then with a force that might have been that of clashing, golden glaciers Misk's jaws tightened and turned and suddenly Sarm was thrown to his back beneath him and in the instant Sarm struck the floor Misk's jaws had slipped their grip to the thick tube about which hung the string of Tola's silverish tools, that tube that separated the head from the thorax of Sarm, what on a human would have been the throat, and Misk's jaws began to close.

In that instant I saw the bladelike projections disappear from the tips of Sarm's forelegs and he folded his forelegs against his body and ceased resistance, even lifting his head in order to further expose the crucial tube that linked thorax with head.

Misk's jaws no longer closed but he stood as if undecided.

Sarm was his to kill.

Though the translator which still hung about Sarm's neck with the string of silverish tools was not turned on I would not have needed it to interpret the desperate odor-signal emitted by the First Born. It was, indeed, though shorter and more intense, the first odor-signal that had ever been addressed to me, only then it had come from Misk's translator in the chamber of Vika. Had the translator been turned on, I would have heard "Lo Sardar"—"I am a Priest-King."

Misk removed his jaws from the throat of Sarm and stepped back.

He could not slay a Priest-King.

Misk slowly turned away from Sarm and with slow, delicate steps approached the Mother, before whom he stood, great chunks of greenish coagulated body fluid marking the wounds on his body.

If he spoke to her or she to him I did not detect the signals.

Perhaps they merely regarded one another.

My interest was more with Sarm, whom I saw lift himself with delicate menace to his four posterior appendages. Then to my horror I saw him remove the translator on its chain from his throat and wielding this like a mace and chain he rushed upon Misk and struck him viciously from behind.

Misk's legs slowly bent beneath him and his body lay on the floor of the chamber.

Whether he was dead or stunned I could not tell.

Sarm had drawn himself up again to his full height and like a golden blade he stood behind Misk and before the Mother. He looped the translator again about his throat.

I sensed a signal from the Mother, the first I had sensed, and it was scarcely detectable. It was, "No."

But Sarm looked about himself to the golden rows of immobile Priest-Kings who watched him and then, satisfied, he opened those great, laterally moving jaws and advanced slowly on Misk.

At that instant I kicked loose the grille on the ventilator

shaft and uttering the war cry of Ko-ro-ba sprang to the Platform of the Mother and in another instant had leaped between Sarm and Misk, my sword drawn.

"Hold, Priest-King!" I cried.

Never before had a human set foot in this chamber and I knew not if I had committed sacrilege but I did not care, for my friend was in danger.

Horror coursed through the ranks of the assembled Priest-Kings and their antennae waved wildly and their golden frames shook with rage, and hundreds of them must have simultaneously turned on their translators for I heard almost immediately from everywhere before me the contrastingly calm translation of their threats and protests. Among the words I heard were "He must die," "Kill him," "Death to the Mul." I almost had to smile in spite of myself for the unmoved, unemotional emissions of the translators seemed so much at odds with the visible agitation of the Priest-Kings and the dire import of their messages.

But then, from the Mother herself, behind me, I sensed once again the transmission of negation, and I heard on the thousand translators that faced me, the simple expression, "No." It was not their message, but that of she who lay brown and wrinkled behind me. "No."

The rows of Priest-Kings seemed to rustle in confusion and anguish but in a moment, incredibly enough, they were as immobile as ever, standing as if statues of golden stone, regarding me.

Only from Sarm's translator came a message. "It will die," he said.

"No," said the Mother, her message being caught and transmitted by Sarm's own translator.

"Yes," said Sarm, "it will die."

"No," said the Mother, the message coming again from Sarm's translator.

"I am the First Born," said Sarm.

"I am the Mother," said she who lay behind me.

"I do what I wish," said Sarm.

He looked around him at the rows of silent, immobile Priest-Kings and found none to challenge him. Now the Mother herself was silent.

"I do what I wish," came again from Sarm's translator.

His antennae peered down at me as though trying to recognize me. They examined my tunic but found on it no scent-markings.

"Use your eyes," I said to him.

The golden disks on his great globular head seemed to flicker and they fastened themselves upon me.

"Who are you?" he asked.

"I am Tarl Cabot of Ko-ro-ba," I said.

Sarm's bladelike projections snapped viciously into view and remained exposed.

I had seen Sarm in action and I knew that his speed was incredible. I hoped I would be able to see his attack. I told myself it would probably come for the head or throat, if only because these were, from his height, easier to reach and he would wish to kill me quickly and with little difficulty, for he would surely regard his main business as the slaying of Misk, who still lay, either dead or unconscious, behind me.

"How is it," asked Sarm, "that you have dared to come here?"

"I do what I wish," I told him.

Sarm straightened. The bladelike projections had never been withdrawn. His antennae flattened themselves over his head.

"It seems that one of us must die," said Sarm.

"Perhaps," I agreed.

"What of the Golden Beetle?" asked Sarm.

"I killed it," I said. I gestured to him with my sword. "Come," I said, "let us make war."

Sarm moved back a step.

"It is not done," he said, echoing words I had heard once from Misk. "It is a great crime to kill one."

"It is dead," I said. "Come, let us make war."

Sarm moved back another step.

He turned to one of the closest Priest-Kings. "Bring me a silver tube," he said.

"A silver tube to kill only a Mul?" asked the Priest-King.

I saw the antennae of several of the Priest-Kings curling.

"I spoke in jest," said Sarm to the other Priest-King, who made no response but, unmoving, regarded him.

Sarm approached me again. He turned his translator down.

"It is a great crime to threaten a Priest-King," he said. "Let me kill you quickly or I will have a thousand Muls sent to the dissection chambers."

I thought about this for a moment. "If you are dead," I asked, "how will you have them sent to the dissection chambers?"

"It is a great crime to kill a Priest-King," said Sarm.

"Yet you would slay Misk," I said.

"He is a traitor to the Nest," said Sarm.

I lifted my voice, hoping that the sound waves would carry to those transducers that were the translators of the Priest-Kings.

"It is Sarm," I called, "who is a traitor to the Nest, for this Nest will die, and he has not permitted the founding of a new Nest."

"The Nest is eternal," said Sarm.

"No," said the Mother, and the message again came from Sarm's own translator, and was echoed a thousand times by those of the other Priest-Kings in the great chamber.

Suddenly with a vicious, almost incalculable speed Sarm's right bladed projection flashed toward my head. I hardly saw it coming but an instant before its flight began I had seen the tremor of a fiber in his shoulder and I knew the signal for its strike had been transmitted.

I counterslashed.

And when the swift living blade of Sarm was still a full yard from my throat it met the lightning steel of a Gorean blade that had once been carried at the siege of Ar, that had met and withstood and conquered the steel of Pa-Kur, Gor's Master Assassin, until that time said to be the most skilled swordsman on the planet.

A hideous splash of greenish fluid struck me in the face and I leaped aside, in the same movement shaking my head and wiping the back of my fist across my eyes.

In an instant I was again on guard, my vision cleared, but I saw that Sarm was now some fifteen yards or more away and was slowly turning and turning in what must have been some primitive, involuntary dance of agony. I could sense the intense, weird odors of pain uncarried by his translator which now filled the chamber.

I returned to the place where I had struck the blow.

To one side I saw the bladed projection lying at the foot of one of the low stone tiers on which Priest-Kings stood.

Sarm had thrust the stub of his foreleg beneath his shoulder and it seemed frozen there in the coagulating green slush that emanated from the wound.

Shaking with pain, his entire frame quivering, he turned to face me, but he did not approach.

I saw that several Priest-Kings who stood behind him began to edge forward.

I raised my blade, resolved to die well.

Behind me I sensed something.

Glancing over my shoulder I saw the welcome, now standing golden form of Misk.

He placed one foreleg on my shoulder.

He regarded Sarm and his cohorts, and his great laterally chopping jaws opened and closed once.

The golden Priest-Kings behind Sarm did not advance further.

Misk's message to Sarm was carried on Sarm's own translator. "You have disobeyed the Mother," said Misk.

Sarm said nothing.

"Your Gur has been refused," said Misk. "Go."

Sarm seemed to tremble and so, too, did those Priest-Kings who stood behind him.

"We will bring silver tubes," said Sarm.

"Go," said Misk.

Suddenly, strangely carried on the many translators in the room, were the words, "I remember him—I have never forgotten him—in the sky—in the sky—he with wings like showers of gold."

I could not understand this but Misk, paying no attention to Sarm, or his cohorts or the other Priest-Kings, rushed to the Platform of the Mother.

Another Priest-King and then another pressed more closely and I went with them to the platform.

"Like showers of gold," she said.

I heard the message on the translators of Priest-Kings who, like Misk, approached the platform.

The ancient creature on the platform, brown and wrinkled, lifted her antennae and surveyed the chamber and her children. "Yes," she said, "he had wings like showers of gold."

"The Mother is dying," said Misk.

This message was echoed by every translator in the room and a thousand times again and again as the Priest-Kings repeated it in disbelief to one another.

"It cannot be," said one.

"The Nest is eternal," said another.

The feeble antennae trembled. "I would speak," she said, "with him who saved my child."

It was strange to me to hear her speak of the powerful, golden creature Misk in such a way.

I went to the ancient creature.

"I am he," I said.

"Are you a Mul?" she asked.

"No," I said, "I am free."

"Good," she said.

At this moment two Priest-Kings carrying syringes pressed through their brethren to approach the platform.

When they made as though to inject her ancient body in what must have been yet another in a thousand times, she shook her antennae and warned them off.

"No," she said.

One of the Priest-Kings prepared to inject the serum despite her refusal to accept it but Misk's foreleg rested on his and he did not do so.

The other Priest-King who had come with a syringe examined her antennae and the brown, dull eyes.

He motioned his companion away. "It would make a difference of only a few Ehn," he said.

Behind me I heard one of the Priest-Kings repeat over and over, "The Nest is eternal."

Misk placed a translator on the platform beside the dying creature.

"Only he," said the Mother.

Misk motioned away the physicians and the other Priest-Kings and set the translator on the platform at its lowest volume. I wondered how long the scent-message, whatever it was to be, would linger in the air before fading into an unrecognizable blur of scent to be drawn through the ventilator system and dispelled somewhere far above among the black crags of the treeless, frozen Sardar.

I bent my ear to the translator.

At the low volume I received the message the other translators in the room would not be likely to pick it up and transduce the sounds into odor-signals.

"I was evil," said she.

I was astounded.

"I wanted to be," said the brown, dying creature, "the only Mother of Priest-Kings, and I listened to my First Born who wanted to be the only First Born of a Mother of Priest-Kings."

The old frame shook, though whether with pain or sorrow, or both, I could not tell.

"Now," she said, "I die and the race of Priest-Kings must not die with me."

I could barely hear the words from the translator.

"Long ago," she said, "Misk, my child, stole the egg of a male and now he has hidden it from Sarm and others who do not wish for there to be another Nest."

"I know," I said softly.

"Not long ago," said she, "perhaps no more than four of your centuries, he told me of what he had done and of his reasons for doing so." The withered antennae trembled, and the thin brown threads on them lifted as though stirred by a chill wind, the passing foot of mortality. "I said nothing to him but I considered what he had said, and I thought on this matter, and at last—in league with the Second Born, who has since succumbed to the Pleasures of the Golden Beetle, I set aside a female egg to be concealed from Sarm beyond the Nest."

"Where is this egg?" I asked.

She seemed not to understand my question and I was

afraid for her as I saw her ancient brown carcass begin to shake with spasmodic tremors which I feared might herald the close of that vast life.

One of the physicians rushed forward and thrust the long syringe deep through her exoskeleton into the fluids of her thorax. He drew out the syringe and held his antennae to hers for a moment. The tremors subsided.

He withdrew and stood watching us from some distance away, not moving, as still as the others, like a thousand statues of tortured gold.

Once again a sound came from my translator. "The egg was taken from the Nest by two humans," she said, "men who were free—like yourself—not Muls—and hidden."

"Where was it hidden?" I asked.

"These men," she said, "returned to their own cities speaking to no one as they had been commanded. In this undertaking on behalf of Priest-Kings they had been united and together had suffered many dangers and privations and had done their work well and were as brothers."

"Where is the egg?" I repeated.

"But their cities fell to warring," said the withered ancient one, "and these men in battle slew one another and with them died the secret as far as it was known among men." The huge, tarnished head lying on the stone platform tried to lift itself but could not. "Strange is your kind," she said. "Half larl, half Priest-King."

"No," I said, "half larl, half man."

She said nothing for a time. Then once again the voice of the translator was heard.

"You are Tarl Cabot of Ko-ro-ba," she said.

"Yes," I said.

"I like you," she said.

I knew not how to respond to this and so I said nothing.

The old antennae stretched forward, inching themselves toward me and I took them gently in my hands and held them.

"Give me Gur," she said.

Amazed, I stepped away from her and went to the great golden bowl on its heavy tripod and took out a few drops of the precious liquid in the palm of my hand and returned to her.

She tried to lift her head but still could not do so. Her great jaws moved slowly apart and I saw the long, soft tongue that lay behind them.

"You wish to know of the egg," she said.

"If you wish to tell me," I said.

"Would you destroy it?" she asked.

"I don't know," I said.

"Give me Gur," she said.

Gently I placed my hand between those huge ancient jaws and with my palm I touched her tongue that she might taste what adhered to it.

"Go to the Wagon Peoples, Tarl of Ko-ro-ba," she said. "Go to the Wagon Peoples."

"But where is it?" I asked.

Then before my horrified eyes the carcass of that ancient she began to shiver and tremble and I stood back as she struggled to my amazement to her feet and reared herself to the height of a Priest-King, her antennae extended to their very lengths as though grasping, clutching, trying to sense something, though what she sought I did not know, but in her sudden fantastic strength, the gasp of her delirium and power, she seemed suddenly the Mother of a great race, very beautiful and very strong and very splendid.

And from a thousand translators rang the message she cried out over those golden heads to the blank stone ceiling and walls of her chamber and I shall never forget it as it was in all the sorrow and the joy of her trembling dying magnificence; I and all could read it in the attitude of her body, the alertness of the forelegs, the suddenly sensing antennae, even in those dull brown disks which had been eyes and now seemed to be for that one last moment luminous again. The voices of the translators were simple and quiet and mechanical. The message was given to my ears as would have been any message. It said: "I see him, I see him, and his wings are like showers of gold."

Then slowly the great form sank to the platform and the body no longer trembled and the antennae lay limp on the stone.

Misk approached her and touched her gently with his antennae.

He turned to the Priest-Kings.

"The Mother is dead," he said.

28
Gravitational Disruption

WE WERE IN THE FIFTH week of the War in the Nest and the issue still hung in balance.

After the death of the Mother, Sarm and those who followed him, most of the Priest-Kings for he was First Born, fled from the chamber to fetch, as it was said, silver tubes.

These were charged, cylindrical weapons, manually operated but incorporating principles much like those of the Flame Death Mechanism. Unused, they had lain encased in plastic quivers for a matter of centuries and yet when these quivers were broken open and the weapons seized up by angry Priest-Kings they were as ready for their grim work as they had been when first they were stored away.

I think with one such weapon a man might have made himself Ubar of all Gor.

Perhaps there were only a hundred Priest-Kings who rallied to the call of Misk and among them there were no more than a dozen silver tubes.

The headquarters for the forces of Misk lay in his compartment and there, pouring over the scent maps of the tunnels, he directed the placement of his defenses.

Thinking to overcome us with little difficulty the forces of Sarm, mounted on transportation disks, swept through the tunnels and plazas, but the Priest-Kings of Misk, hidden in rooms, concealed behind portals, firing from the ramps and the roofs of buildings in the open complexes, soon took fierce toll of Sarm's unwary and overconfident troops.

In such war the much larger forces of the First Born tended to be neutralized and a situation of infiltration and counterinfiltration developed, marked by frequent sniping and occasional skirmishes.

On the second day of the second week of battle, after the forces of Sarm had withdrawn, I, armed with sword and silver tube, mounted a transportation disk and swept through the no man's land of unoccupied tunnels toward the Vivarium.

Although constantly on the alert I saw no sign of enemy forces, nor even of Muls or Matoks of various kinds. The Muls, I supposed, terrified and confused, had scattered and hidden themselves in their cases, living on their fungus and water, while over their heads hissed the weapons of their masters.

Therefore it was much to my surprise when I heard a distant singing in the tunnel that grew louder as I approached and soon I slowed the transportation disk and waited, my weapon ready.

As I waited, the tunnel and, as I later learned, the entire complex, were suddenly plunged into darkness. The energy bulbs, for the first time in centuries perhaps, had been shut down.

And yet there was not an instant's pause in that singing nor the dropping of a beat or tempo. It was as if the darkness made no difference.

And as I waited on the still disk in the darkness, my weapon ready, I suddenly saw far down the tunnel the sudden blue flash of an opened Mul-Torch and then its steady blaze, and then I saw another flash and blaze and another and to my amazement it seemed that these fires hung from the very ceiling of the tunnel.

It was the carriers of Gur but far from the Gur Chamber and I watched with something of awe as the long procession of humanoid creatures, two abreast, marched along the ceiling of the tunnel until they stopped above me.

"Greetings, Tarl Cabot," said a voice from the floor of the tunnel.

I had not even seen him to this moment so intent had I been on the strange procession above me.

I read the mark on his tunic. "Mul-Al-Ka!" I cried.

He came to the disk and seized my hand firmly.

"Al-Ka," said he. "I have decided I am no longer a Mul."

"Then Al-Ka it is!" I cried.

Al-Ka raised his arm and pointed to the creatures above us.

"They too," said Al-Ka, "have decided they will be free."

A thin voice yet strong, almost like that of something that was at once an old man and a child, rang out above me.

"We have waited fifteen thousand years for this moment," it said.

And another voice called out. "Tell us what to do."

I saw that the creatures above me, whom I shall now speak of as Gur Carriers, for they were no longer Muls, still carried their sacks of golden leather.

"They bring not Gur," said Al-Ka, "but water and fungus."

"Good," I said, "but tell them that this war is not theirs, but that of Priest-Kings, and that they may return to the safety of their chambers."

"The Nest is dying," said one of the creatures hanging above me, "and we have determined that we will die free."

Al-Ka looked at me in the light of the hanging torches.

"They have decided," he said.

"Very well," I said.

"I admire them," said Al-Ka, "for they can see a thousand yards in the darkness by the light of a single Mul-Torch and they can live on a handful of fungus and a swallow of water a day and they are very brave and proud."

"Then," said I, "I too admire them."

I looked at Al-Ka. "Where is Mul-Ba-Ta?" I asked. It was the first time I had ever seen the two men separated.

"He has gone to the Pastures and the Fungus Chambers," said Al-Ka.

"Alone?" I asked.

"Of course," said Al-Ka, "we could do twice as much that way."

"I hope to see him soon," I said.

"I think you will," said Al-Ka, "for the lights have been shut down. Priest-Kings do not need light, but humans are handicapped without it."

"Then," I said, "the lights have been shut down because of the Muls."

"The Muls are rising," said Al-Ka simply.

"They will need light," I said.

"There are humans in the Nest who know of these matters," said Al-Ka. "The lights will be on again as soon as the equipment can be built and the power fed into the system."

The calmness with which he spoke astonished me. After all, Al-Ka, and other humans of the Nest, with the exception of the Gur Carriers, would never have known darkness.

"Where are you going?" asked Al-Ka.

"To one of the vivaria," I said, "to fetch a female Mul."

"That is a good idea," said Al-Ka. "Perhaps I too will someday fetch a female Mul."

And so it was a strange procession that followed the transportation disk, now happily piloted by Al-Ka, down the tunnel to the Vivarium.

In the dome of the Vivarium, holding a Mul-Torch, I walked up the ramps to the fourth tier, noting that the cages had been emptied, but I suspected that there would be one that would have remained locked.

And there was, and in this case though it had been seared as if an attempt had been made to open it I found Vika of Treve.

She crouched in the corner of the case away from the door in the darkness and through the plastic I saw her in the blue radiance of the Mul-Torch.

She crept to her feet holding her hands before her face and I could see her trying to see and yet protect her eyes from the glare.

Even shorn she seemed to me incredibly beautiful, very frightened, in the brief plastic sheath that was the only garment allotted to female Muls.

I took the metal key from the loop around my neck and turned the heavy mechanism of the case lock.

I hurled the plastic partition upward opening the case.

"—Master?" she asked.

"Yes," I said.

A soft cry of joy escaped her lips.

She stood before me blinking against the light of the Mul-Torch, trying to smile.

Yet as she stood there she seemed also to be frightened

and to my surprise she dared not approach the door though it now stood open.

She looked rather at me.

Her eyes were apprehensive, not knowing what I would do nor why I had returned to the case.

And her fears were not lessened as she looked beyond me to see the creatures, undoubtedly hideous to her eyes, who clung spiderlike to the ceiling of the Vivarium chamber with their glowing Mul-Torches.

"Who are they?" she whispered.

"Unusual men," I said.

She regarded the small round bodies and the long limbs with the cushioned feet and the long-fingered hands with their heavy palms.

Hundreds of pairs of those great, round dark eyes stared at her.

She shivered.

Then she looked again at me.

She dared ask no question but submissively knelt, as befitted her station, and bowed her head.

The case, I said to myself, has taught Vika of Treve much.

Before her head fell I had read in her eyes the silent, desperate plea of the rightless, helpless slave girl that her master, he who owns her, he who holds her chain, might be pleased to be kind to her.

I wondered if I should take her from the case.

I saw her shoulders tremble as she awaited my decision as to her fate.

I no longer wished her to be confined here now that I better understood how matters stood in the Nest. I thought, even in spite of the cage plastic, she might be safer with the forces of Misk. Moreover, the Vivarium Attendants were gone and the other cages were empty and so it would only be a matter of time before she would starve. I did not wish to return periodically to the Vivarium to feed her and I supposed, if necessary, some suitable confinement might be found for her near Misk's headquarters. If no other choice seemed practical I supposed I could always keep her chained in my own case.

Kneeling before me Vika's shoulders shook but she dared not raise her head to read her fate in my eyes.

I wished that I could trust her but I knew that I could not.

"I have returned for you, Vika of Treve—Slave Girl," I said sternly, "—to take you from the case."

Slowly, her eyes radiant, her lips trembling, Vika lifted her head to me.

"Thank you, Master," she said softly, humbly. Tears welled in her eyes.

"Call me Cabot," I said, "as was your wont."

On Gor I had not minded owning women as much as I should have but I had never been overly fond of being addressed by the title of Master.

It was enough to be Master.

The women I had owned, Sana, Talena, Lara, and others of whom I have not written, Passion Slaves rented for the hour in the Paga Taverns of Ko-ro-ba and Ar, Pleasure Slaves bestowed on me in token of hospitality for a night spent in a friend's compartments, had known that I was master and that had been sufficient.

On the other hand I have never truly objected to the title because I had not been long on Gor before I understood, for some reason that is not yet altogether clear to me, that the word 'Master' can indescribably thrill a girl when she finds it on her lips, now those of a slave girl, and knows that it is true. Whether or not this would be the same with the girls of Earth I do not know.

"Very well, Cabot my Master," said Vika.

As I looked into the eyes of Vika I saw there the tears of relief and gratitude but I saw too the tears of another emotion, infinitely tender and vulnerable, which I could not read.

She knelt in the position of the Pleasure Slave but her hands on her thighs had unconsciously, pleadingly, turned their palms to me, and she no longer knelt quite back on her heels. It was as though she begged to be allowed to lift and open her arms and rise and come to my arms. But as I looked upon her sternly she turned her palms again to her thighs, knelt back on her heels and dropped her head, holding her eyes as if by force of will fixed on the plastic beneath my sandals.

Her entire body trembled with the ache of her desire.

But she was a slave girl and dare not speak.

I looked down at her sternly. "Look up, Slave Girl," I said.

She looked up.

I smiled.

"To my lips, Slave Girl," I commanded.

With a cry of joy she flung herself into my arms weeping. "I love you, Master," she cried. "I love you, Cabot my Master!"

I knew the words she spoke could not be true but I did not rebuke her.

It was no longer in my heart to be cruel to Vika of Treve, no matter who or what she might be.

After some minutes I said to her, rather sternly, "I have no time for this," and she laughed and stepped back.

I turned and left the case and Vika, as was proper, fell into step happily two paces behind me.

We walked down the ramp to the transportation disk.

Al-Ka closely scrutinized Vika.

"She is very healthy," I said.

"Her legs do not look too strong," said Al-Ka, regarding the lovely thighs, calves and ankles of the slave girl.

"But I do not object," I said.

"Nor do I," said Al-Ka. "After all, you can always have her run up and down and that will strengthen them."

"That is true," I said.

"I think someday," he said, "I too will fetch a female Mul." Then he added, "But one with stronger legs."

"A good idea," I said.

Al-Ka guided the transportation disk out of the Vivarium and we began the journey toward Misk's compartment, the Gur Carriers following overhead.

I held Vika in my arms. "Did you know," I asked, "that I would return for you?"

She shivered and looked ahead, down the darkened tunnel. "No," she said, "I knew only that you would do what you wished."

She looked up at me.

"May a poor slave girl beg," she whispered softly, "that she be again commanded to your lips?"

"It is so commanded," I said, and her lips again eagerly sought mine.

It was later in the same afternoon that Mul-Ba-Ta, now simply Ba-Ta, made his appearance, leading long lines of former Muls. They came from the Pastures and the Fungus Chambers and they, like the Gur Carriers, sang as they came.

Some men from the Fungus Chambers carried on their backs great bags filled with choice spores, and others labored under the burdens of huge baskets of freshly reaped fungus, slung on poles between them; and those from the Pastures drove before them with long pointed goads huge, shambling gray arthropods, the cattle of Priest-Kings; and others from the Pastures carried in long lines on their shoulders the ropelike vines of the heavy-leaved Sim plants, on which the cattle would feed.

"We will have lamps set up soon," said Ba-Ta. "It is merely a matter of changing the chambers in which we pasture."

"We have enough fungus to last," said one of the Fungus Growers, "until we plant these spores and reap the next harvest."

"We burned what we did not take," said another.

Misk looked on in wonder as these men presented themselves to me and marched past.

"We welcome your aid," he said, "but you must obey Priest-Kings."

"No," said one of them, "we no longer obey Priest-Kings."

"But," said another, "we will take our orders from Tarl Cabot of Ko-ro-ba."

"I think you would be well advised," I said, "to stay out of this war between Priest-Kings."

"Your war is our war," said Ba-Ta.

"Yes," said one of the Pasturers, who held a pointed goad as though it might be a spear.

One of the Fungus Growers looked up at Misk. "We were

bred in this Nest," he told the Priest-King, "and it is ours as well as yours."

Misk's antennae curled.

"I think he speaks the truth," I said.

"Yes," said Misk, "that is why my antennae curled. I too think he speaks the truth."

And so it was that the former Muls, humans, bringing with them the basic food supplies of the Nest, began to flock to the side of the Priest-King Misk and his few cohorts.

The battle would, I supposed, given the undoubted stores of food available to Sarm and his forces, ultimately hinge on the firepower of the silver tubes, of which Misk's side had few, but still I conjectured that the skills and courage of former Muls might yet play their part in the fierce issues to be decided in that secret Nest that lay beneath the black Sardar.

As Al-Ka had predicted, the energy bulbs in the Nest, except where they had actually been destroyed by the fire of Sarm's silver tubes, came on again.

Former Mul engineers, trained by Priest-Kings, had constructed an auxiliary power unit and had fed its energy into the main system.

When the lights flickered and then burst into clear, vital radiance there was a great cheer from the humans in Misk's camp, with the exception of the Gur Carriers to whom the energy bulbs were not of great importance.

Intrigued by the hardness of the cage plastic encountered in the Vivarium I spoke to Misk and he and I, together with other Priest-Kings and humans, armored a fleet of transportation disks, which would be extremely effective if a silver tube were mounted in them and which, even if not armed, might yet serve acceptably as scouting vehicles or relatively safe transports. The fiery blasts of the silver tubes would wither and wrinkle the plastic but unless the exposure were rather lengthy they could not penetrate it. And a simple heat torch, as I had earlier learned, could scarcely mark the obdurate material.

In the third week of the War, equipped with the armored

transportation disks, we began to carry the battle to the forces of Sarm, though they still outnumbered us greatly.

Our intelligence was vastly superior to theirs and the networks of ventilation shafts provided the quick nimble men of the Fungus Chambers and the uncanny Gur Carriers access to almost anywhere in the Nest they cared to go. Moreover, all former Muls who fought with us were clad in scent-free tunics which in effect supplied them with a most effective camouflage in the Nest. For example, at different times, returning from a raid, perhaps bringing another captured silver tube, no longer needed by one of Sarm's slain cohorts, I would find myself unremarked even by Misk though I might stand but feet from him.

Somewhat to their embarrassment but for their own safety the Priest-Kings who had joined Misk wore painted on the back and front of their thorax the block letter which in the Gorean alphabet would be the first letter of Misk's name. Originally some of them had objected to this but after a few had almost stepped on the silent Gur Carriers, or wandered unbeknownst beneath them, some of the spidery humanoids being armed perhaps with silver tubes, their opinions changed and they became zealous to have the letter painted boldly and repainted promptly if it showed the least signs of fading. It unnerved the Priest-Kings to pass unknowingly within feet of, say, a pale, agile fellow from the Fungus Chambers, who might be crouching in a nearby ventilator shaft with a heat torch, who might have burned their antennae for them if he had pleased; or to suddenly find themselves surrounded by a ring of quiet herdsmen who might at a signal transfix them with a dozen of the spearlike cattle goads.

Together the humans and the Priest-Kings of Misk made a remarkably effective fighting team. What sensory data might escape the antennae might well be discovered by the sharp-eyed human, and what subtle scent might escape the human senses would likely be easily picked up by the Priest-King in the group. And as they fought together they came, as creatures will, to respect one another and to rely on one another, becoming, incredibly enough, friends. Once a brave Priest-King of Misk's forces was slain and the humans who had fought with him wept. Another time a Priest-King braved the fire of a dozen silver tubes to rescue one of the spidery Gur Carriers who had been injured.

Indeed, in my opinion, the greatest mistake of Sarm in the War in the Nest was in his poor handling of the Muls.

As soon as it became clear to him that the Muls of the Fungus Chambers and the Pastures, and the Gur Carriers, were coming over to Misk he apparently assumed, for no good reason, that all Muls in the Nest were to be regarded as enemies. Accordingly he set about systematically exterminating those who fell within the ranges of his silver tubes and this drove many Muls, who would undoubtedly have served him, and well, into Misk's camp.

With these new Muls, not from the Fungus Chambers and the Pastures, but from the complexes of the Nest proper, came a new multitude of capacities and talents. Further, from reports of these incoming Muls, the food sources of the Priest-Kings of Sarm were not as extensive as we had supposed. Indeed, many of the canisters of fungus now in the stores of Sarm were reportedly canisters of simple Mul-Fungus taken from the cases of Muls who had been killed or fled. Rumor had it that the only Muls whom Sarm had not ordered slain on sight were the Implanted Ones, among whom would be such creatures as Parp, whom I had met long ago when first I entered the lair of Priest-Kings.

One of the most marvelous ideas to further our cause was provided by Misk who introduced me to what I had only heard rumored before, the Priest-Kings' mastery of the pervasive phenomena of gravity.

"Would it not be useful at times," he asked, "if the armored transportation disk could fly?"

I thought he joked, but I said, "Yes, at times it would be very useful."

"Then we shall do it," said Misk, snapping his antennae.

"How?" I asked.

"Surely you have noted the unusual lightness of the transportation disk for its size?" he asked.

"Yes," I said.

"It is," he said, "built with a partially gravitationally resistant metal."

I admit I laughed.

Misk looked at me with puzzlement.

"Why do you curl your antennae?" he asked.

"Because," I said, "there is no such thing as a gravitationally resistant metal."

"But what of the transportation disk?" he asked.

I stopped laughing.

Yes, I asked myself, what of the transportation disk?

I looked at Misk. "Response to gravity," I said to him, "is as much a characteristic of material objects as size and shape."

"No," said Misk.

"Therefore," I said, "there is no such thing as a gravitationally resistant metal."

"But there is the transportation disk," he reminded me.

I thought Misk was most annoying. "Yes," I said, "there is that."

"On your old world," said Misk, "gravity is still as unexplored a natural phenomenon as electricity and magnetism once were, and yet you have mastered to some extent those phenomena—and we Priest-Kings have to some extent mastered gravity."

"Gravity is different," I said.

"Yes, it is," he said, "and that is why perhaps you have not yet mastered it. Your own work with gravity is still in the mathematical descriptive stage, not yet in the stage of control and manipulation."

"You cannot control gravity," I said, "the principles are different; it is pervasive; it is simply there to be reckoned with."

"What is gravity?" asked Misk.

I thought for a time. "I don't know," I admitted.

"I do," said Misk, "let us get to work."

In the fourth week of the War in the Nest our ship was outfitted and armored. I am afraid it was rather primitive, except that the principles on which it operated were far more advanced than anything now available to Earth's, as I now understand, somewhat painfully rudimentary science. The ship was simply a transportation disk whose underside was coated with cage plastic and whose top was a transparent dome of the same material. There were controls in the forward portion of the ship and ports about the sides for silver tubes. There were no propellers or jets or rockets and I find it difficult to understand or explain the drive save that it used the forces of gravity against themselves in such a way that the amount, if one may use so inept an expression, of gravitational Ur, which is the Gorean expression for the gravitational primitive, remains constant though redistributed. I do not think force, or charge, or any of the other expressions which occur to one's mind is a good translation for Ur, and I prefer to regard it as an expression best left untranslated, though perhaps one could say that Ur is whatever it was that satisfied the gravitational equations of Misk. Most briefly the combined drive and guidance system of the disk functioned by means of the focusing of gravitational sensors on material objects and using the gravitational attraction of these objects while in effect screening out the attraction of others. I would not have believed the ship was possible but I found it difficult to offer the arguments of my old world's physics against the fact of Misk's success.

Indeed, it is through the control of gravity that the Priest-Kings had, long ago, brought their world into our system, an engineering feat which might have been otherwise impossible without perhaps the draining of the gleaming Thassa itself for its hydrogen nuclei.

The flight of the disk itself is incredibly smooth and the effect is much as if the world and not yourself were moving. When one lifts the craft it seems the earth moves from beneath one; when one moves it forward it seems as though the horizon rushed toward one; if one should place it in reverse, it seems the horizon glides away. Perhaps one should not expatiate on this matter but the sensation tends to be an unsettling one, particularly at first. It is much as if one sat still in a room and the world whirled and sped about one. This is undoubtedly the effect of lacking the resistance of gravitational forces which normally account for the sometimes unpleasant, but reassuring, effects of acceleration and deceleration.

Needless to say, although ironically, the first transportation disk prepared for flight was a ship of war. It was manned by

myself and Al-Ka and Ba-Ta. Misk would pilot the craft
upon occasion but it was, in fact, rather cramped for him
and he could not stand within it, a fact that bothered him no
end for a Priest-King, for some reason, becomes extremely
agitated when he cannot stand. I gathered it would be something like a man being forced to lie on his back when
something of importance is taking place. To lie on one's back
is to feel exposed and vulnerable, helpless, and the nervous-
ness we would feel in such a posture is undoubtedly due as
much to ancient instinct as to rational awareness. On the
other hand, since Misk did not construct the craft large
enough for him to stand in, I suspect he did not really wish
to take part in its adventures. To be sure, a smaller dome
would make the craft more maneuverable in the tunnels, but
I think Misk did not trust himself to do battle with his
former brethren. He might intellectually recognize that he
must slay but perhaps he simply could not have pressed the
firing switch of the silver tube. Unfortunately Sarm's cohorts,
and perhaps fortunately, most of Misk's, did not suffer from
this perilous inhibition. To be so inhibited among a field of
foes, none of whom suffered from the same inhibition,
seemed to me a good way to get one's head burned off.

When we had constructed the ship we felt that now we
had what might prove to be, in this strange subterranean
war, the decisive weapon. The fire of silver tubes could
damage and in time destroy the ship but yet its cage plastic
offered considerable protection to its crew who might, with
some degree of safety, mete out destruction to all that
crossed its path.

Accordingly it seemed to Misk, and I concurred, that an
ultimatum should be issued to Sarm's troops and that, if
possible, the ship should not be used in battle. If we had used
it immediately, decisively, we might have wrought great damage, but neither of us wished to take the enemy by devastating surprise if victory might be won without bloodshed.

We were considering this matter when suddenly without
warning one wall of Misk's compartment seemed suddenly to
blur and lift and then silently to vanish into powder, so light
and fine that some of it drifted upward to be withdrawn

through the ventilator shaft through which used air was drawn from the compartment.

Misk seized me and with the harrowing speed of the Priest-King leaped across the room, buffeting the case I had occupied ten yards across the chamber, bent down and flung up the trap and, carrying me, darted into the passage below.

My senses were reeling but now in the distance I could hear cries and shouts, the screaming of the dying, the unutterably horrifying noises of the broken, the torn and maimed.

Misk clung to the wall below the trap door, holding me to his thorax.

"What is it?" I demanded.

"Gravitational disruption," said Misk. "It is forbidden even to Priest-Kings."

His entire body shook with horror.

"Sarm could destroy the Nest," said Misk, "even the planet."

We listened to the screams and cries. We could hear no fall of buildings, no clatter of rubble. We heard only human sounds and the extent and fearfulness of these were our only index to the destruction being wrought above.

29
Anesthetization

"SARM IS DESTROYING THE UR bonding," said Misk.

"Lift me up!" I cried.

"You will be slain," said Misk.

"Quickly!" I cried.

Misk obeyed and I crawled out of the trap and to my wonder gazed on the patterns of desolation that met my eyes. Misk's compartment was gone, only powdery stains marking the place where the walls had been. Through the very stone of the tunnel which lay outside Misk's compartment, now opened like a deep window, I could see the next large Nest complex which lay beyond. I ran across the flooring of the tunnel and through the swatch of nothingness that had been cut through the stone and looked on the complex. Over it hung ten ships, perhaps of the sort used for surveillance on the surface, and in the nose of each of these ships there was mounted a conelike projection.

I could see no beam extend from these projections but where they pointed I saw material objects seem to shake and shudder and then vanish in a fog of dust. Clouds of particles from this destruction hung in the air, gray under the energy bulbs. The cones were methodically cutting geometrical patterns through the complex. Here and there where a human or Priest-King would dart into the open the cone nearest to him would focus on him and the human or Priest-King, like the buildings and the walls, would seem to break apart into powder.

I ran toward the workshop where Misk and I had left the ship we had fashioned from the transportation disk.

At one point I was faced with a ditch, cut by the disruption cones with geometrical precision in the very stone of the Nest. It lay across my path, perhaps thirty-five feet wide, perhaps forty feet deep.

I cried out with dismay but knew what I must do, and retraced my steps to try the ditch. Gor is somewhat smaller than the earth and, accordingly, its gravitational pull is less. If it were not for that what I intended to hazard would possibly have been beyond human capacity. As it was I could not be sure that I could make the leap but I knew that I must try.

I took a long run and with a great bound cleared the ditch by perhaps two feet and was soon speeding on my way to Misk's workshop.

I passed a group of huddled humans, crouched behind the remains of a wall which had been sheared away about two feet from the floor for a length of a hundred feet.

I saw one man who lacked an arm, lying on the floor, groaning, the limb having been lost to the unseen beam of the ships above. "My fingers," he cried, "my fingers hurt!" One of the humans by the wall, a girl, knelt by him, holding a cloth, trying to stanch the bleeding. It was Vika! I rushed to her side. "Quick, Cabot!" she cried, "I must make a tourniquet!" I seized the limb of the man and pressing the flesh together managed to retard the bleeding. Vika took the cloth from his wound and, ripping it and using a small steel bar from the sheared wall, quickly fashioned a tourniquet, wrapping it securely about the remains of the man's arm. The physician's daughter did the work swiftly, expertly. I rose to leave.

"I must go," I said.

"May I come?" she asked.

"You are needed here," I said.

"Yes, Cabot," she said, "you are right."

As I turned to go she lifted her hand to me. She did not ask where I was going nor did she ask again to accompany me. "Take care," she said. "I will," I said. There was another groan from the man and the girl turned to comfort him.

Had it truly been Vika of Treve?

I raced to the workshop of Misk and flung open the double doors and leaped into the ship and secured the hatch, and in a moment it seemed the floor dropped a foot beneath me and the doors rushed forward.

In less than a few Ihn I had brought the ship into the large Nest complex where the ten ships of Sarm still followed their grim, precise, destructive pattern, as placidly and methodically as one might paint lines on a surface or mow a lawn.

I knew nothing of the armament of the ships of Sarm and I knew I had only the silver tube in my own craft, a weapon far outclassed in destructive potential by the gravitational disruptors mounted in the ships of Sarm. Moreover, I knew that the cage plastic with which my own ship was protected would be no more protection than tissue paper against Sarm's weapons, the nature of which was not to pierce or melt but, from a given center, radiating outwards, to shatter material gravitationally, breaking it apart and scattering it.

I broke into the open and the floor of the complex shot away from beneath me and I hung near the energy bulbs at the very apex of the dome. None of the ships of Sarm had apparently noted me.

I took the lead ship into my sights and dropped toward it, narrowing the range to increase the effectiveness of the silver tube. I was within two hundred yards when I opened fire, attacking from the rear, away from the destructive cone in its bow.

To my joy I saw the metal blacken and burst apart like

swollen tin as I passed beneath it and began to climb rapidly
toward the belly of the second craft which I ripped open with
a sizzling burst of fire. The first craft began to turn slowly,
uncontrollably, in the air and then plunged toward the
ground. I hoped Sarm himself might have been in that
flagship. The second craft shot wildly toward the ceiling of
the complex and shattered on the stone ceiling, falling back
to the ground in a shower of wreckage.

The other eight craft suddenly stopped their destructive
work and seemed to hover in indecision. I wondered if they
were in communication with one another. I supposed so.
Undoubtedly they had not expected to be met with opposition. They may not even have seen me. While they seemed to
hang undecided in space, almost like puzzled cells in a drop-
let of water, I dove again, and the third ship broke apart as
though it were a toy beneath a falling cutlass of fire, and I
climbed once more, the flame of the silver tube stabbing
ahead of me hitting the fourth ship amidships and flinging it
burning a hundred yards from my path.

Now the remaining six ships hovered closely together,
disruptor cones radiating outward in different directions, but
I was above them.

This time, should I dive again, I knew it would be impossible to conceal my position from them, for they would then
know I was below them and at least one of the ships would
be almost certain to cover me with its weapon.

It would be but a moment before they would discover my
position.

Even now two of the ships were moving their place, one to
cover the area beneath the small fleet and the other above. In
a moment there would be no avenue of attack which would
not mean sure death.

The ceiling of the complex leapt away from above me and
I found myself in the very center of the six ships, surrounded
on the four sides, and above and below.

I could see the scanners mounted in the nose of the ships
probing about.

But I was nowhere to be found.

From this distance I could see hatches in the ships, on the
top, and there was sufficient oxygen in the complex to permit

exposed visual observation, but none of the Priest-Kings peered out of any of the hatches. Rather they continued to concentrate on their instruments. They must have been puzzled by the failure of the instrumentation to detect me.

Two hypotheses would seem most likely to explain this phenomenon to them, first that I had fled the complex, second that I was nestled among them, and I smiled to myself, for I was certain that the second hypothesis would never occur to a Priest-King, for it was too improbable and Priest-Kings were too rational a kind of creature.

For half a Gorean Ahn we hung there, none of us moving. Then for a full Gorean Ahn did we remain there, motionless above the complex. Again I smiled to myself. For once I was sure I could outwait a Priest-King.

Suddenly the ship beneath me seemed to quiver and then it blurred and disappeared.

My heart leaped!

Ground fire!

I could imagine Misk hastening to his tools and the vast assemblage of instrumentation in his shop, or perhaps sending an outraged Priest-King to some secret arsenal where lay a forbidden weapon, one to which Misk would never have had recourse were it not for the hideous precedent of Sarm!

Almost immediately the remaining five ships fell into a line and raced down toward one of the tunnel exits that led from the complex.

The first ship to near the exit seemed to burst into a cloud of powder but the next four ships, and myself, who had fallen into line with them, pierced the veil of powder and found ourselves coursing through the tunnel back toward Sarm's domain.

There were now four ships ahead of me in the tunnel, fleeing.

With satisfaction I noted the width of the tunnel did not permit them to turn.

With grim decision I pressed the firing switch of the silver tube and there was a shattering burst of fire and I heard and felt branches of steel and tubing flying back against my armored transportation disk.

Some of the materials flew with such a force that gashes

were cut in the obdurate cage plastic and the ship was buffeted and jostled but it cut its way through this jungle of flying parts and found itself again streaming down the tunnel.

Now the three ships were far ahead and I thrust open the speed valve on the armored transportation disk to overtake them.

Just as the three ships burst into the open of another huge complex I caught up with them and opened fire on the third ship but my fire seemed less effective this time and though I gave it a full burst the charging of the tube seemed at last almost exhausted. The third ship moved erratically, one side black and wrinkled with the scar of my attack. Then it seemed to come under control and turned like a cornered rat to face me. In an instant I would be within the firing radius of the disruptor cone. I took my ship up over the craft and tried another burst, which was even weaker than the last. I tried to keep above the ship, staying away from the disruptor cone on its bow. I was dimly aware of the other two ships now turning to bring me within range.

At that moment I saw the hatch on the injured but threatening ship fly up and the head of a Priest-King emerge. I suppose that some of the scanning instrumentation had been damaged in the ship. His antennae swept the area and focused on me at the same time that I pressed the firing switch, and it seemed the golden head and antennae blew away in ashes and the golden body slumped downward in the hatch. The silver tube might be draining its power but it was still a fearsome weapon against an exposed enemy. Like an angry hornet I flew to the open hatch of the injured ship and blasted away into the hatch, filling the insides with fire. It tumbled away like a balloon and exploded in the air as I dropped my ship almost to the ground. I was quick but not quick enough because the plastic dome of my ship above me seemed to fly away in the wind leaving a trail of particles behind. Now, in the shattered rim of the plastic dome, scarcely protected against the rushing wind, I fought to regain control of the craft. The silver tube still lay intact in the firing port but its power was so considerably reduced that it was no longer a menace to the ships of Sarm. A few yards from the flooring of the plaza I brought the craft again into order and, throwing open the speed valve, darted into the midst of a complex of buildings, where I stopped, hovering a few feet above the street passing between them.

The ship of Sarm passed overhead like a hawk and then began to circle. I would have had a clean burst at the ship but the tube was, for all practical purposes, no longer an effective weapon.

A building on my left seemed to leap into the air and vanish.

I realized there was little I could do so I took the ship up and under the attacker.

He turned and twisted but I kept with him, close, too close for him to use his disruptor cone.

The wind whistled past and I was almost pulled from the controls of the ship.

Then I saw what I would not have expected.

The other ship of Sarm was turning slowly, deliberately, on its fellow.

I could not believe what I saw but there was no mistaking the elevation of the disruptor cone, the calm, almost unhurried manner in which the other ship was drawing a bead on its fellow.

The ship above me seemed to tremble and tried to turn and flee and then sensing the futility of this it turned again and tried to train its own disruptor cone on its fellow.

I flashed my ship to the ground only an instant before the entire ship above me seemed to explode silently in a storm of metallic dust glinting in the light of the energy bulbs above.

In the cover of the drifting remains of the ship shattered above me I darted among the streets of the complex and rose behind the last ship. This time my own craft seemed sluggish, and it was only too clear that it was not responding properly to the controls. To my dismay I saw the last ship turning slowly toward me and I saw the disruptor cone rise and focus on me. It seemed I hung helpless in the air, floating, waiting to be destroyed. I knew I could not evade the wide-angle scope of the disruptor beam. I savagely hurled my weight against the controls but they remained unresponsive. I floated above the enemy craft but it tipped, keeping me in the focus of its beam. Then without warning it seemed the stern of my craft vanished and I felt the deck suddenly give way and as half of the craft vanished in powder and the other half crumbled to the buildings below I seized the silver tube from the firing port and leaped downward to the back of the enemy ship.

I crawled to the hatch and tugged at the hatch ring.

It was locked!

The ship began to bank. Probably the pilots had heard wreckage hit their ship and were banking to drop it into the streets below, or perhaps they were actually aware that I had boarded them.

I thrust the silver tube to the hinges on the hatch and pressed the firing switch.

The ship banked more steeply.

The tube was almost drained of power but the point-blank range and the intensity of even the diminished beam melted the hinges from the hatch.

I wrenched the hatch open and it swung wildy out from its locked side and suddenly I hung there, one hand on the rim, one hand on the silver tube, as the ship lay on its side in the air. Then before the ship could roll I tossed the tube inside and squirmed in after it. The ship was now on its back and I was standing inside on its ceiling and then the ship righted itself and I found the silver tube again. The inside of the ship was dark for its only intended occupants were Priest-Kings, but the open hatch permitted some light.

A forward door opened and a Priest-King stepped into view, puzzled, startled at the sensing of the open hatch.

I pressed the firing switch of the silver tube and it gave forth with a short, abortive scorching blast and was cold, but the golden body of the Priest-King blackened and half sliced through, reeled against the wall and fell at my feet.

Another Priest-King followed the first and I pressed the firing switch again but there was no response.

In the half darkness I could see his antennae curl.

I threw the useless tube at him and it bounded from his thorax.

The massive jaws opened and closed once.

The hornlike projections on the grasping appendages snapped into view.

I seized the sword which I had never ceased to wear and uttering the war cry of Ko-ro-ba rushed forward but as I did so I suddenly threw myself to the ground beneath those extended projections and slashed away at the Priest-King's posterior appendages.

There was a sudden fearful scream of odor from the signal glands of the Priest-King and he tipped to one side reaching for me with his grasping appendages.

His abdomen now dragged on the ground but he pushed himself toward me, jaws snapping, by means of the two forward supporting appendages and the remains of his posterior appendages.

I leaped between the bladed projections and cut halfway through its skull with my sword.

It began to shiver.

I stepped back.

So this was how a Priest-King might be slain, I thought, somehow here one must sever the ganglionic net in mortal fashion. And then it seemed to me not improbable that this might be the case, for the major sensory apparatus, the antennae, lie in this area.

Then, as though I were a pet Mul, the Priest-King extended his antennae toward me. There was something piteous in the gesture. Did it wish me to comb the antennae? Was it conscious? Was it mad with pain?

I stood not understanding and then the Priest-King did what he wished: with a toss of his great golden head he hurled his antennae against my blade, cutting them from his head, and then after a moment, having closed himself in the world of his own pain, abandoning the external world in which he was no longer master, he slipped down to the steel flooring of the ship, dead.

The ship, as I discovered, had been manned by only two Priest-Kings, probably one at the controls, the other at the weapon. Now that it was not being controlled it hovered where the second Priest-King, probably its pilot, had left it, when he had come to investigate the fate of his companion.

It was dark in the ship, except in the vicinity of the opened hatch.

But, groping my way, I went forward to the controls.

There, to my pleasure, I found two silver tubes, fully charged.

Feeling what seemed to be a blank area of the ceiling of the control area I fired a blast upward, using the simple expedient of the tube to open a hole in the craft through which light might enter.

In the light which now entered the control area I examined the controls.

There were numerous scent-needles and switches and buttons and dials, none of which made much sense to me. The controls on my own craft had been designed for a primarily visually oriented creature. Nonetheless, reasoning analogously from my own controls, I managed to locate the guidance sphere, by means of which one selects any one of the theoretically infinite number of directions from a given point and the dials for the height and speed control. Once I bumped the craft rather severely into the wall of the complex and I could see the explosion of an energy bulb outside through my makeshift port, but I soon managed to bring the ship down safely. Since there was, from my point of view, no way of seeing just where I was going, since I could not use the sensory instrumentation of Priest-Kings, without cutting more holes in the ship and perhaps starting a fire or causing an explosion of some sort, I decided to abandon the ship. I was particularly worried about guiding it back through the tunnel. Moreover, if I could bring it to the first Nest complex, Misk would probably destroy it on sight with his own disruptor. Accordingly, it seemed safest to leave the ship and find some ventilator shaft and make my way back to Misk's area by means of it.

I crawled out of the ship through the hatch and slid over the side to the ground.

The buildings in the complex were deserted.

I looked about myself, at the empty streets, the empty windows, the silence of the once bustling complex.

I thought I heard a noise and listened for some time, but there was nothing more.

It was hard to rid my mind of the feeling that I was followed.

Suddenly I heard a voice, a mechanically transmitted voice. "You are my prisoner, Tarl Cabot," it said.

I spun, the silver tube ready.

A strange odor came to my nostrils before I could press the firing switch. Standing nearby I saw Sarm, and behind him the creature Parp, he whose eyes had been like disks of fiery copper.

Though my finger was on the firing switch it lacked the strength to depress it.

"He has been suitably anesthetized," said the voice of Parp.

I fell at their feet.

30
Sarm's Plan

"YOU HAVE BEEN IMPLANTED."

I heard the words from somewhere, vague, distant, and I tried to move but could not.

I opened my eyes to find myself looking into the twin fiery disks of the sinister-appearing, rotund Parp. Behind him I saw a battery of energy bulbs that seemed to burn into my eyes. To one side I saw a brownish Priest-King, very thin and angular, wearing the appearances of age but yet his antennae seemed as alert as those of any one of the golden creatures.

My arms and legs were bound with bands of steel to a flat, narrow, wheeled platform; my throat and waist were similarly locked in place.

"May I introduce the Priest-King Kusk," said Parp, gesturing to the tall, angular figure who loomed to one side.

So it was he, I said to myself, who formed Al-Ka and Ba-Ta, he the biologist who was among the first in the Nest.

I looked about the room, turning my head painfully, and saw that the room was some sort of operating chamber, filled with instrumentation, with racks of delicate tongs and knives. In one corner there was a large drumlike machine with a pressurized door which might have been a sterilizer.

"I am Tarl Cabot of Ko-ro-ba," I said weakly, as though to assure myself of my own identity.

"No longer," smiled Parp. "You are now honored to be as I, a creature of Priest-Kings."

"You have been implanted," came from the translator of the tall, brownish figure beside Parp.

I felt suddenly sick and helpless.

Though I felt no pain nor any of the discomfort I would have expected I now understood that these creatures had infused into the very tissues of my brain one of the golden control webs that could be operated from the Scanning Chamber of the Priest-Kings. I recalled the man from Ar, met on the lonely road to Ko-ro-ba long ago, who like a robot had been forced to obey the signals of Priest-Kings until at last he had tried to throw over the net, and its overload had burned away the insides of his skull, giving him at last the freedom of his own mortal dust.

I was horrified at what had been done and I wondered what the sensations would be or even if I would be aware of what I was doing when under the control of Priest-Kings. But most I feared how I might now be used to injure Misk and my friends. I might be sent back among them to spy, to foil their plans, perhaps even to destroy, perhaps even to slay Misk, Al-Ka and Ba-Ta and other leaders, my friends all. My frame shook with the horror of what I had become and seeing this Parp chuckled. I wanted to get my hands on his fat throat.

"Who has done this?" I asked.

"I," said Parp. "The operation is not as difficult as you might expect and I have performed it many times."

"He is a member of the Caste of Physicians," said Kusk, "and his manual dexterity is superior even to that of Priest-Kings."

"Of what city?" I asked.

Parp looked at me closely. "Treve," he said.

I closed my eyes.

It seemed to me that under the circumstances, while I was still my own master, I should perhaps slay myself. Otherwise I would be used as a weapon by Sarm, used to injure and destroy my friends. The thought of suicide has always horrified me, for life seems precious, and the mortal moments that one has, so brief a glimpse of the vistas of reality, it

seems to me should be cherished, even though they might be
lived in pain or sorrow. But under the circumstances—it
seemed that I should perhaps surrender the gift of life, for
there are some things more precious than life, and were it
not so I think that life itself would not be as precious as it is.

Kusk, who was a wise Priest-King and perhaps aware of
the psychology of humans, turned to Parp.

"It must not be permitted to end its own life before the
control web is activated," he said.

"Of course not," said Parp.

My heart sank.

Parp wheeled the platform on which I lay from the room.

"You are a man," I said to him, "slay me."

He only laughed.

Out of the room he took a small leather box from his
pouch, removed a tiny sharp blade from it and scratched my
arm.

It seemed the ceiling began to rotate.

"Sleen," I cursed him.

And was unconscious.

My prison was a rubber disk, perhaps a foot thick and ten
feet in diameter. In the center of this disk, recessed so I
could not dash my head against it, was an iron ring. Running
from this ring was a heavy chain attached to a thick metal
collar fastened about my throat. Further, my ankles wore
manacles and my wrists were fastened behind my back with
steel cuffs.

The disk itself lay in Sarm's command headquarters and I
think that he was pleased to have it so. He would occasionally loom above me, gloating, informing me of the success of his battle plans and strategies.

I noted that the appendage which I had severed with my
sword in the Chamber of the Mother had now regrown.

Sarm brandished the appendage, more golden and fresh
than the rest of his body. "It is another superiority of
Priest-Kings over humans," he said, his antennae curling.

I conceded the point in silence, amazed at the restorative
powers of Priest-Kings, those redoubtable golden foes against
which mere men had dared to pit themselves.

How much of what Sarm told me in those days was true I could not be sure but I was confident of a few things, and others I learned inadvertently from the reports of Priest-Kings and the few Implanted Muls who served him. There was normally a translator on in the headquarters and it was not difficult to follow what was said. The translator was for the benefit of creatures such as Parp, who spent a good deal of time in the headquarters.

For days in impotent fury I knelt or lay chained on the disk while the battles raged outside.

Still, for some reason, Sarm had not activated the control net and sent me to do his bidding.

The creature Parp spent a great deal of time in the vicinity, puffing on that small pipe, keeping it lit interminably with the tiny silver lighter which I had once mistaken for a weapon.

In the War gravitational disruption was now no longer used. It turned out that Misk, not trusting Sarm from the very beginning, had prepared a disruption device which he would not have used had it not been for Sarm's employment of that devastating weapon. But now that Misk's forces possessed a similar weapon Sarm, in fear, set his own similar devices aside.

There were new ships flying in the Nest, I understood, ships that had been built by Misk's men and disks that had now been armored by those of Sarm. I gathered there were no more available surveillance craft hangared in the Nest. On the other hand the ships of the two forces tended, it seemed, to neutralize one another, and the war in the air, far from being decisive, as Misk and I had hoped, had begun to turn into the same stalemate that had developed on the ground.

Not long after the failure of his gravitational disruption attack Sarm had spread throughout Misk's portions of the Nest various disease organisms, many of which had not had a free occurrence in centuries. On the other hand, vicious as were these invisible assailants, the extreme habitual hygiene of Priest-Kings and Muls, coupled with Misk's use of bacteri-cidal rays, dissolved this new threat.

Most savage and unnatural of all, at least to the mind of a Priest-King, was the release of the Golden Beetles from their various tunnels in the vicinity of the Nest. These creatures, perhaps two hundred or more, were loosed and by means of covered transportation disks, piloted by Priest-Kings using oxygen systems internal to the disks, were driven toward the quarters of the Nest controlled by the unsuspecting Misk and his forces.

The exudate which forms on the mane hairs of the Golden Beetle, which had overcome me in the close confines of the tunnel, apparently has a most intense and, to a human mind, almost incomprehensibly compelling effect on the unusually sensitive antennae of Priest-Kings, luring them helplessly, almost as if hypnotized, to the jaws of the Beetle, who then penetrates their body with its hollow, pincerlike jaws and drains it of body fluid.

Misk's Priest-Kings began to leave their hiding places and their posts of vantage and come into the streets, their bodies inclining forward, their antennae dipped in the direction of the lure of the Beetles. The Priest-Kings themselves said nothing, explained nothing, to their dumbfounded human companions but merely laid aside their weapons and approached the Beetles.

Then it seems that a brave female, a former Mul, unidentified, had grasped the situation and, seizing a cattle goad from one of the confused, puzzled herdsmen, had rushed upon the Beetles jabbing and striking them, driving them away with the long spearlike object, and soon the herdsmen had rushed to join her and prod away the cumbersome, domelike predators, turning them back in the direction whence they had come.

It was not more than a day later before one of Sarm's own scouts laid aside his weapon and, as the Priest-Kings say, succumbed to the Pleasures of the Golden Beetle.

Now the Beetles roamed at random throughout the Nest, more of a threat to Sarm's own forces than Misk's, for now none of Misk's Priest-Kings ventured abroad without a human to protect it should it encounter a Golden Beetle.

In the next days the Golden Beetles began, naturally enough in their hunt for food, to drift toward those portions of the Nest occupied by Sarm's Priest-Kings, for in those portions of the Nest they encountered no shouting humans, no jabbing cattle goads.

The danger became so great that all the Implanted Muls, including even the creature Parp, were sent into the streets to protect Sarm's Priest-Kings.

Oddly enough, to human thinking, neither Misk nor Sarm would permit their humans to slay the Beetles, for Priest-Kings, for a reason which I will later relate, find themselves normally unwilling to slay or order the destruction of the dangerous, fused-winged creatures.

The Golden Beetles, free within the Nest, forced Sarm, in sheer regard for survival, to turn to humans for help, for humans, particularly in the well-ventilated areas of the Nest, are relatively impervious to the narcotic odor of the Beetle's mane, an odor which is apparently almost utterly overpowering to the particular sensory apparatus of Priest-Kings.

Accordingly Sarm broadcast throughout the Nest his general amnesty for former Muls, offering them again the opportunity to become the slaves of Priest-Kings. To this generous proposal he added, sensing it might not in itself be irresistible, a tub of salt per man and two female Muls, to be provided after the defeat of Misk's forces, when presumably there would be captured females to distribute to the victors. To the females of Misk's forces he offered gold, jewelry, precious stones, delicious silks, the permission to allow their hair to grow, and male slaves, the latter again to be provided after the projected defeat of Misk's forces. To these proposals he added the very definite considerations that his forces still substantially outnumbered those of Misk in both number of Priest-Kings and firepower, and that victory would be his inevitably, and that it would be well at such a time to be in his good favor.

Whereas I would not have abandoned Misk and freedom to join the forces of Sarm I was forced to admit that the probable victory in the end would be his, and that his proposals might well be attractive to some former Muls, particularly those who had occupied a position of some importance in the Nest prior to the War.

I should not have been surprised, but I was, when the first deserter from the forces of Misk proved to be the treacherous Vika of Treve.

My first knowledge of this came one morning when suddenly I awakened in my chains to the fierce bite of a leather lash.

"Awake, Slave!" cried a voice.

With a cry of rage I struggled in my chains to my knees, pulling against the metal collar that held me to my place. Again and again the lash struck me, wielded by the gloved hand of a girl.

Then I heard her laugh and knew who was my tormentor.

Though her features were concealed in the folds of a silken veil and she wore the Robes of Concealment there was no mistaking her voice, her eyes, her carriage. The woman who stood over me with the whip, the woman clad in the most marvelous array of the most beautiful silks, wearing golden sandals and purple gloves, was Vika of Treve.

She shook the veil from her face and threw back her head and laughed.

She struck me again.

"Now," she hissed, "it is I who am Master!"

I regarded her evenly.

"I was right about you," I said. "I had hoped that I was not."

"What do you mean?" she demanded.

"You are worthy only to be a slave girl," I said.

Her face was transformed with rage and she struck me again, this time across the face. I could taste the blood from the wound of the whip.

"Do not yet injure him severely," said Sarm, standing to one side.

"He is my slave!" she said.

Sarm's antennae curled.

"He will be delivered to you only after my victory," said Sarm. "In the meantime I have use for him."

Vika threw him a glance of impatience, almost of contempt, and shrugged. "Very well," she said, "I can wait." She sneered down at me. "You will pay for what you did to me," she said. "You will pay," she said. "You will pay as only I, Vika of Treve, know how to make a man pay."

I myself was pleased that it had taken a Priest-King to have me chained at Vika's feet, that it had not been I myself who, in the hope of her favors, had fastened about my own throat the collar of a slave.

Vika turned with a swirl of her robes and left the headquarters chamber.

Sarm stalked over. "You see, Mul," said he, "how Priest-Kings use the instincts of men against them."

"Yes," I said, "I see."

Though my body burned from the whip I was more hurt by the thought of Vika, surprisingly perhaps, hurt by the thought that I had known who and what she was all along, though somewhere in my heart I had always hoped I was wrong.

Sarm then strode to a panel set in one wall. He twiddled a knob. "I am activating your control net," he said.

In my chains I tensed.

"These preliminary tests are simple," said Sarm, "and may be of interest to you."

Parp had now entered the room and stood near me, puffing on his pipe. I saw him turn off the switch on his translator.

Sarm turned a dial.

"Close your eyes," whispered Parp.

I felt no pain. Sarm was regarding me closely.

"Perhaps more power," said Parp, raising his voice so that his words might be carried by Sarm's own translator.

Sarm, at this suggestion, touched the original knob again. Then he reached for the dial again.

"Close your eyes," whispered Parp, more intensely.

For some reason I did so.

"Open them," said Parp.

I did so.

"Lower your head," he said.

I did so.

"Now rotate your head clockwise," said Parp. "Now counterclockwise."

Mystified, I did as he recommended.

"You have been unconscious," Parp informed me. "Now you are no longer controlled."

I looked about myself. I saw that Sarm had turned off the machine.

"What do you remember?" asked Sarm.

"Nothing," I said.

"We will check sensory data later," said Sarm.

"The initial responses," said Parp, raising his voice, "seem quite promising."

"Yes," said Sarm, "you have done excellent work."

Sarm then turned and left the headquarters room.

I looked at Parp, who was smiling and puffing on that pipe of his.

"You did not implant me," I said.

"Of course not," said Parp.

"What of Kusk?" I asked.

"He too is one of us," said Parp.

"But why?" I asked.

"You saved his children," said Parp.

"But he has no sex, no children," I said.

"Al-Ka and Ba-Ta," said Parp. "Do you think a Priest-King is incapable of love?"

Now my imprisonment on the rubber disk seemed less irritating than it had.

Parp had again been sent into the streets to fend off Golden Beetles should they approach too closely any of the Priest-Kings of Sarm.

I learned from conversation in the headquarters room that not many of the humans who fought with Misk's forces had responded to the blandishments of Sarm, though some, like Vika of Treve, had deserted to cast their fortune with what appeared to be the winning side. From what I could gather only a handful of humans, some men, some women, had actually crossed the lines and taken service with Sarm.

Sarm, one day, brought down from the Halls of the Priest-Kings above, all the humans who were quartered there, mostly Chamber Slaves, to aid his cause. The latter, of course, terrified, bewildered, would be of little service themselves, but they were offered as inducements to the males of Misk's forces to encourage their desertion; the girls were, so to speak, a bounty for treachery, and since the beauty of Chamber Slaves was well known in the Nest, I supposed they might well prove quite effective in this role; yet, somewhat to my surprise and pleasure, no more than a half dozen or so men came forth to claim these lovely prizes. As the War continued I became more and more impressed with the loyalty and courage of the men and women serving Misk, who for a bit of fungus and water and freedom, were willing to sell their lives in one of the strangest conflicts ever fought by men, boldly serving one of the most unusual causes that had ever asked for the allegiance of the human kind.

Vika would come to torment me each day but no longer was she permitted to whip me.

I supposed that there was reason for her hatred of me but still I wondered at its depth and fury.

She was later given charge of my feeding and she seemed to enjoy throwing me scraps of fungus or watching me lap at the water in the pan she placed on the disk. I ate because I wished to keep what I could of my strength, for I might have need of it again.

Sarm, who was normally in the room, seemed to take great pleasure in Vika's baiting me, for he would stand by, antennae curling, as she would insult me, taunt me, sometimes strike me with her small fist. He apparently became rather fond of the new female Mul and, upon occasion, he would order her to groom him in my presence, a task which she seemed to enjoy.

"What a piteous thing you are," she said to me, "and how golden and strong and brave and fine is a Priest-King!"

And Sarm would extend his antennae down to her that she might delicately brush the small golden hairs which adorned them.

For some reason Vika's attentions to Sarm irritated me and undoubtedly I failed to conceal this sufficiently because Sarm often required this task of her in my presence and, I noted with fury, she seemed invariably delighted to comply with his request.

Once I called angrily to her. "Pet Mul!"

"Silence, Slave," she responded haughtily. Then she looked at me and laughed merrily. "For that," she said, "you will go hungry tonight!"

I remembered, smiling to myself, how when I was master I had once, to discipline her, refused her food one night. Now it was I who would go hungry, but I told myself, it was worth it. Let her think over that, I said to myself, think over that—Vika of Treve—Pet Mul!

I found myself wanting to take her body in my arms and shatter it to my breast, forcing back her head, taking her lips in the kiss of a master as though I once more owned her.

I shook these thoughts from my head.

Meanwhile, slowly, incredibly, the War in the Nest began to turn against Sarm. The most remarkable event was a delegation of Sarm's Priest-Kings, led by Kusk himself, who surrendered to Misk, pledging themselves to his cause. This transfer of allegiance was apparently the result of long discussion and consideration by the group of Priest-Kings, who had followed Sarm because he was First Born, but had at many points objected to his conduct of the War, in particular to his treatment of the Muls, his use of the gravitational disruption devices, his attempt to spread disease in the Nest and last, his, to a Priest-King's thinking, hideous recourse to the Golden Beetles. Kusk and his delegation went over to Misk while the fighting still hung in stalemate and there was no question, at that time, of their decision being motivated by considerations of personal interest. Indeed, at that time, it seemed they had, almost unaccountably, for reasons of principle, joined a cause which was in all probability a lost one. But not long after this took place other Priest-Kings, startled by the decision of Kusk, began to speak of ending the War, and some others too began to cross the lines. Growing more desperate, Sarm rallied his forces and armored six dozen transportation disks and swept into Misk's domain. Apparently Misk's forces were waiting for them, as might have been expected given the superior intelligence afforded by the numerous humans in Misk's camp and the disks were stopped by barricades and withered in the intense fire from nearby rooftops. Only four disks returned.

It now became clear that Sarm was on the defensive, for I heard orders being issued to block the tunnels leading into the areas of the Nest he controlled. Once I heard the hiss of silver tubes not more than a few hundred yards away. I struggled, enraged, against the chains and collar that held me a helpless prisoner while the issues of the day were being decided by fire in the streets outside.

Then there came a calm in the War and I gathered that Misk's forces had been driven back.

My rations of Mul-Fungus had been cut by two-thirds since I had been captured. And I noted that some of Sarm's Priest-Kings were less golden than I had known them, having now a slightly brownish cast on the thorax and abdomen, signs I knew to be associated with thirst.

I think it was only now that the absence of the supplies captured or destroyed by the Fungus Growers and Herdsmen had begun to make itself keenly felt.

At last Sarm made clear to me why I had been kept alive, why I had not been destroyed long ago.

"It is said that there is Nest Trust between you and Misk," he said. "Now we will see if that is truly so."

"What do you mean?" I asked.

"If there is Nest Trust between you," said Sarm, his antennae curling, "Misk will be ready to die for you."

"I don't understand," I said.

"His life for yours," said Sarm.

"Never," I said.

"No," cried Vika, who had been standing in the background, "he is mine!"

"Do not fear, Little Mul," said Sarm. "We will have Misk's life and you will still have your slave."

"Sarm is treacherous," I said.

"Sarm is a Priest-King," he said.

31
Sarm's Revenge

THE PLACE OF MEETING WAS arranged.

It lay in one of the plazas in the area controlled by the forces of Sarm.

Misk was to come alone to the plaza, to be met by myself and Sarm. No one was to bear arms. Misk would surrender himself to Sarm and I, theoretically, would then be allowed to go free.

But I knew that Sarm had no intention of keeping his part of the bargain, and that he intended to slay Misk, destroying hopefully thereby the effective leadership of the opposition, and then either keep me as a slave for Vika or, more likely, killing me as well, even though that might disappoint the expectations of vengeance nourished in the bosom of his pet Mul.

When I was unchained I was informed by Sarm that the small box he carried activated my control net and at the first sign of disobedience or difficulty he would simply raise the power level—literally boiling my brain away.

I said that I understood.

I wondered what Sarm would say if he knew that Parp and Kusk had not actually implanted me.

In spite of the agreement about arms, Sarm hung from the back of his translator strap, invisible from the front, a silver tube.

To my surprise his pet Mul, Vika of Treve, demanded to accompany her golden master. I supposed that she feared he might slay me, thus depriving her of her revenge for which she had waited so long. He would have refused her, but she pleaded so earnestly that at last he agreed that she might accompany us. "I wish to see my master triumph!" she begged, and that argument seemed to sway golden Sarm, and Vika found herself a member of our party.

I myself was forced to walk perhaps a dozen paces in front of Sarm, who held his grasping appendage near the control box which would, he supposed, activate the golden net he believed to be fused into the tissues of my brain. Vika walked at his side.

At last I saw, far across the plaza, the slowly stalking figure of Misk.

How tender I felt toward the golden giant in that moment as I realized that he, though a Priest-King, had come to give his life for mine, simply because we had once locked antennae, simply because we were friends, simply because there was Nest Trust between us.

He stopped and we stopped.

And then we began to walk slowly towards one another

again across the square tiles of that plaza in the secret Nest of Priest-Kings.

When he was still out of range of the silver tube of Sarm but close enough, I hoped, to be able to hear me, I ran forward, throwing my hands high. "Go back!" I cried. "It is a trick! Go back!"

Misk stopped in his tracks.

I heard Sarm's translator behind me. "You will die for that, Mul," it said.

I turned and I saw Sarm, his entire golden bladelike form convulsed with rage. Two of the tiny hooklike appendages on his foreleg spun the power dial on the control box. "Die, Mul," said Sarm.

But I stood calmly before him.

It took Sarm but an instant to realize he had been tricked and he hurled the box from him and it shattered on the tiles of the plaza.

I stood ready now to receive the blast of Sarm's silver tube which he had whipped from its place of concealment and trained on my breast.

"Very well," said Sarm, "let it be the silver tube."

I tensed myself for the sudden burst of fire, that incandescent torrent that would burst and burn the flesh from my bones.

The firing switch was depressed and I heard the soft click but the tube failed to fire. Once again, desperately, Sarm pressed the firing switch.

"It does not fire!" came from Sarm's translator and his entire frame was startled, shaken with incomprehension.

"No," cried Vika, "I discharged it this morning!"

The girl ran to my side in a swirl of many-colored silks and from beneath the Robes of Concealment she withdrew my sword and kneeling at my side lowered her head and placed it in my hand. "Cabot my Master!" she cried.

I took the blade.

"Rise," I said, "Vika of Treve—you are now a free woman."

"I do not understand," came from Sarm's translator.

"I came to see my Master triumph!" cried Vika of Treve, her voice thrilled with emotion.

Gently I thrust the girl to one side.

"I do not understand," came from Sarm's translator.

"That is how you have lost," I said.

Sarm hurled the silver tube at my head and I ducked and heard it clatter across the tiles of the plaza for perhaps a hundred yards.

Then to my amazement Sarm turned and though I was but a human he fled from the plaza.

Vika was in my arms weeping.

In a moment we were joined by Misk.

The War was at an end.

Sarm had disappeared and with his disappearance, and presumed death, the opposition to Misk evaporated, for it had been held together only by the dominance of Sarm's mighty personality and the prestige that was his in virtue of being First Born.

The Priest-Kings who had served him had, on the whole at least, believed that what they were doing was required by the laws of the Nest, but now with Sarm's disappearance Misk, though only Fifth Born, acceded to the title of highest born, and it was to him now, according to the same laws of the Nest, that their allegiance was now owed.

There was a greater problem as to what to do with the former Muls who had deserted to join the forces of Sarm, for the blandishments he had offered, and because they had thought that his side was the one which was winning. I was pleased to see that there were only about seventy-five or eighty wretches in this latter category. About two-thirds of them were men, and the rest women. None of them, interestingly enough, were Gur Carriers, or from the Fungus Chambers or the Pastures.

Al-Ka and Ba-Ta arrived with two prisoners, female Muls, frightened, sullen girls, lovely, clad now only in brief, sleeveless plastic, who knelt at their feet. They were joined together by a length of chain that had been, by means of two padlocks, fastened about their throats. Their wrists were secured behind their backs by slave bracelets.

"Deserters," said Al-Ka.

"Where now," asked Ba-Ta of the girls, "is your gold, your jewelry and silks?"

Sullenly they looked down.

"Do we kill them now?" asked Al-Ka.

The girls looked at one another and trembled in fear.

I looked at Al-Ka and Ba-Ta rather closely.

They winked at me. I winked back at them. I perceived their plan. I could see that neither of them had the least intention of injuring one of the lovely creatures in their power.

"If you wish—" I said.

A cry of fear escaped the girls.

"Please don't!" said one, looking up, pleading, and the other pressed her head to the floor at Ba-Ta's feet.

Al-Ka regarded them. "This one," he said, "has strong legs."

Ba-Ta regarded the other. "This one," he said, "seems healthy."

"Do you wish to live?" asked Al-Ka of the first girl.

"Yes!" she said.

"Very well," said Al-Ka, "you will do so—as my slave."

"—Master!" said the girl.

"And you?" asked Ba-Ta sternly of the second girl.

Without raising her head she said, "I am your slave girl, Master."

"Look up," commanded Al-Ka, and both of the girls lifted their heads trembling.

Then to my surprise Al-Ka and Ba-Ta, from their pouches, produced golden collars, only too obviously prepared in advance. There were two heavy, short clicks and the lovely throats of the two girls were encircled. I gathered it was the only gold they would see for some time. On one collar there was engraved 'Al-Ka' and on the other 'Ba-Ta'.

Then Al-Ka unlocked the throat chain worn by the female Muls and he went off in one direction and Ba-Ta in the other. No longer did it seem the two former Muls were inseparable. Each departed, followed by his girl, her wrists still bound behind her back.

"And what," laughed Vika of Treve, "is to be my fate?"

"You are free," I reminded her.

"But my fate?" she asked, smiling at me.

I laughed. "It is similar to that of the others," I said, and swept her from her feet and carried her, Robes of Concealment swirling, from the room.

Misk and I had been trying to decide, for the past five days, how to organize the Nest in the wake of the War. The simplest matters had to do with restoring its services and its capacity to sustain both Priest-Kings and humans. The more difficult matters had to do with the political arrangements that would allow these two diverse species to inhabit peaceably and prosperously the same dwelling. Misk was quite ready, as I was afraid he might not be, to allow humans a voice in affairs of the Nest and, moreover, to arrange for the return to their cities of those humans who did not wish to remain in the Nest.

We were considering these matters when suddenly the entire floor of the compartment in which we sat seemed to buckle and break apart. At the same time two walls shattered and fell crumbling in rubble to the floor. Misk covered my body with his own and then with his great strength, reared up, stones falling from his back like water from the body of a swimmer.

The entire Nest seemed to shiver.

"An earthquake!" I cried.

"Sarm is not dead," said Misk. Dusty, covered with whitish powder, he looked about himself disbelievingly at the ruins. In the distance we could hear the domed side of a complex begin to crumble, raining down huge blocks of stone on the buildings beneath. "He is going to destroy the Nest," said Misk. "He is going to break apart the planet."

"Where is he?" I demanded.

"The Power Plant," said Misk.

I climbed over the fallen stones and ran from the room and leaped on the first transportation disk I could find. Though the path it had to travel was broken and littered the cushion of gas on which the disk flowed lifted the vehicle cleanly, though bucking and tilting, over the debris.

In a few moments, though the disk was damaged by falling stone and I could barely see through the powdery drifts of rock hanging in the collapsing tunnels, I had come to the Power Plant and leaped from the disk and raced to its doors. They were locked but it was only a moment's work to find the nearby ventilator shaft and wrench away the screen. In less than a minute I had kicked open another grille and dropped inside the great domed room of the Power Plant. I saw no sign of Sarm. I myself would not know how to repair his damage so I went to the doors of the chamber, which were locked on the inside, and thrust up the latching mechanism. I swung them open. Now Misk and his engineers would be able to enter the room. I had scarcely thrust up the latch when a burst of fire from a silver tube scorched the door over my head. I looked up to see Sarm on that narrow passage that traced its precarious way around the great blue dome that covered the power source. Another flash of fire burned near me, leaving a rupture of molten marble in the floor not five feet from where I stood. Running irregularly, dodging bursts of fire, I ran to the side of the dome where Sarm, from his position somewhere above, would not be likely to be able to reach me with his fire.

Then I saw him through the sides of the blue dome that covered the power source, far above, a golden figure on the narrow walkway at the crest of the dome. He fired at me, burning a hole in the dome near him, exposing the power source, and the same flashing burst of fire tore at the area of the dome behind which I stood. The burst had spent itself and only managed to scorch the dome, but the next, fired through the hole already made above, might do more damage, so I changed my position. Then Sarm seemed to lose interest in me, perhaps thinking I had been slain, more likely to conserve the charge in the silver tube for more important matters, for he then began, methodically, to fire at the paneling across from the dome, destroying one area after another. As he was doing this the entire Nest seemed to shift and the planet convulsed, and fire spurted from the paneling. Then he fired a burst directly down into the power source and it began to rumble and throw geysers of purple fire up almost to the hole which Sarm had burned in the globe. To one side, though I scarcely noticed it at the time, I saw a vague, domelike golden shape, one of the Beetles which, undoubtedly confused and terrified, had crept into the room of the Power Plant from the tunnel outside, through the door I had opened for Misk and his Priest-Kings. Where were they? I surmised the tunnels might have collapsed and they were even now trying to cut their way through to the Chamber of the Power Plant.

I knew that somehow I must try to stop Sarm but what could I do? He was armed with a silver tube and I with nothing but the steel of a Gorean sword.

Sarm kept firing long, persistent bursts of fire at the paneling against the walls, undoubtedly attempting to destroy the instrumentation. I hoped that such firing might exhaust the charge of the weapon.

I left cover and rushed to the walkway and was soon climbing up the narrow path that crept around the surface of the globe that now barely contained the frenzied, bubbling fury, the turbulence of the hissing, erupting substance that leaped and smote against the smooth enclosing walls.

I climbed the walkway rapidly and soon could see Sarm clearly at the very top of the dome, whence he had once displayed to me the majesty of the Priest-Kings' accomplishments, where he had once indicated to me the modifications of the ganglionic net by means of which his people had won to the enormous power they possessed. He was not yet aware of my approach, perhaps not believing I would be fool enough to climb the exposed walkway in pursuit.

Then suddenly he wheeled and saw me and seemed startled but then the silver tube flew up and I threw myself rolling back down the walkway, the steel stairs bubbling away following me. Then I had the curve of the dome between me and the Priest-King. His weapon fired again, slicing through the top of the dome in his vicinity and striking beneath me, melting a hole in the dome below me. Twice more Sarm fired and twice more I scrambled about on the walkway trying to keep the two surfaces of the globe between myself and his weapon. Then angrily I saw him turn away and commence firing again at the paneling. As he did so, I began to climb once more. As I climbed, to my elation, I saw the tube's flame sputter and stop and knew the weapon was at last discharged.

I wondered what more Sarm could do now.

Nothing from his position at the top of the globe, though it had been an ideal vantage point for firing the tube into the instrumentation.

I wondered if he regretted wasting a large part of his weapon's charge on firing at me. To do more damage he would now have to descend the walkway and reach the paneling itself, perhaps that on the other side of the room, but to do this he would have to pass me, and I was determined that I should not, if possible, allow that to happen.

Slowly I climbed the walkway, stepping with care past the ruined portions of the steel steps leading to the crest of the dome.

Sarm seemed in no hurry. He seemed quite content to wait for me.

I saw him toss the silver tube away, and saw it fall through one of the great holes he had blasted in the globe and disappear in the violent, bubbling purple mass seething below.

At last I stood not more than a dozen yards from the Priest-King.

He had been watching me approach and now his antennae focused on me and he drew himself up to his full golden height.

"I knew you would come," he said.

One wall to the left began to crumble, fitted stone from its sides edging outwards and breaking loose to clatter down the ramps and tumble even to the floor so far beneath.

A drift of dust from the rubble obscured Sarm's figure for a moment.

"I am destroying the planet," he said. "It has served its purpose." He regarded me. "It has sheltered the Nest of Priest-Kings but now there are no more Priest-Kings—only I, only Sarm is left."

"There are still many Priest-Kings in the Nest," I said.

"No," he said, "there is only one Priest-King, the First Born, Sarm—he who did not betray the Nest, he who was beloved of the Mother, he who kept and honored the ancient truths of his people."

The bladelike figure of the Priest-King seemed to waver on the walkway and the antennae seemed blown about as though by the wind.

More stones fell from the ceiling of the chamber now, clattering and bouncing off the surface of the blue, scarred seething dome.

"You have destroyed the Nest," said Sarm, looking wildly down at me.

I said nothing. I did not even draw my sword.

"But now," said Sarm, "I will destroy you."

The weapon left my sheath.

Sarm reached to the steel bar that formed the railing to his left on the walkway and with the incredible strength of Priest-Kings with one motion twisted and tore free a length of perhaps eighteen feet. He swung this lightly, as easily as I might have lifted and moved a stick of wood.

The bar he wielded was a fearsome weapon and with it he could strike me from the walkway, hurling me perhaps two hundred feet to the opposite wall, before I could get within yards of him.

I stepped back and Sarm advanced a delicate pace.

"Primitive," said Sarm, regarding the club of steel which he held, and then he looked down at me, his antennae curling, "but fitting."

I knew I could not retreat back down the walkway for Sarm was much faster than I and would be upon me perhaps even before I could turn.

I could not leap to the sides for there there was only the smooth sheer curve of the blue globe and I would slide to my death and fall like one of the stones from the roof above to the dusty, smoking rubble below.

And ahead of me stood Sarm, his club ready. If his first blow missed perhaps I could get close enough to strike but it did not seem probable his blow would miss.

It did not seem to me a bad place to die.

If I had dared to take my eyes from Sarm I might have looked about at the wonder of the Nest and the destruction in which it was being consumed. Drifts of rock powder hung in the air, fitted stone tumbled to the flooring far below, the walls trembled, the very globe and walkway fastened to it seemed to shift and shudder. I supposed there might be tidal waves in the distant Thassa, that crags in the Sardar and the Voltai and Thentis Ranges might be collapsing, that mountains might be falling and new ones rising, that the Sa-Tarna fields might be broken apart, that towers of cities might be falling, that the ring of black logs which encircled the Sardar might rupture and burst open in a hundred places. I imagined the panic in the cities of Gor, the pitching ships at sea, the stampedes of animals, and only I, of all humans, was at the place where this havoc had begun, only I was there to gaze upon the author of the destruction of a world, the golden destroyer of a planet.

"Strike," I said. "Be done with it."

Sarm lifted the bar and I sensed the murderous intensity that transformed his entire being, how each of those golden fibers like springs of steel would leap into play and the long bar would slash in a blur toward my body.

I crouched, sword in hand, waiting for the blow.

But Sarm did not strike.

Rather to my wonder the bar of steel lowered and Sarm seemed frozen suddenly in an attitude of the most rapt perception. His antennae quivered and tensed but not stiffly and each of the sensory hairs on his body lifted and extended. His limbs seemed suddenly weak.

"Kill it," he said. "Kill it."

I thought he might be telling himself to be done with me, but somehow I knew this could not be.

Then I too sensed it and I turned.

Behind me, inching its way up the narrow walkway, clinging with its six small legs, slowly lifting its heavy domelike golden body a step at a time, came the Golden Beetle I had seen below.

The mane hairs on its back were lifted like antennae and they moved as strangely, as softly, as underwater plants might lift and stir in the tides and currents of the cold liquid of the sea.

The narcotic odor emanating from that lifted, waving

mane shook even me though I stood in the midst of free air on the top of that great blue globe.

The steel bar fell from Sarm's appendage and slid from the top of the dome to fall with a distant crash far below in the rubble.

"Kill it, Cabot," came from Sarm's translator. "Kill it, Cabot, please." The Priest-King could not move. "You are human," said the translator. "You can kill it. Kill it, Cabot, please."

I stood to one side, standing on the surface of the globe, clinging to the rail.

"It is not done," I said to Sarm. "It is a great crime to kill one."

Slowly the heavy body with its domed, fused wings pressed past me, its tiny, tuftlike antennae extending towards Sarm, its long, hollow pincerlike jaws opening.

"Cabot," came from Sarm's translator.

"It is thus," I said, "that men use the instincts of Priest-Kings against them."

"Cabot—Cabot—Cabot," came from the translator.

Then to my amazement when the Beetle neared Sarm the Priest-King sank down on his supporting appendages, almost as if he were on his knees, and suddenly plunged his face and antennae into the midst of the waving manehair of the Golden Beetle.

I watched the pincerlike jaws grip and puncture the thorax of the Priest-King.

More rock dust drifted between me and the pair locked in the embrace of death.

More rock tumbled to the dome and bounced clattering to the debris below.

The very globe and walkway seemed to lift and tremble but neither of the creatures locked together above me seemed to take the least notice.

Sarm's antennae lay immersed in the golden hair of the Beetle; his grasping appendages with their sensory hairs caressed the golden hair; even did he take some of the hairs in his mouth and with his tongue try to lick the exudate from them.

"The pleasure," came from Sarm's translator. "The pleasure, the pleasure."

I could not shut out from my ears the grim sound of the sucking jaws of the Beetle.

I knew now why it was that the Golden Beetles were permitted to live in the Nest, why it was that Priest-Kings would not slay them, even though it might mean their own lives.

I wondered if the hairs of the Golden Beetle, heavy with the droplets of that narcotic exudate, offered adequate recompense to a Priest-King for the ascetic millenia in which he might have pursued the mysteries of science, if they provided an acceptable culmination to one of those long, long lives devoted to the Nest, to its laws, to duty and the pursuit and manipulation of power.

Priest-Kings, I knew, had few pleasures, and now I guessed that foremost among them might be death.

Once as though by some supreme effort of will Sarm, who was a great Priest-King, lifted his head from the golden hair and stared at me.

"Cabot," came from his translator.

"Die, Priest-King," I said softly.

The last sound I heard from Sarm's translator was—"The pleasure."

Then in the last spasmodic throb of death Sarm's body broke free of the jaws of the Golden Beetle and reared up once more to its glorious perhaps twenty feet of golden height.

He stood thusly on the walkway at the top of the vast blue dome beneath which burned and hissed the power source of Priest-Kings.

One last time he looked about himself, his antennae surveying the grandeur of the Nest, and then tumbled from the walkway and fell to the surface of the globe and slid until he fell to the rubble below.

The swollen, lethargic Beetle turned slowly to face me.

With one stroke of my blade I broke open its head.

With my foot I tumbled its heavy body from the walkway and watched it slide down the side of the globe and fall like Sarm to the rubble below.

I stood there on the crest of the globe and looked about the crumbling Nest.

Far below, at the door to the chamber, I could see the golden figures of Priest-Kings, Misk among them. I turned and retraced my steps down the walkway.

32
To the Surface

"IT IS THE END," SAID Misk, "the end." He frantically adjusted the controls on a major panel, his antennae taut with concentration reading the scent-needle on a boxlike gauge.

Other Priest-Kings worked beside him.

I looked to the body of Sarm, golden and broken, lying among the rubble on the floor, half covered in the powdery dust that hung like fog in the room.

I heard the choking of a girl next to me and put my arm about the shoulders of Vika of Treve.

"It took time to cut through to you," said Misk. "Now it is too late."

"The planet?" I asked.

"The Nest—the World," said Misk.

Now the bubbling mass inside the purple globe began to burn through the globe itself and there were cracking sounds and rivulets of thick, hissing substance, like blue lava, began to press through the breaks in the globe. Elsewhere droplets of the same material seemed to form on the outside of the globe.

"We must leave the chamber," said Misk, "for the globe will shatter."

He pointed an excited foreleg at the scent-needle which I, of course, could not read.

"Go," came from Misk's translator.

I swept Vika up and carried her from the trembling chamber and we were accompanied by hurrying Priest-Kings and those humans who had accompanied them.

I turned back only in time to see Misk leap from the panel and rush to the body of Sarm lying among the rubble. There was a great splitting sound and the entire side of the globe cracked open and began to pour forth its avalanche of thick, molten fluid into the room.

Still Misk tugged at the broken body of Sarm among the rubble.

The purple mass of bubbling fury poured over the rubble toward the Priest-King.

"Hurry!" I cried to him.

But the Priest-King paid me no attention, trying to move a great block of stone which had fallen across one of the supporting appendages of the dead Sarm.

I thrust Vika behind me and leaped over the rubble, running to Misk's side.

"Come!" I cried, pounding my fist against his thorax. "Hurry!"

"No," said Misk.

"He's dead!" I said. "Leave him!"

"He is a Priest-King," said Misk.

Together Misk and I, as the blue lavalike mass began to hiss over the rubble bubbling towards us, forced aside the great block of stone and Misk tenderly gathered up the broken carcass of Sarm in his forelegs and he and I sped toward the opening, and the blue molten flux of burning, seething, hissing substance engulfed where we had stood.

Misk, carrying Sarm, and the other Priest-Kings and humans, including Vika and myself, made our way from the Power Plant and back toward the complex which had been the heart of Sarm's territory.

"Why?" I asked Misk.

"Because he is a Priest-King," said Misk.

"He was a traitor," I said, "and betrayed the Nest and would have slain you by treachery and has now destroyed your Nest and world."

"But he was a Priest-King," said Misk, and he touched the crushed, torn figure of Sarm gently with his antennae. "And he was First Born," said Misk. "And he was beloved of the Mother."

There was a huge explosion from behind us and I knew that the globe had now burst and the chamber that housed it was shattered in its destruction.

The very tunnel we walked in pitched and buckled under our feet.

We came to the hole where Misk and his fellow Priest-Kings and humans had cut through fallen debris and climbed out through it, finding ourselves in one of the major complexes again.

It was cold and the humans, including myself, shivered in the simple plastic we wore.

"Look" cried Vika pointing upward.

And we looked, all of us, and saw, far above, perhaps more than a mile above, the open blue sky of Gor. A great opening, from the sides of which stones still fell, had appeared in the ceiling of the Nest complex, opening the thick, numerous strata above it until at last through that rupture could be seen the beautiful calm sky of the world above.

Some of the humans with us cried aloud in wonder for never had they seen the sky.

The Priest-Kings shielded their antennae from the radiation of the sunlit heavens far above.

It sprang into my mind suddenly why they needed men, how dependent they were upon us.

Priest-Kings could not stand the sun!

I looked up at the sky.

And I understood as I had not before what must be the pain, the glory and the agony of the Nuptial Flight. His wings, she had said, had been like showers of gold.

"How beautiful it is!" cried Vika.

"Yes," I said, "it is very beautiful."

I recalled that it would have been nine years since the girl had looked upon the sky.

I put my arm about her shoulders, holding her as she wept, her face lifted to the distant blue sky.

At this moment, skimming over the buildings in the complex, no more than a few feet from their roofs, came one of the ships of Misk, piloted by Al-Ka, accompanied by his woman.

It landed near us.

A moment later another ship, piloted by Ba-Ta, appeared and settled by its sister ship. He too had his woman with him.

"It is now time to choose," said Misk, "where one will die."

The Priest-Kings, of course, would not leave the Nest, and, to my surprise, most of the humans, many of whom had been bred in the Nest or now regarded it as their home, insisted also on remaining where they were.

Others, however, eagerly boarded the ships to be flown through the opening to the mountains above.

"We have made many trips," said Al-Ka, "and so have others in the other ships, for the Nest is broken in a dozen places and open to the sky."

"Where will you choose to die?" I asked Vika of Treve.

"At your side," she said simply.

Al-Ka and Ba-Ta, as I would have expected, turned their ships over to others to pilot, for they would choose to remain in the Nest. Their women, too, to my amazement, freely elected to remain by the sides of the men who had fastened golden collars about their throats.

I saw Kusk in the distance, and both Al-Ka and Ba-Ta, followed by their women, began to walk towards him. They met perhaps a hundred yards from where I stood and I saw the Priest-King place a foreleg on the shoulder of each and together they stood and waited for the final crumbling of the Nest.

"There is no safety above," said Misk.

"Nor any here," I said.

"True," said Misk.

In the distance we could hear dull explosions and the crash of falling rock.

"The entire Nest is being destroyed," said Misk.

I saw tears in the eyes of humans.

"Is there nothing that can be done?" I demanded.

"Nothing," said Misk.

Vika looked up at me. "Where will you choose to die, Cabot?" she asked.

I saw that the last ship was preparing to take flight through the hole torn above in the ceiling of the complex. I would have liked to have seen once more the surface of the world, the blue sky, the green fields beyond the black Sardar, but rather I said, "I choose to remain here with Misk, who is my friend."

"Very well," said Vika, putting her head against my shoulder. "I will also remain."

"Something you have said does not translate," said Misk, his antennae dipping towards me.

I looked up into the huge, peering golden eyes of Misk, the left one lined with a whitish seam where Sarm's bladed projection had once torn it open in the battle in the Chamber of the Mother.

I could not even tell him how I felt about him, for his language did not contain the expression I needed.

"I said," I told him, "I choose to remain here with you—and I said something like 'There is Nest Trust between us'."

"I see," said Misk, and touched me lightly with his antennae.

With my right hand I gently pressed the sensory appendage which rested on my left shoulder.

Then together we watched the ship float swiftly upward like a small white star and disappear in the blue distance beyond.

Now Kusk, Al-Ka and Ba-Ta, and their women, slowly walked across the rubble to join us.

We stood now on the uneven, shifting stones of the floor. To one side, high in the domed wall some energy bulbs burst, emitting a cascade of sparks that looped downwards burning themselves out before striking the floor. Some more tons of stone fell from the hole torn in the ceiling, raining down on the buildings beneath, breaking through the roofs, shattering to the streets. Drifting dust obscured the complex and I drew the folds of Vika's robes more about her face that she might be better protected. Misk's body was coated with dust and I felt it in my hair and eyes and throat.

I smiled to myself, for Misk seemed now to busy himself with his cleaning hooks. His world might be crumbling about him but he would not forgo his grooming. I supposed the dust that clung to his thorax and abdomen, that adhered to the sensory hairs on his appendages might be distressing to him, more so perhaps than the fear that he might be totally crushed by one of the great blocks of stone that occasionally fell clattering near us.

"It is unfortunate," said Al-Ka to me, "that the alternative power plant is not near completion."

Misk stopped grooming, and Kusk, too, peered down at Al-Ka.

"What alternative power plant?" I asked.

"The plant of the Muls," said Al-Ka, "which we have been readying for five hundred years, preparing for the revolt against Priest-Kings."

"Yes," said Ba-Ta, "built by Mul engineers trained by Priest-Kings, constructed of parts stolen over centuries and hidden in an abandoned portion of the Old Nest.

"I did not know of this," said Misk.

"Priest-Kings often underestimate Muls," said Al-Ka.

"I am proud of my sons," said Kusk.

"We are not engineers," said Al-Ka.

"No," said Kusk, "but you are humans."

"As far as that goes," said Ba-Ta, "no more than a few Muls knew of the plant. We ourselves did not find out about it until some technicians joined our forces in the Nest War."

"Where are these technicians now!" I demanded.

"Working," said Al-Ka.

I seized him by the shoulders. "Is there a chance the plant can become operational?"

"No," said Al-Ka.

"Then why are they working?" asked Misk.

"It is human," said Ba-Ta.

"Foolish," observed Misk.

"But human," said Ba-Ta.

"Yes, foolish," said Misk, his antennae curling a bit, but then he touched Ba-Ta gently on the shoulders to show him that he meant no harm.

"What is needed?" I demanded.

"I am not an engineer," said Al-Ka, "I do not know." He looked at me. "But it has to do with Ur Force."

"That secret," said Ba-Ta, "has been well guarded by Priest-Kings."

Misk lifted his antennae meditatively. "There is the Ur disruptor I constructed in the War," came from his translator. He and Kusk touched antennae quickly and held them locked for a moment. Then Misk and Kusk separated antennae. "The components in the disruptor might be realigned," he said, "but there is little likelihood that the power loop could be satisfactorily closed."

"Why not?" I asked.

"For one thing," said Misk, "the plant built by Muls is probably fundamentally ineffective to begin with; for another if it is constructed of parts stolen over centuries it would be probably impossible to achieve satisfactory component integration with the elements in the Ur disruptor."

"Yes," said Kusk, and his antennae dipped disconsolately, "the probabilities are not at all in our favor."

A huge boulder fell from the roof and bounded, almost like a giant rubber ball, past our group. Vika screamed and I pressed her more tightly against me. More than anything I began to be exasperated with Misk and Kusk.

"Is there any chance at all?" I demanded of Misk.

"Perhaps," said Misk, "for I have not seen the plant they have built."

"But in all probability," pointed out Kusk, "there is really no chance."

"An extremely small but yet finite possibility," speculated Misk, grooming one foreleg.

"I think so," acknowledged Kusk.

I seized Misk, stopping him from that infernal grooming. "If there is any chance at all," I cried, "you must try!"

Misk peered down at me and his antennae seemed to lift with surprise. "I am a Priest-King," he said. "The probability is not such that a Priest-King, who is a rational creature, would act upon it."

"You must act!" I cried.

Another boulder fell clattering down a hundred yards from us and bounded past.

"I wish to die with dignity," said Misk, gently pulling his foreleg away and recommencing his grooming. "It is not becoming to a Priest-King to scramble about like a human—still scratching here and there when there is no likelihood of success."

"If not for your own sake," I said, "then for the sake of

humans—in the Nest and outside of it—who have no hope but you."

Misk stopped grooming and looked down. "Do you wish this thing, Tarl Cabot?" he asked.

"Yes," I said.

And Kusk looked down at Al-Ka and Ba-Ta. "Do you, too, wish this thing?" he asked.

"Yes," said Al-Ka and Ba-Ta.

At that moment, through the drifting rock dust, I saw the heavy, domed body of one of the Golden Beetles, perhaps fifty yards away.

Almost simultaneously both Misk and Kusk lifted their antennae and shuddered.

"We are fortunate," came from Kusk's translator.

"Yes," said Misk, "now it will not be necessary to seek one of the Golden Beetles."

"You must not yield to the Golden Beetle!" I cried.

I could now see the antennae of both Misk and Kusk turning towards the Beetle, and I could see the Beetle stop, and the mane hairs begin to lift. Suddenly, through the rock dust, I could scent that strange narcotic odor.

I drew my sword, but gently Misk seized my wrist, not permitting me to rush upon the Beetle and slay it. "No," said Misk.

The Beetle drew closer, and I could see the mane hairs waving now like the fronds of some marine plant caught in the currents of its underwater world.

"You must resist the Golden Beetle," I said to Misk.

"I am going to die," said Misk, "do not begrudge me this pleasure."

Kusk took a step toward the Beetle.

"You must resist the Golden Beetle to the end!" I cried.

"This is the end," came from Misk's translator. "And I have tried. And I am tired now. Forgive me, Tarl Cabot."

"Is this how our father chooses to die?" asked Al-Ka of Kusk.

"You do not understand, my children," said Kusk, "what the Golden Beetle means to a Priest-King."

"I think I understand," I cried, "but you must resist!"

"Would you have us die working at a hopeless task," asked

Misk, "die like fools deprived of the final Pleasures of the Golden Beetle?"

"Yes!" I cried.

"It is not the way of Priest-Kings," said Misk.

"Let it be the way of Priest-Kings!" I cried.

Misk seemed to straighten himself, his antennae waved about wildly, every fiber of his body seemed to shiver.

He stood shuddering in the drifting rock dust, amid the crashings of distant rocks. He surveyed the humans gathered about him, the heavy golden hemisphere of the approaching Beetle.

"Drive it away," came from Misk's translator.

With a cry of joy I rushed upon the Beetle and Vika and Al-Ka and Ba-Ta and their women joined me and together, kicking and pushing, avoiding the tubular jaws, hurling rocks, we forced away the globe of the Golden Beetle.

We returned to Misk and Kusk who stood together, their antennae touching.

"Take us to the plant of the Muls," said Misk.

"I will show you," cried Al-Ka.

Misk turned again to me. "I wish you well, Tarl Cabot, human," he said.

"Wait," I said, "I will go with you."

"You can do nothing to help," he said. Misk's antennae inclined toward me. "Go to the surface," said Misk. "Stand in the wind and see the sky and sun once more."

I lifted my hands and Misk touched the palms gently with his antennae.

"I wish you well, Misk, Priest-King," I said.

Misk turned and hurried off, followed by Kusk and the others.

Vika and I were left alone in the crumbling complex. Over our heads it seemed suddenly that, splitting from the hole already there, the entire roof suddenly shattered apart and seemed for a moment to hang there.

I seized Vika, sweeping her into my arms, and fled from the chamber.

With uncanny speed it seemed we almost floated to a tunnel entrance and I looked behind us and saw the ceiling descending with incredible softness, almost like a snowfall of stones.

I sensed the difference in the gravitation of the planet. I wondered how long it would take before it broke apart and scattered in a belt of dust across the solar system, only to bend inward at last and spiral like a falling bird into the gases of the burning sun.

Vika had fainted in my arms.

I rushed onwards through the tunnels, having no clear idea of what to do or where to go.

Then I found myself in the first Nest Complex, where first I had laid eyes on the Nest of Priest-Kings.

Moving as though in a dream, my foot touching the ground only perhaps once in thirty or forty yards, I climbed the circling ramp upward toward the elevator.

But I found only the dark open shaft.

The door had been broken away and there was rubble in the shaft. There were no hanging cables in the shaft and I could see the shattered roof of the elevator some half a hundred feet below.

It seemed I was trapped in the Nest, but then I noted, perhaps fifty yards away, a similar door, though smaller.

With one slow, strange bound I was at the door and threw the switch which was placed at the side of the door.

It opened and I leaped inside and pushed the highest disk on a line of disks mounted inside.

The door closed and the contrivance swiftly sped upward.

When the door opened I found myself once more in the Hall of Priest-Kings, though the great dome above it was now broken and portions of it had fallen to the floor of the hall.

I had found the elevator which had originally been used by Parp, whom I had learned was a physician of Treve, and who had been my host in my first hour in the domain of Priest-Kings. Parp, I recalled, with Kusk, had refused to implant me, and had formed a portion of the underground which had resisted Sarm. When he had first spoken to me I knew now he would have been under the control of Priest-Kings, that his control net would have been activated and his words and actions dictated, at least substantially, from the Scanning

Room below, but now the Scanning Room, like most of the Nest, was demolished, and even if it had not been, there were none who would now care to activate his net. Parp would now be his own master.

Vika still lay unconscious in my arms and I had folded her robes about her in order to protect her face and eyes and throat from the rock dust below.

I walked before the throne of Priest-Kings.

"Greetings, Cabot," said a voice.

I looked up and saw Parp, puffing on his pipe, sitting calmly on the throne.

"You must not stay here," I said to him, uneasily looking up at the remnants of the dome.

"There is nowhere to go," said Parp, puffing contentedly on the pipe. He leaned back. A puff of smoke emerged from the pipe but instead of drifting up seemed instead almost immediately to pop apart. "I would have liked to enjoy a last, proper smoke," said Parp. He looked down at me kindly and in a step or two seemed to float down the steps and stood beside me. He lifted aside the fold of Vika's robes which I had drawn about her face.

"She is very beautiful," said Parp, "much like her mother."

"Yes," I said.

"I wished that I could have known her better," said Parp. He smiled at me. "But then I was an unworthy father for such a girl."

"You are a very good and brave man," I said.

"I am small and ugly and weak," he said, "and fit to be despised by such a daughter."

"I think now," I said, "she would not despise you."

He smiled and replaced the fold of the garment over her face.

"Do not tell her that I saw her," he said. "Let her forget Parp, the fool."

In a bound, almost like a small balloon, he floated up, and twisting about, reseated himself in the throne. He pounded on the arms once and the movement almost thrust him up off the throne.

"Why have you returned here?" I asked.

"To sit once more upon the throne of Priest-Kings," said Parp, chuckling.

"But why?" I asked.

"Perhaps vanity," said Parp. "Perhaps memory." Then he chuckled again and his eyes, twinkling, looked down at me. "But I also like to think," he said, "it may be because this is the most comfortable chair in the entire Sardar."

I laughed.

I looked up at him. "You are from Earth, are you not?" I asked.

"Long, long ago," he said. "I never did get used to that business of sitting on the floor." He chuckled again. "My knees were too stiff."

"You were English," I said.

"Yes," he said, smiling.

"Brought here on one of the Voyages of Acquisition?"

"Of course," he said.

Parp regarded his pipe with annoyance. It had gone out. He began to pinch some tobacco from the pouch he wore at his belt.

"How long ago?" I asked.

He began to try to stuff the tobacco into the bowl of the pipe. Given the gravitational alteration this was no easy task. "Do you know of these things?" asked Parp, without looking up.

"I know of the Stabilization Serums," I said.

Parp glanced up from the pipe, holding his thumb over the bowl to prevent the tobacco from floating out of it, and smiled. "Three centuries," he said, and then returned his attention to the pipe.

He was trying to thrust more tobacco into it but was having difficulty because the tiny brown particles tended to lie loosely about a quarter of an inch above the bowl. At last he wadded enough in for the pressure to hold it tight and, using the silver lighter, sucked a stream of flame into the bowl.

"Where did you get tobacco and a pipe?" I asked, for I knew of none such on Gor.

"As you might imagine," said Parp, "I acquired the habit originally on Earth and, since I have returned to Earth several times as an Agent of Priest-Kings, I have had the opportunity to indulge it. On the other hand, in the last few years, I have grown my own tobacco below in the Nest under lamps."

The floor buckled under my feet and I changed my position. The throne tilted and then fell back into place again.

Parp seemed more concerned with his pipe, which seemed again in danger of going out, than he did with the world that was crumbling about him.

At last he seemed to get the pipe under control.

"Did you know," he asked, "that Vika was the female Mul who drove away the Golden Beetles when Sarm sent them against the forces of Misk?"

"No," I said, "I did not know."

"A fine, brave girl," said Parp.

"I know," I said. "She is truly a great and beautiful woman."

It seemed to please Parp that I had said this.

"Yes," he said, "I believe she is." And he added, rather sadly I thought, "And such was her mother."

Vika stirred in my arms.

"Quick," said Parp, who seemed suddenly afraid, "take her from the chamber before she regains consciousness. She must not see me!"

"Why?" I asked.

"Because," said Parp, "she despises me and I could not endure her contempt."

"I think not," I said.

"Go," he begged, "go!"

"Show me the way," I said.

Hurriedly Parp knocked the ashes and sparks from his pipe against the arm of the throne. The ashes and unused tobacco seemed to hang in the air like smoke and then drift apart. Parp thrust the pipe in his pouch. He seemed to float down to the floor and, touching one sandaled foot to the ground only every twenty yards or so, began to leave the chamber in slow dreamlike bounds. "Follow me," he called after him.

Vika in my arms I followed the bounding body of Parp, whose robes seemed to lift and flutter softly about him as he almost floated down the tunnel before me.

Soon we had reached a steel portal and Parp threw back a switch and it rolled upward.

Outside I saw the two snow larls turn to face the portal. They were unchained.

Parp's eyes widened in horror. "I thought they would be gone," he said. "Earlier I freed them from the inside in order that they might not die chained."

He threw the switch again and the portal began to roll down but one of the larls with a wild roar threw himself towards it and got half his body and one long, raking clawed paw under it. We leaped back as the clawed paw swept towards us. The portal struck the animal's back and, frightened, it reared up, forcing the portal up, twisting it in the frame. The larl backed away but the portal, in spite of Parp's efforts, now refused to close.

"You were kind," I said.

"I was a fool," said Parp. "Always the fool!"

"You could not have known," I said.

Vika's hand went to the folds of the robe and I could feel her squirm to regain her feet.

I set her down and Parp turned away, covering his face with his robe.

I stood at the portal, sword drawn, to defend it against the larls should they attempt to enter.

Vika now stood on her feet, a bit behind me, taking in at a glance the jammed door and the two unchained larls without. Then she saw the figure of Parp and cried out with a tiny gasp, and looked back again at the larls, and then to the figure.

Out of the corner of my eye I saw her put out her hand gently and approach Parp. She pulled aside the folds of his robe and I saw her touch his face which seemed filled with tears.

"Father!" she wept.

"My daughter," he said, and took the girl gently in his arms.

"I love you, my Father," she said.

And Parp uttered a great sob, his head falling against the shoulder of his daughter.

One of the larls roared, the hunger roar that precedes the roar of the charge.

This was a sound I knew well.

"Stand aside," said Parp, and I barely knew the voice that spoke.

But I stood aside.

Parp stood framed in the doorway holding that tiny silver lighter with which it seemed I had seen him fumble and light his pipe a thousand times, that small cylinder I had once mistaken for a weapon.

Parp reversed the cylinder and leveled it at the breast of the nearest larl. He turned it suddenly and a jolt of fire that threw him five feet back into the cave leapt from that tiny instrument and the nearest larl suddenly reared, its paws lifted wildly, its fangs bared, its snowy pelt burned black about the hole that had once housed its heart, and then it twisted and fell sprawling from the ledge.

Parp threw the tiny tube away.

He looked at me. "Can you strike through to the heart of a larl?" he asked.

With a sword it would be a great blow.

"If I had the opportunity," I said.

The second larl, enraged, roared and crouched to spring.

"Good," said Parp, not flinching, "follow me!"

Vika screamed and I cried out for him to stop but Parp dashed forward and threw himself into the jaws of the startled larl and it lifted him in its jaws and began to shake him savagely and I was at its feet and thrust my sword between its ribs plunging it deep into its heart.

The body of Parp, half torn apart, neck and limbs broken, fell from the jaws of the larl.

Vika rushed upon it weeping.

I drew out the sword and thrust it again and again into the heart of the larl until at last it lay still.

I went to stand behind Vika.

Kneeling by the body she turned and looked up at me. "He so feared larls," she said.

"I have known many brave men," I said to her, "but none was more brave than Parp of Treve."

She lowered her head to the torn body, its blood staining the silks she wore.

"We will cover the body with stones," I said. "And I will cut robes from the pelt of the larl. We have a long way to go and it will be cold."

She looked up at me and, her eyes filled with tears, nodded her agreement.

33
Out of the Sardar

VIKA AND I, CLAD IN robes cut from the pelt of the snow larl I had slain, set out for the great black gate in the somber timber palisade that encircles the Sardar. It was a strange but rapid journey, and as we leaped chasms and seemed almost to swim in the cold air I told myself that Misk and his Priest-Kings and the humans that were engineers in the Nest were losing the battle that would decide whether men and Priest-Kings might, working together, save a world or whether in the end it would be the sabotage of Sarm, First Born, that would be triumphant and the world I loved would be scattered into fugitive grains destined for the flaming pyre of the sun.

Whereas it had taken four days for me to climb to the lair of Priest-Kings in the Sardar it was on the morning of the second day that Vika and I sighted the remains of the great gate, fallen, and the palisade, now little more than broken and uprooted timbers.

The speed of our return journey was not due primarily to the fact that we were now on the whole descending, though this helped, but rather to the gravitational reduction which made it possible for me, Vika in my arms, to move with a swift disregard for what, under more normal conditions, would have been at times a dangerous, tortuous trail. Several times, in fact, I had simply leaped from one portion of the trail to float more than a hundred feet downward to land lightly on another portion of the trail, a point which, on foot, might have been separated by more than five pasangs from the point above from which I had leaped. Sometimes I even neglected the trail altogether and leaped from one cliff to another in improvised short cuts. It was late in the morning of the second day, about the time that we sighted the black gate, that the gravitational reduction reached its maximum.

"It is the end, Cabot," said Vika.

"Yes," I said. "I believe so."

From where Vika and I stood together on the rocky trail, now scarcely able to keep our feet on the path, we could see vast crowds, robed in all the caste colors of Gor, clustered outside the remains of the palisade, looking fearfully within. I supposed there might have been men from almost all of Gor's cities in that frightened, teeming throng. In the front, several deep, in lines that extended as far as I could see in both directions, were the white robes of the Initiates. Even from where we stood I could smell the innumerable fires of their sacrifices, the burning flesh of bosks, smell the heady fumes of the incense they burned in brass censers swinging on chains, hear the repetitious litanies of their pleas, observe their continual prostrations and grovelings by which they sought to make themselves and their petitions pleasing to Priest-Kings.

I swept Vika again to my arms and, half walking, half floating, made my way downward toward the ruins of the gate. There was a great shout from the crowd when they saw us and then there was enormous quiet and every pair of eyes in that teeming throng was fixed upon us.

It suddenly seemed to me that Vika was a bit heavier than she had been and I told myself that I must be tiring.

I descended with Vika from the trail and, as I floated down to the bottom of a small crevice between the trail and the gate, the bottoms of my sandals stung when I hit the rock. I had apparently slightly misjudged the distance.

The top of the crevice was only about thirty feet away. It should take one leap and a step to clear it, but when I leaped my leap carried me only about fifteen feet and where my foot scraped the side a pebble, dislodged, bounded downward and I could hear it strike the floor of the crevice. I took another leap, this time putting some effort into it, and cleared the top of the crevice by some ten feet to land between it and the gate.

In my heart something seemed to be speaking, but I could not dare to listen.

Then I looked through the ruins of the palisade and over the fallen gate, at the smoke from the countless sacrificial fires that burned there, at the smoke from the swinging censers. No longer did it seem to pop apart and dissipate. Now it seemed to lift in slender strands toward the sky.

A cry of joy escaped my lips.

"What is it, Cabot?" cried Vika.

"Misk has won!" I cried. "We have won!"

Not stopping even to set her on her feet I now raced in long, soft bounds toward the gate.

As soon as I reached the gate I placed Vika on her feet.

Before the gate, facing me, I saw the astonished throng.

I knew that never before in the history of the planet had a man been seen to return from the Sardar.

The Initiates, hundreds of them, knelt in long lines to the crags of the Sardar, to the Priest-Kings. I saw their shaven heads, their faces distraught in the bleak white of their robes, their eyes wide and filled with fear, their bodies trembling in the robes of their caste.

Perhaps they expected me to be cut down by the Flame Death before their very eyes.

Behind the Initiates, standing, as befits the men of other castes, I saw men of a hundred cities, joined here in their common fear and plea to the denizens of the Sardar. Well could I suppose the terror and upheavals that had brought these men, normally so divided against one another in the strife of their warring cities, to the palisade, to the dark shadows of the Sardar—the earthquakes, the tidal waves, the hurricanes and atmospheric disturbances, and the uncanny lessening of the gravitational attraction, the lessening of the bonding that held the very earth together beneath their feet.

I looked upon the frightened faces of the Initiates. I wondered if the shaven heads, traditional for centuries with Initiates, held some distant connection, lost now in time, with the hygienic practices of the Nest.

I was pleased to see that the men of other castes, unlike the Initiates, did not grovel. There were men in that crowd from Ar, from Thentis, from Tharna, recognized by the two yellow cords in their belt; from Port Kar; from Tor, Cos, Tyros; perhaps from Treve, Vika's home city; perhaps even from fallen, vanished Ko-ro-ba; and the men in that crowd were of all castes, and even of castes as low as the Peasants, the Saddle Makers, the Weavers, the Goat Keepers, the Poets and Merchants, but none of them groveled as did the Initiates; how strange, I thought—the Initiates claimed to be most like Priest-Kings, even to be formed in their image, and yet I knew that a Priest-King would never grovel; it seemed the Initiates, in their efforts to be like gods, behaved like slaves.

One Initiate stood on his feet.

I was pleased to see that.

"Do you come from Priest-Kings?" he asked.

He was a tall man, rather heavy, with bland soft features, but his voice was very deep and would have been quite impressive in one of the temples of the Initiates, constructed to maximize the acoustical effects of such a voice. His eyes, I noted, in contrast with his bland features, his almost pudgy softness, were very sharp and shrewd. He was no man's fool. His left hand, fat and soft, wore a heavy ring set with a large, white stone, carved with the sign of Ar. He was, I gathered, correctly as it turned out, the High Initiate of Ar, he who had been appointed to fill the post of the former High Initiate whom I had seen destroyed by the Flame Death years earlier.

"I come from the place of the Priest-Kings," I said, raising my voice so that as many could hear as possible. I wanted to carry on no private conversation with this fellow, which he might later report as he saw fit.

I saw his eye furtively flit to the smoke of one of the sacrificial fires.

It was now ascending in a gentle swirl to the blue sky of Gor.

He knew!

He knew as well as I that the gravitational field of the planet was being re-established.

"I wish to speak!" I cried.

"Wait," he said, "oh welcome messenger of Priest-Kings!"

I kept silent, waiting to see what he wanted.

The man gestured with his fat hand and a white bosk,

beautiful with its long, shaggy coat and its curved, polished horns, was led forward. Its shaggy coat had been oiled and groomed and colored beads were hung about its horns.

Drawing a small knife from his pouch the Initiate cut a strand of hair from the animal and threw it into a nearby fire. Then he gestured to a subordinate, and the man, with a sword, opened the throat of the animal and it sank to its knees, the blood from its throat being caught in a golden laver held by a third man.

While I waited impatiently two more men cut a thigh from the slain beast and this, dripping with grease and blood, was ordered cast upon the fire.

"All else has failed!" cried the Initiate, weaving back and forth, his hands in the air. Then he began to mumble prayers very quickly in archaic Gorean, a language in which the Initiates converse among themselves and conduct their various ceremonies. At the end of this long but speedily delivered prayer, refrains to which were rapidly furnished by the Initiates massed about him, he cried, "Oh Priest-Kings, let this our last sacrifice turn aside your wrath. Let this sacrifice please your nostrils and now consent to hear our pleas! It is offered by Om, Chief among all the High Initiates of Gor!"

"No!" cried a number of other Initiates, the High Initiates of various other cities. I knew that the High Initiate of Ar, following the policies of the High Initiate before him, wished to claim hegemony over all other Initiates, and claimed to possess this already, but his claim, of course, was denied by the other High Initiates who regarded themselves as supreme in their own cities. I surmised that, pending some form of military victory of Ar over the other cities or some form of large-scale political reordering of the planet, the Initiate of Ar's claims would remain a matter of dispute.

"It is the sacrifice of all of us!" cried one of the other High Initiates.

"Yes!" cried several of the others.

"Look!" cried the High Initiate of Ar. He pointed to the smoke which was now rising in an almost natural pattern. He jumped up once and came down, as though to illustrate a point. "My sacrifice has been pleasing to the nostrils of Priest-Kings!" he cried.

"Our sacrifice!" cried the other Initiates, joyfully.

A wild, glad shout broke from the throats of the assembled multitude as the men suddenly began to understand that their world was returning to its normal order. There were thousands of cheers and cries of gratitude to the Priest-Kings.

"See!" cried the High Initiate of Ar. He pointed to the smoke which, as the wind had changed somewhat, was now drifting toward the Sardar. "The Priest-Kings inhale the smoke of my sacrifice!"

"Our sacrifice!" insisted the other High Initiates.

I smiled to myself. I could well imagine the antennae of the Priest-Kings shuddering with horror at the very thought of that greasy smoke.

Then somewhat to his momentary embarrassment the wind shifted again and the smoke began to blow away from the Sardar and out towards the crowd.

Perhaps the Priest-Kings are exhaling now, I thought to myself, but the High Initiate had more practice in the interpretation of signs than myself.

"See!" he cried. "Now the Priest-Kings blow the breath of my sacrifice as a blessing upon you, letting it travel to the ends of Gor to speak of their wisdom and mercy!"

There was a great cry of joy from the crowd and shouts of gratitude to the Priest-Kings.

I had hoped that I might have used those moments, that priceless opportunity, before the men of Gor realized the restoration of gravity and normal conditions was occurring, to command them to give up their warlike ways and turn to the pursuit of peace and brotherhood, but the moment, before I realized it, had been stolen from me by the High Initiate of Ar, and used for his own purposes.

Now as the crowd rejoiced and began to disband I knew that I was no longer important, that I was only another indication of the mercy of Priest-Kings, that someone—who had it been?—had returned from the Sardar.

At that moment I suddenly realized I was ringed by Initiates.

Their codes forbade them to kill but I knew that they hired men of other castes for this purpose.

I faced the High Initiate of Ar.

"Who are you, Stranger?" he asked.

The words for 'stranger' and 'enemy' in Gorean, incidentally, are the same word.

"I am no one," I said.

I would not reveal to him my name, my caste, nor city.

"It is well," said the High Initiate.

His brethren pressed more closely about me.

"He did not truly come from the Sardar," said another Initiate.

I looked at him, puzzled.

"No," said another. "I saw him. He came from the crowd and only went within the ring of the palisade and wandered towards us. He was terrified. He did not come from the mountains."

"Do you understand?" asked the High Initiate.

"Perfectly," I said.

"But it is not true," cried Vika. "We were in the Sardar. We have seen Priest-Kings!"

"She blasphemes," said one of the Initiates.

I cautioned Vika to silence.

Suddenly I was very sad, and I wondered what would be the fate of humans from the Nest, if they should attempt to return to their cities or the world above. Perhaps, if they were silent, they might return to the surface, but even then, probably not to their own cities, for the Initiates of their cities would undoubtedly recall that they had left for, and perhaps entered, the Sardar.

With great suddenness I realized that what I knew, and what others knew, would make no difference to the world of Gor.

The Initiates had their way of life, their ancient traditions, their given livelihood, the prestige of their caste, which they claimed to be the highest on the planet, their teachings, their holy books, their services, their role to play in the culture. Suppose that even now if they knew the truth—what would change? Would I really expect them—at least on the whole—to burn their robes, to surrender their claims to secret knowledge and powers, to pick up the hoes of Peasants, the needles of the Cloth Workers, to bend their energies to the humble tasks of honest work?

"He is an impostor," said one of the Initiates.

"He must die," said another.

I hoped that those humans who returned from the Nest would not be hunted by Initiates and burned or impaled as heretics and blasphemers.

Perhaps they would simply be treated as fanatics, as daft homeless wanderers, innocent in the madness of their delusions. Who would believe them? Who would take the word of scattered vagrants against the word of the mighty Caste of Initiates? And, if he did believe them, who would dare to speak out that he did so?

The Initiates, it seemed, had conquered.

I supposed many of the humans might even return to the Nest, where they could live and love and be happy. Others, perhaps, to keep the skies of Gor over their head, might confess to deceit; but I suspected there would be few of those; yet I was sure that there would indeed be confessions and admissions of guilt, from individuals never within the Sardar, but hired by Initiates to discredit the tales of those who had returned. Most who had returned from the Sardar would, eventually at least, I was sure, try to gain admittance in new cities, where they were not known, and attempt to work out new lives, as though they did not keep in their hearts the secret of the Sardar.

I stood amazed at the greatness and smallness of man.

And then with shame I realized how nearly I myself had come to betraying my fellow creatures. I had intended to make use of that moment myself, pretending to have come with a message from Priest-Kings, to encourage man to live as I wished him to live, to respect himself and others, to be kind and to be worthy of the heritage of a rational animal, and yet of what worth would these things be if they came not from the heart of man himself, but from his fear of Priest-Kings or his desire to please them? No, I would not try to reform man by pretending that my wishes for him were the wishes of Priest-Kings, even though this might be effective for a time, for the wishes that reform man, that make him what he is capable of becoming, and has not yet become, must be his own and not those of another. If man rises, he can do so only on his own two feet.

And I was thankful that the High Initiate of Ar had interfered.

I thought how dangerous might be the Initiates if, intertwined with their superstitious lore and their numerous impressive ceremonies, there had been a truly moral message, something that might have spoken to the nobility of men.

The High Initiate of Ar gestured to the others who crowded about, pressing in on me.

"Stand back," he said, and he was obeyed.

Sensing that he wished to speak to me I asked Vika to withdraw somewhat, and she did so.

The High Initiate of Ar and myself regarded one another.

Suddenly I did not feel him as an enemy any longer and I sensed that somehow he did not regard me either as a threat or foe.

"Do you know of the Sardar?" I asked him.

"Enough," he said.

"Then why?" I asked.

"It would be hard for you to understand," he said.

I could smell the smoke from the burning thigh of the bosk as it hissed and popped on the sacrificial fire.

"Speak to me," I said.

"With most," he said, "it is as you think, and they are simple, believing members of my caste, and there are others who suspect the truth and are tormented, or who suspect the truth and will pretend—but I, Om, High Initiate of Ar, and certain of the High Initiates are like none of these."

"And how do you differ?" I asked.

"I—and some others—" he said, "wait for man." He looked at me. "He is not yet ready."

"For what?" I asked.

"To believe in himself," said Om, incredibly. He smiled at me. "I and others have tried to leave open the gap that he might see it and fill it—and some have—but not many."

"What gap is this?" I asked.

"We speak not to man's heart," said Om, "but only to his fear. We do not speak of love and courage, and loyalty and nobility—but of practice and observance and the punishment of the Priest-Kings—for if we so spoke, it would be that much harder for man to grow beyond us. Thus, unknown to most members of my caste, we exist to be overcome, thus in our way pointing the way to man's greatness."

I looked at the Initiate for a long time, and wondered if he spoke the truth. These were the strangest things I had heard from the lips of an Initiate, most of whom seemed interminably embroiled in the rituals of their caste, in the arrogance and archaic pedantry of their kind.

I trembled for a moment, perhaps from the chill winds sweeping down the Sardar.

"It is for this reason," said the man, "that I remain an Initiate."

"There are Priest-Kings," I said at last.

"I know," said Om, "but what have they to do with what is most important for man?"

I thought about it for a moment. "I suppose," I said, "—very little."

"Go in peace," said the Initiate, stepping aside.

I extended my hand to Vika and she joined me.

The High Initiate of Ar turned to the other Initiates about. He raised his voice. "I saw no one emerge from the Sardar," he said.

The other Initiates regarded us.

"Nor did I," said several of them.

They parted, and Vika and I walked between them, and through the ruined gate and palisade which had once encircled the Sardar.

34
Men of Ko-ro-ba

"MY FATHER!" I CRIED. "MY father!"

I rushed to the arms of Matthew Cabot who, weeping, caught me in his arms and held me as though he might never let me go.

Once again I saw that strong, lined face, that square jaw, that wild, flowing mane of fiery hair so much like my own, that spare, ready frame, those gray eyes, now rimmed with tears.

I felt a sudden blow on my back and nearly lost my breath

and twisted to see the gigantic brawny Older Tarl, my former
Master at Arms, who clapped me on the shoulders, his hands
like the talons of tarns.

There was a tugging at my sleeve and a blubbering and I
looked down and nearly poked a scroll in my eye which was
carried by the small blue-clad figure at my side.

"Torm!" I cried.

But the little fellow's sandy hair and pale, watery eyes
were hidden in the vast sleeve of his blue robe as he leaned
against my side and wept unabashedly.

"You will stain your scroll," I cautioned him.

Without looking up or missing a sob he shifted the scroll
to a new position under his other arm.

I swept him off his feet and spun him around and the robes
flew from his head and Torm of the Caste of Scribes cried
aloud in joy and that sandy hair whoofed in the wind and
tears ran sideways down his face and he never lost hold of
the scroll although he nearly batted the Older Tarl with it in
one of his orbits and then he began to sneeze and I gently put
him down.

"Where is Talena!" I begged my father.

Vika, as I scarcely noted, stepped back when I had said
this.

But in that instant my joy was gone, for my father's face
became grave.

"Where is she!" I demanded.

"We do not know," said the Older Tarl, for my father
could not bring himself to say the words.

My father took me by the shoulders. "My son," he said,
"the people of Ko-ro-ba were scattered and none could be
together and no stone of that city might stand upon another
stone."

"But you are here," I said, "three men of Ko-ro-ba."

"We met here," said the Older Tarl, "and since it seemed
the world would end we decided that we would stand together one last time—in spite of the will of Priest-Kings—that we
would stand together one last time as men of Ko-ro-ba."

I looked down at the little scribe, Torm, who had stopped
sneezing, and was now wiping his nose on the blue sleeve of
his robes. "Even you, Torm?" I asked.

"Of course," said Torm, "after all a Priest-King is only a Priest-King." He rubbed his nose meditatively. "Of course," he admitted, "that is quite a bit to be." He looked up at me. "Yes," he said, "I suppose that I am brave." He looked at the Older Tarl. "You must not tell other members of the Caste of Scribes," he cautioned.

I smiled to myself. How clearly Torm wished to keep caste lines and virtues demarcated.

"I will tell everyone," said the Older Tarl kindly, "that you are the bravest of the Caste of Scribes."

"Well," said Torm, "thus qualified, perhaps the information will do no harm."

I looked at my father. "Do you suppose Talena is here?" I asked.

"I doubt it," he said.

I knew how dangerous it would be for a woman to travel unattended on Gor.

"Forgive me, Vika," I said, and introduced her to my father, to the Older Tarl and Torm, the Scribe, and explained as briefly as I could what had befallen us in the Sardar.

My father, the Older Tarl and Torm listened amazed to my account of the truths of the Sardar.

When I had finished I looked at them, to see if they believed me.

"Yes," said my father, "I believe you."

"And I," said the Older Tarl.

"Well," said Torm, thoughtfully, for it did not behoove a member of his caste to volunteer an opinion too rapidly on any matter, "it does not contradict any text with which I am familiar."

I laughed and seized the little fellow by the robes of his caste and swung him about.

"Do you believe me?" I asked.

I swung him about by the hood of his garment twice more.

"Yes!" he cried. "I do! I do!"

I set him down.

"But are you sure?" he asked.

I reached for him again and he leaped backwards.

"I was just curious," he said. "After all," he muttered, "it is not written down in a text."

This time the Older Tarl lifted him up by the scruff of his robes and held him dangling, kicking, a foot from the ground. "I believe him!" cried Torm. "I believe him!"

Once safely down Torm came over to me and reached up and touched my shoulder.

"I believed you," he said.

"I know," I said, and gave his sandy-haired head a rough shake. He was, after all, a Scribe, and had the proprieties of his caste to observe.

"But," said Matthew Cabot, "I think it would be wise to speak little of these matters."

All of us agreed to this.

I looked at my father. "I am sorry," I said, "that Ko-ro-ba was destroyed."

My father laughed. "Ko-ro-ba was not destroyed," he said.

I was puzzled, for I myself had looked upon the valley of Ko-ro-ba and had seen that the city had vanished.

"Here," said my father, reaching into a leather sack that he wore slung about his shoulder, "is Ko-ro-ba," and he drew forth the small, flat Home Stone of the City, in which Gorean custom invests the meaning, the significance, the reality of a city itself. "Ko-ro-ba cannot be destroyed," said my father, "for its Home Stone has not perished!"

My father had taken the Stone from the City before it had been destroyed. For years he had carried it on his own person.

I took the small stone in my hands and kissed it, for it was the Home Stone of the city to which I had pledged my sword, where I had ridden my first tarn, where I had met my father after an interval of more than twenty years, where I had found new friends, and to which I had taken Talena, my love, the daughter of Marlenus, once Ubar of Ar, as my Free Companion.

"And here, too, is Ko-ro-ba," I said, pointing to the proud giant, the Older Tarl, and the tiny, sandy-haired scribe, Torm.

"Yes," said my father, "here too is Ko-ro-ba, not only in the particles of its Home Stone, but in the hearts of its men."

And we four men of Ko-ro-ba clasped hands.

"I understand," said my father, "from what you have told

us, that now once more a stone may stand upon a stone, that two men of Ko-ro-ba may once again stand side by side."

"Yes," I said, "that is true."

My father and the Older Tarl and Torm exchanged glances. "Good," said my father, "for we have a city to rebuild."

"How will we find others of Ko-ro-ba?" I asked.

"The word will spread," said my father, "and they will come in twos and threes from all corners of Gor, singing, each carrying a stone to add to the walls and cylinders of their city."

"I am glad," I said.

I felt Vika's hand on my arm. "I know what you must do, Cabot," she said. "And it is what I want you to do."

I looked down at the girl from Treve. She knew that I must search out Talena, spend my life if need be in the quest for she whom of all women I had chosen for my Free Companion.

I took her in my arms and she sobbed. "I must lose all," she wept. "All!"

"Do you wish me to stay with you?" I asked.

She shook the tears from her eyes. "No," she said. "Seek the girl you love."

"What will you do?" I asked.

"There is nothing for me," said Vika. "Nothing."

"You may return to Ko-ro-ba," I said. "My father and Tarl, the Master-of-Arms, are two of the finest swords on Gor."

"No," she said, "for in your city I would think only of you and if you should return there with your love, then what should I do?" She shook with emotion. "How strong do you think I am, dear Cabot?" she asked.

"I have friends in Ar," I said, "even Kazrak, the Administrator of the City. You can find a home there."

"I shall return to Treve," said Vika. "I shall continue there the work of a physician from Treve. I know much of his craft and I shall learn more."

"In Treve," I said, "you might be ordered slain by members of the Caste of Initiates."

She looked up.

"Go to Ar," I said. "You will be safe there." And I added, "And I think it will be a better city for you than Treve."

"Yes, Cabot," she said, "you are right. It would be hard to live now in Treve."

I was pleased that she would go to Ar, where she, though a woman, might learn the craft of medicine under masters appointed by Kazrak, where she might found a new life for herself far from warlike, plundering Treve, where she might work as befitted the daughter of a skilled, courageous father, where she might perhaps forget a simple warrior of Ko-ro-ba.

"It is only, Cabot," she said, "because I love you so much that I do not fight to keep you."

"I know," I said, holding her head to my shoulder.

She laughed. "If I loved you only a little less," she said, "I would find Talena of Ar myself and thrust a dagger into her heart."

I kissed her.

"Perhaps someday," she said, "I will find a Free Companion such as you."

"Few," I said, "would be worthy of Vika of Treve."

She burst into tears and would have clung to me but I handed her gently into the arms of my father.

"I will see that she gets to Ar safely," he said.

"Cabot!" cried Vika and broke away from him and hurled herself into my arms weeping.

I held her and kissed her again, gently, tenderly, and then wiped the tears from her eyes.

She straightened herself.

"I wish you well, Cabot," she said.

"And I," I said, "wish you well, Vika, my girl of Treve."

She smiled and turned away and my father gently put his arm about her shoulder and led her away.

For some unaccountable reason tears had formed in my own eyes, though I was a Warrior.

"She was very beautiful," said the Older Tarl.

"Yes," I said, "she was very beautiful." I wiped the back of my hand across my eyes.

"But," said the Older Tarl, "you are a Warrior."

"Yes," I said, "I am a Warrior."

"Until you find Talena," he said, "your companion is peril and steel."

It was an old Warrior saying.

I drew the blade and examined it.

The Older Tarl's eyes, like mine, ran the edge, and I saw that he approved.

"You carried it at Ar," he said.

"Yes," I said. "The same."

"Peril and steel," said he.

"I know," I said. "I have before me the work of a Warrior."

I resheathed the blade.

It was a lonely road that I now had to walk, and I wished to set out upon it as soon as possible. I told the Older Tarl and Torm to say good-bye to my father, as I did not trust myself to see him longer, for fear that I would not wish so soon to part from him again.

And so it was that I wished my two friends well.

Though I had met them only for a moment in the shadow of the Sardar, we had renewed our affection and comradeship, one to the other, in the timeless instant of friendship.

"Where will you go?" asked Torm. "What will you do?"

"I don't know," I said, and I spoke honestly.

"It seems to me," said Torm, "that you should come with us to Ko-ro-ba and wait there. Perhaps Talena will find her way back."

The Older Tarl smiled.

"It is a possibility," said Torm.

Yes, I said to myself, it is a possibility, but not a likely one. The probability of so beautiful a woman as Talena finding her way through the cities of Gor, over the lonely roads, among the open fields to at last return to Ko-ro-ba was not high.

Somewhere even now she might be facing danger that she would not face in Ko-ro-ba and there might be none to protect her.

Perhaps she was even now threatened by savage beasts or even more savage men.

Perhaps she, my Free Companion, even now lay chained in one of the blue and yellow slave wagons, or served Paga in a tavern or was a belled adornment to some warrior's Pleasure Gardens. Perhaps even now she stood upon the block in some auction in Ar's Street of Brands.

"I will return to Ko-ro-ba from time to time," I said, "to see if she has returned."

"Perhaps," said the Older Tarl, "she attempted to reach her father, Marlenus, in the Voltai."

That was possible, I thought, for Marlenus, since his deposition from the throne of Ar, had lived as an Outlaw Ubar in the Voltai. It would be natural for her to try to reach him.

"If that is true," I said, "and it is heard that Ko-ro-ba is being rebuilt Marlenus will see that she reaches the city."

"That is true," said the Older Tarl.

"Perhaps she is in Ar," suggested Torm.

"If so, and Kazrak knows of it," I said, "he will return her."

"Do you wish me to accompany you?" asked the Older Tarl.

I thought his sword might indeed have been welcome, but I knew his first duty lay to his city. "No," I said.

"Well then," said Torm, shouldering his scroll like a lance, "that leaves only two of us."

"No," I said to him. "Go with Tarl, the Master-of-Arms."

"You have no idea how useful I might be," said Torm.

He was right, I had no idea.

"I am sorry," I said.

"There will be many scrolls to examine and catalog when the city is rebuilt," observed the Older Tarl. "Of course," he added, "I might do the work myself."

Torm shook with horror. "Never!" he cried.

The Older Tarl roared with laughter and swept the little scribe under his arm.

"I wish you well," said the Older Tarl.

"And I wish you well," I said.

He turned and strode off, saying no more, Torm's chest and head sticking out behind from under his arm. Torm hit him several times with the scroll but the blows seemed not to phase him. At last Torm, before he disappeared from sight, waved his scroll in farewell.

I lifted my hand to him. "I wish you well, little Torm," I

said. I would miss him, and the Older Tarl. And my father, my father. "I wish all of you well," I said softly.

Once more I looked to the Sardar.

I was alone again.

There were few, almost none on Gor, who would believe my story.

I supposed that there would be few on my old world— Earth—too, who would believe it.

Perhaps it was better that way.

Had I not lived these things, did I not know whereof I speak, I ask myself if I—Tarl Cabot himself—would accept them, and I tell myself frankly, in all likelihood, No. So then why have I written them? I do not know, save that I thought these things worth recording, whether they are to be believed or not.

There is little more to tell now.

I remained some days beside the Sardar, in the camp of some men from Tharna, whom I had known several months before. I regret that among them was not the dour, magnificent, yellow-haired Kron of Tharna, of the Caste of Metal Workers, who had been my friend.

These men of Tharna, mostly small tradesmen in silver, had come for the autumn fair, the Fair of Se'Var, which was just being set up at the time of the gravitational lessening. I remained with them, accepting their hospitality, while going out to meet various delegations from different cities, as they came to the Sardar for the fair.

Systematically and persistently I questioned these men of various cities about the whereabouts of Talena of Ar, hoping to find some clue that might lead me to her, even if it might be only the drunken memory of some herdsman of a vision of beauty once encountered in a dim and crowded tavern in Cos or Port Kar. But in spite of my best efforts I was unable to uncover the slightest clue to her fate.

This story is now, on the whole, told.

But there is one last incident which I must record.

35
The Night of the Priest-King

IT OCCURRED LATE LAST NIGHT.

I had joined a group of men from Ar, some of whom remembered me from the Siege of Ar more than seven years before.

We had left the Fair of Se'Var and were making our way around the perimeter of the Sardar Range before crossing the Vosk on the way to Ar.

We had made camp.

We were still within sight of the crags of the Sardar.

It was a windy, cold night and the three moons of Gor were full and the silvery grasses of the fields were swept by the chill blasts of the passing wind. I could smell the cold tang of approaching winter. There had already been a heavy frost the night before. It was a wild, beautiful autumn night.

"By the Priest-Kings!" shouted a man, pointing to a ridge. "What is it?"

I and the others leaped to our feet, swords drawn, to see where he had pointed.

About two hundred yards above the camp, toward the Sardar, whose crags could be seen looming in the background against the black, star-shattered night was a strange figure, outlined against one of the white, rushing moons of Gor.

There were gasps of astonishment and horror from all save myself. Men seized weapons.

"Let us rush on it and kill it!" they cried.

I sheathed my sword.

Outlined against the largest of Gor's three hurtling moons was the black silhouette, as sharp and keen as a knife, of a Priest-King.

"Wait here!" I shouted and I ran across the field and climbed the knoll on which it stood.

The two peering eyes, golden and luminous, looked down at me. The antennae, whipped by the wind, focused themselves. Across the left eye disk I could see the whitish seam that was the scar left from the slashing bladelike projection of Sarm.

"Misk!" I cried, rushing to the Priest-King and lifting my hands to receive the antennae which were gently placed in them.

"Greetings, Tarl Cabot," came from Misk's translator.

"You have saved our world," I said.

"It is empty for Priest-Kings," he said.

I stood below him, looking up, the wind lifting and tugging at my hair.

"I came to see you one last time," he said, "for there is Nest Trust between us."

"Yes," I said.

"You are my friend," he said.

My heart leaped!

"Yes," he said, "the expression is now ours as well as yours and you and those like you have taught us its meaning."

"I am glad," I said.

That night Misk told me of how affairs stood in the Nest. It would be long before the powers of the broken Nest could be restored, before the Scanning Chamber could function again, before the vast damages done to the Nest could be repaired, but men and Priest-Kings were even now at work, side by side.

The ships that had sped from the Sardar had now returned, for as I had feared, they were not made welcome by the cities of Gor, nor by the Initiates, and those who had ridden the ships had not been accepted by their cities. Indeed, the ships were regarded as vehicles of a type forbidden to men by Priest-Kings and their passengers were attacked in the name of the very Priest-Kings from which they had come. In the end, those humans who wished to remain on the surface had landed elsewhere, far from their native cities, and scattered themselves as vagabonds about the roads and alien cities of the planet. Others had returned to the Nest, to share in the work of its rebuilding.

The body of Sarm, I learned, had been burned in the Chamber of the Mother, according to the custom of Priest-Kings, for he had been First Born and beloved of the Mother.

Misk apparently bore him not the least ill will.

I was amazed at this, until it occurred to me that I did not either. He had been a great enemy, a great Priest-King, and had lived as he had thought he should. I would always remember Sarm, huge and golden, in the last agonizing minute when he had pulled free of the Golden Beetle and had stood upright and splendid in the crumbling, perishing Nest that he was determined must be destroyed.

"He was the greatest of the Priest-Kings," said Misk.

"No," I said, "Sarm was not the greatest of the Priest-Kings."

Misk looked at me quizzically. "The Mother," he said, "was not a Priest-King—she was simply the Mother."

"I know," I said. "I did not mean the Mother."

"Yes," said Misk, "Kusk is perhaps the greatest of the living Priest-Kings."

"I did not mean Kusk," I said.

Misk looked at me in puzzlement. "I shall never understand humans," he said.

I laughed.

I truly believe it never occurred to Misk that I meant that he himself, Misk, was the greatest of the Priest-Kings.

But I truly believe he was.

He was one of the greatest creatures I had known, brilliant, courageous, loyal, selfless, dedicated.

"What of the young male?" I asked. "Was he destroyed?"

"No," said Misk. "He is safe."

For some reason this pleased me. Perhaps I simply was pleased that there had not been further destruction, further loss of life.

"Have you had the humans slay the Golden Beetles?" I asked.

Misk straightened. "Of course not," he said.

"But they will kill other Priest-Kings," I said.

"Who am I," asked Misk, "to decide how a Priest-King should live—or die?"

I was silent.

"I regret only," said Misk, "that I never learned the location of the last egg, but that secret died with the Mother. Now the race of Priest-Kings itself must die."

I looked up at him. "The Mother spoke to me," I said. "She was going to tell me the location of the egg but could not."

Suddenly Misk was frozen in the attitude of utter attention, the antennae lifted, each sensory hair alive on his golden body.

"What did you learn?" came from Misk's translator.

"She only said," I told him, "'Go to the Wagon Peoples.'"

Misk's antennae moved thoughtfully. "Then," he said, "it must be with the Wagon Peoples—or they must know where it is."

"By now," I said, "any life in the egg would surely have perished."

Misk looked at me with disbelief. "It is an egg of Priest-Kings," he said. Then his antennae fell disconsolately. "But it could have been destroyed," he said.

"By this time," I said, "it probably has been."

"Undoubtedly," said Misk.

"Still," I said, "you are not sure."

"No," said Misk, "I am not."

"You could send Implanted Ones to spy," I suggested.

"There are no more Implanted Ones," said Misk. "We have recalled them and are removing the control nets. They may return to their cities or remain in the Nest, as they please."

"Then you are voluntarily giving up a valuable surveillance device," I said.

"Yes," said Misk.

"But why?" I asked.

"It is wrong to implant rational creatures," said Misk.

"Yes," I said, "I think that is true."

"The Scanning Chamber," said Misk, "will not be operational for an indefinite period—and even so we can scan only objects in the open."

"Perhaps you could develop a depth scanner," I suggested, "one that could penetrate walls, ground, ceilings."

"We are working on it," said Misk.

I laughed.

Misk's antennae curled.

"If you should regain your power," I asked, "what do you

propose to do with it? Will you still set forth the law in certain matters for men?"

"Undoubtedly," said Misk.

I was silent.

"We must protect ourselves and those humans who live with us," said Misk.

I looked down the hill to where the campfire gleamed in the darkness. I could see human figures huddled about it, looking up at the hill.

"What of the egg?" asked Misk.

"What of it?" I asked.

"I cannot go myself," said Misk. "I am needed in the Nest and even so my antennae cannot stand the sun—not for more than a few hours at most—and if I so much as approached a human being it would probably fear me and try to slay me."

"Then you will have to find a human," I said to him.

Misk looked down at me.

"What of you, Tarl Cabot?" he asked.

I looked up at him.

"The affairs of Priest-Kings," I said, "—are not mine."

Misk looked about himself, and lifted his antennae toward the moons and the wind-swept grass. He looked down at the distant campfire. He shivered a bit in the cold wind.

"The moons are beautiful," I said, "are they not?"

Misk looked back at the moons.

"Yes," he said, "I think so."

"Once you spoke to me," I said, "of random elements." I looked up at the moons. "Is that—" I asked, "—seeing that the moons are beautiful—is that a random element in man?"

"I think," said Misk, "it is part of man."

"You spoke once of machines," I said.

"Howsoever I spoke," said Misk, "words cannot diminish men or Priest-Kings—for who cares what we are—if we can act, decide, sense beauty, seek right, and have hopes for our people?"

I swallowed hard, for I knew I had hopes for my race, and I sensed how Misk must have them for his, only his race was dying, and would sooner or later, one by one, meet with accident or succumb to the Pleasures of the Golden Beetle.

And my race—it would live on Gor—at least for the time, because of what Misk and Priest-Kings had done to preserve their world for them.

"Your affairs," I told him, but speaking to myself, "are your affairs—and not mine."

"Of course," agreed Misk.

If I should attempt to help Misk, what would this mean, ultimately? Would it not be to surrender my race to the mercies of the people of Sarm and the Priest-Kings who had served him, or would it be ultimately to protect my race until it had learned to live with itself, until it had reached the maturity of humanity, until it, together with the people who called themselves Priest-Kings, could address itself to a common world, and to the galaxy beyond?

"Your world is dying," I said to Misk.

"The universe itself will die," said Misk.

He had his antennae lifted to the white fires that burned in the black night over Gor.

I surmised he was speaking of those entropic regularities that apparently prevailed in reality as we know it, the loss of energy, its transformation into the ashes of the stellar night.

"It will grow cold and dark," said Misk.

I looked up at him.

"But in the end," said he, "life is as real as death and there will be a return of the ultimate rhythms, and a new explosion will cast forth the primitive particles and we shall have another turn of the wheel, and someday, sometime, in eons which defy the calculations even of Priest-Kings, there may be another Nest, and another Earth, and Gor, and another Misk and another Tarl Cabot to stand upon a windy hill in the moonlight and speak of strange things."

Misk's antennae looked down at me.

"Perhaps," he said, "we have stood here, on this hill, thusly together, unknown to either of us, already an infinite number of times."

The wind seemed now very cold and very swift.

"And what did we do?" I asked.

"I do not know what we did," said Misk. "But I think I would now choose to do that action which I would be willing that I should do again and again with each turning of the wheel. I would choose so to live that I might be willing that I should live that life a thousand times, even forever. I would choose so to live that I might stand boldly with my deed without regret throughout eternity."

The thoughts that he had spoken horrified me.

But Misk stood, the wind whipping his antennae, as though he were exalted.

Then he looked down at me. His antennae curled. "But I speak very foolishly," he said. "Forgive me, Tarl Cabot."

"It is hard to understand you," I said.

I could see climbing the hill towards us, a warrior. He grasped a spear.

"Are you all right?" he called.

"Yes," I called back to him.

"Stand back," he cried, "so I can have a clean cast."

"Do not injure it!" I called to him. "It is harmless."

Misk's antennae curled.

"I wish you well, Tarl Cabot," he said.

"The affairs of Priest-Kings," I said to him, more insistently than ever, "are not my affairs." I looked up at him. "Not mine!" I cried.

"I know," said Misk, and he gently extended his antennae towards me.

I touched them.

"I wish you well, Priest-King," I said.

Abruptly I turned from Misk and rushed down the hill, almost blindly. I stopped only when I reached the side of the warrior. He was joined by two or three more of the men from the camp below, who were also armed. We were also joined by an Initiate, of unimportant ranking.

Together we watched the tall figure on the hill, outlined against the moon, not moving, standing in the uncanny, marvelous immobility of the Priest-King, only its antennae blowing back over its head in the wind.

"What is it?" asked one of the men.

"It looks," said the Initiate, "like a giant insect."

I smiled to myself. "Yes," I said, "it does look like a giant insect."

"May the Priest-Kings protect us," breathed the Initiate.

One of the men drew back his spear arm but I stayed his arm. "No," I said, "Do not injure it."

"What is it?" asked another of the men.

How could I tell him that he looked, with incredulity and horror, on one of the awesome denizens of the grim Sardar, on one of the fabulous and mysterious monarchs of his very world, on one of the gods of Gor—on a Priest-King?

"I can hurl my spear through it," said the man with the spear.

"It is harmless," I said.

"Let's kill it anyway," said the Initiate nervously.

"No," I said.

I lifted my arm in farewell to Misk, and, to the surprise of the men with me, Misk lifted one foreleg, and then turned and was gone.

For a long time I, and the others, stood there in the windy night, almost knee-deep in the flowing, bending grass, and watched the knoll, and the stars behind it, and the white moons above.

"It's gone," said one of the men at last.

"Yes," I said.

"Thank the Priest-Kings," breathed the Initiate.

I laughed and the men looked at me as though I might be mad.

I spoke to the man with the spear. He was also the leader of the small group.

"Where," I asked him, "is the land of the Wagon People?"

THE CHRONICLES
OF COUNTER-EARTH

John Norman

TARNSMAN OF GOR
OUTLAW OF GOR
PRIEST-KINGS OF GOR
NOMADS OF GOR
ASSASSIN OF GOR
RAIDERS OF GOR
CAPTIVE OF GOR

Here is the magnificent world of Gor, known also as Counter-Earth, a planet as strangely populated, as threatening, as beautiful as any you are likely to encounter in the great works of fiction. Here too is Tarl Cabot—the one picked out of millions to be trained and schooled and disciplined by the best teachers, swordsmen, bowmen on Gor . . . Toward what end, what mission, what purpose?

Only Gor holds the answer

To order by mail, send $1.50 per book plus 50¢ per order for handling to Ballantine Cash Sales, P.O. Box 505, Westminster, Maryland 21157. Please allow three weeks for delivery.

Edgar Rice Burroughs

MARS NOVELS

A PRINCESS OF MARS

THE GODS OF MARS

THE WARLORD OF MARS

THUVIA, MAID OF MARS

THE CHESSMEN OF MARS

THE MASTER MIND OF MARS

A FIGHTING MAN OF MARS

SWORDS OF MARS

SYNTHETIC MEN OF MARS

LLANA OF GATHOL

JOHN CARTER OF MARS